Praise for the Canon (

'An absolute joy . . . fun[...]
plotted. Praise be!'
Adam Kay

'All the elements that make up a classic detective story:
a pitch-perfect setting, a genuine puzzle, a gruesome
murder (or more) and engaging characters'
Philip Pullman

'I've been waiting for a novel with vicars, rude old
ladies, murder and sausage dogs . . . et voila!'
Dawn French

'The Reverend Richard Coles gives us a serpent in
England's pastoral Eden – and whodunit fans can give
praise and rejoice'
Ian Rankin

'You'll want to take a front row pew in Champton
while this delicious series unfolds'
Janice Hallett

'Perfect for those who like their cosy crime to have a
cutting edge'
Ben Aaronovitch

'Even better than I knew it would be. Really well
plotted . . . beautifully written, charming without
being twee, funny, intelligent and mordant too'
India Knight

Also by The Reverend Richard Coles:

FICTION
Murder Before Evensong

NON-FICTION
Fathomless Riches
Bringing in the Sheaves
The Madness of Grief

A DEATH IN THE PARISH

A Canon Clement Mystery

The Reverend
RICHARD COLES

W&N
WEIDENFELD & NICOLSON

First published in Great Britain in 2023 by Weidenfeld & Nicolson
This paperback edition first published in Great Britain in 2024 by
Weidenfeld & Nicolson
an imprint of The Orion Publishing Group Ltd
Carmelite House, 50 Victoria Embankment
London EC4Y 0DZ
An Hachette UK Company

1 3 5 7 9 10 8 6 4 2

A CIP catalogue record for this book is
available from the British Library.

ISBN (Paperback) 978 1 4746 1 2685
ISBN (eBook) 978 1 4746 1 269 2
ISBN (Audio) 978 1 4746 1 270 8

Typeset by Input Data Services Ltd, Bridgwater, Somerset

Printed and bound in Great Britain by Clays Ltd, Elcograf S.p.A.

MIX
Paper from
responsible sources
FSC
www.fsc.org
FSC® C104740

www.weidenfeldandnicolson.co.uk
www.orionbooks.co.uk

For Martin

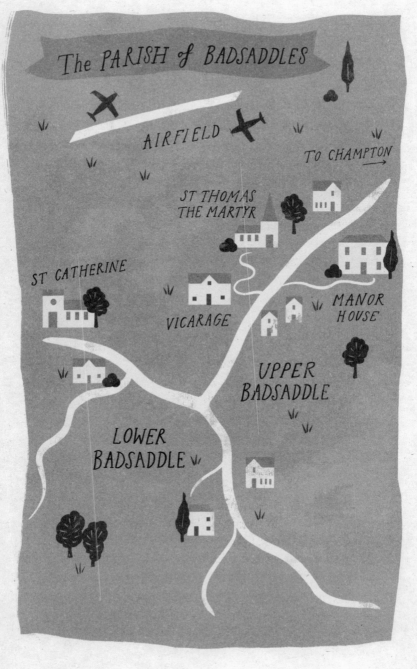

Children, obey your parents in the Lord:
for this is right. Honour thy father and mother;
which is the first commandment with promise;
that it may be well with thee, and thou mayest
live long on the earth.

Ephesians 6: 1–3

I

Audrey Clement did not flinch when half a bread roll, thrown with force from one side of Lord de Floures' dining table to the other, just missed her.

In the silence that followed she pretended to study the monogram on her dining plate – a 'de F' entwined by a circlet of flowers; whether the eyebrow she slowly raised was the result of that study or a silent comment on the interruption was uncertain.

Sunday lunch at Champton House was not going as everyone had hoped. At the head of the table the host, Lord de Floures, looked up as Audrey looked down, his fork – laden with a thick slice of pink venison – paused between plate and mouth. His eyes narrowed.

The missile had landed harmlessly on the parquet floor and skidded like a duck landing badly on a frozen pond. Imperfectly smothered sniggers rose on both sides of the table as it came to a halt.

'Joshua, please. Lydia, don't encourage him . . .' said Sally Biddle to her teenaged son and daughter, but that only made them snigger more. She gave a look to her husband, Chris.

'You can't take them *anywhere*!' he said in a jocular tone of voice (Audrey winced at that) and got up from the table to retrieve the roll. He was tall and coltish, like a distance runner, with hips that were too far forward and skinny shoulders that his blond curly hair almost touched. He was older than he looked from his dress and manner, like a primary school teacher in a progressive London borough.

'Do leave it,' snapped Lord de Floures. 'The mice will have it if the housekeeper doesn't.'

'All right for some!' said Chris, looking around the table for signs of comradeliness, or even an indulgent smile. 'The housekeeper!'

His lordship blinked, then returned wordlessly to his meat, its juices by now dripping onto his regimental tie, as bloodstained and frayed as a battle standard. Daniel Clement, Rector of Champton, Audrey's son and co-habitee at the lovely Queen Anne rectory at the edge of the park, coughed gently and attempted to change the subject.

'The venison is excellent, Bernard.'

'Bit tough, don't you think?' said his lordship. 'Don't know if that's down to the cook or the keeper.'

'I remember once,' said Audrey, 'your father and I were having Sunday lunch in a restaurant . . . I think it was Norfolk, yes, Brancaster . . . and it was not very busy, quite quiet, when suddenly a lady started to choke. The dining room fell silent — aghast — and, without thinking really, I got up, grabbed her round the waist from behind and heaved and heaved. And then this piece of beef simply flew out of her mouth and hit the opposite wall with a thwack like a squash ball. *That* was tough. This venison is really very good.' She turned to the bread-throwing boy. 'You would have enjoyed it, I think, dear. Ballistically speaking.'

Joshua Biddle did not know what to make of that and looked back at her blankly.

Then his sister said, 'Sorry, I keep thinking of Bambi,' and pushed her plate away.

'We're vegetarians,' mumbled her brother.

Bernard's eyes narrowed again, then with a little shrug he went back to eating his lunch.

Daniel exchanged a look with his mother. This was not good. The new associate vicar the bishop had forced Bernard to accept, by adding the parishes of Lower and Upper Badsaddle to Champton St Mary, had not passed the Sunday-luncheon test. His children were uncivil, his meat was declined, his welcome curtailed.

Around them, hung on the walls of the Rudnam Room, where smaller family lunches were served, were two dozen paintings of magnificent shorthorns, as unlike real cattle as apostles in mannerist art. Their virtues — of pedigree, bulk and potency — distorted their appearance, so they looked as unlikely as minotaurs standing in the park with the house in the background, tended by cattlemen who seemed as subservient to

THE REVEREND RICHARD COLES

them as to the then Lord de Floures. Farmer Hugh, as he was known, also larger than life in the paintings, looked over them proprietorially, protectively, like a football chairman his new foreign signings.

'Have the deer been here . . . long?' asked Sally, a little desperately.

'Long?' Bernard thought about it. 'There has been a deer park here for centuries, probably since my Norman ancestors settled here, but most of what you see now' – he waved his unfreighted fork at the window – 'are descended from sires and hinds we were given by the Duke of Bedford in my great-grandfather's day. I think he gave us a pair of everything – sika, muntjac, Père David's – after we gave them some of our girls.'

'Does?'

'Daughters. For their sons to marry.'

'It's all about pedigree, then?' said Chris, a comment in which Audrey detected a note of challenge.

'Yes,' said Bernard, 'in a way. Bloodline. So you have some idea about what you're going to get.'

Silence.

'Sounds a bit feudal,' said Chris.

'Well, it would.'

Audrey changed the subject.

'Mrs Biddle, or is it—'

'Sal, please.'

'. . . or is it the Reverend Mrs Biddle?'

'Oh, I suppose it is. But I'm a deacon.'

'Deaconess?'

'I think we say deacon now, Audrey. And I'm not stipendiary, like Chris. I volunteer.'

'Not quite two for the price of one, then?' said Bernard, whose interest had been stirred by a possible economy of scale.

'Well, of course I'll help out,' said Sally, 'but I'm not a priest, so it's limited.'

'Not yet,' said Audrey. 'Don't you think it will come?'

'I suppose so . . .' Sally looked a little uncomfortable at being invited into a conversation she did not want to have. Daniel wondered if there was dissent in their clerical ranks.

Audrey, in her musing-aloud voice, said, 'It just seems a little quaint, now we've all got used to a female prime minister, that we can't have women vicars.'

'Priests, Mum,' said Daniel. 'Women cannot – yet – be ordained as priests.'

'You look like a vicar,' said Bernard pointedly. 'More than some men do nowadays.'

Sal had made the most effort to dress suitably for lunch at Champton, in the serviceable Laura Ashley dress she wore for the Clergy Wives' Lunches at the Bishop's Palace, when that distinguished prelate's wife sought to encourage the spouses of the lower clergy in their distaff ministries.

'Thatcher's a man,' said Lydia Biddle. 'A man in drag.'

Audrey grimaced. 'I don't think so, dear. She *can* be

a bit pantomime dame, but she's made it to the top; a woman in a man's world.'

'She's no feminist. That's what I meant.'

'Lady vicars', mumbled Bernard, 'before we know it. How long, Mrs Biddle, before you're up at the altar as well, waving your hands about, hocus pocus, and all that?'

'I like being a deacon, actually. It's a very valuable and important ministry in its own right.'

Audrey raised an eyebrow. 'Church of England communion lady?'

'It's so much more than that . . .'

'But you can't . . . what's the word, Daniel?'

'Preside.'

'What about you, Audrey?' Chris interjected. 'Has home and hearth been enough for you?'

'Oh, I had a little job before I met Daniel's father.'

'What sort of jobs did well-brought-up young ladies do before marriage and motherhood claimed them?'

'I was a nurse. At St Thomas' Hospital. During the Blitz.' She smiled brightly, enjoying a moment of triumph.

Mrs Shorely, housekeeper at Champton, appeared in a doorway. She was in her sixties, slight and rather fragile-looking, but she ran the house with an expert and unflexing rule. 'Are you done, m'lord?' she said in her customary tone (flat, with just a hint of irritation), and without waiting for an answer she began to take the plates from the table. She put one down with the faintest '*tsk*' when she saw the thrown bread roll with its skid of crumbs on the parquet floor and went to retrieve it.

Joshua and Lydia sniggered again.

The Rudnam Room, which took its name from the de Floures' estate in Norfolk, while not the largest or most splendid in the house, was still large enough to have an echo. Every sound had a short delay, so a laugh overdubbed itself, a dropped fork ricocheted around and a comment took time to release its energy. Daniel sometimes wondered if the Whiggish salons of the 1700s had produced such memorable conversation, so aphoristic and quotable, not only because of the wit of the participants, but because of the acoustics too. Those who are used to such places trim their speech and deportment accordingly — and those unused to them are sometimes wrongfooted by the unexpected patterns of sound and silence.

The young Biddles' sniggers hung in the silence like a puff of smoke, as Mrs Shorely bent down, over-laboriously, to scoop up the missile.

'Will you have dessert now, m'lord, or will you wait?'

'Right away, Mrs Shorely, thank you. And coffee in the library.'

'Very good, m'lord.'

Mrs Shorely padded away, glancing with a faint suggestion of implacable judgement at the Biddle children as she went.

Bernard broke the silence.

'You're settling in, Mrs Biddle? Vicarage satisfactory?'

'Oh, it's far too big for us. Heaven knows how we'll be able to maintain it. Or heat it.'

Daniel winced. The vicarage of Lower Badsaddle was one of the finest in the diocese of Stow, a neat and quietly splendid Georgian box built by Smith of Warwick for a clerical third son in 1730.

'It is not in good repair?'

'A bit neglected, actually,' said Chris. 'The windows need a bit of attention, and I guess the diocese wouldn't put in double glazing.'

'Couldn't,' said Audrey, 'it's listed; but I sympathise, there's a hell of a draught in our drawing room when the wind whistles in from the Fens. But that's what woollens are for, isn't it . . .?'

Daniel thought of his predecessor, Canon Dolben, who had the central heating removed from his cottage after he retired, for it made him feel 'like a hothouse orchid after thirty years in the rectory'.

'. . . but the estate is very good at sending someone to paint the woodwork or fix a gate when it needs doing.'

'Ah,' said Chris, 'who do I need to talk to about that?'

Bernard interrupted. 'A matter for the Parsonages Board in your case, I'm afraid . . .'

'Oh,' he said, disappointed, 'but with you as patron of Champton St Mary—'

'And *only* Champton St Mary. You see, the Badsaddles were added – lumped in – with the benefice by the bishop as a cost-cutting exercise. Naturally, he is not the only person who has to cut costs.' Bernard said all this without looking up from his place mat, which showed a rather plain nineteenth-century engraving of the house. 'And here's Mrs Shorely with our pudding.'

The sound of Mrs Shorely's approaching footsteps, faint but getting louder, filled the uncomfortable silence that followed.

'Just leave it on the table, would you, Mrs Shorely?' said Bernard, and the dish, hot from the oven, was placed before him with a jug of custard to the side.

Bernard served – apple and blackberry crumble: 'Our apples too. The custard is courtesy of Mr Bird.'

Audrey passed the bowls along and the jug of custard followed – its skin, she noted, as wizened as a St Tropez grandame's face.

Daniel, at Bernard's request, took the bottle of Sauternes, premier cru, from the sideboard and poured a glass for his mother.

'Mrs Biddle?'

'I won't, thanks, we don't really take wine.'

'*Take* wine?' said Bernard. 'What an odd way of putting it – makes it sound like cod liver oil . . .'

'Perhaps it's your livers you're thinking about?' said Audrey.

'I don't like the taste of alcohol,' said Chris Biddle. 'I never have.'

9

Bernard looked at the wine in his glass — golden, luscious — and swirled it once so it left a syrupy tidemark. 'I don't think I could live without wine.' He took a mouthful and sat back in his chair, savouring it.

'Oh, look, there's Honoria . . .' said Audrey brightly.

The Hon. Honoria de Floures was riding in the park. She had declined her father's last-minute invitation to lunch and taken out her favourite horse instead. It was a lively chestnut mare with a flaxen mane and tail, and even in clothes and kit she had put together from spares in the stables, Honoria managed to look in every sense coordinated as she trotted past.

'. . . Doesn't she look marvellous! I could never get the rhythm, the bounce in the saddle. It's like a yo-yo. I could never get that either.'

'She makes everything look effortless,' said Daniel admiringly, and his mother for a moment wondered if he might sigh like a swain.

He quoted a song instead.

> 'Surely you see My Lady
> Out in the garden there,
> Riv'ling the glittering sunshine
> With a glory of golden hair . . .'

'It's red hair, Daniel,' said Audrey, who found it hard to resist an opportunity to slacken his sails. 'She's starting to look quite the countrywoman. Wasn't she here only last week?'

'She comes up quite often now,' said Bernard. 'When

she's not at work. My daughter,' he added for the benefit of the Biddles; 'she lives in town. She has a job.'

'Oh, what does she do?' asked Sally.

Bernard thought about it for a moment and then
said, 'I don't really know. Something to do with a
hotel.'

'She's an "events planner",' said Audrey. 'She plans
. . . events, like grand weddings or . . . corporate
launches . . .' The phrase sounded freshly minted on
Audrey's lips. 'She's the reason Daniel is here.'

'How so?'

'I was at St Martin's Kinnerton Square in town before
I came here,' said Daniel, 'and Honoria works at the
Motcombe next door, so we got to know each other
negotiating the often highly unreasonable demands of
Belgravia's brides.'

'Like what?' asked Chris Biddle with the heightened
tone of interest one cleric shows another when they
start to talk shop.

'Oh, it was all about the reception. The church part
was a picturesque prelude to it, on a par with the flowers
and the canapés. If we gently asserted the law – or the
sacrament – they were sometimes rather taken aback.
Not everyone.'

'It can't have been a big parish . . .'

'No, tiny, the size of a stamp.'

'So, why so many weddings?'

'Lovely church, posh Belgravia, handy for the
grander hotels.'

'But how did so many couples qualify to get married there?'

The law permitted only those resident in the parish, with one or two exceptions, to get married in the parish church.

'We took a rather . . . latitudinarian line over the qualifying criteria.' There was a silence, and Daniel felt a blush rise in his cheeks. 'A custom established in the incumbency of my predecessors, you understand.'

'Oh, I see,' said Chris.

'Yes,' said Audrey, 'in the registers half the marriage couples gave the vicarage as their address. More over-crowded than one of Mr Rachman's slums.'

Daniel winced. 'It was a bit more complicated than that, Mum. Often they were from families who had London houses in the parish, or once had London houses in the parish, so there was a connection . . .'

'The only connection, I seem to recall you saying, was from their bank account to St Martin's. A roaring trade!'

Daniel glanced at Chris, who said nothing, but there was a slight air of a grimace about him.

It was Lydia who spoke. 'How C of E, bending the rules for the rich and privileged.'

'It's weddings, dear, not subjugating the poor,' said Audrey. 'Wouldn't you want to temper rigour with discretion under those circumstances?'

'It's actually the law,' said Chris, 'and tempering rigour with discretion is a breach of it.'

There was an awkward pause, and Daniel said, 'We just adapted to circumstances. Like mission priests, only in darkest Belgravia rather than Africa.'

'Are you saying Belgravia is like Ethiopia?' asked Josh, with undisguised scorn.

'No, but I was in Belgravia, not in Ethiopia.'

Audrey spoke up brightly. 'Well, Jesus said feed my sheep and this sheep is ready for coffee. In the library?'

Bernard stood up and led the way – his guests falling in behind him – from the table of plenty through the Great Hall, so grand, so splendid. The Biddles paused and looked around a little self-consciously, trying to resist its magnificence.

The Biddles had been in the new joint benefice of Champton St Mary with the Badsaddles not even a fortnight, arriving at Michaelmas, which falls at the end of September. It is a time for ends and beginnings, as England shifts from summer to autumn, a time of the turning of the leaves, of a faint presage of winter in the early mornings, of blackberries and conkers, of new academic and legal terms, and of a return to work after holidays. In the Church calendar it com- memorates the battle of the devil with St Michael the Archangel, a cosmic bout in which the battalions of heaven are mobilised and Satan is vanquished, cast into hell by the fiery sword of truth and righteousness – a triumph often seen in stained-glass windows with a winged warrior, in unaerodynamic armour, trampling a sort of dragon beneath his spurred feet.

It was Audrey Clement's favourite season of the year. When she had been a girl she had loved the thrill of a new pencil case, new shoes, and her strapped trunk on the platform at Grantham waiting for the train to take her back to her austere boarding school in Scotland. Her mother had provided sandwiches, cake and – it never occurred to her that this was unusual for a twelve-year-old – a half-bottle of sherry for the journey. With her school mates she had thrown a penny out of the window as the train went over the Forth Bridge, a rather superstitious tradition for girls en route to a Presbyterian school in the Twenties, but an offering needed to be made to the gods of chance, for the favour to face the opportunities and challenges of a new school year.

She also rather liked the theme of the battle with the forces of darkness, a theme uppermost in her mind as she walked with her son up the path through the park from Champton House to Champton Rectory after the lunch of awkward welcome for the Biddles. It was a sunny Sunday; the park looked lovely, the green of the trees turning to red and gold and russet, fretted by an intermittent wind, a hint of cold and, Daniel noticed, a perceptible lengthening of the shadows in this pre-tea hour.

'*He's* a lot of fun,' said Audrey, 'and what a cheek, ticking you off for *marrying* people!'

'He does have a point, Mum. It was a bit naughty.'

'Naughty? Pah!'

'They don't cope very well with naughty.'

'Who?'

'Evangelicals.'

'We're not Brownies, Daniel. Aren't we all naughty? Isn't that the point of someone like you? To make us good little boys and girls?'

'Yes, but it's a bit different for someone like me. *I* think we're always a work in progress, beguiled by the old Adam to the old ways. Sin, self-regard and so forth. Chris, I think, would want to make a complete distinction between the person before and after' – he put on the lugubrious voice he used for pieties that were not his own – '*an encounter with the living Jesus*. They're born again, you see.'

'I've never understood what that means.'

'The first birth is into sinful life, thanks to the disobedience of Adam and Eve. The second birth is into the life of Jesus Christ, and that is once and for all. Not just in this life, but in eternity.'

'Don't you think that?'

'I think we're forever turning this way and that and life is essentially *Come Dancing* until we finally waltz into heaven, and that can take not only a lifetime, but more than a lifetime. That's why we pray for those who have died, to help them along. Chris would think that *very* naughty.'

'Why? How could anyone object to helping people into heaven?'

'Because that's not ours to do, it's God's. And when you die you're done. And if you have not . . . *received the Lord Jesus into your heart* . . . then it's damnation for you.'

'Goodness, how very fiery! You wouldn't think so to look at him.'

'It's not unusual for the soppiest-looking people to espouse the sternest doctrines.'

They walked on towards the rectory. It stood to the east of the parish church, which had started quite plainly as Norman and 350 years later acquired a perpendicular makeover. The present rectory followed in the reign of Queen Anne, another handsome example of its kind, built splendidly for the third son of whichever de Floures was incumbent at the time (inheritance and the army claimed the first and second), leaving Daniel and his mother the parallel, if reduced, challenge of maintaining the style of life it called for. Not even that now, in these straitened times; merely keeping hypothermia at bay in winter was challenge enough. Daniel noticed with foreboding a cloud formation not quite scudding across the sky but certainly hurrying, at summer's pace.

'What were they dressed up for?'

'The kids?'

'Yes. They looked like they'd turned up for Hallowe'en a month early.'

'They're Goths, I think.'

'Goss?'

'Goths. As in Goths and Vandals.'

'I doubt very much that whey-faced child could bring about the fall of Rome.'

'It's just the name of their . . . subculture. It came out of punk, I think, but they dress up like vampires. It's a critique of, you know, the status quo.'

'They look undernourished. No wonder, if they throw their food around rather than eat it.'

'That was a bit much, wasn't it?'

'A bit much? I could feel Bernard going glacial before it hit the floor. What terrible manners! And the *parents*? Not a word of reproach! If you had thrown a bread roll at a Sunday lunch, you would have been sent home.'

'I never would have.' Like many whose instinct it is to conform, Daniel felt a flicker of admiration for those who didn't. 'I suppose it's their hippy-dippy way of doing things, or not doing things. Did you see he was wearing beads?' Daniel had noticed Chris's bangle, threaded with wooden beads. 'They spelt something – wasn't his name. I think it was WWJD. What Would Jesus Do?'

'Not what *they* think.'

'Not what any of us think,' muttered Daniel, who had become reluctant even to speculate what Jesus would make of the weather, let alone the devices and desires of the human heart.

'He just seems so . . . unvicarish. So unlike *you*.'

'He doesn't have to be like me. There is more than one way of skinning a cat, Mum. I'm sure he's very effective pastorally . . .'

'Wearing beads and playing catch with Holy Communion? In the Badsaddles? I can't see Mrs Hawkins taking to him, can you?'

'Perhaps not, but it's about the whole community. I expect he will be able to reach people I couldn't reach. He has children.'

'Weird, wan things,' said Audrey again. 'They need feeding up and bringing to heel. Bit of carrot, bit of stick. They won't get either from her.'

'I quite liked her. She spoke up.'

'But she bit her lip, did you notice, when women's ordination came up?'

'Probably didn't want to upset Bernard.'

'Do you think?'

'But imagine what it's like for them, new in the parish, new to . . . all this . . .'

'What did they expect?' said Audrey. *Jesus Christ Superstar*?'

A wind stirred the trees and they rustled noisily. It felt, for a moment, rather ominous.

'Jesus Christ!' sang Audrey. *'Superstar! Looks like Chris Biddle and he wears a bra!'*

As the Clements walked home, the Biddles drove back to the Badsaddles in their creaking campervan. Its livery, improvised for Greenbelt one year, was tatty now, but proclaimed a gaiety that did not match the mood onboard.

Sally Biddle's son and daughter sat on the bench seat behind her, looking out of opposite windows. She, in the passenger seat, was looking fixedly at the road ahead, and in silence since they had said a slightly more hurried goodbye to Lord de Floures – 'I must leave you now, so kind of you to come. The rector will lead the way' – than she had hoped for.

It was her husband who spoke. 'That was . . . interesting.'

'Interesting?' she said. 'It was *excruciating*.'

'What were we supposed to do? Turn up looking like the Quiverfulls of Barchester?'

'I mean your children throwing a bread roll across the table at a lunch with a peer of the realm who just so happens to be patron of your living.'

'He's not *our* patron, I thought he made that very clear.'

'Patron of the living we depend on.'

'He's just one of the neighbours . . .' said Lydia.

Sal said, 'It doesn't matter who he is, it matters that you behave when we're guests at someone else's dining table. For goodness' sake!'

'I'm not going to be the perfect little Christian child you want me to be. I didn't ask for this.'

'Hold on, Lydia, you're sixteen,' said Chris, 'so is your twin brother, and you will do what you are told . . .'

'*Christian children all should be*', sang Josh sarcastically, '*mild, obedient, good as he.*'

Chris hit the brakes and the van, and the verse from 'Once in Royal David's City', came to a sudden stop.

'*Enough.* Or there'll be real trouble.'

Sal said, 'When we get home you both write a letter of apology to Lord de Floures.'

'But I'm not sorry.'

'Then try harder.'

'Thou shalt not bear false witness.'

Chris turned to face his son, blond, curly reproach facing raven-black impertinence. 'Try Exodus, chapter twenty, verse twelve. Honour your father and mother? The Fifth Commandment?'

He started up the van again and it wheezed and creaked up to a steady thirty as they sat in silence for the rest of the way home.

2

In one of the characteristic reversals of the season, the next day dawned like it was still summer. The sky was cloudless, the sun strong, and Audrey's favourite late-blooming rose, full and pink, was flush with its third show of flowers. The variety was called 'Sexy Rexy', which Audrey pronounced in a comedy voice that made Daniel blush pinkly too. He preferred whites, or the palest peach, for the rectory garden – roses named after characters from the *Canterbury Tales* or grand-daughters of Queen Victoria – but he supposed a last hurrah, before the first frosts, might be forgiven.

It was a little after seven, and he stood in the walled garden at the back of the house with a mug of coffee bearing a Union flag and the legend 'I'M BACKING BRITAIN' as his two dachshunds, Cosmo and Hilda, circled and sniffed in the first security sweep of the day. Badgers had found a way in and were using his garden as a shortcut. Shy and nocturnal, they were usually elu-sive, but sometimes on his way back from Compline he would see an old bruiser who looked back at him with an unmistakable air of challenge. His mother had started calling him Tyson, after the boxer, and Daniel feared if Cosmo and Hilda should ever attack, as dachshunds — badger hounds — are bred to do, they might bite off more than they could chew.

He thought of the day ahead, and while he did not mutter a curse, he did sigh. His new associate vicar had requested a breakfast meeting, bidding him to Lower Badsaddle Vicarage at eight for 'fellowship, praise and breaking bread'.

'Why?' Daniel said to his mother. 'Why spoil a breakfast to talk about the assembly rota?' But Chris Biddle was keen: keen to face the challenges of evangelism, keen to seek God's blessing on their mission day by day and keen, Audrey said, 'to come over like Richard bloody Branson'.

But Daniel felt it proper to support his new 'colleague' and was so temperamentally mild that he tended to yield to any pious assertion made with conviction. Chris Biddle was full of conviction, and when he was with him Daniel sometimes felt like a genial Liverpudlian Fabian being hectored by Militant Tendency. He sighed again and called for the dogs, who reluctantly returned from their reconnaissance of the perimeter. He would normally go to church and say Matins, vested properly, for the doubtful benefit of his congregation — Cosmo and Hilda — who slept through it in a reassuringly C of E way. But this would not happen today, for Chris wanted worship before muesli, and although he was far more devout than Bernard, Daniel did not think a double dose of the '*Te Deum*' necessary or even advisable.

The dogs pattered past him, muted at first, and after a short clatter of claws on the flagstoned kitchen floor they jumped into their bed by the Aga. 'Don't get comfortable,' he said, 'you're coming with me.' He took their leads down from the hook by the door and Cosmo, drama queen to Hilda's sphinx, squealed with excitement. They followed him to the front door, exchanging glances at this stroke of good fortune — a walk at an unwonted time.

His Land Rover, a terrible creaking beast, awaited in the drive. He lifted the dogs onto the passenger seat, still covered with the pages from the *Telegraph* that his mother insisted on laying down before getting in. Oh, he thought, I would like to read that, seeing a report of druids being arrested at Stonehenge for revelling at the solstice. As the dogs sat on it, he wondered when anyone had last been arrested for enthusiastically attending Church of England worship. He got in, turned the improbably small key in the ignition and the Land Rover coughed and shook into life.

You might think that eight years' experience driving the vehicle, which had been given to him in a fit of slightly passive-aggressive generosity by Bernard, might have improved his performance behind the wheel, but, alas, it had not. Daniel drove like an inquisitive child playing with a shotgun, uncertain of the operation of its parts and ignorant of the consequences of a misplaced finger. No matter how hard he'd tried to master the elements, his driving had not improved; if anything, it had got worse, most noticeably worse after his new friend Neil Vanloo, detective sergeant at Braunstonbury CID, had offered a course of driving lessons. They had met after church on a Sunday in the fields to the north of Champton House's park, where the concrete runway laid in the Second World War offered a suitably uncluttered surface for their manoeuvres. Neil had explained, patiently at first, how the pedals and the buttons and the levers connected to gears and pistons and brakes, expecting that showing their workings would lead to crisper execution. It had not. If anything, it had made Daniel even more self-conscious; his lurching zig-zags across the concrete were somewhere between clownish and dangerous. In the end, it was Neil who did the driving on their trips out and about to the lovely churches and historic houses of the county, with Daniel as guide, and also to the rugby – Neil's choice – the mysteries of which had begun to enthral his unsporty companion. But these diversions lay ahead, and before them lay the necessities of ministry.

Although the morning was summery there was something of the coda about it, not unpleasant to Daniel, who, like his mother, had always enjoyed the return to school after the summer holidays, his new pencil case loaded with sharpened HBs, fountain pen and Quink. That anticipation took on a note of anxiety as he approached Lower Badsaddle Vicarage, its hedge untidy and lawn unmown, the campervan in hippy homespun livery parked even more incongruously outside than the Land Rover outside his rectory.

He let the dogs out and they rushed into grass so long they had to jump up and down like ponies at a gymkhana to see where they were going.

Chris Biddle appeared at the door and waved. 'Come on in, Daniel. Lovely morning!' and he extended his arms to the creation like one of those druids, thought Daniel, arrested at Stonehenge.

Daniel had made an effort that morning to dress in a way that would make his new associate vicar feel comfortable. He had put on his sports jacket, bought by his mother for his unsuccessful Oxford entrance exams, its elbows patched with leather, its sleeves – also hemmed with leather – a little too short after he had experienced one final, if diffident, growth spurt. He had matched this with brown shoes, which poked out from the faded charcoal-grey turn-ups of the trousers he thought might go with the sports jacket. The overall effect was that of an undergraduate trying to look like C. S. Lewis.

Chris was wearing cotton dungarees the colour of peas, the bib half undone to reveal a clashing red T-shirt that looked, to Daniel's inexpert eye, a bit like the kind of thing Alex de Floures, Bernard's artist son, wore in the heyday of punk; '100%' it said, but '100%' of what?

'Daniel. Dan. Good to see you, come in, come in. You brought your dogs?'

'Yes. Is that all right?'

'Of course. Come in.'

Daniel called Cosmo and Hilda, and the long grass wavered and switched, marking their progress back to the gravel drive.

'It's like *Children of the Corn*,' said Chris.

'Children of the what?'

'The film, did you see it? Based on that Stephen King book about a demon that lives in a cornfield – the American kind of corn, you know, tall. And he enslaves these children, and when they come for you all you see at first is the corn moving. Scary!'

The dogs burst out of the long grass and without breaking stride ran past the two clerics into the hall.

'Cosmo! Hilda! I'm sorry,' said Daniel.

'It's fine, we love dogs.'

They followed the dogs into the hall, smaller but showier than Daniel's, its symmetry and formality disrupted by bicycles leaned carelessly against the wainscoting, and a row of coat hooks so overladen they looked like they might bring the wall down. The black-and-white tiled floor was scattered with wellington boots and bats and balls and a guitar and a skateboard poised ominously, Daniel thought, for slapstick. A cry came from behind a door and Cosmo and Hilda burst out and skidded to a halt in front of Chris, who bent to pat them until Cosmo barked and backed away and Hilda did a sort of victory roll onto her back and up again, then sat looking at Chris as if unsure of his status.

'They do tricks,' said Chris. 'How clever.'

'I don't think I've ever seen her do that before,' said Daniel.

'I'm honoured. Good girl . . . did you say Hilda?'

'Yes, Hilda after Hilda of Whitby. She arrived on the feast. November 19th. And you'll know who Cosmo's named after.'

'Cosmo Smallpiece.'

'Smallpiece?'

'The Les Dawson character?' He pursed his lips as if for a kiss and said in a comic voice, 'Knickers, knackers, knockers!'

'Cosmo Gordon Lang,' said Daniel. 'The Archbishop of Canterbury.'

'Oh.'

'During the abdication crisis.'

Sal Biddle, the source of the cry, poked her head round the door. 'Daniel, hello! I thought it must be you. You brought the dogs!'

Just a hint of irritation in the unnecessary statement, thought Daniel, so he offered to leave them in the Land Rover.

Sal said, 'No,' brushing the suggestion away with her hands, which, he noticed, were floury. 'I'm sure they'll be fine, they just made me jump. They're so . . . eager. Made the cat jump too.'

'Mum!' a voice floated down the stairs. 'Bat's just run up the tree again!'

'Come through, Daniel, we're in the kitchen.'

The kitchen was a chaos of books, papers, china, bags, clothes left to dry, mismatched chairs, boots, a bowl of slightly decomposing fruit and competing smells: from the Aga, a pantry with an open door, piled plates next to the sink and a cat litter tray that Daniel suspected had done double or even triple duty. But here and there were small islands of orderliness: two places laid at the cleared half of a large kitchen table, and a floured countertop where Sal was in the middle of kneading dough.

'You're a bread maker,' said Daniel. 'How lovely!'

'Sal makes all our bread. And she does workshops at festivals. Her crusty cobblers are famous at Keswick.'

'You can have one if you like, Daniel. You could use it at communion. Bread baked in the parish, almost, for the parish.'

Daniel frowned. 'That's very kind of you, Sal, but it wouldn't really do. I'd love a loaf for the rectory, if you can spare one?'

'Why not communion?'

'Um,' he looked flustered, '*crumbs*.'

'Worried about mice?' said Chris with a hint of mischief.

A DEATH IN THE PARISH

'No. Well, not in the first instance. It's just that we use wafers – unleavened bread as the rubrics proscribe – and it would not do to have crumbs of Our Lord . . . in the form of a crusty cobbler . . . flying around.'

There was a silence.

Sal said, 'I don't understand.'

'Transubstantiation,' said Josh, who had appeared in the doorway in the uniform of Bishop Oakley, the C of E secondary school in Braunstonbury. For school, Daniel noticed, he wore less make-up than he had at Sunday lunch.

Josh pointed to the school crest on the breast pocket of his blazer, a host and paten, the large round wafer hovering like a halo over the cup of wine for the Eucharist. 'The teaching that a priest at Mass turns bread and wine literally into the flesh and blood of Jesus. We did it in RS. I thought it was Catholics only.'

'Most people do, but there are others. Some Anglicans believe it too. Or something like it. Bishop Oakley, whom your school is named for, was a great theologian of the Eucharist in the days when that was quite a controversial thing.'

'Why?'

'Why controversial? Well, it looked to many like "popery".'

'It's juju.'

Chris said sharply, 'Josh . . .'

'It is *literally* juju. Bread and wine into flesh and blood. I love it.'

29

Daniel looked puzzled. 'I wouldn't call it juju. Not least because I think that is a sort of dark magic . . .'

'That's the kind of magic I like. Magic *blood* and eating flesh . . .'

Sal sighed. 'It's a bit early for vampirism, Joshua. And I need to get you to school. Where's your sister?'

'She's trying to get the cat down from the tree.'

'I should really put the dogs in the Land Rover,' said Daniel, embarrassed.

'It might make rescuing the cat a bit easier,' said Sal.

He gathered the dogs up, one under each arm, as they wriggled in protest at being taken away from the possibility of chasing a cat. He got them into the Land Rover and left them looking accusingly at him through the window.

Sal and the twins were on the steps, leaving for school. Lydia said, 'I missed your dogs!' and cooed with pleasure when she saw their little brown faces looking out at her; she was suddenly different — sentimental instead of cynical.

Her brother pulled a face. 'Lyds, we gotta go. Leave the priesthood to its craft.'

'Oh, can't you let them out?' She ran over to the Land Rover making coochy-coo sounds and they got excited again.

'Lydia, campervan, now!' her mother said.

Lydia made one more kissy face at the dogs and as she passed said to Daniel, 'Please can I come to see them?'

'Of course. We could take them for a walk if you like. If that's all right with your parents?'

'When?'

'Perhaps after school?' He looked at Sal.

'Are you sure? I could drop her at yours at, say, four? But really?'

'Really. I'll bring her home. Half past five? Would you like to join us, Josh?'

'I can't. I've got a band rehearsal.' He held up what Daniel assumed was a cased electric guitar, as if evidence were needed.

'OK,' said Sal, 'that's very kind, Daniel. See you later.'

Daniel waved them off and, to the receding sound of his dogs' complaining barks, went back inside. Chris was in the kitchen, scattering what, to Daniel, looked like birdfeed from a Kilner jar into two bowls. He invited Daniel to sit down and placed a bowl in front of him.

'Muesli,' he said. 'My own.'

'How interesting,' said Daniel. 'What's in it?'

'Rolled oats. Wheatgerm. Some sultanas, I think. Nuts. Desiccated coconut. Brown sugar. Full of goodness.'

Daniel reached for the milk jug. Chris held out a restraining hand.

'Shall we first offer thanks?'

'Oh, yes, of course.'

Chastened, Daniel closed his eyes in expectation.

'Father God, we thank you for your *bounty*, for your *loving* generosity to us your children . . . for food and drink, and fellowship, and for our partnership in *your gospel* . . .'

'Ame—'

'. . . and I want to thank you for my family, and for Daniel, and his family, and ask you to b-*less* our homes, our parishes, this joint benefice of Champton and the *Bad*-saddles . . .'

'Ame—'

'. . . and Father God, gracious God, we want to thank you, too, for the opportunities we have in *this* place to share your Word, and to b-*ring all* people into your *loving* care . . .'

'. . .'

'. . . and, loving God, we pray for *strength* to *serve* you . . . and when we fail in zeal . . . or grow tired . . . when our salt has lost its savour . . . when the way is too *narrow* and the path too *hard* . . . we pray that you continue to b-*less* us with your gifts, that we may not stumble or wander from *your* ways, and to know, always, that serving you is never a burden . . . but a *gift* . . .'

Daniel said nothing. Chris opened an eye.

'Would you like to offer a prayer?'

'Oh. Almighty and everlasting God, from whom cometh every good and perfect gift: send down upon our bishops, and other clergy, and upon the congregations committed to their charge, the healthful Spirit of thy grace: and, that they may truly please thee, pour upon them the continual dew of thy blessing. Grant this, O Lord, for the honour of our Advocate and Mediator, Jesus Christ . . .'

Chris said nothing.

'Amen.'

It was not only the muesli that was indigestible, thought Daniel as the Land Rover rattled its way home to Champton St Mary. Breakfast had improved with the appearance of a passable marmalade, made by Sal, but no matter how thickly he had spread it on the slice of toast — so dense with goodness it could resurface the controversial stretch of Mrs Thatcher's M25 that rumbled like thunder when you drove over it — he could not lift it from wholesome virtue to indulgent pleasure. Chris had then made him a second mug of coffee, Mellow Bird's 'to make you smile' as the advert trilled, but even that ineffectual effort to approximate the taste of cafetière coffee came with a caveat. It was produced unjustly, to the detriment of the growers in Mexico, an inequity that Chris wished to challenge through signing up the parish to a commitment to serve only coffee that was ethically sourced when available. Daniel thought it entirely admirable, but he could not feel keenness for anything much at breakfast, save Arbroath Smokies, and these were served only on his birthday as a treat.

This had been but an overture to a suite of exhortations that followed when Chris had produced a Filofax so fat with documents that Daniel feared it would burst open and scatter its contents like a deposed dictator's filing cabinet. He had laid on the table his equivalent, the Parson's Pocketbook, a diary published each year especially for the parish clergy, containing useful data like the Collect for the Day, the lectionary readings, and the addresses of church suppliers and diocesan HQs. The diary section had seemed rather meagre compared with Chris's, and when Daniel had opened it to a week that was completely bare, save an appointment at the vet in Braunstonbury for Cosmo and Hilda to get their claws clipped, he'd tipped it towards his chest, lest he be judged.

He did not think a single virgin page now remained until the Feast of Stephen. There were meetings to discuss carol services, nativities, something called a Christingle, which he had never heard of but at least sounded like something he might like to do. There were meetings about strategies, for upbuilding lay ministries and forming positive partnerships with maintained sector schools, and something called the Sheffield Formula, which at first he thought might be a tonic for sickly cutlers. Worst of all, he had conceded to a weekly meeting, Tuesday mornings at half past seven, a prayer and muesli sandwich alternating between rectory and vicarage. Daniel thought it unlikely his mother would allow for muesli so Chris said he would bring his own, enough for two. An even more lowering feeling fell upon him.

He had come the back way from the Badsaddles. He preferred not to return home by the route he took on his outward journey, a peculiarity his friend Neil had remarked was also a habit of criminals and spies. The route took him along Champton's ambitiously named Main Street, past the grand east gates of the big house, with their neat lodges facing the short row of shops in what Bernard called the Enterprise Zone. One of the lodges looked occupied, Daniel noticed, which he hoped meant that Alex de Floures was home. Alex, Bernard's second son, had spectacularly come out as gay the previous year, when murder had come to Champton and revealed a number of unsettling truths.

Distracted by this, he failed at first to notice a woman who had stepped onto the zebra crossing. When he did, he slammed on the brakes, and the Land Rover came to a halt about three feet from the woman, who was so surprised she dropped her bag.

'You absolute . . . *BUFFOON*!' she shouted, raising her hand magnificently in a V-sign. Then she saw Daniel's collar and pretended she was brushing something off her blouse instead.

Daniel got out. 'I'm so terribly sorry, all my fault, I wasn't paying attention. May I help you?'

The woman, in fight mode because of the near miss, was also involuntarily cowed by the clerical status of the perpetrator. 'It's quite all right, I'm fine. Please don't make a fuss' – her hands flapped around in a windmill of confusion. She was wearing gloves, of dark-blue leather, like the ones his mother wore when she went to Braunstonbury Library.

'But your milk,' said Daniel, noticing a white leak from her shopping bag. 'You must let me replace it. And may I take you to your home? I'm afraid I gave you rather a shock.'

'I'm fine, Vicar, thank you, and I'm only going to the other side of the road. And we shall have our coffee black; it is . . . slimming.' She patted herself down, and only then Daniel noticed that she was young, in her thirties or even twenties, he thought, though she was dressed in a peculiarly old-fashioned way, like a Norland Nanny who had lost her pram.

'But you must . . .'

She smiled in a thin, muscular way, took her bag and walked away, not noticing, or choosing not to notice, the trail of dribbled milk behind her.

On the other side of the street a face disappeared from the window of Stella's High Class Ladies' Fashion. He thought it Anne Dollinger's, who used to work there as an assistant to Stella Harper, not only her employee but her aide-de-camp in the Flower Guild, until Stella was killed by a slice of walnut cake adulterated with poison in last year's murderous Ascensiontide. But what was Anne doing back in the shop, its shutters opened, its blind furled?

The sound of Cosmo barking alerted him to the fact that he was obstructing the zebra crossing. The little dog was sitting up, his paws on the dashboard, making a racket, but a solo racket. Hilda, usually quickest to add her voice to any controversy, was asleep on the passenger seat and barely stirred when he got in. 'Are you all right, my darling doglet?' he said, and stroked her ears, eliciting a single lick in response. How unlike her, he thought.

He let the dogs out at the rectory and Hilda reassuringly scooted to the back door in step with Cosmo. His mother was in the kitchen grinding an unfashionable cut of beef in the aluminium mincer that she had clamped to the tabletop with such unnecessary force over the years that its imprint was as permanent as the grain.

'I nearly ran someone down on the zebra crossing in the village and she dropped her shopping bag.'

'That was careless. Who did you nearly run down?'

'I don't know. Unusual-looking woman. Dressed like she was in the 1950s but she can't have been thirty.'

'Tall, thin, rigid?'

'Yes.'

'Miss March. Sounds like a glamour model but she's definitely not that. She's taken over Stella's. Mrs Braines told me. Didn't you know?'

'Miss March? That's a bit old-fashioned.'

'Well, yes. Or perhaps it's actually rather lovely?'

Daniel wondered if it really was lovely. 'What does she intend for Stella's? I can't see you in bobbysocks and a muff.'

'Not *that* sort of old-fashioned. Classic. Just what the ladies of Champton are looking for.'

'Can I take a pint of milk, Mum?'

'Yes, there's plenty. Why?'

'I'm going to drop it round at Stella's for the admirable Miss March. Replace the one she lost when I nearly ran her over.'

'Not gold top.'

He took a bottle of plain in one of the old bottles Mr Farmer the milkman still delivered – taller and slenderer than the stubby bottles that were replacing them, and with rather an elegant slope to the shoulder, which, it occurred to him, was not dissimilar to the recipient. 'Modigliani,' he muttered to himself. 'She looks like a figure from a Modigliani.'

'Mince, Daniel. Mince with tatties and peas. Hearty fare for lean lunches. One o'clock. And we have visitors.'

'Who?'

'Your brother and your policeman.'

'Theo and Neil?'

'Yes. Theo's calling in on his way up to York, I think he said, and Neil telephoned to say he wants to see you about something. So I said come to lunch. You don't mind?'

'Mind? No, not at all.'

But he did mind a little, or felt a certain apprehension, for he preferred to keep his brother separate from his life outside the family. Theo was an actor, a profession many would think remote from Daniel's vocation, and in personality the two were opposites. Daniel was self-controlled, cautious, restrained; his brother was impulsive, reckless and generous, and ever since they were little boys it was Daniel's job to deal with the messes his younger brother made. It had become a family joke, but family jokes exist in part to moderate difficult truths, in this case that Theo lived life in its fullness — messy and sometimes injurious, but full — the kind of life Daniel was supposed to proclaim but in reality denied himself. His brother's exuberance and unboundedness made Daniel feel like a gamekeeper on watch for poachers. And he was certain, although not sure why, that he did not want this poacher getting anywhere near his friendship with Neil. Perhaps because he also knew that one similarity between clergy and actors was acute powers of observation.

'Well, see you at one sharp, please. I don't want to be left making small talk with your brother and your policeman. Not after the last time.'

There had been an awkwardness when Theo and Neil had first met, in the middle of a murder inquiry, in a sequence of events that had led to them clashing when Daniel was about to be driven to the police station to answer questions about the whereabouts of the prime suspect. He winced at the thought and felt a peak of anxiety at the prospect of the two meeting again.

'I'll be there, don't worry.'

The sign on the door to Stella's High Class Ladies' Fashion said 'CLOSED' so Daniel knocked tentatively, and then a little more forcefully, and its tinny bell gave a feeble ding. A figure moved within and Anne Dollinger, wearing a tape measure round her neck and a pinny over her dress, opened it.

'Yes, Daniel?'

'Good morning, Anne, I've come to see Miss March.'

'Have you?'

'Yes.'

'Miss March?'

'Yes. She is here, I think.' He could hear the sound of someone in the shop moving furniture.

'I will enquire,' Anne said in the voice she usually used for reading the lesson in church. 'Would you kindly wait?'

How peculiar, he thought, like something out of George Eliot; but then he reflected how Anne had withered since Stella's death had left her without someone to serve. If Miss March was to replace her then Anne might very well wish to make a special show of fealty and have a special interest in protecting her from unannounced callers, even if the caller was someone used to passing without let or hindrance through every door in Champton.

Anne returned. 'Miss March will see you now,' she said, and stepped to one side. Daniel half expected her to curtsey as he passed.

The shop was all but empty, the rails bare of frocks, the racks of shoes and bags. It felt deserted, ghostly almost, and Miss March seemed ghostly too, he thought. She was standing in front of the counter, one hand resting on it, one foot turned out, a symphony in grey: grey jacket and skirt, grey eyes and neat hair that looked so much greyer than her years Daniel wondered if it could be dyed to make her seem older. She extended her other hand.

'Rector.' (She had done her homework.)

'Miss March.' Daniel took her hand and found himself bowing as if her steely antiquity was sufficient to force a parallel reaction in him. 'I hope you will allow me to replace the bottle of milk I made you drop.' He offered her his spare pint like a teetotal suitor.

'Quite unnecessary, but how kind.' She took it and glanced at Anne, who took it from her in turn. 'And now I can offer you coffee. Or tea?'

'Thank you. Coffee, if you have it.'

'I would not have offered it if I did not. Anne, would you?'

'Very good, Miss March.' She scuttled off to the kitchen at the back of the shop where once she stirred Lift for Stella.

'I'm afraid I cannot offer you anywhere to sit, or not

yet. I haven't quite decided what I'm going to do with the space.'

'Did you know the shop when Stella kept it?'

'No, but I can imagine what it was like.' There was the suggestion of a purse about her lips.

'She is very much missed, and so is the shop. My mother was one of her stalwart customers. All the ladies of Champton were, or most of them. And of course, her reputation spread further than the village.'

'I should not want to do anything to impair that, of course. But we must adapt, don't you think?'

Daniel recalled saying the same thing to Dora Sharman when the lavatory controversy engulfed them last year. 'We must, where possible. Have you had a dress shop before?'

'Shoes,' said Miss March. 'I had the shoe shop at Stow. You must know it; it was just round the corner from the cathedral close.'

'Oh, yes. March's. A lovely shop. What became of it?'

'Dolcis. Clarks. Cheap imports. My father held on, and so did I after he died, but not for long. Why sell rubbish after three generations of selling the best? I sold up. It's a Scottish knitwear shop now, though they're probably all made in Pakistan.'

'I'm sorry to hear it.'

'So it's dresses now. And you? How long have you been here?'

'Nearly ten years now. I was in London before. Belgravia.'

'How very smart.'

'Yes, it was smart, though people are people.'

'Indeed so. Ah, our coffee.'

Anne appeared with a tray of matching teacups and saucers, a milk jug, a sugar bowl and a tall coffee pot, all with sunflower motifs, so it looked like it had been a prize on *Sale of the Century*. 'Where shall I put it, Miss March?'

'Just leave it on the counter, Anne. Thank you.' The 'thank you' was pronounced with firmness, as a dismissal rather than an expression of gratitude.

'I'll just . . . tidy up the kitchen.'

'Bless you. Oh, that's your business, Rector, not mine, do forgive me.'

Miss March produced the thinnest of smiles and poured the coffee. It gave off not so much an aroma as a threat, the disappointment of chicory, and Daniel could see for a moment the bottle of Camp Coffee – labelled with a kilted Gordon Highlander being served a cup, improbably, by a magnificently attired Sikh – which his mother had started to use when the price of coffee had become extravagant in the 1970s. He wondered if Miss March was similarly motivated by thrift or by the plain old-fashionedness of a coffee substitute that was unsatisfactory in every other way.

'Are you intending to move to Champton, Miss March? Perhaps you already have.'

'Flat above the shop. Not ready yet, but as soon as it is suitable I will. Perhaps, if I like it, I might make it more . . . permanent? I still have the house at Stow – it didn't seem right to sell it as well as the business after everything Father went through, but, well, we adapt. I should make that my motto. Bandit?'

'I'm sorry?'

'A biscuit. They're Bandits. I got them from the post office, with the milk. They survived, I'm pleased to say.'

'Oh, yes, please. And again, I'm so sorry I gave you such a fright.'

'No matter. But if I were to think of settling here, I imagine houses don't come up for sale that often?'

'There's Stella's house. Do you know it? The modern house, chalet-style, set back from the street? I don't think that's sold.'

'The house she was murdered in?'

'Yes. There is that. Of course.' Daniel remembered an estate agent once telling him that three things made a house unsaleable: the smell of dogs, the smell of fags and a murder.

'I shouldn't mind that, but chalet-style? I don't think so. We're not in Zermatt. I was thinking more of an old house. Is everything still owned by the estate?'

'Not everything, but most. You could rent something from the estate? The Factor's House is lovely, and it was only done up a couple of years ago. It's vacant.'

'Not a crime scene too?'

'No . . . but it was where Anthony Bowness lived, who, as you probably know, was unfortunately, ah . . .'

'He was murdered in church, wasn't he?'

'Yes. He was.' Daniel thought of Cosmo and Hilda running towards him, their paws wet with Anthony's blood. He had dreamt of it once or twice too.

'I'm sorry,' said Miss March, 'it must have been dreadful.'

'It is still raw for those of us who were caught up in it.'

'We must face forward,' said Miss March, 'and keep going, don't you think?'

'If we can.'

Miss March sipped her coffee and bit off a corner of her Bandit as daintily as anyone could, thought Daniel. 'Whom should I see about the Factor's House?'

'Call the estate office. Mr Meldrum takes care of the property and letting, I think. Nicholas Meldrum.'

'Very good.'

He sensed that his work, whatever it might be, was done. 'I must be on my way, Miss March . . .'

'Of course, Rector.'

'And do call me Daniel.'

'I would prefer not to. I have such a terrible memory for names.'

'As you wish, Miss March.' He extended his hand, which she shook in the briefest way. He half expected Anne to appear holding his hat and coat (he had brought neither) to show him to the door.

★

'She's quite extraordinary, like a character from Barbara Pym.'

'I remember her,' said Audrey, 'from the shoe shop at Stow. "The Grey Lady" we called her, just there suddenly, gliding in and out, and always with an air of disapproval. Knew her shoes, mind.'

Daniel, his mother and brother, and Neil Vanloo, detective sergeant from Braunstonbury and now Daniel's friend, were lunching in the dining room at the rectory. The room was not used often and had the faint air of a furniture warehouse, its fine table and chairs so seldom being put to service.

'You can tell a lot about someone from their shoes,' said Neil, who was on second helpings already of Audrey's mince, which had emerged robustly from the Aga, insufficiently tenderised even in its reliable and even heat. But Neil was robust himself, stocky and sporty, with the suggestion of muscles beneath the drapery of his not well-fitting suit. He always looked uncomfortable in it, thought Audrey, like a cowman on his wedding day. And his face looked northern, she thought, which it was, though to her that was, if not quite a handicap, something to be regretted. She sometimes thought he had stepped out of a black-and-white film, set in a deprived Lancashire mill town where he had got a girl in the family way and was thinking of doing a runner.

'Yes,' said Daniel. 'I always look at people's shoes.'

'Beryl Reid', said Theo, 'always begins creating a character with the shoes. Get that right and the rest follows. You know who I mean?' he said grandly to Neil.

'Connie Sachs in *Tinker Tailor Soldier Spy*?'

'Wasn't she marvellous?'

There was a pause, then Neil said, 'What were Miss March's like, Dan?'

'Actually, they were penny loafers, but rather well made and impeccably looked-after. A little more dashing than I was expecting. Fashionable.'

'Penny loafers are VERY *à la mode*,' said Audrey, 'but more Honoria's thing than mine. A curious name for shoes, penny loafers.'

'Originally,' said Daniel, 'in the Thirties, I think, American phone boxes took pennies – two pennies – and you could tuck a penny in the slit over the bridge of each shoe so you would have enough to call home if you were stranded after a night out.'

'Is that right?'

'Yes, I think so. I read about it somewhere.'

'Doesn't sound like this Miss March is likely to be stranded after a night out,' said Theo.

'I don't know. There's something quite unusual about her. I felt she was playing a part. Actually, more than that. I felt she was having fun with it. Does that make sense?'

'*A propos* mysterious ladies,' said Theo, 'is Honoria here?'

'She is,' said Daniel a little hesitantly, for Theo's life overlapped with Honoria's and Alex's in London's loucher social networks, and that made him mildly anxious. 'Why do you ask?'

'*Well*,' said Theo, 'love matches, family dramas, dynastic matters.'

'What love match?' asked Audrey.

'She has to prepare Bernard for the wedding.'

'What wedding?' said Audrey. 'Honoria's getting married? I thought there was a bloom on her!'

'No,' said Daniel, 'Hugh's getting married. To the Canadian.'

It would fall to him to officiate at the coming wedding of the Hon. Hugh de Floures, Bernard's eldest son and heir, who was to return, reluctantly, from Canada with his bride for the event. Her first visit to the house and estate of which she would one day be chatelaine was coming in a couple of weeks, and everyone was a little nervous about it.

'Not quite what Bernard had in mind, I suppose,' said Theo, 'but disappointment at the love matches of your heirs and successors is an occupational hazard for aristocrats.'

'He doesn't have a say, though, does he?' said Neil. 'It's not the Middle Ages.'

'No,' said Daniel, 'but marrying into this, even if it's faded, brings expectations.'

'And Bernard's blessing would certainly be highly

preferable, if not necessary,' said Audrey. 'And there's the question of honour due.'

'Honour due?'

'Yes. Honour thy father and mother. Well, father in this case; I don't suppose Hugh's mother gets much of a look-in. But I think it would mean something to his father.'

'Not so much of that about recently,' said Neil.

'No. And better a Canadian for a daughter-in-law than a gay gypsy boy for a son-in-law,' said Audrey, 'from Bernard's point of view.' Last year Alex de Floures surprised even himself by admitting a love affair with the grandson of Edgy Liversedge, a former gypsy prize-fighter who had ended up living a quieter life as a sort of unofficial gamekeeper on the Champton estate. 'Shame, in a way; he was so *handy*.'

'Who knows what lies ahead for the house of de Floures?' said Theo in a portentous voice.

There was a silence.

'A wedding', said Neil, 'of the first born. Big day at t'big house,' he added in a comedy northern accent.

'It will be a very big day,' said Daniel, 'and a tricky one. I've never known the de Floures to be quite so exercised by something. It's one of the ways you notice that they're different from the rest of us. The succession question.'

'I've always known they were different from the rest of us,' said his mother tartly. 'I mean for Bernard' – whom she never addressed, Daniel thought, by

49

his Christian name in person — 'it's not only a new daughter-in-law; it's securing the future of the dynasty. Can't be *anyone,* can it?'

'When Hugh announced he'd met someone, and a Canadian, Bernard said at least it's not some hatchet-faced Portuguese duchess.'

'I thought they hadn't met yet,' said Neil, pushing his fork through his lunch like a builder's trowel through a stiff mortar.

'They haven't, but I don't think a match of this kind is made without . . . enquiries. Especially if you can't look them up in *Burke's,* or the *Almanach de Gotha.*'

'Neil, please don't feel you have to finish that,' said Audrey. 'Let me take it. There's pudding.' She scooped up the plates with a touch more briskness than she normally did, a cue for Theo to get up too and help carry the dishes out to the kitchen.

'I hope I haven't offended her,' said Neil.

'It was awful,' said Daniel. 'Why did you ask for seconds?'

'I was trying to be polite.'

'I don't think even the most gallant of diners would ask for more from Dennis the butcher's economy tray. We're in a time of famine, rather than plenty, at the rectory. My stipend and her pension don't stretch like they used to. But you wanted to see me?'

'Yes. It's not only the de Floures who are having to mind dynastic issues at the moment. Mrs Hawkins at Upper Badsaddle Manor?'

'I know her, yes.'

'She's not well.'

'So I gathered.'

'Seriously unwell, in fact.'

'I'm sorry to hear it.'

There was a pause.

'Why are you telling me this, Neil?'

'There are concerns that she is vulnerable.'

'About as vulnerable as my mother, I would say.'

'She's not what she was. And she's on her own. She's wealthy, she has no immediate family and the vultures are circling.'

'Anyone I know?'

'The Tailbys.'

Daniel had met Jean and Roy Tailby when he'd first arrived at Champton. He had been asked to conduct a funeral for a woman who had died alone; her husband was long dead, she had no children, no close family, so she had been looked after in her decline by neighbours, the Tailbys, who had been so kind and helpful they had practically moved in. It was them he met in her little house, and they who told him about her life – 'There was a nephew and a niece, but she never saw them or heard from them . . . some sad family business. She did tell me, but . . . private, you know? In the end we were all she had . . . We'll miss her ever so much . . .' It was they who chose the readings and the hymns – '"All Things Bright and Beautiful" and that one about the bread of heaven they do at the rugby' – and they who inherited her savings and her house.

Six months later an undertaker had called him with another job and he had gone to the deceased's house and found Jean and Roy Tailby there again. They had befriended the lonely widow who lived there too, and she had left everything to them, to the surprise and disappointment of the NSPCC, which had been promised a generous legacy.

'I don't think the Tailbys will get anywhere near her,' said Daniel, 'they like easier prey.'

'She's old, dying, alone and a prize, and I hear Jean Tailby has offered her services as cook-housekeeper after Mrs Hawkins sacked the last one.'

'I see,' said Daniel. 'I should perhaps ask my new colleague to call in on his parishioner.'

'Thanks. And I wondered if you fancy the football on Saturday?'

'Rugby?'

'No, the other kind. Association. The one where they don't use hands much.'

'Who's playing?'

'It's a big match, Stow at home to Stratton, Daniel, local derby. Longstanding rivals meet on the field of play. Should be . . . lively.'

'I'd love to come . . .' – a sudden memory of the misery of games at school, of being the last to be picked (*Not YOU, Clement*), humiliation in the cold, pitiless rain, the agony of changing, Gordon Ashby banging his boots against a wall so the compacted mud between the studs flew off and hit him in the eye. 'How much are the tickets?'

'Free. Got them from work. I'll pick you up about twelve.'

'Let me pick you up. You always do the driving.'

'No, you're all right. And don't wear your dog collar.'

'Why not?'

'Just don't.'

'OK. But let me do the driving.'

'That's a lot of excitement for one day, Daniel.'

Audrey and Theo reappeared with a trio of baked apples, so mottled from the rectory Aga they looked more decayed than cooked. 'Season of mists and mellow fruitfulness!' Audrey declaimed, digging one out with a serving spoon and depositing it so emphatically in Neil's bowl that it slowly settled in on itself, like a dismantled marquee.

'You look like you've been plotting,' said Theo as he poured a stiff custard over it. 'What have I missed?'

'You don't miss much, Theo, do you?' said Neil quietly. 'We're going to the football. Is that a first for Dan?'

'I would have thought mud wrestling in the Limpopo more likely,' said Audrey. 'Perhaps you have that planned too?'

Theo noticed Daniel and Neil exchange a look, like naughty boys at the back of the class.

53

'Football, Dan? *Football*?'

'Yes. Behold, I will do a new thing; now it shall spring forth; shall ye not know it?'

'It certainly is a new thing. I don't remember you having much fondness for it when we were at school.'

'Those terrible shorts,' said Audrey. 'Dark-blue serge-like stuff, elasticated waist. I spent hours sewing in name tapes. You looked like borstal boys.'

'Wasted effort, Mum,' said Theo, then to Daniel: 'You can't have played more than a couple of games of football in all my time there. And I still remember your cricket protest.'

'What cricket protest?' asked Neil.

'Dan hated cricket so much that when he was made to do it – for a house match when everyone was ill – he walked out to the crease and before the ball was bowled he knocked the bails off with his bat, turned round and walked straight back to the pavilion.'

'How did that go down?'

'There was a chorus of boos.'

'Not my finest hour,' said Dan, 'but I was not going to play cricket. It just wasn't for me. And when they made me . . . . I did what I had to do.'

'You know,' said Theo, 'I think it *was* your finest hour.'

Next to the front door of Champton Rectory was a brass sign put up by a Victorian predecessor. It said 'THE RECTOR IS NOT AT HOME IN THE

AFTERNOON', and though the era when rectors devoted their afternoons to butterfly collecting or archaeology or croquet had passed, Daniel still liked to maintain a cordon round the hours between lunch and tea. Two hours, if he was lucky, to devote to his 'studies', which at the moment meant reading his way through the new revised edition of H. P. Lovecraft's *The Horror in the Museum* and teaching himself the accordion. A parishioner who played in a folk band had died and left him his instrument, knowing he liked its reedy noise. Perhaps this was because of its slight resemblance to the organ: the ingenuity and neatness of its operation, the melody played on the miniature keyboard with the right hand, bass notes and chords on dozens of tiny buttons with the left? It pleased him to conjure a jolly dance tune from this lacquered contraption, even when Audrey said it sounded like 'a massacre at an Albanian wedding'.

This struck him as quite a fitting description, for his parishioner had Lithuanian heritage and left him an album of Baltic wedding dances, invoking the moon, or an old windmill, or a turbulent river. They had a remorseless jollity to them, which was as unsettling, in its way, as clowns.

Daniel was three-quarters of the way through a very approximate evocation of spring in Livonian Courland when he noticed the Biddles' campervan coming up the drive. In the excitement of nearly mowing down Miss March and the unexpected lunch with Neil, he had completely forgotten his arrangement to walk the dogs with Lydia after school. It was entirely his fault, but the surprise and the necessary adjustment to his immediate plans made him resent her, so when she and Sal came to the door he had to resist the temptation to indulge a slight testiness. Instead, he was too fulsome in his greeting, a more subtle C of E way of indicating irritation, but not subtle enough for Sal, who had been collaterally damaged by it through marriage.

'You did remember, Daniel? That you and Lydia arranged to take the dogs out?'

'Of course, and I'm delighted! Do you have time for a cup of tea, Sal?' he offered, again with an obviously contrived enthusiasm that Sal did not have the patience to field with parallel insincerity.

'No. You'll bring Lydia back?'

'Of course. To the vicarage?'

'Yes, please.'

A door opened behind Daniel, followed by the sound of claws clattering on the black-and-white tiles in the hall, then Cosmo burst out from behind him and skidded to a halt and sat up to bark at the intruders. Lydia dropped to her knees.

'Oh, you little beauty, aren't you *gorgeous*?' she cooed and reached out to the little dog; he backed away at first, but Cosmo knew a good thing when he saw one and was soon standing by her feet, tail whirring like a strimmer. But where is Hilda? thought Daniel. She's usually in the vanguard when visitors come to call.

She was with Audrey, hiding almost behind her as she approached to see who it was at the door. 'Mrs Biddle! And . . . Miss Biddle, sorry, *Ms* Biddle! How nice to see you. And so unexpected!'

'Hello, Audrey – please, it's Sal, and this is Lydia, and we arranged for her to come and walk the dogs.'

'Of course you did. Daniel forgot to tell me, but we're only too pleased to see you.' With that, Hilda walked forward uncertainly from behind Audrey and went to sit with Cosmo, looking up at the visitor. Lydia gave another exclamation: 'And YOU'RE gorgeous too!' and went to scratch her head. This had given the postman, the man from Christian Aid and the window cleaner cause for regret, for Hilda was typical of the breed: protective, aggressive, fearless, and if anyone got too near without sufficient warning or permission, she would nip. She had once nipped Daniel for getting close while she was chewing a bone she had confiscated from Cosmo, her pack due, she thought, which not even Daniel could deprive. But now she just allowed Lydia to stroke her head and ears and scratch her under the chin. Then she rolled onto her back in a gesture of submission so extravagant it made Daniel think of a vassal chieftain making obeisance to his unrivalled king.

'Ooh, aren't you scrumptious, scrumptious?' said Lydia, which to Audrey, coming from beneath a mound of hair dyed jet black so that it looked from a distance like a bearskin, sounded as if it were perhaps in anticipation of eating Hilda. And then it occurred to her, too, that the dog's behaviour was not what she expected, and a thought stirred in her not-yet-conscious mind. 'Do you have time for a cup of tea, Mrs Bid— Sal?'

'Thank you, but no, I have . . . something in the oven. Another time?'

'Any time.'

'We have a house group tonight, Daniel, so it's an early supper at six,' said Sal.

'OK, I'll make sure she's back in time. Let me see you out.'

He walked her to the campervan. 'What a splendid machine!' he said in the traditional manner of a Church of England parson trying to hide a plain truth behind gratuitous praise.

'It's a rusty old pile of junk, Daniel,' Sal said. 'We got it for Greenbelt when the kids were small. And for Greenham Common. Before rectories and vicarages and lunches at the big house.'

'I see. It was rather a baptism of fire?'

'We don't . . . live like that.'

'You may have to find a way of accommodating it.'

'Are you suggesting we enrol at a finishing school?'

'No.'

'We know how to behave, Daniel. But there are more important things than good behaviour.'

'Like what?'

'Being faithful.'

'Yes. We must always be faithful.'

'I suppose I'm saying I didn't give myself to Christ in the expectation of aperitifs in the library.'

'What did you expect?'

'Not *this*.'

'Oh, that's good.'

She looked puzzled. 'What do you mean?'

'Well, if we got what we expected it wouldn't be worth our time and trouble.'

'One of your riddles. Chris said you liked riddles.'

She got into the campervan and started coaxing it into unpromising life. 'Thanks for taking the trouble with Lydia, though,' she said through the open window. 'It's kind of you.'

He waved her off with the faint satisfaction of one bad driver watching another.

Lydia was on her hands and knees in the study playing with the dogs when he closed the front door behind him. Audrey was waiting for him.

'She's sharp, isn't she?'

'I thought a bit on edge. Do you think she might not like dogs?'

'Imagine!'

'Or perhaps she just doesn't want to be part of what we are.'

'I expect she must feel bitter.'

'About what?'

'Not being allowed to be a lady vicar. Do you think

59

she looks at that soppy husband droning on and longs to throw her plasticine at him?'

'I don't know. I don't suppose Chris would be in favour of lady vicars.'

'Really?'

'Very unlikely. His lot are rather against all that.'

'I thought they were all trendy?'

'Not about this. Because Scripture tells us, rather it tells *them*, that women may not take leadership roles. Only men can.'

Audrey gave a little yelp of laughter, which made Hilda come waddling out of the study. 'How very quaint!'

'Indeed. But I must get these dogs walked.'

'Where are you going to take them?'

'Up to the old airfield, let them run. And I want to get to know Lydia. It might help me make sense of her parents.'

'There's something not quite right about her . . .'

'Mum, she's sixteen and likes Goth music, and dyes her hair, and she's a feminist . . .'

'Not her, you fathead, *her*,' and she pointed at Hilda still sitting meekly on the threshold of adventure, rather than hurling herself into it with her usual yelping battle cry.

Daniel drove Lydia and the dogs up to the old airfield where Neil had been giving him 'advanced motoring' lessons. It lay to the northwest of the Champton estate, on de Floures land, but in the Badsaddle parishes, and had been built in 1941 for the Flying Fortresses of the United States Air Force. The airmen had brought chewing gum and Lucky Strikes and nylons and the vague promise of a better life elsewhere to the ladies of Champton and the Badsaddles and Braunstonbury, some of whom indeed had 'bagged a Yank' and were now living in the spreading suburbs of Florida and North Dakota and New Mexico. Others had not been so lucky and, bereaved of that promised life, kept a thin packet of letters tied with ribbon hidden under a different marital bed.

Also left behind were buildings – derelict concrete sheds now, once barracks and gun emplacements and fuel dumps and messes – the temporary town with an even more temporary population, and a phantom infrastructure of roads and runways now fringed with nettles and thorns.

It was not the loveliest place in Champton to walk the dogs, but its spaces were wide enough for Daniel to let them off their leads but keep them within sight, and here they were less likely to chase hares or pheasants into the woods – excursions which could last for hours and leave him helplessly calling their names into some unresponsive glade. He also wanted to keep a close eye on Hilda; she seemed fine now, but the frequency of her out-of-character moments was increasing, or so he thought. He was also interested in talking to Lydia.

'I hope you don't mind that I brought you here, Lydia. It's perhaps not what you were thinking of, but the dogs like it and I think it's interesting too.'

Lydia looked around as if it had not occurred to her yet that this was a site of Second World War archaeology. 'Why do the dogs like it?'

'They like to run, I like to keep an eye on them, and the place is lively with interest for all of us.'

'What do they like about it?'

'Smells. Nosing around in inaccessible places. Indulging their curious natures.'

'I see. They're definitely the right shape for that.'

'Exactly. You can let them off if you like.' Cosmo and Hilda were already pulling at their leads and were too impatient for Lydia to unlatch them, so they kept straining and making it harder for her to do what they wanted.

Once freed, they ran off in a wide circle of reconnaissance.

'Why sausage dogs?'

'Dachshunds?' he said in the C of E way of correcting someone by replying with the right word to their wrong. 'I've always had them, from when I was a little boy.'

'Do you remember the first?'

'Yes, I do. Caspar was the first, a little red, but he didn't last long, I'm afraid; he was run over when he was only a puppy really.'

'Oh *no*,' said Lydia, and tears appeared in her eyes.

'I'm afraid so. But more followed. Cosmo and Hilda are five and six.'

'What were the others called?'

'After Caspar we had Gusty – Augustus, but my brother couldn't say his name properly, so he became Gusty. Then I had Isolde when I was at theological college, who practically lived under my cassock, then she was joined by Tristan, obviously.'

'Why Tristan?'

'Tristan and Isolde, from the opera by Wagner.'

'Is that the same as Tristan and Iseult?'

'Same source, yes. But how do you know that?'

'It's in one of my favourite books. *The Sword and the Circle*. Rosemary Sutcliff.'

'The *Eagle of the Ninth* author? I read them when I was a boy.'

'She's related to Dad. I think her father and Dad's grandfather were cousins. And they served together in the navy.'

'I didn't know that. Then Cosmo and Hilda came after my mother moved in with me; she thought they would be good company. And they are good company.'

'I don't think your mother likes us very much.'

'Why do you say that?'

'Because Josh threw a bread roll at me at the snobby lunch.'

Daniel noticed Hilda, some distance away, stop and stiffen. He knew that look.

'Hilda!' She suddenly rolled onto her long back and then squirmed left and right, so that whatever thrillingly pungent deposit she had found would be thoroughly worked into her fur. She had once done this just before he and Audrey had set off in the car for the long drive home from her Scottish cousins on the Kyle of Lochalsh. They were nine hours kippered in the stink of fox droppings; it was so bad Audrey had refused to let him stop at a service station and he'd had to jump out in a lay-by for a pee.

'Oh, Hilda!'

'Don't be cross with her! She's only doing what nature made her for.'

'Wait for the drive home.'

'But did you see the way she did it? She was being a dog! Not just a pet. She was being what God intended her to be, right? I think it's beautiful when they do that.'

'Civilisation is all about training instincts, don't you think? It's why my mother would . . . raise an eyebrow . . . at bread-roll fights at Sunday lunch.'

'Sorry about that, it wasn't very cool. It's Josh. He can't help it when he's meant to be on his best behaviour. And you know how it is for vicarage kids.'

'Is that why you're Goths?'

She sighed. 'We're not Goths. We're semi-Goths. You can't really be a Goth at school because of the rules about make-up and what you can wear.'

'What sort of make-up?'

'You know, black lipstick, eyeliner, powder . . . and that's just Josh.'

'Isn't he in a band?'

'Yes, he's the bass player.'

'What's the band called?'

'Castle of Otranto.'

'Ah, Walpole.'

'We love that book.'

'Let me show you something.' Daniel called the dogs. They swerved back towards him, and he led them down one of the service roads through the trees, then down another very wild path that led to a collection of semi-derelict buildings. There were what had once been Nissen huts, and what he supposed was a canteen, and then a curious little building, half buried, with an arched roof that was still intact. Some sort of bomb shelter? Perhaps it had originally been that, but when they went down the steps into the damp and musty interior what Lydia saw came as a surprise.

'This was the chapel,' Daniel said. 'You made me think of it when you said Castle of Otranto, with the crypt church – do you remember, all that business with Manfred and Matilda?'

'Oh, wow!'

'It was built by the men who flew from here. Adapted by them, I suppose. Somewhere to pray, somewhere to come to Mass, or to sing hymns; it was for all denominations – I met an American chap in the village not long ago who had been one of the padres here.'

'Did he bless their bombs and their guns too?'

'I don't know. But do we know what it was like for them to fly out to bomb Cologne knowing they had a fifty-fifty chance of returning? I wouldn't begrudge them whatever comforts they could come by,' and he remembered the old padre telling him that they also had dances, amply attended by women from town in those straitened times, with recreational opportunities afterwards and such exchanges as suited both parties – no sermonising required.

'Would you bless bombs and guns?' Lydia asked.

'No, I wouldn't.' One of his trickiest moments when he'd arrived at Champton was when the invitation came to bless the hounds of the Muscott Hunt on St Hubert's Day, an ancient tradition which, like so many ancient traditions, had long died out but was re-stored when a vogue for ecclesiastical antiquity briefly peaked, and everyone had to Beat the Bounds again or climb the tower on Ascension Day. He could not, in conscience, do what he was asked to do, but he did not want to alienate the hunting set and was at a loss until he consulted his predecessor, Canon Dolben, who offered to do it in his place on the grounds that he was a priest of good standing in the Confraternity of St Hubert, and therefore should have been their first choice, and actually he was rather wounded they had not come to him. Daniel conveyed this to the Master of Hounds, who was mortified, and immediately called on Canon Dolben to make amends and invited him to preside. Neither told him that the Confraternity of St Hubert consisted of one member, Canon Dolben, and that they had made it up expressly for this purpose.

The dark space was mouldy and chilly, but you could still make out a table at the end with a low rail in front of it and almost indecipherable paintings, blurred by time and damp, which he realised were the Stations of the Cross painted directly onto the walls. He shivered.

'Are you all right?'

'Yes. It just makes the people who worshipped here, who made this, seem so vivid. Shall we?' He stepped aside to let her out, and the dogs weaved between them out into the light. 'It's . . . um . . . getting on; I should get you home.' They walked on in silence, the dogs just ahead of them, like motorcycle outriders for a slow convoy.

Lydia said, 'Do you remember the war?'

'Barely. I was only a little boy when it ended. I think I remember that, but I may have appropriated other people's memories for my own. Everyone in Braunstonbury was celebrating – VE Day – but one house, neighbours of ours, had all the curtains drawn. They'd lost a son in Burma, I think. I can remember rationing. And the winter of 1947. I remember that very clearly. What about you? What's the first thing you remember?'

'In the news?'

'Yes.'

'I think it was when John Lennon got shot. Mum cried. And "Imagine" was on the radio for weeks. And then Greenham Common.'

'Oh, yes. It seemed to be constantly on the news.'

'We went. Mum took us. I remember staying in a tent and everyone dancing in the mud and then lots of policemen in black coats standing on the other side of the fence and we tried to make them laugh.'

'Did you succeed?'

'No. Josh made all the women laugh, though; he stuck his tongue out at the police and did a V-sign, but Mum stopped him.'

'So you started young?'

'What do you mean?'

'Giving two fingers to authority.'

'I suppose so. But then we saw Uncle Will.'

'A whole family of protesters?'

'No, he was one of the policemen. He's Mum's cousin really, not brother, but we call him Uncle Will. It was quite funny: one minute we were singing "Give Peace a Chance" through the fence at the guards, then Will shouted hello and Mum ended up inviting him to tea on Boxing Day.'

Daniel laughed.

'I made you laugh,' said Lydia.

'It's so C of E,' he said.

The drive to Lower Badsaddle Vicarage was fortunately short. Hilda, banished to the very back, was so pungent with the stink of fox droppings, even with all the windows open, that Daniel had to breathe through his mouth lest he gag. When he dropped Lydia off he saw her mother's nose wrinkle as soon as she stepped out of the Land Rover, and when she made to pet Hilda goodbye they both raised a restraining hand.

'Sorry, Sal,' said Daniel, 'she rolled in fox poo – it's dachshunds being dachshunds.'

'I don't know why people love dogs – they can be so . . . dirty.'

Daniel felt something cold begin to form within him, like the first crust of ice on a puddle in November.

'I thought you liked dogs?'

'Did Chris tell you that? We officially like dogs, for pastoral reasons. But I'm more of a cat person. Less needy.'

'I suppose so, but then one thinks of them bringing in half-dead birds, or squirrels, or mice.'

Sal laughed. 'I know, I wasn't being . . . doggist.' She looked flummoxed for a second. 'I would rather not have another year of Lydia pleading for a puppy. Anyway, thanks for taking her, Daniel. I'd better . . .' She looked towards her daughter, who was already disappearing through the front door.

Daniel took the dogs to the back door when he got home. His mother was in the kitchen, beating flour and eggs and butter at the kitchen table. He opened the door an inch. 'Mum,' he shouted, 'look out! Hilda's rolled in fox do again . . .' but Cosmo, in the vanguard, pushed through the gap and Hilda followed, and the comforting smell of Audrey's baking was almost instantly overlaid with searing top notes of ammonia and goat's cheese.

'Get that filthy hound out of here, Daniel!'

He tried to shoo Hilda out, but flapping his arms at her had the opposite effect, driving her further in, while Cosmo, thinking it a game, ran round and round the kitchen in aimless pleasure.

'I am NOT having that stink on my Victoria sponge!' said Audrey, her tone of command causing Cosmo to stop and Hilda to turn back towards her. 'Right,' she said, 'bathtime for YOU,' and she picked up the now-compliant Hilda, wrinkled her nose and took her outside. There was a stable out the back with a cold-water tap and an old tin bath reserved for washing the dogs when they were exceptionally muddy or exceptionally foul, a job that Audrey secretly rather liked because it allowed her to show care, but robustly, without the sentimentality she abhorred. When Daniel and Theo were little boys, Audrey would brush their hair with such force that Daniel thought it more a punishment than a benefit. 'And there's a message for you by the telephone!'

Audrey disliked answering machines, saying if she wished to listen to recorded voices she would go to a discotheque. So a note in her old-fashioned writing informed him that Mrs Hawkins from Upper Badsaddle Manor had telephoned and could Daniel please call her at his earliest convenience – 'earliest' underlined three times.

The telephone, which Audrey insisted on keeping in the hall on its own table and with an accompanying chair, was one of the old Marmite-coloured Bakelite models with silver buttons that now did nothing, a little tray you pulled out to reveal important numbers and an artfully wound cord, which curled itself into Gordian knots the dogs liked to chew. Daniel disliked the telephone, not as an object, but as a means of communication. He wanted to see whom he was talking to, so he could interpret what their faces and gestures revealed about them; but there was no need of supplementary information for his conversation with Mrs Hawkins.

'Rector, I wonder if you would be so kind in future – not that there's a lot of that in store for me – if you wish to consult me, to come yourself rather than send the . . . person who came to see me today, at your behest, he said.'

'Oh. Would that be Mr Biddle?'

'I don't recall his name, but his appearance I will not forget. Now, I don't expect the vicar to wear a top hat on a visit to a dying parishioner, but I draw the line at play clothes.'

'Oh dear.'

'How would you feel, should you be about to compose yourself in anticipation of meeting your maker, if a man in a green boiler suit and rattling beads attempted to offer words of consolation?'

'I cannot imagine.'

'You don't have to, for I will tell you. Aggrieved. Very aggrieved indeed.'

'I am sorry to hear that, Mrs Hawkins. Perhaps, if you will allow me, I could come to see you?'

'I will most certainly allow it. When can you come?'

'I could come now, if you wish?'

'Certainly. And I would be very much obliged if you would bring a prayer book and a Bible rather than a space hopper or spinning top.'

'Of course. I will be with you very soon, Mrs Hawkins. Goodbye.'

He telephoned Chris.

'Badsaddle Vicarage?'

'Chris, it's Daniel.'

'Hi, Daniel.'

'Chris, I've just had a telephone conversation with Mrs Hawkins.'

'Ah.'

'She's asked me to go and see her. I hope you don't mind, but I wondered if you could tell me what happened?'

'No need for you to go, Daniel, I can handle it.'

'I'm quite sure you can, but she has asked to see me.'

'Oh, for . . . Pete's sake!'

'Go on.'

'I went to see her, as you asked me to, all very last

minute, but you asked so I did, and she was extremely rude. So be it, but then she refused even to let me pray with her. When I insisted, she threw a box of tissues at me and told me to leave. I did try, but there was no point. What could I do?'

'Well, possibly nothing, but you should have telephoned me.'

'Why? Do you want me to bother you over every time waster?'

'Time waster?'

'And whoever shall not receive you or hear your words, shake off the dust of your feet when you depart from that house.'

'She's a parishioner, Chris, she's dying, she's frightened.'

'She didn't seem very frightened to me. And she's my parishioner, so I don't see what it's got to do with you.'

'My responsibility too, I'm the Team Rector' – how Daniel disliked that title – 'and technically we share the cure of souls.'

There was a silence.

'Daniel, may I be straight with you?'

'Such an ominous phrase, but yes, if you must.'

'I am not happy to dance attendance on a rude old woman who is not a churchgoer, or barely, nor a Christian of any authentic kind, when I could be going where God wants me to go, to do what God wants me to do.'

Daniel took a breath. 'Remember, Chris, "How great a treasure is committed to your charge. For they are the sheep of Christ, which he bought with his death, and for whom he shed his blood."'

Chris took a breath. 'Cast not your pearls before swine, Daniel. And . . .'

'Go on.'

'I'm sorry, I don't mean to be offensive, but I have to say that if it were not Mrs Hawkins of the Manor House but Doris Bloggs of Back Lane, I wonder if you would be quite so punctilious.'

'Oh. This is not a conversation for the telephone, I think. I am going round to see Mrs Hawkins now. May I call on you afterwards?'

'It's really not convenient.'

'Nor for me, especially considering I just dropped off Lydia at your vicarage. It won't take a minute.'

Chris sighed. 'OK, if you must.'

'I fear I must,' he said. 'Till later, then; goodbye.' Daniel put down the receiver without waiting for Chris to respond — a rather regrettable way, he thought, of terminating the conversation, but necessary, too, to be clear about where the negotiables and non-negotiables lay.

But before that, another tricky visit. He checked himself in the mirror. All was seemly, but he decided to change out of his sports jacket and slacks and put on a cassock in a gesture of respect, not only for the sensibilities of Mrs Hawkins, but for his associate vicar's too, although he didn't suppose Chris would see it that way. He kept a cassock – not his best cassock with the scarlet piping and buttons he was entitled to wear as a Canon of Stow, but a plain one – on the hook on the back of his study door, along with the full-length black Melton cloak he wore for funerals. Once, wearing it on a cold day walking back from the cemetery to church, a man in a white van leaned out as he drove past and shouted, 'Oi! Count Dracula! Shouldn't you be in your coffin?' He picked up his prayer book and his oil stock – the three little screw-together silver pots of holy oils – and quietly went out of the front door to avoid both Cosmo and his mother, who he knew would be flushed from her lustrations and probably feeling combative.

The drive to the Badsaddles was becoming rather a frequent experience, and an irritating one for a man with a mildly obsessive dislike of retracing his steps. But then the road forked right for Upper Badsaddle instead of left for Lower, and – enjoying the novelty – soon he was driving through the gateposts, now unhung with gates, of Manor House.

Manor House was a generous description of Mrs Hawkins's home. It was indeed built on manor land, but in the 1930s the Tudor house had burnt down, leaving only the Victorian dower house, which looked like the rectory of one of the better-off clergy of Barsetshire. Rear Admiral Hawkins, Mrs Hawkins's father-in-law, simply transferred the name from the greater to the lesser, conferring a dignity that the structure could not quite support. In fact, the structure could only barely support itself, and the house, though handsome and well situated, looked faded. The drive was weedy, the laurels on either side shaggy; all the windows of the third floor were shuttered, and there was a general look of greyness about its south front, as if it had been dressed in a thin layer of ash from a distant volcanic eruption.

He rang the doorbell and unhurried footsteps approached. It was Dora Sharman. Her twin sister, Kath, had last year murdered three of his parishioners and died in a fire she had set herself. Wouldn't such terrible events, and the suspicions they caused, make her twin's continuing presence in the neighbourhood awkward? But the waters of Champton, once the troubling currents had subsided, had returned almost immediately to their accustomed state of tranquillity, and the catastrophe sank beneath the surface almost as if it had never occurred.

'Rector.'

'Dora. I didn't expect to see you.' She put her head slightly to one side. 'Oh. I'm here to see Mrs Hawkins.'

'She's expecting you. Come in.'

Dora, tiny and wearing a cross-over housecoat that made him think of a shroud, led him into the hall. It was gloomy, with portraits of Hawkinses in navy uniforms from the age of Nelson to the Cod Wars looking out from the walls. The furniture was dark brown and massive, built for another age but still here, solid and enduring. On the stairs and on the sideboard and the hall table were boxes, and scrunched-up pieces of newspaper, stacked and scattered, telling a different tale of impermanence.

'I'm helping out Mrs R,' said Dora, 'in case you were wondering.'

'Mrs R?'

'Mrs Reginald Hawkins – this Mrs Hawkins. Not Mrs Hawkins her mother-in-law. She was Mrs Hawkins.'

'How is she?'

'Dying. But not fading especially.'

'What will you do?'

'What will I do?'

'When she's gone.'

'Go home. But I'm not waiting for her to die to do that. I'm only here to help with the bits and bobs, packing things up and the like. No, she has someone to look after her. Shall I see if she's ready to see you?'

'If you would.'

Dora padded away up the stairs, which creaked loudly even under her bantamweight. Daniel sat in a space on a hall bench. He noticed only then that his cassock was not entirely up to the task of conferring dignity. It was shiny where the pile had worn, and many of the buttons were loose – thirty-nine according to tradition, one for each of the Articles of Religion in the prayer book, only there weren't thirty-nine, but nobody could be bothered to count, so it stuck.

A voice sounded from a landing above. 'Daniel? I mean, Rector?'

'Yes, Dora?'

'Come up.'

Daniel made his way up the creaky stairs, past the half-filled boxes and onto the landing. The sickroom smell of balm and bandages and bedpans wafted from an open door.

'She's in there.'

The room was even gloomier than the hall; the curtains were drawn, and a little crooked, across the wide bay window. And there in bed, propped up on pillows, was Mrs Hawkins in a bed jacket, her hair suddenly whiter, her arms as thin as pipe cleaners, but her eye steady and unblinking. And there, sitting next to her in an armchair, was Jean Tailby with a bit of crochet stuffed down the side of a cushion.

'Ah, Reverend Clement,' she said, 'I *am* pleased it's you!'

'I wondered when we'd meet again, Mrs Tailby,' he said.

'It's me you're here to see, Rector, not her,' interrupted Mrs Hawkins in a voice with barely a wobble.

'Mrs Hawkins,' he said. 'You look encouragingly well.'

'I'm dying, but the curtains are drawn, and Mrs Tailby's brushed my hair and found me a bit of lipstick. And I am glad to see you. Will you have tea? Or a drink? I shall have a sherry.'

Mrs Tailby smiled and said, 'Dora? Sherry for the vicar and Mrs R?'

'Get it yourself, Jean, you know where it is. And it's rector, not vicar,' and Dora turned and left.

With a little laugh, Mrs Tailby smoothed her lap and struggled out of the chair. She, too, was small, but broad to Dora's thin, and her cream knitted sweater was a little stretched over her bust. Her legs, in brown slacks, paddled up and down as she tried to rise, revealing two shoes so tiny they looked like a child's. Daniel leaned in to offer her his arm.

'Thank you, Reverend,' she said. 'I'm quite the tortoise!' Once she was safely vertical, she fussed at her sleeves and her neckline for a second or two and then smiled, hugely. 'Sherry for *you*, and for *you* . . . won't be a minute.' She shuffled out of the room.

'I didn't know you were acquainted with the Tailbys,' Daniel said.

'You know the husband too?'

'I do. Roy, I think.'

'He's making himself useful, driving, tidying up, fetching things.'

'I'm sure he is. How did you . . . come by them?'

'They came by me. Word got out – you know what people are like – and she came to see me. And while Dora's a dear, she's not exactly busting her guts to help out. And I need things tidy, Rector, before I die.'

'Things?'

'My affairs, the house, business. That's what I wanted to see you about.'

'I thought you wanted to see me about Mr Biddle?'

'That wretched curate?'

'He's not a curate, actually, but the clergyman who came to see you.'

'Clergyman? He looks like he presents *Blue Peter*.'

'He's . . . um . . . a new generation.'

'I don't want a new generation; I want the old generation. I want a parson who looks like a parson, talks like a parson – you know, someone like you.'

'I can assure you there is nothing I can offer you that Mr Biddle cannot also offer you.'

'Really? Do you know what he offered me?'

Daniel tensed. 'No, I don't.'

'He offered to lay his hands upon me.'

Daniel was silent.

'Yes. To lay his hands upon me. Do I look like a Tiller Girl?'

Daniel coughed. 'I think, Mrs Hawkins, the offer would have been for the laying on of hands.'

'Exactly, like I said.'

'It isn't what I think you suspect. It's actually a charism, a gift . . . It's a means of giving healing.'

'I'm sure the magistrate will take that kindness into consideration.'

'Magistrate?'

'No, of course not, but really, Daniel, am I to be

groped because some well-meaning fool thinks he can make me all better?'

'I am sure Mr Biddle would not do anything you did not wish him to do.'

'Are you? He then attempted to pray for me.'

Daniel frowned. 'That is not an entirely unexpected offer from a clergyman, surely?'

'Words of consolation I want, Rector, not some made-up rubbish asking God to take away my cancer. Stow Royal Infirmary can't take away my cancer, nor all the wise heads of Harley Street. So why would a man with a bubble-cut perm and a simpering manner succeed where chemotherapy has failed? But he wouldn't take no for an answer.' She propped herself up on her elbows. 'Rector, I want you to promise me something.'

Oh dear, thought Daniel, and said, 'If I can, I will.'

'I don't want him anywhere near my funeral.'

'Mrs Hawkins, he is your parish priest.'

'You're my parish priest, aren't you? Now we're jumbled in together?'

'Not really. Mr Biddle has responsibility for the Badsaddles, and I have an . . . I think the bishop called it an "executive role". I don't really know what that means, but I don't think it would be right for me to interfere in another priest's pastoral duties. And – please let me assure you – I am certain his intentions today were *entirely* good.'

Mrs Hawkins slapped the counterpane with both

hands. 'I don't care about his intentions! I don't care what the plumber's intentions are, or the gardener's; I just want them to stop the tap dripping and keep the slugs off my hostas!' Now there was a more noticeable wobble in her voice and a bead of light reflected from the bedside lamp formed in the corner of her eye.

Daniel went to sit in the chair vacated by Jean Tailby. 'Mrs Hawkins, I am sorry. This must be a very difficult time for you. What can I do for you?'

'And he was rude, RUDE. No apology, the brusquest of goodbyes. And I'm *dying* . . .'

'Are you frightened?'

'Of course I'm frightened. Are you going to tell me not to be?'

'No. I was going to say you are not alone.'

She suddenly sobbed. He took her hand. It was tiny and frail, like a moth.

In a quiet but steady voice, Daniel said:

'Tarry no longer! Toward thine heritage
Haste on thy way, and be of right good cheer;
Go each day onward on thy pilgrimage;
Think how short time thou shalt abide thee here.
Thy place is built above the starre's clear;
None earthly palace wrought in so stately wise . . .'

Mrs Hawkins sobbed, and he took from his pocket the oil stock and unscrewed the section marked I for Infirmarium. He pressed his thumb into the oily wad

it contained and traced with it the sign of the cross on
her forehead.

'Muriel,' he said, 'I anoint you in the name of God,
Father, Son and Holy Ghost. The Lord bless thee, and
keep thee. The Lord make his face to shine upon thee,
and be gracious unto thee. The Lord lift up his countenance upon thee, and give thee peace, both now and
evermore.'

'Amen,' she said, and her sobbing subsided. He took
her hand again.

'Ooh,' said a voice from the shadows beyond the
bed, 'you're a Muriel?'

'Not to you, Mrs Tailby, if you don't mind.'

'No, dear, of course not. I've brought your sherry.'

She moved into the light holding a tray, on which
stood two Madeira glasses – Daniel winced at the sole-
cism – which were filled to the brim with a liquid the
colour of garnets.

'Where do you want them, Mrs R?'

'Just put mine on the bedside table. Rector, help
yourself.'

'I will. Thank you, Mrs Tailby. I wonder . . . were
you there long?'

'Where, dear?'

'In the room. Listening in?'

'Oh, bless you, I wasn't listening!'

'You heard "Muriel",' snapped Mrs Hawkins.

'Oh, just a tiny bit. It's such a pretty name.'

She stood beaming at them. Daniel eventually said, 'Perhaps you could leave us, Mrs Tailby.'

'Of course, of course. I'll be in the kitchen if you need anything, Mrs R. And just to let you know, Roy's got your prescription.' And with that she reversed out, still beaming.

Daniel took a sticky sip of sherry. 'Goodness,' he said, 'it's sweet!'

'You don't have to drink it, Rector. Now, there is something else.'

'Yes?'

'I have no family left and I need to know that the administration of my affairs is in good hands. Rector, I want to appoint you my executor.'

'Oh. I see.' He wondered if this was something he could do.

'Yes, who better? And your mother could be co-executor. Keep it under one roof, you see?'

'I am not sure I can be your executor, Mrs Hawkins. It might look improper. Especially if – how to put this? – the Church were to benefit from your generosity?'

'The Church? No, it's all going to Distressed Gentle-folk. Can you think of a more deserving cause?'

Daniel swallowed. 'A challenge indeed. But what an extraordinarily generous gift! And there need be no concern over any pecuniary advantage to St Mary's.'

'Exactly. Well, may I rely on you?'

'I need to find out if I can. Are you sure there's no one else?'

Mrs Hawkins looked up at the ceiling. 'There's the Tailbys, I suppose.'

'Oh, do you think that would be wise?'

'Why not?'

'You, I think, have not known them long and perhaps have not had an opportunity to conduct the fullest and most rigorous assessment of their bona fides?'

'What are you suggesting, Rector?'

Daniel blushed, although it could not be seen in the pale light cast by the lamp. 'I am not suggesting anything, Mrs Hawkins, just that one should always be prudent when it comes to one's financial affairs.'

Mrs Hawkins laughed. 'Oh, do I look like I was born yesterday? I'd die before I gave Jean Tailby a fiver, let alone all my worldly goods.'

Daniel said nothing but wondered long after if it would have made any difference if he had.

Dora was still there when he left. She was in the hall, wrapping the plates from a porcelain dinner service in newspaper and putting them in boxes. 'Can I give you a lift home, Dora?'

'I've got my bike, Rector. But let me see you out.'

An unusually solicitous gesture, Daniel thought, but in the driveway she said: 'I take it you have met the Tailbys before.'

'I have. Once or twice.'

'I see.' She crossed her arms against the cold and said,

'I can always stay on with Mrs R a bit longer, if you think that would be right.'

'How kind you are, Dora.'

'Not especially. But you were kind to me when I needed it. I don't forget things like that.'

'And you will let me know if you have any concerns about Mrs Hawkins? I can always make a pastoral visit if you do.'

'The good shepherd.'

'Something like that.'

'Beware of those who come to you in sheep's clothing, but inwardly are ravening wolves.'

'Exactly that, Dora.'

'Are you here to give Chris a bollocking?' said Sal, opening the door to his ring, the second of that day.

'Good evening, Sal,' Daniel said. 'No, but I would like to see him.'

'He's in the study, expecting you. Don't be long, we have a house group tonight. Perhaps you would like to stay?'

'Umm . . .'

'I'm joking, Daniel. Do you know where the study is? It's the door right opposite.'

Daniel wondered if he should knock, but there was something about that he wanted to resist, so instead he said through the door, which stood ajar, 'Chris, may I come in?'

'Daniel!' Chris opened the door. 'Come in, come in

. . .' He indicated a sofa, which looked like it had been made from hay bales and was covered in a light grey cloth, now stained and torn. 'Daniel, I'm sorry about earlier today, I should not have said what I said, but I was really jolly cross. I'm sorry.'

'No need to apologise to me, Chris. That's not why I'm here.'

'OK. Thanks.'

A black cat appeared from behind the door and approached Daniel. He absentmindedly went to stroke it, but the cat recoiled suddenly and ran up the back of an armchair. It perched there and stared at him, its two bright-green eyes looking somehow affronted against the black fur.

'This must be . . . did I hear Lydia call it Bat?'

'Yes, Bat. Careful, she's not very good with strangers.'

'Why Bat?' As he said it the cat pricked its ears.

'It was Lyds who called her that. I thought it was from "Come into the Garden, Maud" . . .'

'. . . "*for the black bat, night, has flown*" . . .'

'. . . Sal used to sing it to her when she was a child, but no, it is from a Goth fantasy the kids are into, I think. How was your walk today?'

'I enjoyed getting to know her a bit. She's very good with animals.'

'Yes, I love that about her. It has endured even through the, er, passions of teenagehood and the Goth thing. I hardly recognise her brother sometimes, not now. But teenagers, they need to find their own way, yes? And for clergy kids it can be really difficult. Are you one?'

'No. My father was in business.'

'I am. Father and grandfather before me. I never wanted to be anything else. We had a talk when I was at theological college from someone who went on about the vocation of clergy wives and children. I thought that was quite normal, but I don't think my kids do. Or my wife.'

Daniel paused for a moment, then said, 'Mrs Hawkins.'

'*Dear* Mrs Hawkins.'

'You don't have to like her, Chris. But you do have to love her.'

Chris opened his mouth to speak, but then closed it to think for a moment. (That's good too, thought Daniel.) 'What do you mean, love her?'

'Be to her as Christ.'

'And what does that mean?'

'To win her for salvation whatever the cost.'

'You make it sound so straightforward.'

'The simple but difficult thing.'

Chris let out an exasperated sigh. 'You can be . . . I mean, your type . . . can be so annoying sometimes.'

'So I am told. But what do you mean?'

He turned to face him. 'Your refusal to do the simple thing. You only like the difficult thing. You're good at that, the paradoxes, the poetry. Sometimes, Daniel, ministry is prose. And you only really do poetry. And it

. . . impairs your vision. I think it impairs our mission.'

'Oh dear.'

'"Oh dear." There you go. Where's your fight? Where's your shaking the dust from your shoes, where are your sheep and your goats, your wheat and your tares? You're so . . . Anglican.'

'Aren't you?'

'I'm a Bible Christian, Daniel. Aren't you?'

'We could argue forever about what that means. But we must be concerned first with the state of the immortal soul of Muriel Hawkins. And you cannot abandon her, Chris.'

'She threw me out.'

'Because you got in a fight. Because she was looking for a fight, someone to be angry with, and you gave her that opportunity. Avoid it, because she is in need of what we have, and we have to be available.'

'So you think we have to take her nonsense, pacify her, long enough to get a communion wafer down her, and call it job done? Is that what we are called to do?'

'Yes, I do. We may think differently about these matters, naturally, but remember our charge: to love and serve the people, caring alike for young and old, strong and weak, rich and poor. To preach, to declare God's forgiveness to penitent sinners, to pronounce God's blessing. You do remember?'

'I seem to remember something about admonishing too. When was the last time you admonished anyone?'

'Why do you think I'm here?'

There was another silence. Chris sat down. 'What do you want me to do?'

'Pray for her.'

'Should I go round and eat humble pie?'

'I don't think that would help, really. Leave Muriel Hawkins to me. There's no point in making things worse. But there is something.'

'Yes?'

'What did you make of her companion?'

He thought for a moment. 'Fat or lean?'

'The . . . um . . . better-nourished one, Mrs Tailby.'

'A bit creepy. I didn't like the husband much either.'

'Why?'

'Something fake about him. A bit too keen to profess his dutiful care of Mrs Hawkins. Whom he barely knows.'

'Could you keep your ears open? Village gossip would be helpful.'

'Yes. Anything in particular?'

'I believe it was La Bruyère who observed that widows, like ripe fruit, drop easily from their perch.'

'That really does sound ominous.'

'No immediate cause for alarm, and I have confidence in Mrs Hawkins's ability to take care of herself. But she is rich, and dying, and alone in the world, and that always brings the jackdaws and the crows. But now, I must leave you to your house group.'

Daniel got up. Bat jumped off the back of the chair and scooted behind it.

Chris said, 'Shall we pray?'

'Let us say the grace together.'

'The grace of our Lord Jesus Christ, and the love of God, and the fellowship of the Holy Spirit, be with us all evermore. Amen.'

The words were together, but the choreography was not. Daniel, with eyes closed, concluded by crossing himself. Chris, meanwhile, looked around the room, searching for others to make eye contact with, so the holy sentiment might be more sincerely vouchsafed.

It was surprisingly dark – the arrival of autumn, hardly unpredictable, was always surprising – when Daniel turned up the lane to Champton Rectory, now with the first thin drifts of fallen leaves on either side.

Audrey was waiting for him in the kitchen, her Noilly Prat, normally drunk in the drawing room, on the table.

'Where did you get to?' she asked, in a slightly pressing tone.

'I had to go to see Mrs Hawkins at Upper Badsaddle Manor,' he said. 'She doesn't have very long to live, I'm sorry to say.'

'In the midst of life we are in death, dear,' said his mother, in an unusually philosophical turn.

'Quite so.'

'How suitable for the autumn.'

'I was just thinking the same thing.'

'But the opposite is also true – in the midst of death we are in life.'

'In a very *real* sense, mother,' he said in the over-parsonical tone he liked to use when she stepped into his territory.

She paused.

'I've discovered what's wrong with Hilda.'

'Is she all right?'

'She's pregnant, Daniel.'

3

Daniel wondered why it was so difficult to get men to sing hymns in church. If it were an old favourite, re-membered from school or military service, a growl like a bear waking from hibernation would rise from the male section of the congregation. '*E-ter-nal fa-a-ther, strong to save . . .*' And then in the second line, as the melody rose higher, the sound subsided as the sing-ers realised they were going to have to climb into a register that was heading towards baritone, with its perils of strain and – worse – sounding effete, and there was already enough to emasculate in church without that. If it were possible to go down an octave, then down they would go. Daniel had one parishioner, Councillor Staveley, a natural bass, who would drop when the melody nudged above a B flat, so when they sang '*Holy, Holy, Holy, Lord God Almighty!*' it sounded like Feodor Chaliapin had come to Trinity Sunday.

But here, in Stow's venerable football stadium,

Ellington Road, no such anxieties prevailed. On the contrary, a roar, not a growl, rose above the rickety stands – a roar like a jet attempting to break the sound barrier. Ten thousand men, old and young, fat and thin, Siegfrieds in supermarket jeans holding hot pies, were singing at the tops of their voices. But what were they singing?

'*SUMMERS GODDA HOLDAHIZ NUTTS*
HOLDAHIZ NUTTS
HOLDAHIZ NUTTS!'

The last syllable of each line was sung in a shrieking falsetto that would have soared high above the descant even for 'Once in Royal David's City'.

'Neil,' Daniel shouted, 'what are they singing?'

'You don't want to know.'

'Yes, I do.'

'It's not very seemly.'

'I rather thought not. But it is *tremendous*.'

Neil pointed out a player standing in the lordly way of a star, seemingly unaffected by the pelting rain while around him his teammates stretched and warmed up on the slippery pitch. He was dressed in the colours of the opposite side, the red, white and blue of Stratton United, which seemed to Daniel rather more *en fête* than the pale blue and white of Stow City, even under the low grey sky, which lay over the stadium like a prep-school dormitory blanket.

'You see that man standing on his own looking

towards us, the tall guy in the red, white and blue?' said Neil.

'He looks like he's in charge.'

'He's Darren Sumner, he's their star midfielder, the guvnor, dominates play, dominates other players, but he's not renowned for his sportsmanship.'

'Oh dear.'

'He likes to grab his opponents by the balls and then squeeze them as hard as he can.'

'I imagine that would put them off their stride.'

'Very nasty. There's a famous photograph of him practically castrating another player during a play-off. It makes your eyes water. That's what they're singing about.'

'I can't make it out.'

'I know you're not interested in pop music, Daniel, but there was a big hit this year, a new version of an old Gene Pitney song that even you might have noticed. "Something's Gotten Hold of My Heart"? Marc Almond, from Soft Cell . . .? Never mind. He did a cover version of Gene Pitney's old song but as a duet with Gene Pitney now. It was Number One.'

'How does it go?'

Neil leaned in to Daniel and sang tentatively in his ear: '"*Something's gotten hold of my heart, keeping my soul and my senses apart . . . Something's gotten into my li-i-i-ife, da da da daa, da da da da da daaa*". Do you recognise it?'

'No, I don't think so.'

'Never mind. What they're singing is the same tune,

but they've changed the words. It's a thing football fans
do.'

'What words?'

'Sumner's gotten hold of his nuts.'

'Nuts?'

'Balls. It's why they go falsetto at the end.'

'Oh, I see! How clever!'

'Very inventive. Hymns of the common man.'

'Thrilling,' said Daniel, as his heartbeat slowed
down.

Football, like all sport, had never held much attrac-
tion for Daniel. At school he had been obliged to play
it (then cricket and eventually softball, remedial sport
for the hopeless cases), but he was so comprehensively
bad (*Not YOU, Clement*) he was told to stand at the
back, and should a ball accidentally come towards him,
to move out of the way. He had once been asked to
bring on the quartered oranges at half-time for a house
match, but, running onto the pitch, he had dropped
the plate and to the amusement of both players and
spectators had trodden on most of the oranges he was
trying to rescue. He was so bad that even the masters joined in ridiculing his efforts, and as soon as he
was able, he obtained exemptions. Fortunately, his
school was musical as well as sporty, and the prestige
distinction in music conferred on the nerdy boys who
couldn't swing a bat was valued, so his housemaster,
who was head of music and not without pity, signed
him off contact sports lest his piano-, organ- and

violin-playing fingers be damaged. Hours of organ practice filled his Wednesday and Saturday afternoons, when through the chapel windows the odd adolescent roar interrupted his first adventures in the preludes and toccatas and fugues and passacaglias of J. S. Bach. So he ceased even to notice sport at about the same time his peers ceased to notice religion – the point at which it was no longer compulsory – and apart from in croquet, which was played at his theological college primarily as a means of moderating the drinking of Pimm's, the athlete's garland was no more likely to encircle his head than the Imperial State Crown.

This changed when he became friends with Neil Vanloo. His new friend loved sport, played sport with the athlete's unselfconscious grace, radiated a strength and freshness that Daniel found so exhilarating he sometimes wanted to sniff him to be energised by his vapour. Something restless but hidden within him was beginning to stir, seeking to make itself known, a version of himself that he had so neglected it had become a pale stranger. What was it? Masculinity, he thought. Now in his late forties, he knew, in the indistinct but unignorable way of knowing that comes in middle age, that a stranger was turning to face him.

At the same time Neil, fifteen years younger, had discovered in Daniel a guide to the mysteries of worlds he wanted to know but could not yet enter – music, art, architecture – and, even more important, someone who could open up the half-forgotten landscape of his childhood. He had grown up in the Moravian Brethren, a church of exiled Protestants from Bohemia, some exiled as far from home as Oldham, where the Vanloos had settled, part of a community still shaped by the belief that it existed on earth to live the life of heaven – communally, around the chapel and the Men's Institute, the football club and cricket club, the dramatic and musical societies, which he loved and which were his whole world until adolescence had provoked rebellion and inevitably departure. To leave the church was to close its door behind you, but we never leave anything entirely, and in his thirties Neil had started to want to look behind that closed door again.

So Daniel and Neil's friendship surprised everyone. Audrey, notable for lacking introspection, was exceptionally clear-eyed when it came to extrospection, and said once, 'I saw that nice policeman of yours again today. He's here so often you'd think Champton was Dock Green.' Their friendship surprised them also, for their affinity was not at first clear, but it was profound, and as each became more sharply focused to the other, so they grew more sharply focused to themselves.

The shrill sound of the referee's whistle cut through the surrounding din and the symmetry of the two teams facing each other across the jewel-green pitch instantly broke. Daniel's grasp of football was unformed and unorthodox. He liked the set plays, the patterns, the display of a team's colours, which he once described, to Neil's undisguised delight, as being like 'the Montagues and Capulets in Zeffirelli's *Romeo and Juliet*'. And he loved the way the pattern deformed and reformed as a team's tactics began to show, and the skill with which the players shaped those patterns by playing the ball, and the way each movement shifted the next movement and the movement after that. While his grasp of technical matters was growing, he had not yet acquired a share of the tribal loyalty that others felt for their teams. Neil was for Stow City today, really for Chorley FC above all others in football, and Rochdale above all others in rugby, but Daniel was by nature uncomfortable with passionate commitments to the powers of this world. This meant that he rarely understood, and never reacted to, advantageous or disadvantageous play for either side. He delighted in skill, whether to his team's benefit or detriment, and this was what caused the trouble that afternoon.

Neil had seats in the heart of the Stow supporters' section, for it would not occur to him to sit anywhere but in the middle of the action. Here, among the loyalists, every kick of a Stow player was legitimate and sporting, and every kick of an opposing player a dastardly foul or pathetically incompetent. This determination of merit or demerit by allegiance alone was completely unintelligible to Daniel. He was put out to hear the referee described ungallantly as 'the bastard in the black' for decisions that seemed to him to be Solomonic in their magnificent detachment, and one man sitting behind them was so ungenerous in his attitude to a free kick given against Stow, after an obvious foul, that Daniel turned to give him a reproachful look. The man looked back at him and nudged a lad to his side, who also looked at him with a sort of questioning hostility.

Daniel turned round again to see if Neil had noticed, but he had not, so engrossed was he in the game. It was at Neil's suggestion that he had prepared for this game by watching *Match of the Day* on the television, much to his mother's derisive scorn. She thought it 'barbaric, like watching adolescent boys bursting their spots', and demanded in a quid pro quo a budget of programmes she wanted to watch, mostly gardening, cookery and *Sale of the Century*, live from Norwich every Sunday until ITV unaccountably took it off. Her dislike of football surprised him a little, for she adored watching the sports she liked: cricket, hockey, the ITV wrestling on a Saturday afternoon – 'COME ON, HAYSTACKS, *FLATTEN* HIM' – and above all Wimbledon, into which she would settle like Queen Victoria into her reign, untroubled by interruption, let alone dissent. In that long fortnight the television, normally not permitted during hours of daylight, was relentlessly on, and he would from time to time bring his mother smoked salmon sandwiches and strawberries and cream, a diet which so stretched the household budget for June and July that he had started to dilute the Pimm's to an all-but-spiritless pop. Audrey, meanwhile, became so engaged with the tournament that she would start shouting at the television in the second round, mostly at Boris Becker, whom she particularly disliked for his blond eyelashes, for being too good too young and for 'looking like that Nazi postman from *The Sound of Music*'.

Daniel was once visiting the Logan Botanic Garden in Scotland and had there fallen into conversation with a woman his mother's age about an echium, 'Pride of Madeira', that surprisingly flourishes in the balmy microclimate of the Rhins of Galloway. He discovered the woman had been at school with his mother, in their dourly Presbyterian boarding school of granite and Gregory's Powder. 'We were in the same house!' she said. What did she remember of her? She thought a bit, and then said, 'Mostly that she was unusually violent.'

Suddenly everyone around him, and Neil too, stood up and erupted into a wordless cry, which sounded a bit like the 'OWZAT' that rose above the cricket club on Saturday afternoons in the summer. It sounded to him like 'YA-BAAUW!' But what could it mean? The ref made a gesture like the hokey cokey, and play, which had halted, resumed, and with another cry – this time of unambiguously angry disappointment – everyone sat down.

'What just happened?' he asked Neil.

'Handball. Didn't you see it?'

'No, I didn't.'

'It happened very quickly and it's raining. Easily missed.'

Although Daniel was incapable of seeing a handball even when it occurred directly in front of him, and the offside rule was as opaque to him as the Schleswig–Holstein question to Chopper Harris, he was beginning to discern in the dynamics of the game how advantage went one way, then the next, and was starting to recognise players not from their extraordinary haircuts and hot-pant shorts, but from their style of play, their movement across the pitch.

That movement was halted again by the sound of the whistle. A cry of outrage rose again from the seats around him, intensifying when the ref gave a decision about a brutal tackle against Stow. It led to Stratton scoring a goal and Daniel was the only person who stood up among the Stow supporters to applaud.

'Bravo!' he shouted. 'Bravo!'

It did not help that he was wearing a red, white and blue striped tie, which his mother had bought for him in the belief that it was suitably sportif. These were the colours of the opposing side, at a grudge match, with tempers high and circumspection narrowed. Daniel did not even notice that he alone was standing and applauding, and it was only when Neil took his arm that he realised anything was wrong.

'Daniel,' he said, 'I would . . . you might want to sit down.'

But before he could, the indignant man sitting behind him said, 'Bravo? It's not the last night of the fucking Proms.'

Daniel turned. 'I beg your pardon?'

The man said, 'I beg your pardon, fuck off. What are you doing here anyway? Fuck off to your own end.'

The lad sitting next to him said 'fuck off' too to add emphasis.

It was the tenderness of his years – he must have been in his early twenties – that provoked Daniel, and he said, 'I have no end. And I can sit where I like.'

Another man on the other side of the indignant fan said, 'All right, all right, let's just leave it.'

By now a few other heads were turned towards Daniel. 'There is no need', he said to the indignant man, 'to be offensive' – a turn of phrase that made him more indignant rather than less.

'Fuck off, prof,' he said, 'you shouldn't be here.'

'I have a ticket. And what business is it of yours?'

Daniel went to sit down but the lad, in a gesture of bravado, slapped the back of his head, not hard, but contemptuously.

Neil stood up. He held up a finger and said, quietly but audibly, 'Enough.'

'You can't tell me what to do,' said the young man.

'I'm not telling you what to do,' said Neil. 'I said that's enough. You decide what you're going to do.'

'Fuck off,' said the older man, 'and take Prof Plum with you.'

'I said enough.'

The man squared up to him and the young man pushed his chest forward and stood on the balls of his feet in a way that was intended to be menacing, thought Daniel, but actually made him think of the Dance of the Cygnets in *Swan Lake*.

'Are you trying to be funny?' said Neil.

The older man raised his hand, but Neil took his wrist. 'Don't be naughty. Sit down.'

People around them were turning to watch.

'You *can't* tell me what to do, you prick. And get your hand—'

But with that Neil shifted his weight forward and forced the man's hand back so he started to sit down whether he wanted to or not. There was a professionalism about it that impressed not only the man, but his friends too. 'All right, all right . . .' he said with a tone of wounded righteousness.

The younger man shrank a little, taking a cue from the older, but as he sat down he gave Daniel a cold look.

'Thank you, gents,' said Neil. 'Enjoy the rest of the match,' and in one of the mysterious switches in current that flows through crowds, the tension slackened. Everyone sat down and attention returned to the pitch.

Daniel said, 'Neil, I think that was my fault.'

'Don't worry about it. We're all friends now.'

'I don't understand the rules.'

'Rituals, Dan, it's more your field than mine. You'll get the hang of it.'

And then a police officer in uniform was at the end of their row. The men who a minute ago had been menacing pretended not to notice.

'Oh, good Lord,' said Daniel, 'what have I done now?'

'DS Vanloo?'

Neil was already out of his seat. They stood in the gangway in a tense conference. Neil came back to his seat. He was terse.

'I've got to go, Daniel.'

'Why? What's happened?'

'Um, you might want to make your way over to Upper Badsaddle.'

'Neil . . .'

But he had gone.

It was beginning to get dark by the time Daniel finally got out of the car park at Ellington Road. Leaving the stadium had been awkward enough. Without Neil, he'd suddenly felt exposed to the hostility of the people in the row behind. He'd politely paused on the steps to let them out. The older one nodded grudgingly, but the younger one gave him a cold look again, as if he were leaving a marker for a future settling of a score. Daniel did not flinch and the boy looked away.

Leaving the car park, without the assistance of Neil and with hundreds of disappointed Stow fans disinclined to offer any obliging courtesies at all, was a trial. In the end two stewards told him to wait until the crush had dwindled. 'I can't wait, it's an emergency,' he said.

'You're not going anywhere, mate, not for a while.'

'I'm a priest. I have an urgent pastoral matter in my parish.'

'Then I suggest you pray, sir,' said the other.

Daniel had already prayed to counter the apprehension rising within him, for he knew what Neil looked like when a suspicious death was called in; and for Muriel Hawkins, whom he suspected had been cheated of the death that was nearly upon her; and for forgiveness, for not having seen sooner or understood earlier how gravely dangerous the Manor House at Upper Badsaddle had become.

The Land Rover lurched and stopped and started again and lurched again, for impatience was driving him, but the car had no sense of urgency and he kept stalling like a learner on his first lesson. 'Come on, come ON!' he snapped, but they were moving so slowly they would have been overtaken by the Vatnajökull glacier.

Eventually the traffic thinned, and the edge of the city was reached, the main roads out lit with the horrible orange light of sodium lamps. The rain had stopped, but it was now dark and cold, and as he chugged to the roundabout over the still-busy motorway, Daniel noticed that the road ahead, on the other side of the roundabout, was empty. This was the road that took him home and, while not quite putting his foot down, he went as fast as he dared the fifteen miles to Braunstonbury and the Badsaddles turning.

What would he find when he got there? He felt for

a moment what he always felt before arriving at the worst day of someone else's life. He needed to prepare, to arm himself against another's anguish, to concentrate on the upturned world that person had just been forced to occupy. So he would pause in Reception at Intensive Care, or on the corner before the house with too many cars outside and too many flowers in the window, and ask for grace and clarity. He would ring on the bell or walk through a door into a hospital side room and see confirmed in the faces of those gathered the unspeakable, unthinkable fact of the death of the person they loved. *The vicar's here* . . .

He saw a distant flicker of blue light through the trees that fringed the road as he approached and drove along Upper Badsaddle's main street. Light from opened curtains fell across the front gardens as he passed. *The vicar's here* . . .

A car was parked awkwardly, half on and off the verge, very near to the opening to the Manor House. It looked peculiar, a perfectly ordinary little saloon but with marks of grandeur – a grille like a Rolls-Royce and a two-tone livery – which made Daniel think of stone lions on bungalow gateposts; there was a figure sitting in the driver's seat, who turned away in the lights from the Land Rover, perhaps because the headlights were dazzling, or perhaps because they did not want to be seen. Daniel slowed down as he went past and looked in but could make out only an outline of shadowy grey. He turned up the drive to the Manor House, its windows lit up, and there were people silhouetted in what he realised was Mrs Hawkins's bedroom window. But there was only one car, unmarked, parked in front of the house. He supposed the ambulance had been and gone, but where were the SOCOs – scene of crime officers – the tape, where was the constable on the door? They should be here by now. The inconsequential thought occurred to him that perhaps they had all been at the football too.

The door to the Manor House opened and a figure, lit from behind so Daniel could not see who it was, stood on the threshold.

'Hello, Reverend Daniel. You remember me?'

It was Roy Tailby.

'Mr Tailby. I do.'

'You've heard the news?'

'Why else would I be here?'

Mr Tailby nodded. 'You had better come in.' He stood to the side and gestured rather quaintly with his spare hand.

Daniel hesitated. 'Mr Tailby, I don't understand. Why are you answering the door? Where are the police?'

'Attending the crime. And who else would be answering the door?'

'So a crime has been committed?'

'It looks like it, yes.'

'Are you aware of what you have just said?'

'Uh?'

A voice came down from the landing. 'Roy, who is it?'

'It's Reverend Daniel.'

There was a pause. 'I'm coming down.'

'Are you going to stand there all night, Reverend?'

Daniel felt for a moment like a virgin answering the door of her chamber to a vampire. He did not want to do Roy Tailby's bidding; it would relinquish to him a status he did not deserve and yield to a manipulativeness that was so sinister it seemed almost to colour the air around him. What actually did surround him was the smell of Old Spice, a dapper note on the nose for a dapper man in slacks and moccasins decorated with leathery tassels that looked like flaring tulips, and a cardigan that appeared to be made out of the carpet from a Berni Inn. Jean appeared at his side.

'Such awful news, Reverend Daniel. We're all stunned. Come upstairs.'

'I would like to see whoever's in charge.'

'Muriel?'

'Mrs Hawkins? No, of course not. Where's Detective Sergeant Vanloo?'

'I don't know.'

'But he came directly here from Stow – I was with him. He told me to come too.'

Jean looked puzzled. 'I expect he's at the old airfield.'

'Why would he be there?'

'Because there's been a murder. That's what people are saying. But he'll be able to tell you about that.'

Roy then looked puzzled. 'But why would you arrange to meet him here?'

Realisation began to dawn. Daniel looked down, then up again, and said, 'Is Mrs Hawkins all right?'

'She's fine. Dora just took up her tea. She's with her now. Faithful as a little dog, that one.'

Daniel shook his head. 'But who . . . who's been murdered?'

Roy said, 'Don't know. I *do* know a body has been discovered up at the airfield. Dora heard it from someone who knows whoever discovered it, but I don't know any details. I still don't see why you came here. Unless you have an unusually suspicious mind?'

'I must go.' Daniel walked away and heard as he retreated the music, rather than the words, of Roy's overdone indignation. He cringed to hear it, cringed at having made such a mistake and having revealed his private thoughts to the Tailbys. He had been so concerned about Muriel Hawkins he had just assumed that if anyone was going to be murdered in the Badsaddles it would be her, and he'd chided himself for not having seen more clearly the urgency of the danger she was in. He should have realised the blue lights he had seen through the trees were not from the Manor House – they could not have been – but from the airfield.

Anxious, he crunched the gears and made a mess of turning in the drive – a five-point turn when only one was really necessary – and he could feel Roy Tailby's judging look upon him. As he turned into the street he forgot this time to slow down and peer into the peculiar little car parked outside, but he noticed there was still a figure in the driving seat, a figure that again turned away.

He drove between the two Badsaddles and turned off at the little road that led to the airfield. Already he could see lights where no lights should be, and signs of recent arrivals – the convoy of tragedy that attends unexpected deaths.

Up ahead there was a patrol car, a jam sandwich with its blue light on (red, white and blue he thought, like Stratton), parked in the road. Two uniformed officers, with a professional air of accustomed boredom, were leaning against it. One held up a hand. Daniel stopped and the policeman approached, shining a torch through the windscreen, which flashed in Daniel's eyes.

'You're the vicar, aren't you?'

'Daniel Clement, Rector of Champton.'

'You're Neil's friend. Solved the murders last year? Secret friend, we used to say, he was so mysterious about it. We thought he was having a fling with a Champton girl.'

'Is he here?'

'Yes, you'll see where. Just follow the lights.'

He waved Daniel on, and he anxiously started to manoeuvre the Land Rover past them. The policemen watched as he went by, not in an unfriendly way, but not generously, as if they were waiting to see what would happen before they put themselves out.

The light ahead began to intensify as he approached it along the bumpy service road. He could see cars and vans parked like a stockade, and beyond them floodlights on stands, and what he supposed was the sound of a generator powering them. A blue tarpaulin hung over the entrance to the old chapel that he had shown to Lydia Biddle while walking the dogs only a few days ago. It lifted to let figures in the baggy white overalls and blue spats of crime scene investigators in and out. Daniel felt a terrible anticipation. He parked, composed himself and spoke some words from the Bible against the thrum of the generator and the sound of distant voices: 'Whether we live, we live unto the Lord; and whether we die, we die unto the Lord: whether we live therefore, or die, we are the Lord's.'

There was an officer with a clipboard standing near the tarpaulin entrance making notes as people came and went. 'Officer, is DS Vanloo here?'

'Inside, sir. Are you the vicar?' Daniel nodded. 'You'll have to wait until someone goes in and I'll get them to say you're here. Over there, please.' He pointed with his pen – a utility Biro with a chewed end, Daniel noticed – to a spot far enough away not to have to interact with him. Soon, two men dressed in different paper suits and carrying briefcases gave their names to the officer, who nodded towards Daniel. They turned to look at him, and Daniel felt for a moment as though he was being assessed by a pair of Michelin Men before the officer opened the flap. 'Shouldn't be too long, sir,' he said, 'ideally.'

It was cold, and felt colder, he thought, standing at the edge of the pool of light, not sufficiently official to enter into it, but official enough not to be sent entirely beyond it. It reminded him of something Archbishop Ramsey had said when he came to give a talk to the leavers at Daniel's theological college. 'The priest', he'd said, 'stands on the manward side of God and the God-ward side of man.' Daniel had rather liked that, and still did years later, though occupying border territory, facing both ways, was not without cost. Chris Biddle, he thought, his Low Church associate, would take a different view, seeing himself not as a priest, dressed in sacramental mystery, but as a minister, dressed in the formal informality of his affiliation. Not for him the beauty of liturgy, but the clarity of Scripture, only Daniel found Scripture to be rarely so clear, especially when people insisted it was. 'Thou seagreen incor-ruptible,' he said out loud, which caused the officer to look up from his clipboard. That made him pause for a second, and check an uncharitable feeling about Chris, and resist the temptation to indulge an impulse of competitive churchmanship, beloved sport of Anglican clerics. He thought instead of the football that after-noon, and his dislike of the tribalism that made your side always right and the other side always wrong and the ref an unjust antagonist to both. He suddenly felt an affinity with that other figure in black who stands at the border and faces both ways, and realised that he could never be the fan that Neil was, without self-consciousness or even an effort to suspend disbelief.

'Daniel!' Another Michelin Man had stepped out from behind the blue tarpaulin. 'Come with me!' It was Neil. 'We need to get you suited up if you want to see this and I think you should.'

'Who is it, Neil?'

Neil said nothing.

'Who is it?'

It was Joshua Biddle. Daniel did not recognise him at first, for he was crumpled beside the table that had served as the altar, and now, he wondered with sickening dread, perhaps had served again. Two candles had been fixed to the ends of the table, stuck into pools of wax, one burnt down, the other extinguished before it had got there. Josh's face was obscured by what looked like a dark mantle drawn half across it. It was blood, which had come from a cut in his neck, a gash; blood that had flowed, then thickened. Daniel wondered if he was yet missed in the vicarage at Lower Badsaddle, if Chris and Sal and Lydia knew what had happened yet.

'You know him?'

'Yes. It's Joshua. He's the Biddles' son. My associate vicar and his wife – she's a deaconess. He's sixteen.'

'Why this?'

'I can't think of any reason at all.'

'What does it look like to you?' asked Neil.

Daniel thought, for a second, that Neil in his crime-scene overalls looked like Andy Pandy, before, by an effort of will, he forced his mind to engage with the horror in front of him. 'I wonder if there's something ritualistic about it. His throat cut, an altar, like the lamb of sacrifice in the Jewish temple, or a child sacrifice on an Aztec pyramid.'

'What do you know about him?'

'He was a Goth, or like a Goth. I don't really know what that is, but there are bands, and a way of dressing and an outlook . . .'

'I know what Goths are, Dan.'

'. . . and he was interested in horror — vampires, rituals, the dead — and ceremonial. But it was more a style than a doctrine, I think. He was too cynical to take anything like that seriously. And too young, only sixteen. His sister, Lydia, his twin, she's one too, and . . . Neil, I showed her this place only a few days ago.'

'What? Why?'

'She loves dogs and she asked to come on a walk with Cosmo and Hilda. I brought her here and I was explaining the history of the air base and showed her the chapel.'

'What did she say?'

'Nothing much. She was more interested in the dogs.'

'Do you think she told Josh about it?'

'I don't know, but I should think so. They're very

close. And I wonder if they look out for places to do
. . . whatever it is they do. A coven of witches from
Braunstonbury used to meet at Tom Tower on the
estate. You know the building at the top of Beacon
Hill? You can't get into it now, it's too dangerous, but
then you could, and they would come and perform
their rituals.'

'Did you exorcise them?'

'No, it didn't look like the sort of thing to worry
about. And they stopped using it because there was
no banister and some of the witches weren't up to the
stairs . . . But, no matter about that . . . Neil, can I
touch the body?'

'No. Why?'

'I want to bless him.'

'Can you do it from here?'

Daniel turned to face the altar and said, 'The Lord
God lives in his holy temple, yet abides in our midst.
In baptism Joshua became the Lord's temple and his
dwelling place, and so we bless his body' – he made
the sign of the cross. 'Into your hands we entrust our
brother Joshua, that he be welcomed into paradise,
where there is no sorrow, nor pain, nor sighing, but
life everlasting. In the name of the Father and of the
Son and of the Holy Ghost. Amen.'

Neil said, 'Amen.' One of the pathologists looked up
from the pool of blood he was kneeling beside on the
floor. He stared at Daniel for a moment, then wearily
shook his head.

Outside, Daniel shuffled off his overalls and got back into his jacket and shoes.

'Daniel,' said Neil, 'we're going to need to talk to the family.'

'Of course. When?'

'We need to notify them first.'

'That's not happened yet?'

'No . . . Not *yet*.'

And Daniel realised he was going to have to tell them.

Daniel and Neil were sitting at the kitchen table at the rectory. Audrey had poured them both a whisky from the bottle that Bernard had brought round on the night Daniel discovered Anthony Bowness's body in church. It was a twelve-year-old Macallan, not that its distinction meant much to either of them in that moment, and Daniel had started to think of it as a distillation not of grain, but of grief.

He and Neil had gone straight to the vicarage from the airfield. He'd wondered what Sal was thinking when the doorbell went at an unusual time – although there is no unusual time for a vicarage doorbell to be rung – and, opening the door, what she made of him and Neil standing on the step, not in clericals, not in uniform; a plain-clothes deputation but on official business. Grave faces. 'May we come in?' By what increments did puzzlement turn to suspicion, to anxiety, to dread?

Chris, summoned from his study and his sermon, two thousand unsparing words on lepers and repentance.

Lydia, left undisturbed in her room listening to Bauhaus. '*UNDEAD UNDEAD UNDEAD*,' sang Peter Murphy, as loudly as she dared play it, so at first she mistook her mother's voice, howling in the kitchen, for backing vocals.

4

Sunday services that terrible weekend were plain and
short. As soon as he could, Daniel telephoned Bernard,
then Bob Achurch, the sexton-cum-tower captain, and
Jane Thwaite who played the organ; he stood them
down, and cancelled the ten-thirty Parish Eucharist at
Champton, so anyone who wished to receive the sacrament that day at St Mary's would need to get up for the
eight o'clock, which disobliged those who were hoping
for a lie-in, and disobliged in turn those who attended
the eight o'clock precisely to avoid the people who went
to the ten-thirty. The Badsaddles would have a joint
service at eleven, taken by Daniel – a said service, their
choir and organist stood down also out of respect for
the vicar's family. A said service also meant a homily
of a few words rather than a full-blown sermon, and
Daniel knew what he wanted to say, what needed to
be said: not a discourse on the nuances of the synoptic
gospels' harmonisation of the parables, but a prayer for
the departed and a prayer for those who mourn.

It was a fine morning, sunny but cool, nearly cold, and there were hats and coats worn to the eight o'clock at Champton, which was unusually well attended, for the news of Josh Biddle's murder had arrived at Upper Badsaddle Manor before it reached Lower Badsaddle Vicarage. Thence, via Dora Sharman, to Champton, and as soon as the first telephone had trilled there it would have been as impossible to contain the news as Spanish flu. There was tension already in the air when the swelled numbers of worshippers arrived at the church door, and it was wound up when those used to occupying a particular place at the ten-thirty found it occupied by those who took them at the eight, and vice versa. Neither felt their claim to that particular place was in any way lessened by the alteration of the hour, and when obvious irritation was met by an en-quiring look from the usurper, delivered with an air of innocent query, it was returned in kind, with a non-chalant shrug as if nothing could matter less in all the world, and they would search for another place with an exaggerated display of exploration. The form for the early service used traditional language derived from the Book of Common Prayer, so those used to the more contemporary language of the ten-thirty were derailed in the *Gloria* where the versions diverged; but they never diverged sufficiently for either party to be certain theirs was correct, and both doggedly persisted with yous instead of thous, and Holy Spirits instead of Holy Ghosts. The effect was to make an already unsettling experience even more unsettled, for the familiarity of the service normally had a solvent effect on the troubles of the moment, so Daniel had to try to enforce the calmness the occasion required with his own apparent unflappability.

He had, of course, done this before, three times between Easter and Pentecost last year, when murder had destroyed the tranquillity Champton and its neighbours usually enjoyed. He had preached then that tranquillity would be restored, and with the revelations that flowed from the murders, and the reckoning that followed, he had hoped it was so. But now it had happened again, tranquillity was again destroyed, and in some ways the second time around felt worse than the first, for what was a wildly anomalous horror had been repeated. And it had been repeated not only in the fact, but in the execution. Rumour had spread overnight of a brutal death, of dark ritual, of the profanation of a sacred space.

Daniel would make no specific mention of what had happened but would speak instead about the enduring faith of Israel through fear and tribulation. Bernard, a vanishingly infrequent visitor to the eight o'clock, had come to 'show my face' and offered assistance by reading, as of right, the first lesson, from Lamentations. It was set for the twenty-first Sunday after Pentecost, and would have been read whatever the headlines in Champton's news round-up, but it was apt for the occasion (as, Daniel thought, the lectionary readings so often were).

'The thought of my affliction and my homelessness is wormwood and gall!' read Bernard in fluent Old Etonian.

'My soul continually thinks of it and is bowed down
    within me.
But this I call to mind, and therefore I have hope:
The steadfast love of the Lord never ceases, his mer–
    cies never come to an end;
they are new every morning; great is your
    faithfulness.'

After the reading of the Gospel, Daniel kept the silence for longer than he would normally, until the mild stirring of infrequent worshippers who thought something must have gone wrong, and that maybe it was because of them, told him it was time to speak. And then he prayed for those who were taken from this world by violence, for those who grieved, for those who were damaged by the merciless unfolding of its consequences, and for communities lost to anxiety and confusion and remorse.

He kept the churchyard parliament short after the service.

Bernard was first out, as usual. 'Come to tea? Bring your mother?' Daniel said thank you, and Bernard gave him a comradely grimace. Whether this was in acknowledgement of the crisis that was again upon them, or at the prospect of entertaining Audrey with her list of matters she 'would like to raise about the state of the rectory', Daniel could not decide.

As soon as he could get away, he drove to Upper Badsaddle. Although he had overall responsibility in the newly joined benefices for the Badsaddles, he had devolved his powers to Chris and Sal and did not know the people there with the same familiarity as those in Champton St Mary, only a mile or two distant. He recognised many in the clumps that were making their way from the village towards the church, which was set back a little from the end of the road. St Thomas the Martyr was very different from St Mary's, with its grand tower and pinnacles and de Floures tombs. St Thomas's was older, or most of it was, and had not been given any makeover with the rising fortunes of the patron. It was twelfth century, with a later stepped chancel, and at the other end was the broach spire so typical of this diocese. The church was originally set in an ensemble of three with the Manor House and the vicarage, but the loss of part of the former unbalanced it like a stool that has lost a leg. The vicarage had been sold off and was now lived in by a misanthropic man of business with a younger second wife and teenage daughter. He had built a swimming pool in its walled garden and was reputed to bathe in it naked.

There was, as he had expected, a bigger crowd than usual coming to church that morning, some arriving

in cars, which had already filled the spaces outside, so
he turned the Land Rover into the drive of the Manor
House. At the end there was only the Tailbys' estate
parked near the front door (he noticed there were
boxes loaded in the back); mindful that he had no specific invitation to park there, and lest he be observed
from Mrs Hawkins's bedroom window, he tried to
park in a way that acknowledged sufficiently that he
was not visiting, or not straight away, and knew that
this was not an entitlement but a favour. He got out,
giving a courteous nod in the direction of the bedroom
window, fetched his surplice and stole from the passenger seat and walked through the arriving congregation
to the vestry door, which had not been unlocked, so
he had to go round to the south entrance and make his
way through the small press again. It was then that he
saw the peculiar car with the mysterious driver he had
noticed the night before coming up the street towards
the church. It looked even more peculiar in the light
of day: small, chunky and familiar. He saw it was an
Allegro – Audrey had one ten or so years ago; a car so
poorly finished and unreliable she described it as 'the
three-day week on wheels' – but as he'd noticed before,
this Allegro had an unusual distinction: it was two tone,
the colour of tobacco and the colour of cream, and had
a grille that looked like it had come from a grander car,
complete with what looked like a Garter Star but was
really the insignia of the Royal Automobile Club. The
chrome glittered, the paintwork shone, and it drove

up the street at such a graceful pace that people parted to let it through, like the Queen at a garden party. As it passed, he saw that it was driven by Miss March — the Grey Lady from the dress shop — in Sunday best with a hat and, he could see against the oddly shaped steering wheel, gloves. She was looking for somewhere to park and did not notice his wave of acknowledgement. What brought her to church today in Upper Badsaddle?

He winced when he came inside, for the first thing he saw was the east window, which was dedicated to the church's patron, St Thomas the Martyr. There were several Thomases in the martyrology, but this was our own, Thomas Becket, Archbishop of Canterbury in the reign of Henry II. He looked serene at first, in richly stained glass, the morning sun making brilliant his full-length figure in episcopal vestments, and wearing the pallium — a white yoke with black crosses given by popes to archbishops as a sign of their authority and retained in the arms of the archbishops of Canterbury and York, despite being no longer under the old authority. The image told the story not only of Thomas's prestige as a churchman, but as a faithful servant of God. As a bishop he wore a mitre, signifying the tongues of flames that danced on the heads of the apostles at Pentecost, and that was encircled by a halo, signifying not only a man but a saint, but both were pierced by a sword — an awkward cluster of symbols, but a graphic reminder of how this archbishop had met his death: in church, an innocent cut down by armed men, profaning sacred space with his blood. Daniel shuddered. Thomas's death, violent and recounted in grimly vivid detail by one of the monks who had witnessed it, had been the work of the king, his patron and friend, who grew exasperated by the archbishop's refusal to bow to his worldly power. Knights were despatched to Canterbury and the troublesome cleric was murdered. But Josh's murder was not an act of political expediency, or the blunt exercising of power. It was an unimaginably savage and calculated act inflicted on an innocent boy for no reason that Daniel could discern.

He had lain awake all night trying to work out how such a vicious death could have come Josh's way. He was sixteen, a schoolboy, a teenager, and his passions may have been intense, as teenage passions are, but could they have been sufficient to cause his murder? Perhaps the answer had something to do with his being a Goth? But they were teenagers, and the method of the death was surely the work of someone who was, if not professional, then horribly capable, though that was too troubling to think of for long. And Lydia had told him that she and her brother were not fully Goth, but aspiring Goths, junior Goths, and even if there were someone in the ranks capable of such a terrible act, why would they have inflicted it on someone not yet fully fledged? Neil and his team would be drawing up lists of them, and they would all be questioned, and perhaps something that made sense would be discovered in what they said. Before then came the awful job of interviewing Josh's family, whose lives had just exploded, but who the police needed to treat as potential witnesses and even suspects.

'Morning, Reverend Daniel. We saw you park – that's absolutely fine.'

It was the Tailbys.

'The whole village is upset. We all need to hear your words of comfort.'

I'm not sure I have words of comfort, Daniel thought, or not what you mean. But he said, 'Good morning, Mrs Tailby, Mr Tailby . . .'

'Jean and Roy, please!'

'. . . and how is Mrs Hawkins?'

'She's struggling a bit at the moment. Dora's with her. But it can't be long now.'

'She seemed quite her old self the other day.'

'Oh, in spirit, yes, but she's physically fading. That's the cancer for you, it takes you cell by cell.' Jean made a sad face. 'Be sure to pray for her; that's all we can ask for now,' and she placed her hand against her breast, as if to calm a surge of feeling. Daniel noticed she was wearing a diamond and sapphire engagement ring that had belonged to another widow she had befriended in her decline.

Roy said, 'Eyup, Jean, look who's here.'

Miss March had arrived in the porch. She was collecting her little Book of Common Prayer and the photocopied news sheet from the sidesman, but when she turned into the aisle to look for a place in the crowded pews she saw Daniel with Jean and Roy Tailby, a sight that seemed to produce conflicting reactions: polite for Daniel, wary for the Tailbys.

'It's that Miss March,' said Jean. 'What a peculiar-looking lady she is.'

Miss March had no choice but to approach, for the only vacant places were beyond them. 'Good morning, Rector,' she said to Daniel, 'and good morning to you,' to Jean and Roy, but there was something a little forced about the latter greeting, which told Daniel they had form.

'Miss March,' said Roy, 'we meet again!'

'Happier circumstances today,' said Jean, then remembered where she was and why. 'Only not for that poor boy and his family, of course.'

Daniel said good morning. Miss March nodded and walked away. 'I must get ready,' he said to the Tailbys, then followed Miss March down the aisle towards the vestry. She went left, to sit in one of the seats at the very side, in the north transept, normally used only for an overflowing wedding or funeral from where she would see nothing of what was happening at the altar, and where he couldn't see her. He wanted to, for her presence in church this morning had made him curious, and he resolved to catch her at the door after the service.

The same service, the same reaction, with a stir at the apposite words from Lamentations, but Daniel felt jarred slightly by the colonisation of the west end of the church by the new regime. Carpet had been put down (which for him was as unwelcome in a church as ground elder in a lawn) and a sign put up saying 'Kiddies Space', minus the apostrophe he would have liked to see qualifying the cheery childish writing. On hooks, which once would have served to hang up the cloaks of wintering churchgoers, striped drawstring bags now hung under another sign saying 'FUNBAGS', containing the toys and props required for telling Bible stories to children. This was the pet project of Sal Biddle, who had been a primary school teacher before she was a deaconess, and who brought these two commitments together for the purpose of catechising the young. By the time they had reached teenagehood, she had discovered it was too late to try to catechise them at all, so she liked to teach younger children through the medium of play. There had been an awkward moment when a guest at their youth group had tried to illuminate the mystery of the Trinity by using balloon animals, which he was not very expert in manipulating. Halfway through his squeaky attempt to set forth the procession of the Holy Spirit, sniggering had broken out among some of the parents – sniggering which had mystified him until afterwards, when Sal had told him the half-completed sausage dog he was waving around resembled a penis and testicles so splendid they reminded her of the Cerne Abbas Giant. Toys and felt and sand and bean bags had been less controversial – effective, in fact – for telling the story of Moses leading the Israelites through the Red Sea, for the story of Joseph and his brothers, and the Flood, so Chris had surrendered the back of St Thomas the Martyr to her. To Daniel it looked like a kindergarten had staged a small invasion. He had no difficulty with the church hall being surrendered to tiny tots, and understood the importance of engaging children with the necessary business of their salvation, but the back of the church already had a purpose and he winced when it was converted into floor space for games of Twister. He checked himself, remembering how his plans to change the way the back of the church was used at Champton had unintentionally caused havoc there. Move a pew at your peril.

Also seen by him but not by others were the two men who arrived towards the end of the service. They came in, declined the offer of a prayer book and stood at the back. One had a notepad and was writing things in it. Journalists, he thought. Word is out.

After the service the men were waiting for him at the porch. 'Reverend Clement?' One of them gave a name and the name of a paper, but it was spoken so quickly he couldn't tell which one. 'I was wondering what it's like to have another murder here so soon after the last one?'

'We cannot say murder, we don't know. And I can't

say anything about it, apart from how sorry we all are to be facing another terrible loss. And to assure all who are mourning today, or frightened today, of our prayers. All three churches will be open and available for prayer. Thank you.'

'You solved it last time. Will you be turning detective this time?'

'Braunstonbury CID solved it, and I am confident they will do so again.'

'Will you be offering your assistance?'

'I'm not Sherlock Holmes, Mr . . .?'

'Mind if we have a picture?'

Before Daniel could say yes, the other man produced a camera with a flash and took his picture in one movement like a hitman with a gun. The two men nodded and went away.

Miss March was next out. She must have half run to beat the crowd heading for the door after the dismissal and there was the faintest suggestion of disarray about her. 'Rector, I hope you did not think me rude before the service, but I did not want to interrupt your conversation.'

'Not at all,' said Daniel, 'but I was not expecting to see you. What brings you to the Badsaddles?' and then he wished he had phrased it differently, for it sounded like he was accusing her of curiosity rather than piety.

'Oh, nothing more than a desire to get to know the area. The villages are so lovely. Especially after three weeks in Braunstonbury, I thought perhaps there might be somewhere here.'

'How is your house hunting proceeding?'

'I've seen one or two places that might be suitable. But I'm sorry, you won't be interested in that. It must be very difficult for you.'

'We had only just begun to recover from last year's terrible events, and now . . .'

'I am very sorry to hear it.' She made as if to go, but paused and said, 'Rector . . . I wonder if I might come to see you at your convenience?'

'Yes, of course. About anything in particular?'

'It's delicate.'

'Does this have anything to do with Mr and Mrs Tailby?'

'Is that their name? But . . .' Suddenly she looked down, then started to walk away.

Roy and Jean Tailby appeared. They looked as if they, too, had been in a hurry to get to Daniel. 'Do you know each other?' said Jean, looking at Miss March as she made her way through the lines of yews that stood on either side of the churchyard path.

'We have met,' said Daniel.

'She's new to the area, I believe. Do you know much about her?'

'I couldn't say.'

'Something not quite right about her,' said Roy. 'I don't care what anyone says!'

★

When Daniel arrived back at the rectory his mother was making lunch. 'Nothing special today, darling, it's just a casserole. It can wait if you have to go out.' She had harvested the Champton gossip that he had missed after the service, gossip he very much disliked to hear personally, for it embarrassed him, but he was also glad his mother had no such scruples, for she was an attentive listener and provided a useful précis.

'Majority view? The boy was into weird things – the vampire club they were part of – whatever it's called – and they were high on drugs – you know he's in a pop band? – and things got out of hand. Some dissenting voices. Bob Achurch – who is the only person here who knows what it's like to cut someone's throat, apart from Kath, but she's no longer with us – said it didn't sound to him like the work of teenagers. But Alex said to Honoria, this from Bernard, that these groups are caught up in drugs and all sorts of nonsense, and might have fallen foul of some very nasty people indeed. And Anne Dollinger has taken to her bed she's so upset, and would you go and see her?'

He made an excuse that he had some letters to write, left his mother in the kitchen and went to his study. He sat in the chair and looked down at his desk, which he found in its customary order. Pens, pencils, hole-punch, reinforcers, treasury tags, the blue-and-gold tin of Oxford Mathematical Instruments. These were for him tokens of the orderly world that had again been disrupted, and were normally for him also the means to assert and reassert the elements of order, administrating away the minor ills of this or any community. But this was not a minor ill. This was evil, with its unknowable power and unpredictable reach, once again bringing chaos to Champton and its neighbours.

Daniel did not know, at that moment, if he had the resources to confront it. The evening before was as bad and bleak as any in all his years of ministry. It was not the first time he had told a family that something terrible had happened. When he was a new curate he had been summoned to the primary school and informed that the father of one of the children had been killed in an accident. The little girl's mother had died of cancer the year before. Would he please tell her what had happened? She was nine. Someone went to fetch her. When she came into the office, emptied for the purpose, and saw him she said, 'My dad's dead, isn't he?' He had gone home later to an empty house – the vicar was away, on holiday with his wife – and paced from room to room, upstairs and downstairs, unable to settle for hours. It was seeing the realisation in her face that a life already deformed by loss was about to fall apart again. 'God will give you grace', the vicar had said when he'd returned, 'to do what you have to do, to carry what you must carry. Remember, it is not yours to keep; you must offer it up.'

His role, when catastrophe visited a parishioner, was defined: to be there, to know what he was doing (or to look like it), to make the necessary arrangements, to preside over the ceremonies, and to offer the assurance of continuing prayers and pastoral care. He sometimes felt he was the GP for matters of the soul rather than the body. At Champton one of his predecessors in the eighteenth century had been particularly close to the surgeon, in an era when curiosity about soul and body were in alignment, and the de Floures archive preserved their affectionate correspondence on matters such as the pox, how disturbance to the soul provoked apoplexies and the causes of lunacy in women, which continued until the rector died. His last letter to the physician was written to entrust him with his body after his death to dissect and examine, 'lest my children and grandchildren be afflicted with such agues as have caused me such torment in my last years'.

Daniel now felt he had more in common with the detective than the doctor, concerned with the agues of the community rather than the body. When Kath Sharman last year had embarked on her murderous spree it had fallen to him to discern what was faltering in Champton's vital signs – the irregularities in its pulse, the unexplained limp, the clammy appearance – and from that to diagnose not only its ills, but their causes. He had been unusually good at it, the skills of ministry and the components of his own character being excellently suited to the task; but when the truth was discovered, and order restored, he had wanted, more than anything, to get back to being the good shepherd of a flock that fell out over mowing the churchyard, the kind of mince pies to be served after the carol service, whether a new hymn that nobody knew was a favourite that had not yet established itself in the congregational repertoire or should be left to deserved obscurity.

That was beginning to happen – the restoration of the untumultuous ordinary – and next week it was Harvest Festival, with swelling marrows on the windowsills, boxes of cauliflowers and carrots propped up at the chancel steps, and a display of sheaves of wheat between the candlesticks on the gradine behind the altar, with the harvest loaf displayed in front of it. The former had been the work of Stella Harper, the latter of Kath Sharman, a victim and her murderess, so finding volunteers to take over those responsibilities had been a work of some delicacy. His mother, unusually willing to take on a task which had once been Stella Harper's, had agreed to do the arrangements for the gradine. 'I'm bringing in the sheaves, darling, like the Moabitish damsel in what's-his-name's field!' she had trilled. 'Boaz,' he'd said, 'and she gleaned rather than reaped, but thank you.' The baking of the harvest loaf went to Sal, but he could not ask her to do that now, for the seasonal metaphors of the Lord taking his harvest home, of the fruitful ears to be stored in the garner, of the tares cast into the fire would be brutally insensitive.

In all these duties he knew what he was doing.

He had enough of a sense of what to say and when, of the currents that rose and fell in a family and a community visited by catastrophe, of what people thought they needed and what they actually needed, to be confident about doing an adequate job. But he did not feel confident about what he was obliged to do for those mourning the death of Josh Biddle. In everyday circumstances the constant tension between him and Chris about even the most fundamental matters of faith and practice was manageable, or had been so far. But how could he manage what needed to be managed with a father of a murdered son who felt, as all grievously bereaved people feel, that having been deprived of something so lovely and so rare, any further deprivation would be outrageous and intolerable? Chris Biddle would want the funeral to be an example of how faithful Christians, beloved of the Lord, live in anticipation of his favour. That was a stretch at the best of times, but at the funeral of a child? Who had died so horribly?

Something stirred against Daniel's ankles and he looked under his desk where Hilda had tucked herself. She was so still he had forgotten she was there, but now she crawled out again, suddenly alert. He could see she was bigger, her body barrel-shaped now, and hauling it around must tire her more quickly than usual, though not enough to stop her waddling with an unusual show of speed to the window, where she began to growl. Daniel heard steps coming to the front door and then the sound of something pushed through the letter flap. Hilda immediately started barking in full voice, and Cosmo, who came running from the kitchen, started barking too. Audrey followed from the kitchen as the sound of steps retreated down the drive. And then the creaky, squeaky sound of a bicycle, was it?

He heard his mother say, 'Oh!' And then she came in, without knocking. 'A note for you, from Alex de Floures.'

'Oh, may I see?'

'You may.'

It was a postcard: on one side was an invitation to join Honoria and him for drinks at the lodge after Evensong; on the other was a black-and-white photograph of a seedy-looking man wearing what seemed to be a pair of waders with the seat cut away. Inexplicably, he had inserted one end of a bullwhip into his bottom.

'Oh!' Daniel said, surprised by this unexpected image.

'That's what I said too. Oh!'

'I'm not sure what this is supposed to be,' he said, and turned it over. 'It's a self-portrait, apparently, of the photographer. A Mr Mapplethorpe.'

'Well, I shan't be asking him to do my passport,' said Audrey. 'But Alex is home, I see?'

'Yes, Honoria too. I wonder what this is about.'

'Perhaps they want you to fill them in on the latest tragedy to befall us?'

'I hope not. But I suppose everyone's talking about it.'

'Have you talked to Bernard?'

'Yes, I spoke to him this morning. He was . . . very Bernard about it.'

'Will you be calling in on the Biddles today?'

'I think so. I should see how Chris and Sal are. And I thought I'd ask Lydia if she'd like to walk the dogs.'

'I think it better to keep Hilda at home at the moment, in her condition. We don't want to tire her out. But would you take them something? I've cooked for them. A casserole. A pie. And tell them we have beds if they need to put people up.' Audrey's method of caregiving was strictly practical. Bed. Board. Baking. 'Do you want some lunch? The Biddles' will need to cool so we might as well have ours now. It's game, from the estate. Pheasant. Rabbit. I think there may be pigeon, I can't remember.'

'Thanks. And Bernard's invited us to tea later, if you fancy it?'

'Oh, it's like old times!' said Audrey with undis-guised pleasure, she who had so loved the Blitz, and rationing, and the winter of discontent, and the trouble the year before.

Audrey had wrapped the casserole in tea towels and put it in a big wicker basket with a foil-covered apple pie balanced on top. Smells of the most delicious kind of autumn filled the Land Rover, and if tantalising for Daniel, then how much more so they must have been for Cosmo, who had not looked back when he closed the door on Hilda on his way out. Her incredulous barking, outraged at being denied the outing Cosmo was permitted, followed them down the drive. Cosmo, who would normally sit with his paws on the dash-board so he could see out, instead strained to get into the back, where the basket of mellow fruitfulness had been stowed.

Lower Badsaddle Vicarage looked like it, too, was in mourning; the curtains drawn, bunches of flowers, and cards, and most incongruous of all a giant teddy left on the steps. The campervan looked wretched, like a partygoer after the ball had ended, and parked next to it was Neil's dark-blue police saloon, sleekly sombre.

Daniel left Cosmo in the Land Rover, retrieved the basket and knocked on the open door. 'Hello!' he said, too softly to be heard, but he did not want to shout into a house still ringing with shock. He could hear voices coming from the kitchen, so he knocked gently on that door and opened it. 'Forgive me for interrupting . . .'

Neil was sitting at the kitchen table with Sal and Chris. Lydia was sitting slightly away from them on a bench with Bat the cat on her lap. The cat saw Daniel, hissed and scooted off, digging a claw into Lydia's thigh. She started: she had fallen asleep, finally exhausted after a night and day awake, and when she

saw Daniel she smiled in welcome. He saw the smile
stall, then fail as she remembered what had happened,
and that it was not a nightmare she was waking from,
but a dreadful reality she was waking into. Daniel
opened his mouth to say something, but she crumpled
and began to cry. His impulse to go towards her was
crossed by Sal, whose attention was immediately and
entirely focused on her daughter. 'Lyds, Lyds,' she said
as she came to the bench and sat beside her. She put her
arm round her shoulders and hugged her as tightly as
she could while Lydia sobbed.

Daniel said nothing. Neil and Chris were suddenly
silent too. Chris looked almost unrecognisable. He was
pale but with dark smudges under his eyes; he looked
winded, as if all the fight had been knocked out of
him and he had nothing left to offer but unfocused
pain.

'Daniel,' he said. 'You're back.'

'Yes,' he said. 'Mum asked me to bring you these.' He
put the basket on the kitchen table. 'It's a casserole and
a pie. I don't suppose you're hungry now, but when you
are, it's here.' He unpacked the basket and unwrapped
the casserole from the tea towels. One commemorated
the Royal Wedding and showed the Prince and Princess of Wales looking out hopefully from framed ovals,
like any other bride and groom, were it not for the
three feathers of his arms and the three scallop shells
of hers to remind us that this was not romantic, but
dynastic.

'I'm starving,' Chris said, 'but I don't want to eat anything. There's something cold and hard in my stomach, like I've swallowed a packet of frozen peas.'

'I think that's everything I need for now, sir,' said Neil. 'We'll keep in touch. Call us if you remember something, or if you hear something, or if you notice anything unusual, no matter how unimportant it seems. And – please – don't make any plans to leave the area for now. And if the press starts causing you any bother, let us know and we'll do what we can to keep them away. Daniel,' he nodded, 'could we talk later?'

'Yes, of course. Oh, I'm out to tea, then I have Evensong, then I have to see someone. Could it be around nine?'

'That's fine, speak then. I'll let myself out.'

Daniel went to sit opposite Chris. There was a long silence, broken only by the faint creak of the bench as Sal rocked Lydia gently to and fro. Eventually Sal said, 'She's completely exhausted. We've been up all night.'

'What do you need?' he said. 'The food will keep if you don't want it now. And my mother says if you need to put anyone up, we've got room at the rectory.'

'Will you thank her for me, Daniel? I think we're all right . . . but I'm not really thinking straight.'

'Would you like me to speak to anyone? Services are all covered, of course, so don't worry . . . about that.'

'Chris's parents are coming later – my brother's picking them up after the evening service. We've got enough room here. Something to be said for living in a mausoleum after all.'

'How are the dogs?' asked Lydia in a small voice.

'They're fine. Cosmo's in the Land Rover, actually.' Sal started. 'Um, and you remember I said Hilda was not herself? We found out she's going to have puppies.'

'Puppies!' said Lydia.

Daniel checked himself. 'Not for a while yet, she's early on.'

Sal stirred. 'I think you should try to get some rest, Lydia. You're falling asleep.'

'Can I sleep in your bed, Mum?'

'Yes. I'll take you up.'

'Daniel, can I see Cosmo?'

'If that's all right with your parents?'

'I don't think so, Lyds, Bat won't like it,' said Sal and gave Daniel a questioning look. Then, very gently, she disentangled herself from her daughter and helped her up. Daniel smelt the staleness that clings to people who have been up all night. 'I'll be down in a minute,' she said, 'as soon as she's settled.'

Chris waited until his wife and daughter had left. Then he said, 'What are people saying? Does everyone know?'

'Yes. They know something. The . . . details are not known, but there is some lurid speculation, and I'm sorry but I have to tell you the press were at church this morning.'

'Yours or mine?'

'Yours.'

'I suppose we will have to talk to them. What do we say?'

'Nothing. Or as little as possible at the moment.'

'You've been through this before. What do I need to know?'

Daniel thought for a while. 'There is not much you can do. And what you can, you will do imperfectly because the world is upside down. I would say, not from my own experience, but from observing the experience of others, that you will be incapable with grief. Allow yourself to be incapable. Ask for help if you need help; we will all help you. If you can stand up and face forward, and if Sal and Lydia can too, then you are doing as well as you possibly can.'

Chris nodded. 'Thank you. We have to talk about the funeral at some point.'

'When the time is right; and I'm afraid when there is a police investigation, it can cause a delay.'

'That's what your policeman friend said. He interviewed us all.'

'I'm sorry. That must have been an ordeal.'

'Not really. There isn't much to say. Sal was here, baking. Lydia was upstairs in her room. I was out on my prayer walk. When it happened. Imagine that, praying for all the farms on the Champton road while half a mile away Josh was . . . Josh was . . . I was praying for the farmers and their families. For Harvest Festival, and all involved in food production and distribution, and for those who do not have enough . . .' There was something rote-like about Chris's list, the familiar pattern overlaying the chaos of what he was feeling. 'We thank you then, Creator, for all things bright and good . . .' He faltered, and choked, and began to cry.

'I am so very sorry, Chris,' Daniel said, 'so very sorry. And I want you to know that we are all praying for you and for your family, and for Jo—' He checked himself again.

Chris looked up. 'Praying for Josh? You know we don't pray for the dead, Daniel.'

'Yes, I'm sorry.'

'What good would it do?'

Daniel would in normal circumstances have had a lot to say about that, but now was not the time.

'Seriously, what good would it do? I would love to know.'

Daniel looked at the tabletop. 'Chris, I don't want to say anything that will make things difficult between us.'

'It won't make any difference now. It's like watering a dead plant.'

Daniel thought if anything could make a difference now it would be prayer, the prayer of those living for those who have died but are not beyond the redeeming love of God. Chris's theology allowed no room for that. Those who died estranged from God would remain estranged for all eternity. How agonising it must be not only to have lost a child, but to fear that child is lost forever.

'You saw him?'

Daniel nodded.

'Tell me. Tell me before Sal comes back.'

'I can't.'

'You can. I need to know.'

'What did the police tell you?'

'That he died as the result of a stab wound to the neck.'

'I can't tell you any more than that.'

'Did he suffer?'

'I don't know.'

'He must have suffered. You know that. You would have said no if he hadn't.'

It would be hard to think of a more terrifying experience. 'I don't want to tell you something that I don't know to be true.'

'You can't . . . the police have a form of words. I think they're meant to spare you – to spare them – the horrors. I need to know.'

'I think there are also investigative reasons why they cannot share details of how someone died.'

'What sort of reasons?'

'There may be distinctive elements to the crime that only the murderer or an accomplice would know. If the murderer were to . . . commit the offence again he might repeat certain actions, which would help identify him. You see?'

'But they don't know anything yet?'

'I don't know, Chris.'

'I suppose we will find out eventually.'

They were silent for a while. Then Chris said, 'The person who discovered the body.'

'The police were notified anonymously.'

'Yes,' he said. 'Who do you think it was?'

'I don't know. I suppose if it were just someone who stumbled across it, they would probably not have stayed anonymous.'

'So it was someone who was involved?'

'I don't know.'

'You are a cloud of unknowing, Daniel.'

Before Daniel could answer the door swung open. It was Sal.

'She fell asleep as soon as she got into bed. I just hope she stays asleep.'

'I thought the dog might comfort her.'

'Thank you, that's thoughtful. But I'd rather a kindly doctor came to give us something to help us sleep. Daniel, would you like a cup of tea? I'd offer you a drink, but we don't drink.'

'Let me make you a cup of tea.'

'I would rather make it myself. It gives me some-thing to do.' She went to the sink and started filling the kettle. 'What's your policeman friend called?'

'Detective Sergeant Vanloo.'

'I meant his Christian name.'

'It's Neil.'

'Is he a Christian?'

'I'm not sure how to answer that.'

'Have a go.'

'It's not my place to say, Sal.'

'Daniel, I just want to know if he believes in Jesus Christ.'

'Sal . . .'

'I want to know if he believes in salvation.' She twisted the tap off but with more force than it needed or she intended.

Daniel realised that he did not know. It had not occurred to him to enquire, and in matters of faith he disliked saying to people, 'Anything to declare?' preferring to leave it to them to declare what they wanted to declare. He even disliked asking people if they were baptised and confirmed when he was filling in the forms for school entry, or to be godparents, or to be considered for training for ordination. It was not that he thought it unimportant; on the contrary, it was because he believed it to be of such sublime importance that he did not want to force people to put a value on something so precious, so elusive, so mysterious.

'You will have to ask him, Sal. I don't actually know.'

She took a tea bag from a box of PG Tips, put it in a mug and poured on boiling water. 'Do you want milk?'

'Yes, please.'

'I'll leave it to brew. Biscuit?'

'No, thank you.'

'It's not quite high tea at Champton House.'

'I don't expect it to be. I really just want to know if there's anything I can do for you.'

She went to the fridge and took out a bottle of milk and poured a splash into the mug. She stirred the bag in the milky tea, waiting, he supposed, for it to go sufficiently brown. There was something deliberate and focused about each action, as if she had planned it and was concentrating, trying to get it right. Then she fished the tea bag out with the spoon and dropped it onto the draining board. For a moment she seemed to concentrate on the bag releasing its liquid as it trickled slowly towards the sink. Then she seemed to recover her awareness, brought him the mug; she sat down opposite, next to Chris, and put her hand in his. He looked up, and Daniel wondered if the gesture was unusual. 'I don't know how we're going to get through the next five minutes,' she said. 'What does the next week look like? The next month?'

'There are some things you have to do. Registering the death, for one. If you need to be taken into town, or . . . perhaps you would like to talk to some other parents who have been through what you are going through? Anything, really, anything at all. Please tell me.'

'Pray for us.' Sal held out her hand to Daniel. He took it in his right hand. He offered his left to Chris, who took it in his, and they sat in silence for a moment. He felt the warmth of their hands in his and felt their unequal pressure, more from her than from him.

'Oh, merciful Father,' he said, 'who hast taught us in thy holy Word that thou dost not willingly afflict or grieve the children of men, look with pity upon the sorrows of thy servants for whom our prayers are offered . . .'

'Daniel, what about you? What do you feel?'

'. . . Remember them, O Lord, in mercy. Nourish their souls with patience, comfort them with a sense of thy goodness . . .'

'Daniel, what do you feel?'

'. . . I feel such deep sorrow I don't think I can . . . lift up thy countenance upon them, and give them peace, through Jesus Christ our Lord. Amen.'

'Amen.'

Sal Biddle would have been disappointed by how low high tea at Champton House could be. It was served in the library, or rather left in the library, by Mrs Shorely. Another stainless-steel pot, of tea this time, sat on a hot plate on a sideboard table by William Hamilton, with a jug of milk and a decent cake on a stand next to it. The china was exquisite but handled by Bernard like mugs from Habitat, which made both Daniel and Audrey wince. Alex and Honoria were also there. Alex looked surprised to see them.

Honoria hurried over and said *sotto voce* to Daniel, 'Don't mention you're coming to the lodge for drinks, I don't want Dad to know.'

'Why ever not?' said Daniel, who hated being

obliged to collude in an untruth even if it were for the
most innocent of ends.

'I'll tell you later . . . shh!'

Bernard approached carrying a plate of slices of cake.
It was a Dundee cake, 'a fiddly sort of cake to serve
without a plate,' Audrey observed, 'all flyaway almonds
and sticky crumbs. Especially one of Dora's.' He was
followed by Jove, his favourite white cat, an imperious
beast who normally lay on the library steps, but when
the house was full, instead of sloping off to find a quiet
corner, he attached himself to Bernard like a squire to
a knight.

'Daniel,' he said, 'a word?' and turned towards
the billiard room. A common element in Daniel and
Bernard's relationship was their intimate occupancy
of historic buildings. Daniel knew every quoin, every
corbel and every flagstone of St Mary's, but he also knew
his feet were just the latest, as the fifty-ninth rector, to
tread those flags and wear down the little hollow in
the middle of the aisle. Bernard had lived at Champton
from childhood, and he knew intimately its rooms and
corridors and cellars and attics – and its effects, not just
the intended ones of splendour in its baroque parts, or
of leisured ease in its eighteenth-century wing, but also
the unintended: the jarring effect of opening a grand
door and finding behind it the narrow, unadorned
back stairs to the attics; the change in acoustics when
moving from space to space. Bernard at this moment
wanted to be seen but not heard. He did not want to

look like he had abandoned his guests at tea, for that would be discourteous. But he did want to speak privately to Daniel and the billiard room, visible through open double doors to the library, was distant enough for their conversation to be seen but not heard.

'Been to see the Biddles?'

'I went this afternoon.'

'What state are they in?'

'Shock.'

'Should I go?'

'I don't think that would be necessary. A letter, of course. The offer of help?'

'Already done. But not necessary to call round?'

'No.'

'I don't want to give a misleading impression.'

'In what way?'

'To expect too much. I don't want them to think I owe them what I would owe you, as patron. Condolences, yes, but I am not going to replace their windows. It's all the fault of your damn bishop, Daniel, confusing matters with his wretched reorganisation.'

'I think a letter of condolence and the assurance of help with something specific? Perhaps you could offer to host the wake? That would be generous but not open-ended.'

'Those bloody children . . .'

'One, Bernard.'

'Oh. Yes. Awful.'

★

Daniel had little time to debrief with Audrey after tea, for the hour of Evensong was nigh, and she gave a summary of the intelligence she had gathered on her circuit of the library as he got into his cassock and cincture. It was cold outside and he felt the stirrings of something at the back of his throat, so he took a preventative Zubes lozenge from the box on his desk and started to suck it.

'Cahoots. Honoria and Alex. Something's up. Did they think I wouldn't see her corner you before Bernard did? He's worried about something. Won't you say? You know, don't you? Or is it the wedding? Why would Honoria and Alex both be here at the same time? And why the invitation to drinks? And apropos weddings, you will have to take Hilda to the vet on Tuesday. I want her to take a look, make sure everything's all right . . .'

'Yes, what time?'

'Ten-fifteen – I'll leave you a note. How long will you be this evening?'

'I don't know, not long; it's drinks, not supper.'

'Soup and a sarnie later? Pheasant and bread sauce and a game broth with . . . whatever needs eating?'

'That would be lovely.'

After Evensong Daniel's sinuses felt a little flushed by the mentholated fumes from his Zubes sweet. He must have smelt like a eucalyptus tree, he thought, as he intoned the Collect for Peace: 'O God, from whom all holy desires, all good counsels, and all just works do proceed; give unto thy servants that peace which the world cannot give . . .' And now he stood at the porch, in the night air, definitely chilly now; it felt almost sharp when he breathed in. He thought perhaps he had the beginnings of a cold, and blamed the football, which had been not only chilly, but damp and crowded. It was not crowded in church – seven in the congregation and eight in the choir: four sopranos, two basses and a soprano who was forced to be an alto and a bass who was forced to be a tenor. They were supposed to sing the setting of the Evening Canticles in the key of A by Sumsion, the organ part played bravely by Jane Thwaite, so what was intended as a four-part harmony was more two-and-three-fifths. 'Such a lovely *open* sound,' Audrey remarked as she scooted past to attend to the broth that was barely bubbling half-on and half-off an Aga hot plate whose thermodynamic properties were a mystery known only to her.

Anne Dollinger, soprano forced to sing alto, was first of the choir to leave. 'Daniel,' she said, 'how *is* Mrs Hawkins?'

'Mrs Hawkins? She is not very well, I'm afraid. Are you acquainted?'

'From the shop. A valued customer for many years. We were so sorry to hear she was so poorly. And I suppose Mr Biddle will be on leave for the foreseeable future?'

'Yes.'

'I was wondering – we were wondering – if pastoral

provision has been made for Mrs Hawkins in these critical weeks.'

'Yes, of course. Is that what you wanted to see me about? I have called in and will go again.'

'Only she is so . . . vulnerable . . .'

Daniel had to quell a bristling feeling. 'Anne, I will go again.'

'Of course you will, I know you will, but we are so worried about her.'

Anyone might be worried about a dying woman, thought Daniel, but there was something unusually insistent in Anne's tone. 'Is there any particular reason why you are so worried?'

'She has no family, no one to take care of her. Or no one . . . properly qualified.'

'Anne, is there something you would like to tell me? In confidence?'

She blinked three times. 'Just passing on our concerns, Daniel.' She did up the buttons on her coat. 'Do pass on our very best wishes to Mrs Hawkins when you see her.'

'I will.'

She nodded, then trotted down the darkening path to a tray and a jigsaw and Richard Stilgoe on the wireless.

Jane Thwaite was out next. 'Sorry about the Magnificat, Daniel. It's just too hard.'

'I hardly noticed anything out of place,' he said.

'You're very sweet, but we both know it sounded like *Coronation Street*.'

'I am so very glad that you play for us Jane, really.'

Her eyes were suddenly shiny. 'Thank you. It gets me out of the house, you see, on Sunday evenings, which are so long when you're on your own.'

'You know you could come to us when you're lonely?'

'Thank you. But I loved him. I miss him. Of course I'm lonely. I *should* be lonely. Anyway, sweet of you. Bye.'

And back she went to the house she had shared with her husband Ned – until he had stumbled across a truth his murderer wished to keep concealed.

Bob Achurch appeared. 'Shall I lock up, Rector? You want to get away?'

'Thanks, Bob.' Daniel slipped round the side of the church so he did not get slowed by conversation, and ducked into the vestry via the outside door. He slipped his black preaching scarf over his head and onto its hook in one move, which gave him a similar sort of pleasure, he imagined, to a cowboy lassoing a steer. He undid the loop that fastened his academic hood to his cassock button, flicked that over his head and hung it up too, then he pulled the long, voluminous surplice over his head and pulled his arms out of its enormous sleeves and hung it on a hanger and then on the rail. He filled in the register using what he called a Vicar's Count (lest not one of the flock be overlooked) and let himself out by the vestry door, which he locked behind him with the heavy old key.

It was too far to walk to the lodges through the park so he took the Land Rover. Alex must have seen his headlights coming towards the lodges, for he was at the little front door of the North Lodge, which he used for entertaining, when Daniel arrived. The other lodge, the South Lodge, was where he bathed and slept, and he was often seen walking from one to the other in his dressing gown, or sometimes pyjamas, oblivious to the visitors who arrived on Open Day.

'Dan!' he said. 'Don't you look magnificent in your cassock! Sorry about the subterfuge earlier.'

'There is something you wish to keep from your father?'

'Come on in and I'll tell you what. You won't blame me, either! But mind the logs.' Split logs, cut for the fire, were half stacked in a pile by the door. Daniel stepped around them and along a tiny dark corridor into what Alex grandly called 'the drawing room'. It was poky, and overfilled not with an abundance of things, but with things too good for the meagre accommodation it afforded. There were chairs from Champton's attics that had been made for the de Floures' London house and rescued from the Blitz; there were plates and bowls and tureens with the family arms in various iterations; there were portraits on the walls of once-loved, now-forgotten cousins and paintings of once-no-less-loved shorthorns. Even the cutlery seemed too big for the dining table, set for two, as if Brobdingnagian butlers had done the best for Lilliputian guests.

The table was set for Alex and for Honoria, who was sitting on the little two-seater sofa in front of the fire, lit for the first time this year, thought Daniel; the cold chimney released little handfuls of soot, which rattled onto the gently burning logs. 'Dan,' she said, 'thanks for coming. It's important.' The light from the fire flickered across her face and the red in her hair flickered back.

'Drinks first,' said Alex. 'What would you like? There's a Chardonnay open if you don't mind oaky Aussie stuff? I'm sure I could find a sherry, which of course simply *screams* you.'

'I'm driving,' said Daniel. 'Nothing for me.'

'Only through the park,' said Honoria. 'No one will catch you.'

'Really, I'm fine.'

'You can't, Dan, can you? You can't drive on a small sherry even through the park, even though it has less alcohol than one of Mrs Shorely's mince pies. You're *so* unlike your brother.'

'He can *only* drive when he's drunk,' said Alex, 'in that little hot hatch of his.'

'He drives beautifully . . .' said Honoria, '. . . well, *dramatically*.'

'You've been seeing quite a lot of each other,' said Daniel, trying not to sound more interested than he should.

'We bump into him out and about. He gets every-where, especially now he's on the telly.'

'And isn't he enjoying it!' said Alex.

'He would,' said Dan, 'it's what he's made for.'

'Rather a fixture on the after-hours scene. Carousing. Full of drink and Charlie.'

Honoria gave him a look. 'And a lady friend. Lots of lady friends.'

'Not like you *at all*, Dan.'

Alex was right, Daniel was no more likely to infringe a regulation than defy the laws of gravity. For if we are just in small things, he thought, we will be just in great things.

'Cup of tea?'

'No, I really don't want anything. But what did you want to see me about?'

Honoria shifted to one side of the sofa. 'Daniel, come and sit next to me . . . Now, we've had some intelligence arrive that we think indicates a problem.'

'Oh dear.' The sofa was lower and smaller than Daniel would have liked and a cassock is not a forgiving garment. 'That sounds intriguing.'

'It's about Hugh.' Hugh was their elder brother, heir to Champton and the de Floures barony.

'It's about Hugh's *fiancée*,' said Alex.

'I think she's called Michelle?'

'Yes. Michelle Giasson.'

'French Canadian?'

Alex put his head to one side and said, 'In *part*.'

Daniel thought for a moment. 'What are you . . . trying to say?'

159

'Friend of Hugh's from agricultural college ran into them in Canada. She's a Red Indian.'

'A Red Indian?'

'Mohawk. You know, pow-wows, smoke signals, scalping.'

There was a silence, then Daniel said, 'I don't think that's a very helpful way of describing the original peoples of Canada, Alex, if I may say so.'

'Oh, Daniel, of course it isn't, I don't *mean* it. She's a vet, not Hiawatha. But I don't know what Daddy is going to say. Honoria, back me up?'

'Of course it doesn't matter, Dan, if she's a Mohawk or a Mauritanian, not to you and me, but it does to Daddy.'

'I'm sure Bernard would not be so short-sighted as to judge someone on their nationality.'

'That's a noble sentiment, Dan, but like lots of people of his age and background – actually just *lots* of people – he would.'

Daniel flinched. 'I find it difficult to believe that your father would be so . . . ungenerous, so unimaginative . . . to think someone of another ethnicity as any less than a white person.'

'He wouldn't. It's not about their character, it's about their suitability.' Honoria pointed to the portrait over the fireplace. 'Look at him.'

Daniel looked. 'I can see he's a de Floures.'

'Yes, you can. Red hair, blue eyes.'

'Face like a frog,' said Alex.

'And two hundred years old. We still look like that. And we did for centuries before that, probably since the Vikings. Not because red hair is smart. It isn't when you think about it. I was mocked for mine when I was at school. But it's like Farmer Hugh's shorthorns: we're not a single instalment, we belong to a line, and the line must be preserved.'

Daniel said, 'But isn't a line strengthened by the addition of new blood?'

'Yes,' said Alex, 'but it's no good if it doesn't come with certain attributes. And I don't mean appearance, I mean experience.'

'I don't understand.'

'Hugh's wife is going to have to be chatelaine of Champton,' said Honoria. 'She's going to have to do . . . all this.' She waved her hand at the paintings hanging on the walls.

'She doesn't have to be happy. She doesn't have to love her husband. She doesn't have to be alabaster white,' said Alex, 'but she does have to be able to carry this off. Perhaps she is a princess of her tribe, the Catherine the Great of the Prairies for all we know, but what if she's . . . just a horse vet?'

'There is nothing wrong with being a horse vet,' said Honoria, 'it would be very useful in the stables, but could she manage everything the role requires? Running the house? Looking after the tenantry? Looking the part? That's what Daddy will be thinking.'

Daniel felt one of those occasional moments of

recognition when their world – which he moved in, and was part of, and thought he understood, and found so congenial – was suddenly strange. It had not occurred to him until that moment that Alex and Honoria – not just Bernard – thought dynastically about Hugh's choice of wife. And those elements of the role that she was destined for were not only outward, they were inward too; the successful candidate for the post of chatelaine of Champton would need to know, not just learn, how it worked. He thought again of Hugh and his intended, settled in the wide, open plains of Canada rather than the wheat-stacked fields of his birth.

'What do you want me to do?'

'What you always do, Dan,' said Alex. 'Prepare the way. Make straight in the desert a highway. For Hiawatha.'

'Alex!' snapped Honoria. 'You really *must* stop doing that.'

'You want me to talk to your father and tell him that his prospective daughter-in-law is Mohawk?'

'Who better than you, Dan?'

'It will be better for everyone,' said Honoria, 'if it does not come as a complete surprise.'

Daniel did not know very much about Mohawks. He remembered a marvellous film he'd once seen at the British Film Institute on a day off in London about skywalkers – not, as he thought, the young man in judo kit in *Star Wars*, but the men who built the skyscrapers of New York. They were Mohawks from

Quebec, French speakers, he thought, who, oddly for people who lived on the plains, were fearless working at altitude, and hopped from girder to girder a thousand feet above Manhattan without even a hint of vertigo. There were so many during that city's boom that they had their own neighbourhood in Brooklyn. Hardly teepees and bison, and he wished Alex would tire of the joke that had already wilted for Honoria.

'It seems not to have occurred to you what it might be like for her. Do you wonder what she will make of it? If she would like to take on the role? Your older brother hardly seems to view his destiny with relish. If she's made to feel unwelcome, perhaps they will return to Canada and not come back.'

'Hugh *has* to come back.'

'Why?'

'Because he inherits. Title and estate. Primogeniture, Daniel. You know how it works.'

'What if he doesn't want it?'

'He doesn't want it. But he has no choice. It can only be him.'

'I understand he inherits; but does he have to come back and run the show? Couldn't somebody else do it, if he's happy in Canada and wants to stay there?'

Alex and Honoria looked puzzled, as if the thought had never occurred to them. Then she said, 'I have sometimes thought he'd be better off as an *ordinary* landowner.'

Alex shrugged. 'People don't walk away, Daniel.

Look at what we've got. And the history. You've got to keep it going. Wouldn't you?'

'I don't know. But I'll think about how best to approach this with your father. Anyway, I must go.'

He struggled to get up from the sofa and had to rock forward to get enough momentum so his knees could do the work of getting him vertical. As he did, he discovered the tassels on his cincture had got tangled with his cassock buttons.

Honoria said, 'Oh, Daniel, let me help.' She picked away at the tangle and eventually freed him.

Daniel produced the Land Rover key from his pocket. She said, 'Dan, I can't be bothered to walk back to the house, could you drop me?'

'Of course.'

Alex, with unusual gallantry, stood up to see them out and they all had to squeeze round one another. It caused Daniel to knock the table, and the light reflected by the silverware shivered across the ceiling.

At the rectory Sunday supper awaited, a ritual he and Audrey observed with the same diligence as he would Evensong. It was, as she had promised, a broth made from the regular supply of pheasants Bernard left hanging on the rectory door. The tithe once exacted by the rector from the parish was no longer paid, and had not been for centuries, but there persisted a custom of providing out of one's first fruits for the needs of the clergy. In the old days his predecessors kept a meticulous record of who had paid what, and in one of his predecessor's tithe books from the seventeenth century, every farthing, every ounce of wheat, every turnip was recorded in a tiny, cramped hand. The ink had faded to brown, but the parsimony was undiminished, and Daniel often wondered how the rector conducted pastoral relationships with those from whom he exacted a tenth part of what was really theirs.

Most of what was theirs was not theirs, of course, or rather the labour they gave was not to fill their own storehouses, but those of whichever Lord de Floures they served, and whom they depended on for employment and lodging and their means of existence. For some of his parishioners, even today, that was still the reality, although most of the tenants in the village were now retired, the days of underbutlers and grooms and gardeners' boys as distant as the parson sending his men to take a cow from a farmer who was short on what he owed. But the memory of those relationships endured in the deference still shown to Bernard – still 'my lord' to those who worked, or had worked, in the house or on the estate – and, Daniel realised, it endured in the minds of those on the other side of that grossly disproportionate equation: Alex and Honoria. He had thought that the de Floures, like the rectors of the parish, had started to live lives in which those assumptions and privileges and obligations had faded into the past, but they were surprisingly persistent, especially when they conferred privileges. Perhaps Alex was right, and Hugh would not walk away from his inheritance but return like the prodigal son. And if he did return with Michelle as his wife and his lady, then he would not be the first to transplant a North American to a family seat in an English shire, even if it did not always work out well. He remembered not that long ago visiting a parishioner in a private psychiatric hospital, the old County Asylum only now with a chef and en-suites, and one of the nurses pointing out to him a woman born with a famous American society name who married a duke but fell from his affection and the altitude of her position, and eventually landed in their care. He would have to work out a way to prepare Bernard for his first encounter with his pro-spective daughter-in-law.

Before any of that, supper. He joined his mother in the drawing room, the fire lit with logs from the estate – another free dole for which he was with each more straitened year grateful. The dogs were curled up in front of it, in a nose-to-tail yin and yang, only he could now see that Hilda's curve was shallower than it used to be. Three or four puppies were normal for a first litter, Audrey said, so her insides were getting crowded. Her feistiness (so like his mother, he thought) was less in evidence, gestation taking its toll on her energies, and he wondered if hormones were stirring within her to produce motherly feelings that had not so far been much in evidence. He thought of his own mother, who would be unlikely to strike anyone as motherly; but when he thought of that term, 'motherly', it was Jean Tailby who came to mind: her fussiness and sentimentality and calculation. Audrey had none of those. She was steady, reliable; he had never doubted her love for him or his brother, nor had she failed to provide, but she never felt it necessary to make a fuss of her feelings.

Provision this evening was laid out on the trolley she had wheeled in from the kitchen, an impulse buy at the end of the Swinging Sixties; it was by Ercol, in beech, with wings that extended to turn it into a small table, and it was laid this evening with a plate piled with pheasant sandwiches, smeared with bread sauce and redcurrant jelly, and two soup bowls she had bought from a pottery in Norfolk around the same time. It was typical, Daniel thought, of vicarage furniture, out of keeping with the rooms it inhabited, for buying on-trend is not a one-off enterprise; it is a work of constant revision and they had not the means to upgrade every time, or any time, the fashion changed. He thought of all the other vicarages with horrible crockery, and ugly sofas, and bathrooms that looked like they were used for an unpolished form of Victorian hydrotherapy.

Audrey had put on the television – almost a ceremony in itself, for it was only on Sunday evenings that supper could be eaten in front of 'the set'. *Howards' Way* was on, one of her favourite programmes – a British answer to *Dallas*, only about yacht builders on the Solent rather than oilmen in Texas and made with considerably less in the budget.

They sat and watched in the bluish flicker from the screen and the reddish flicker from the fire. Then Audrey asked, 'How's poor Mrs Hawkins?'

'Still with us. Oh, that reminds me. She has asked me to be her executor, and you to be co-executor. She has no family, and no one close, apart from the vultures.'

'Oh, good, a generous legacy for the church, I hope. But won't that be awkward?'

'Nothing for the church, nothing for anyone apart from the Distressed Gentlefolk's Association.'

'I wonder if I qualify for that. Charity begins at home, doesn't it?'

'I think you have to be more distressed than we are, Mum.' And more gentle, he thought but didn't say.

Audrey harrumphed. 'I know we're hardly poor, Daniel, but it's not getting any easier to live on your stipend and my pension. If it weren't for the estate, I don't know how we would manage. And that's not an endless source of largesse. Since Nathan Liversedge disappeared there's been no one to mend things.'

'What needs to be mended?'

'Everything! The roof, the windows, the gutters. I know a homosexual gypsy boy is perhaps not Bernard's idea of a suitable match for Alex, but he was so . . . helpful. And no one's replaced him.'

'Do you need me to have a go?'

'As a suitable match for Alex?'

'Mother!'

'It might ease our money worries . . .'

'I meant, do you want me to have a look at the gutters?'

'I can more readily see you as a gay gypsy, darling.'

Daniel blushed – invisibly, he hoped, in the firelight – and pretended to be fascinated by yacht movements in the Solent.

Daniel was in his study after supper. He had a new amusement thanks to the gift of a music centre from a former parishioner, complete with a record player, a cassette-tape machine built in and twin stereophonic speakers – a great improvement on the little Dansette he had taken to college and never got round to replacing. It sat incongruously on a leaf table with barley-sugar legs, sleek and in stainless steel, like a medical device intruding into a dying country squire's bedroom. It was not the only phonographic device in the rectory; his mother's Roberts radio in the kitchen reliably delivered *The Archers* when she was cooking, and she had brought with her to the rectory the radiogram that had stood in the sitting room at the house Daniel grew up in for years, a sideboard wired for sound. It, too, had a record player built in, but his father, who did not like music, had only one album, a recording of the speeches of Winston Churchill, which he would play whenever a patriotic mood fell upon him. His parents had installed it for the wireless, permanently tuned to the Home Service, so the revolving disc with its rubber mat, which had rather beguiled Daniel as a child, was hardly ever used. Daniel loved music, and when he went to college he asked for the Dansette, which was given to him as a present, and on it he listened to the Karajan recordings of the Beethoven symphonies, Martha Argerich playing Chopin, Jacqueline du Pré in Elgar's cello concerto, Solti's *Ring* and, because he did not want to be seen as lacking a lighter side, Flanders and Swann's *At the Drop of a Hat*. He listened to them over and over again, and with such concentration, that now, if he was at a concert where one of these pieces was played, when the conductor lifted the baton he heard in his mind's ear the faint pre-echo the scratchy vinyl produced before the first chord sounded. He loved these recordings, knew every note of them, wore them almost to the condition of unplayability, and they remained in his collection, shelved according to a system of his own, by era or genre, and then alphabetically within that category.

This evening, which he had devoted to administration, he was listening to Janet Baker singing Mahler's *Kindertotenlieder* – a transportingly beautiful recording with Barbirolli conducting – to which he was sharpening the coloured pencils he used to show the correct liturgical colour for the vestry servers' rota. Daniel, particular in all things, was particular almost to a fault in this. He would use only Derwent Rexel Cumberland Artists' Pencils, series nineteen, which afforded far more colours than the Church's calendar required, even if he included – and he did – the two Sundays of the year when rose vestments were permitted, Gaudete Sunday in Advent and Laetare Sunday in Lent, which gave a day's relief from the weeks of austerity that characterised those two seasons. Some churches (he shuddered to think of it) wore pink on those days, even shocking pink, but that was not correct. Rose, which symbolised the Virgin Mary, was redder, more like salmon, and less . . . camp. There was a pencil in precisely the right colour, called 'Rose Pink', in the range and he was making sure it was sharpened properly, to his standard, so he would not be caught out with a blunt and uneven tip when Advent began in only seven or so weeks.

'*Oft denk' ich, sie sind nur ausgegangen* . . .' sang Janet Baker – 'I often think they have just stepped out . . .' – the orchestra sounding like a drunk town band, when, with jarringly bad timing, the phone went. Cosmo, who was sleeping at Daniel's feet, sat up as Daniel took the needle carefully off the record and went to answer it. 'Champton Rectory?'

'It's me.'

Neil. On that unusually busy evening he had quite forgotten he was supposed to see Neil. 'Hello, Neil. We're supposed to meet, I think?'

'Yes, won't take long. Can I call in? I'm only round the corner.'

'Yes, come round. I'll see you in a minute.'

'On my way.'

He heard his mother's voice from the hall. 'Have you got to go out?'

'No,' he said, 'but someone's coming round. I'll see to it.'

He heard nothing at first, then the drawing-room door closing on the television's din, surges of laughter and the distant but unmistakable sound of Liverpudlians being verbally brilliant.

He did not want Audrey to know Neil was coming round. He did not yet know why he did not want Audrey to know, but he did not have to think about it when she called to him from the hall. It was a new kind of discretion, he realised that; not professional, but personal. He remembered with almost unbearable embarrassment how one day she had walked in on him in his bedroom with a pile of washing while he was experimenting with an early and infrequently repeated attempt at masturbation. He'd pretended he was having a dream, and she did not so much as break stride; she put the folded clothes in his chest of drawers and left. After supper that night his father had asked him to come to his study and there, even more excruciatingly, he had laid out the facts of life and warned him against 'playing with yourself', for it 'saps a man's strength, physical and moral'. As an adult, he was no more willing to share the sparse details of his intimate life with his mother than she was hers with him. Other people's sex lives came to the rectory door, in one form or another. Audrey was blithely unembarrassed by them. He was no longer surprised by who did what with whom, and was as generous and as gentle in his attitude to people in messes of a sexual nature as he was with those caused by money or dishonesty or addiction. But when they told him of their own misadventures he offered nothing of himself in return, partly because he felt a certain opacity was necessary for authority, partly because he thought it bad manners, and partly because he knew they did not want to hear it.

Daniel heard a car coming up the drive and, lest the ring on the doorbell should summon his mother from the television, he slipped out to meet Neil at the door. He was wearing his Sunday best, the kind of suit worn by those attending court.

'Come in. You look smart.'

'I've been with the Biddles.'

'I can't think of anyone less likely to appreciate the formal gesture than the Biddles, poor souls.'

'I suppose not, but I like to observe the formalities. Like you.'

Cosmo had followed Daniel to the door and was trying to haul himself up Neil's trousers to say hello, but the material was so shiny his claws could find no purchase. Neil bent to greet him. 'Where's Hilda?'

'She's with Mum. Now she's pregnant she seems to have transferred her affection from me to her. Perhaps it's a maternal hormone.'

'I guess pregnancy makes them go crazy too.'

'Can I get you anything?'

'No, I've had gallons of tea. I just wanted to fill you in on where we are. And see if you have any ideas.'

Daniel gestured to the Sofa of Tears, where those visiting the rector would sit and talk and sometimes weep. Neil sat down and picked up the record sleeve on the coffee table. 'What were you listening to?'

'Mahler. The *Kindertotenlieder*.'

'What does that mean?'

Daniel was about to reply but checked himself. 'It means . . . it means songs for dead children. How apt. And how horrible. It hadn't occurred to me until just now.'

He turned the chair in front of his desk round, an unconscious choice that put him a few inches higher than his interviewee and preserved his authority.

'That would not be my first choice to listen to on the weekend,' said Neil.

'I suppose not. But why did you want to see me?'

Neil produced a little notebook from his inside pocket with what to Daniel looked like an undistinguished Biro held by the elastic band round the middle. He flicked through it and found a page covered in script. 'I want to go over what we've got. Now, Josh Biddle left the vicarage yesterday to go to band practice at eleven.'

'Oh, yes, Castle of Otranto. Such a peculiar name for a pop group.'

'That's right. We've talked to the other members of the band and they said there was no band practice. Two of them were in bed at home and the other was at Burton in Braunstonbury trying on suits for job interviews.'

'So Josh was using it as an excuse?'

'Don't know. He took his bass with him, though.'

'Wouldn't be a very effective excuse if he had not.'

'No. We found it at the scene.'

'Where?'

'Stashed behind the altar table.'

'Why do you say stashed?'

'It had been hidden, I think. But not very well. Quickly. And we found the case – no guitar.'

'I wonder what became of that?'

'Don't know. Forensics are taking a look. Of course, he might have set out with an empty case, if all he needed was to look like he was going to band practice.'

'What about the other Biddles?'

'His father was out on a prayer walk – do you know about that?'

'I think he likes to walk round the parish praying for people as he goes. The houses and the farms and the bus shelter, I think. He's comprehensive.'

'What does that involve?'

'I don't really know. I do something like it, too, but not in an organised way; it's habitual. Sometimes, when I take the dogs out, just seeing where people live puts them in mind, prompts me that perhaps there is something in their lives which is troubling them, so I pray for them.'

'Specific things?'

'Not really, I hold them in prayer before God. I don't ask for things. I don't try to put anything in words. Chris would, though.'

'That's interesting. Would that mean his route would be predictable?'

'I think it would be methodical. I wouldn't be surprised if he had a list, or a route. He told me he was walking the parish boundaries, the farms, the farm cottages.'

'The airfield?'

'Possibly, only no one lives there, and I don't think he would bother unless they did. Did anyone see him?'

'Not at the airfield. It was raining, though. The lady at Southfield Farm, out towards Champton House – I don't remember her name – saw him. She said he was soaking wet, and if she'd known he was the vicar she'd have asked him in. No dog collar. She didn't approve.'

'What time was that?'

'Dinner time.'

'You mean lunch time?'

Neil gave him a look. 'I mean midday. Twelve exactly. Gerald Harper had just come on the radio. He comes on at noon on a Saturday. Off at one.'

'Time of death?'

'Could be about then, maybe an hour or two later. So we know where Chris is at twelve, but not between eleven and twelve. And he got home at three.'

Daniel frowned. 'I don't think he would have been near the airfield at those times.'

'Why?'

'Methodical. He'll plan his prayer walk and it wouldn't make sense to head out towards Champton, then double back to the airfield. I would expect him to have an itinerary written down.'

'He did, we've seen it. But nobody saw him. He could have doubled back, done the deed, and resumed. Can you think of a motive?'

'No, I can't. What about Lydia and Sal?'

'Sal was in the kitchen baking all morning, Lydia was in her room listening to records. She came down for a sandwich around half past one and they talked for twenty minutes, then she went back to her room.'

'Did anyone call round?'

'Lady from the village dropped off some photocopying about two. Rang the doorbell but no one answered – there was loud pop music playing, she says – and it was raining so she left it in the porch. Chris found it when he got back at three.'

'What about Josh's friends? What about the band practice?'

'No one knew anything about it. I asked them if he could have made a mistake and they said yes, they do sometimes practise on a Saturday, and they were going to next week. He might have got it wrong. But he would have found out as soon as he got there; they practise in the drummer's garage, in Braunstonbury.'

'How would he get to Braunstonbury?'

'On the bus.'

'From Lower Badsaddle?'

'Leaves at quarter past eleven from the bus shelter.'

'Did he catch it?'

'Don't know. We'll find out.'

'And were his friends able to tell you anything about Goths?'

'They're not fully fledged, Daniel, they're like the Cubs to the Scouts.'

Daniel wondered for a moment what a Grand Howl by Goth Scouts might sound like. 'Is there anyone among them who you think might be capable of murder, or involved in murder?'

'We don't think so. Maybe if you look at the wider circle, but we haven't been able to establish any direct link so far. The only one people seem to have had worries about was Josh.'

'What sort of concerns?'

'He was difficult, confrontational, had no respect for authority.'

'Typical child of a vicarage.'

'Yes, I can see how that could happen. And Lydia?'

'A gentle girl, really, for all the attitude.'

'But they were twins. Close.'

'Yes, but they were *different*. How is she?'

'In shock. She's hardly taken it in. If we ask questions – very, very gently – she falls apart.'

'Were you able to ask her about the chapel?'

'Yes, she said she told Josh about it. When I pressed her she just crumbled, and her mum said we had to stop.'

'Guilt.' It occurred to Daniel that if he had not shown the chapel to Lydia, she wouldn't have told Josh about it and he wouldn't have gone. 'Did the others know about the chapel? In the band?'

'Yes, Josh had told them, and he'd taken a couple of them to see it. He wanted to do a photo session there.'

Daniel thought of the police photographers and the light of their flash guns illuminating Josh's body so graphically. 'Is there anything from forensics?'

'He died of blood loss, from a severed carotid artery. A clumsy cut, though, not the work of an expert.'

'Murder weapon?'

'Very sharp knife, thin blade. A butcher's knife? Something specific to a task? We don't know yet. Nothing's been found. It was drawn across his neck more than once. Untidy cuts, someone feeling his way, we think. First couple tentative, last was deeper, inflicted with more violence. That was the fatal one, cut the artery. No sign of the weapon.'

'What about footprints?'

'Two distinct sets in the blood, both standard, male, we think, approximately a size nine and a size ten, probably wellingtons – we'll know more later. We think the size tens were present after the size nines, because our blood man thinks the deposits were more coagulated when he stepped in them. The size nines looked much more slippery, more of a mess.'

'So probably left by the murderer?'

'That's likely, yes.'

'So we're looking for a man with size nine feet and wellingtons.'

'We may be. There are lots and lots of them.'

'Not so many with a taste for ritual throat-cutting.'

'Any more thoughts about that?'

'Yes. My first thought was that the motive might be religious – the altar, a sacrificial offering – but now I'm not so sure. There was something staged about it, something not *authentic*.'

'You know what a real child sacrifice would look like?'

'No, of course not. I mean, perhaps the killer was trying to make it look like it had a ceremonial purpose, but it was as if he'd read something in a book. It was like an outline, a caricature. So I wonder if it's more likely to have something to do with the Goths. They love to make up rituals, they love the imagery, the language, but it's ersatz. The question is what possible reason could they have for actually killing Josh?'

'All the usual reasons, maybe? Money? Drugs? A warning? Behave, or you will get what's coming? There was a hint, some talk, that Josh was connected to something higher up the chain than the others he was hanging out with. We're looking into it. They would need to be very nasty, very worried, if they're prepared to hack away at a lad's throat until he's bled to death.'

Daniel wondered how Neil could reel off the gruesome details of a death like this without flinching. He supposed it was repeated exposure, and after time the existential drama of a life cut short fades from the plain litany of facts. Neil dealt in facts, Daniel in drama; both contributed to the picture, hazy at first, then gradually more detailed and more focused, that told the fuller story about how and why and who. Nothing was coming into focus yet, but could there be something that was not yet in focus but in which the very faintest shape was beginning to muster mass, and angle, and volume, and distinctiveness? He did not know, but the fact that he was even thinking it suggested that on the furthest edges of awareness a faint pressure, a breath of wind, a ripple, was felt.

'What was he doing there?'

'Don't know. No sign of a forced abduction, so it looks like he went there willingly. To meet someone who wasn't a stranger?'

Daniel thought of the moment Josh would have realised what was about to happen. He flinched.

'Are you all right?'

'It's so horrible . . .'

'It is horrible. Murder is horrible.'

'*Ritual* murder. The candles . . .'

'Yes, I need to tell you about that. The candles were the kind you find in churches.'

'How do you know?'

'Forensics. But didn't you recognise them?'

'Recognise them?'

'They're the kind you use in your church.'

Daniel flinched again. 'St Mary's?'

'Yes, I checked with the suppliers.'

'They're standard issue, Neil; everyone – or nearly everyone – uses them.'

'And they could be from any church that uses them. I guess from any supplier. If they did come from you, how easy would it be to get hold of them?'

'Someone could just walk in and help himself from the candlesticks.'

'Aren't they too big?'

'The ones on the altar, yes; I don't mean them. I mean the ones we use on the side altars. And the big ones aren't real. They're plastic fakes, with little phials that you fill with oil and put a wick in that fits in a hole at the top.'

'Smoke and mirrors?'

'Stage management. Thrift.'

'Wouldn't you notice if someone stole the candles from the side altars?'

'Not necessarily. It's not my job to look after them, it's Bob Achurch's. You could ask him. But he keeps a box of them under the altar. You would only have to look.'

'Who looks under altars?'

'What do you mean?'

'Aren't they supposed to be holy?'

'They are holy – I put ashes that come in for burial under the main altar; nothing else – but they're also convenient places to store things like candles.'

'Who would know that?'

'Sacristans. Clergy. Churchwardens. Anyone who spends time around churches, backstage people.'

Neil made a note in his notebook with the stubby Biro that was beginning to bother Daniel. 'Would you like something better to write with?'

'No, thanks, this fits in the elastic . . . . Daniel, it's not pretty, but it's functional.'

'I don't see any reason why functional can't be beautiful. In fact, I wonder if it *can* be functional and *not* beautiful?'

'It's standard issue, Daniel, I get it from a cupboard at work. It's not what I would choose . . .'

'Inspector Morse gets to drive that lovely car.'

'That's not real life. It's all Escorts and Maestros now. Look, I should go.' He stuck the Biro in the notebook and put them in his pocket. 'Keep your ear to the ground?'

'Of course. Is the airfield out of bounds?'

'It will be for a while. Why do you ask? Do you want to take a look?'

'I was thinking of our driving lessons, actually.'

'Aren't we down for Sunday?'

'Not next Sunday, it's Harvest Festival and we're having a parish lunch. I don't suppose you want to come to that?'

'We're going to be working round the clock until we get this guy. But if I can get away . . . Can I let you know?'

'You can.'

Daniel saw Neil to the door and stood with Cosmo on the step. He waved as he watched him drive away in the modest saloon that came with the job. He had never really noticed the prose of it compared with the poetry of Morse's Jaguar. Nor did he notice his mother watching from the kitchen.

5

Hilda, who had seemed until now much preoccupied with pregnancy, recovered something of her old self as she sat on Daniel's lap in the waiting room at the vets in Braunstonbury on Tuesday. Dogs and cats were separated there, like gentlemen from ladies in a mosque, in an effort to reduce the hostilities that famously attend their encounters. Hilda, however, could be almost as hostile to other dogs as to cats and, with the idiot pluck of her breed, cared not whether the object of it was a toy poodle or a pit bull terrier. It was an Alsatian that was making her growl and snap – fortunately rather a placid one, thought Daniel, and he made what he hoped were mollifying expressions to the owner, a farmer who was not as placid and looked at Daniel with the contempt countrymen reserve for those insufficiently in control of their pets. When Daniel loosened his scarf to reveal a dog collar, a tactic he sometimes used if the object of hostility, the farmer went red, not from choler but embarrassment, and nodded at him.

A vet in a green smock appeared in the doorway. She was in her late twenties, thirty perhaps, and solid – 'Hilda Clement?' – from Yorkshire, he thought, and looked like the kind of vet you could imagine delivering calves on a windy dale.

Daniel got up, holding Hilda and her snapping jaws out of range of the Alsatian, nodded to the farmer and followed the vet through to a booth.

'I'm Lizzie,' she said, and Daniel put Hilda on the stainless-steel table, which so reminded him of a mortuary, and unclipped her lead.

'How's the mum-to-be?' said Lizzie.

'I think she's all right,' said Daniel, 'physically. Her behaviour has changed, quite noticeably.'

'What have you noticed?'

'She's less playful, she's less aggressive, though that Alsatian might not think so. And she does things she has not done before.'

'Like what?'

'She's treading her bed more than she used to. She's spending more time with my mother. And she's expanded her repertoire of . . . I don't know quite how to describe them . . . physical tics – rolling and sniffing the air when there's nothing to sniff?'

'Sounds like pregnancy.'

'Typical for dachshunds?'

'I was thinking of mine. Let's have a look at her . . .'

She felt Hilda's belly, an indignity the little dog

seemed rather to enjoy, and said, 'Nipples like chapel hat pegs. If that's a helpful image?'

'I'll take that in the ecumenical spirit with which it was intended. How far gone is she?'

'A fair way. Is she eating more?'

It was hard to imagine Hilda eating anything less than the maximum amount possible in any situation, but his mother, who was the grossest offender when it came to feeding her titbits from her plate, had said she definitely was. 'Yes, we think so.'

'And trying to nest?'

'She's collecting cushions and blankets and burrowing into them, and trying to keep the other one out of it.'

'A male?'

'Yes. Four years old. Her nephew as a matter of fact.'

'I don't think we need worry about degrees of kindred, vicar.'

That was an insider phrase, Daniel thought. He said, 'You grew up in a vicarage?'

'I did. The vicarage of St Hilda's Ravensburn.'

A dark little mill town, shadowy with soot, and an ugly Victorian vicarage with a modern church next to it. It looked like the Addams Family had built a squash court in the garden.

'Are you Leonard Livesley's daughter?'

'I am.'

'You're not . . . Dorcas?'

She glanced towards the open door. 'Not NOW. I changed it to Lizzie. Wouldn't you?'

'I used to come to your vicarage for Deanery Chapter when I was a curate in Hartburn and your father was rural dean.'

Lizzie squinted at him. 'I don't remember you. But there were so many curates . . .'

'It's quite all right. In fact, I like to be unremarkable. I remember you. You must have been about twelve or thirteen. But how is your father?'

'Um, anxious.'

'About what?'

'About women priests.'

St Hilda's was so High that even by the standards of the slum churches of the industrial North it was accounted stratospheric. Its liturgy would have induced helpless raptures in Pope Pius X; so rare and so refined, it drew congregations from far and wide. Once a Low Church archdeacon, bidden to Solemn Evensong and Benediction, was so upset by the billowing incense, the numberless candles and a sung Latin litany that was liturgically eccentric and canonically doubtful that he declared it worthy of the prophets of Baal and took a bus home to Bradford before the monstrance had even been lifted up.

'I imagine he would have difficulty in reconciling to a change in the status quo.'

'It seems so clear to him. To me, the opposite seems so clear. What do you think, if it isn't a tricky question?'

'It is a tricky question. I used to think like your father, but now I think more like you. I do not know what the outcome will be, but change will come at a cost. I don't know how high a cost, and how it will be paid.'

He felt the sadness fall on him that he only felt when the prospect reared of people falling out whom he respected and cared for equally. Lizzie looked sad too.

'I've never known Dad so low.'

Hilda barked, as if to remind them that she was the purpose of the visit, not the gloomy prospect of impaired communion within the Church of England.

'Hilda', Daniel said more cheerfully, 'shares her name with your father's church. I named her after Hilda of Whitby, for she arrived on her feast.'

'The nineteenth of November. I still know the prayer for the day by heart. O God, by whose grace the blessed Abbess Hilda, enkindled by the fire of your love, became a burning and shining light in thy Church: grant that we may be inflamed with the same spirit of discipline and love and ever walk before thee as children of light; through Jesus Christ our Lord. Amen.'

'Amen,' said Daniel.

After the vet Daniel made his second errand of the day, to Our Price in Market Street, a shop he had not visited before because he invariably bought his records from the specialist in Stow, where he did not have to

explain who Gesualdo was, or how to spell Janáček.
The shop always reminded him of a Wimpy's bright-
red livery and promise of beef burgers – a dish he had
no desire to eat, though Neil had taken him once to
McDonald's and laughed at him when he'd asked for
cutlery. He had no desire, until now, to buy anything
from Our Price either, and he felt the same sense of
apprehension as he approached the desk, where two
young men stood. One looked like a road mender but
with close-cropped hair; the other was wearing baggy
jeans and a T-shirt with long sleeves. They looked at
him with a mixture of surprise and dislike.

'Good morning,' he said.

The one in baggy jeans said, 'Hello, Fath—' but
didn't finish the sentence.

Daniel said, 'I'm looking for a record.'

'I would say you're in the right place, but it depends
on the record,' he said.

'I'm looking for "Something's Gotten Hold of My
Heart", by Marc Almond and Jim Pitney.'

The other one snorted. Something about him was
familiar.

'Gene Pitney, not Jim. You'll find that in the chart
singles section. Unless you want the twelve-inch?'

'Just the normal one. The one for normal record
players.'

'They're both normal, but one is like the version you
hear on the radio, the other is the longer version for
fans.'

'Oh, I wonder if I could have one of each, please.'

'Would you like me to get them for you?'

'Yes, please. I don't really know my way around.'

The boy sloped off and Daniel stood at the counter trying to ignore his uncommunicative colleague, who turned away from him and started looking through a thick folder, so he went and inspected a rack of records – twelve-inches as the boy had called them, the size of long-playing albums, but they appeared to have only one song on them, which he imagined made them very long versions indeed.

'I thought you wanted me to get it?' said the first boy.

'I don't really know what I am looking at,' said Daniel. 'Is it one of these?'

'It is,' and he reached across Daniel and withdrew from a densely packed section a white sleeve with a picture of a brooding young man with black slicked-back hair printed on the front.

'Is that Marc Almond?'

'It's not Jim Pitney.'

'But he sings on it too?'

'He sang the old version back in the Sixties, then when Marc Almond asked him, he came out of retirement for this version. I think that's what happened. It's not the first recording I thought a vicar would go for, if you don't mind me saying.'

'No, it's a present for a friend. The long version is; the short version is for me.'

'Oh. *Special* friend.'

Daniel said nothing.

At the desk the uncommunicative boy was communicating with a customer. 'It's shit. Why have that when you could have *Disintegration*?'

'I want that too, but my brother got *Kiss Me, Kiss Me, Kiss Me.* I love it. He got it on vinyl and I want it on cassette. For me.'

'We've got it in stock. Sure I can't get you *Disintegration* too? It's a return to form, proper Cure, not the pop shit.'

'I haven't heard it.'

'Do you want to hear it?'

'Yeah.'

'I've got it. You could come round to mine?'

'Er . . .'

'I'm Brandon. What's your name?'

'Lydia.'

It was Lydia Biddle. Daniel leaned onto the counter. 'Hello.'

She took a moment to recognise him, so unexpected was his appearance in a record shop. 'Daniel! Hello. What are you doing here?'

'I'm buying a record.'

'Yeah, Jim Pitney and Marc Walnut,' said Brandon, with a sneer.

'What about you?' said Daniel.

'Same. But not your kind.'

'Perhaps not. But I'm curious.'

'I'm getting *Kiss Me, Kiss Me, Kiss Me*. It's an album by a band called the Cure.'

'Is it Goth?'

The boy gave Daniel a stare, and then he knew where he had seen him before.

'It's *the best*. The Cure are *the best*,' said Lydia.

'Why do you like them?'

'Their music. I love it. Josh loved it. He discovered it and then he played it to me.' She began to crumple.

'When you listen to it perhaps you feel connected to him?'

'Yes. I think so. And it . . . speaks to me. It's like they're my friends. I hear my own life in their music. Do you get that?'

'I do. I feel the same about Janáček.'

'I don't know what that is.'

'A composer. From Czechoslovakia. He was an organist and a professor in Brno, and about sixty years ago, when he was already old, he started producing the most beautiful music . . . which speaks to me and . . . well, I hear my own life.'

'Organ music?' said the boy. 'But you're buying, not what's-his-name, but Marc Almond and Gene Pitney.'

'I didn't know you were a Marc Almond fan,' said Lydia, sounding surprised.

'I just like that record.'

The helpful boy appeared on the other side of the till with the twelve-inch and the seven-inch singles. 'Lyds,' he said, and he searched for his words: 'I'm really sorry about Josh.'

She looked down. 'Thanks.'

'I didn't know him long, but I thought he was a . . . good bloke.'

'Thanks.'

'You something to do with Josh Biddle?' said Brandon.

'I'm his sister.'

'Really bad . . . what happened.'

'Thanks.'

'So do you want to come round? I could play you that album. Make you a tape.'

'I don't know.'

The other boy rang up Daniel's records at the till. 'That's £3.98.'

Daniel took out his wallet and handed him a five-pound note.

'Thanks. Do you want a bag?'

Daniel nodded. 'Yes, please. And thank you for your help. Lydia, do you want a lift home?'

'Oh, yes. Thanks! I'm just going to pay for this.'

Brandon took her money and bagged the packaged cassette.

'There you go . . . Lydia.'

'Thanks, Brandon.'

'And come round sometime?'

'Yeah. Brandon Redding?'

'Yeah.'

'Josh talked about you.'

'Did he?'

'Yeah, nothing bad. I don't remember anything bad. Anyway, see you.'

'Yeah. See you around. You know where I am.'

At the door Daniel said, 'Lydia, I forgot my receipt, I won't be a minute.'

Brandon was at the desk. He didn't look up. 'Yeah?'

'Could I have your undivided attention, Brandon?'

Then he looked up.

Daniel said, 'That hostile stare of yours – I remember it from the football – it neither becomes you nor creates the intended effect, which I suppose is menace? It's not menacing, it's ridiculous, but that's not important. This is what is important: I know who you are; I know where you are; I know what you want. Are we clear?'

'Uh . . . OK.'

Daniel left, ignoring the stifled expletive that followed.

On the way home Daniel called in at the post office. Anne Dollinger was at the shop counter talking to Mrs Braines. They both hushed as soon as the little bell over the door jingled as he came in.

'Good morning, Mrs Braines. Anne.'

'Rector.'

'Hello, Daniel. Anyway, Norah, best keep a packet or two in for her. She's hardly a bonfire, but she does like one with her coffee in the morning.' Anne gathered up her purse and a paper bag, which Daniel saw contained a packet of Consulate cigarettes.

'I'll put in an order, Anne.'

'Toodle-oo.'

Anne made rather a show of squeezing past Daniel – 'Breathe in!' – lest anyone should think it her intention all along to rub against the rector, and the little bell jingled again as she stepped out onto the pavement.

'I wonder, Mrs Braines . . . if you . . .'

'I have it here, Rector.' She produced a *Church Times* from under the counter, which made Daniel think he had asked her for indecent material rather than the Church of England's weekly digest of news and comment and listings of clerical appointments, retirements and deaths, known in the trade as 'Jezebel's Trumpet'. It arrived at Champton post office in the morning, too late for the paper boy, and Daniel liked to read it after lunch before the afternoon paper boy arrived with the Braunstonbury *Evening Telegraph*.

Mrs Braines was another rich source of news and comment, uniquely placed behind her twin counters – shop and post office – to receive and disseminate. She was almost lusty in her appetite for the comings and goings of Champton and its neighbours, and tireless in sharing her view of the merits or otherwise of the individuals who made the headlines.

He glanced at the front page – another debate about

divorce in Synod, a sticky issue at the Tory Conference concerning South Africa, a call to prayer for Terry Waite, captive in Beirut—

'It looks like Anne Dollinger's found a new mistress, Rector.'

'Would that be Miss March, Mrs Braines?'

'It would. On the counter all day and every day, and she even sends her out for her fags. Consulate. The menthol ones.'

Daniel wondered why anyone would mentholate a cigarette, adding something that assists breathing to something that impedes it, but it seemed to fit Miss March, with her meticulous calibration of distinction, her Joan Fontaine way of dressing, her Rolls-Royce Allegro.

'Does she come in herself?'

'Sometimes, if Anne's off. Fags, a magazine, biscuits. It's like stepping back in time. I half expect her to ask for a tin of snoek.'

'How's her shop doing?'

'She knows how to sell, she knows how to deal with customers. Lovely dresses too, though I could never afford them. But what she wears! She looks like she's stepped out of *Brideshead Revisited*.'

'I understand she has been looking for somewhere to live. Here? The Badsaddles?'

'Anne said she'd been looking at something in Upper Badsaddle, a cottage on manor land. I don't know if it's still Mrs Hawkins's; it might have been sold off. I know she's been back to see it a couple of times, but I wouldn't . . . you know.'

'What?'

'It's so close to the airfield, a murder place; it's not very nice, is it? And no one caught?'

'I understand the feeling of nervousness, but it is very unlikely that such a thing should recur . . .' He put his hand to his mouth.

'It recurred here, Rector, didn't it? And only a year ago.'

'Yes, it did, how silly of me.'

'They say lightning and all that never strikes twice, touch wood.' She pressed her hand onto the wood of the counter. 'But I began to worry we were turning into St Mary Mead.'

Daniel paid for his *Church Times* and tucked it into his cincture. 'Thank you, Mrs Braines.'

'Give my regards to your mother, Rector. And tell her that box of United biscuits is going to go out of date and if she doesn't want them, I shan't be ordering them again.'

United biscuits, his brother Theo's favourites; his visits to the rectory had become less frequent since he had started filming his new drama series, and his consumption of the Uniteds Audrey kept for him had declined. Daniel resolved to telephone and see if he could get him to come down for her birthday in November, which fell on St Cecilia's Day, the patron saint of music, although her intercession had not yet granted to Audrey's inaccurate soprano the beauty she, but only she, thought it evidenced. One of the sounds that haunted Daniel's childhood was the descant to 'O Little Town of Bethlehem', which she had learnt as a girl at school. It was among her proudest accomplishments and made its appearance at the carol service as reliably as candlelight, which flickered thanks to the sheer projectile force of her G in 'we hear the Christmas angels the great glad tidings tell'.

Daniel decided to call in to see Miss March. She had wanted to speak to him after the service at Upper Badsaddle, and the Tailbys had seen her off, but not before asking if she could come to see him. She had not – nor telephoned, nor written – and while he would normally wait for someone to pluck up the courage to do so, he decided to take the initiative.

Outside the shop a new sign had been hung up: 'Elite Fashions' it proclaimed in black copperplate script on a pale grey background. The window, carefully dressed to tempt the ladies of Champton with the latest modes, was freshly painted too, and the door, which opened onto a scene transformed since Daniel had last seen it. There were mannequins and mirrors and hats on stands and rails of dresses and jackets and coats, and there were bags and belts and three curtained booths, and a long counter at which Miss March, in a grey ensemble that suddenly looked more battleship than dove, was dealing with a customer. The customer was

Jean Tailby. She was brandishing a dress as if it were a crucial piece of evidence in a trial.

'Miss March, I am very disappointed in you.'

'I am sorry to hear it, Mrs Tailby, but—'

'But, but, but – I don't want buts, I want to return this dress. It's not right for me. You knew it was not right for me when you sold it to me.'

'Not at all, Mrs Tailby. It is a very nice dress indeed – one any lady would be happy to wear to a luncheon. In town. Midweek.'

'Never mind that . . .'

'I sold quite a few dresses and jackets last week to ladies who were attending the NSPCC luncheon yesterday at the Assembly Rooms in Braunstonbury. Perhaps you know about it?'

'That is neither here nor there. The dress does not suit, I want a refund.'

Miss March paused and then said in a voice of icy calm, 'Mrs Tailby, the garment is neither crisp enough nor fresh enough for me to offer it for resale. That, I'm afraid, is that.'

Jean Tailby stuffed the dress back into a bag, then leaned across the counter and said, 'I can see why you're still a Miss,' and turned to leave. She pretended not to see Daniel, partly because it might make her look less magnificent in retreat, and partly because she did not want to have to be nice to him after she had been so nasty to Miss March. With a ding of the bell over the door and the suggestion of a slam, she was gone.

'Miss March,' Daniel said, and went to lift the hat that again he was not wearing.

'Rector,' she said, 'I am so sorry you had to see that. She's such an angry woman.'

'I did not quite understand what the contretemps was about.'

'She came in on Saturday for a dress. I showed her a classic crossover, Windsmoor, lovely belt and buckle, purple, and honestly, I *did* think it not quite suitable, but she liked it and she bought it. Then today, the day after the ladies' luncheon in Braunstonbury, which I knew all about because lots of my ladies went, she brought it back in saying it was not quite right. It was right enough for her to wear to that luncheon, and I would not be running this shop if I did not know what a soup stain half sponged out of a polyester mix looks like.'

'Isn't that rather dishonest?'

'It is rather dishonest, and it happens every day. And that is what the world looks like, Rector, to a dress shop proprietress in a little place like Champton in Middle England at the end of the 1980s.'

'I see,' said Daniel, 'I see.'

'But what may I do for you?'

'I was thinking more of what I could do for you. We were interrupted after church on Sunday, and I was so sorry not to catch up with you. Then I saw Anne in the post office so . . . here I am.'

'Anne, dear?' said Miss March.

Anne appeared from behind the curtain that separated the staff room from the shop floor. 'Yes, Miss
March?'

'Would you do me a great favour and take the gloves
round to Mrs Staveley at the Old School House? I
promised I'd have them to her by lunchtime, and it is
nearly past lunchtime.'

'Where are they?' she asked.

'On the front seat of the Vanden Plas. You'll need
my keys.'

She retrieved them from the till and, when Anne
appeared in her coat, dropped them rather grandly into
her offered hand. 'No need to rush, dear.'

'Yes, Miss March. Daniel.' And she scooted off to the
ding of the little bell.

'I did intend to come and see you, Rector, but . . . I
feel a little awkward.'

'Is there anything I can do for you?'

'I have not been completely frank with you. My reasons for being here are not simply to do with the retail
opportunity.'

'I wondered if that might be the case.'

'You did?'

'Only in the most general terms.'

'Well, I feel it my duty – and I am reluctant to do so
in spite of what you just witnessed – to pass on my concerns about the welfare of Muriel Hawkins at Upper
Badsaddle Manor.'

'Mrs Hawkins in the care of Jean Tailby?'

'Yes, and Mr Tailby. Rector, in retail you learn very quickly to spot someone who is not entirely . . . straight.'

'And you think Mrs Tailby is not entirely straight?'

'I do. And while Muriel Hawkins is no wilting flower, she is old and ill and – this is none of my business, of course – to be quite honest with you I am concerned for her safety.'

'Mrs Hawkins and you are . . .?'

'She is an old customer of mine, of many years. She and Mr Hawkins were regulars at the shoe shop. I could not say we were friends, but you get to know someone over the years when you sell them their shoes. They are curiously revealing items.'

Daniel nodded. 'I always look at people's shoes too. My family were in the shoe trade.'

'I know, we used to stock Clements of Caswell. There was a lovely brown Oxford, Goodyear welted, that my father loved and wore for decades. In the end they became his gardening shoes.'

'But could you tell me any more about your concerns for Mrs Hawkins?'

Miss March paused and then took a breath. 'I am conscious that to make an accusation, or even to allow someone to infer, that the motives of another may be very concerning indeed is no small—'

The door swung open. The bell rang. Audrey Clement stood in the doorway.

'Daniel! I see you are getting acquainted with the marvellous Miss March?'

'Mum. Miss March, you know my mother, I see?'

'Mrs Clement, how nice to see you again.'

There was a pause. After a while, Audrey smiled more determinedly. 'If I may, I wonder if I could prevail upon you for professional advice, Miss March?'

'Yes, Mrs Clement, of course.'

Another pause. Then Audrey said, 'Daniel, perhaps you would permit us to discuss matters not suitable for a son and a clergyman?'

Daniel calculated that if he were to ask for his mother to wait, she would do so within earshot and that would imperil the confidentiality of the conversation he wished to have with Miss March. That was not something he would even consider negotiating with his mother, for it would excite her curiosity, and Audrey's excited curiosity was as a roaring lion that walketh about, seeking whom he may devour.

'Miss March, perhaps you would like to call at the rectory at your convenience?'

'Thank you, Rector. Your telephone number is in the book, I presume?'

'It is.'

'Then I shall ring you up.'

'You have to hand it to her, it's a very personal style . . .' Audrey was speaking on the telephone. 'Yes, very personal. But I can tell you what it is. I remember it from school . . . Yes, Scotland. No, not in the Thirties. It's posh Presbyterian, but later, the Fifties. It's what the better class of minister's wife would wear . . . My best friend, Kitty Muirden, her people were from Ross-shire – lawyers, ministers; her grandfather was a professor of something at Glasgow – she dressed like that too. Not flashy, not look-at-me. Quiet, but quality . . .'

Daniel found it impossible not to listen. His mother, he thought, could easily have been a professor at Glasgow, if there were a Chair for Social Class. Her powers of analysis of dress, accent, gait, affiliation were so fine-tuned that any noble child stolen from his cradle would have needed no identifying tattoo to be restored to his rightful inheritance. She had no *Burke's*, no *Almanach de Gotha*, partly because she knew the aristocratic families of England and Scotland and Ireland better than she knew her own, but also because those powers were principally directed towards the upper middle classes of her homeland, in their ranks of farmers who farmed their own land, solicitors, clergy, doctors, possibly dentists (Wimpole Street preferred), Members of Parliament, bank managers and – a more recent addition – manufacturers, merchants, the proprietors of department stores, the select end of trade. These complicated connected networks were not recorded in any guide, but in her memory and sensibility – the latter detecting an uncertain diphthong, an incomplete educational pedigree, the unpolished handling of cutlery; the former assigning it to a place in the League of

Distinction. This is where Audrey ultimately assigned everyone, including herself, and she needed nothing more to know where she, and everyone else, was in the world. The one complicating factor was money. In the old days, there had always seemed to be sufficient funds to maintain the style of life one's place required. Now a gap had appeared, and opened up, and got wider, in her case noticeably so. This was why she had become interested in Miss March, whom she immediately identified as a woman who knew how to look like one of her customers, rather than one of their ancillaries.

'Oh yes, Kitty's mama went to Campbell's of Beauly. I stayed with them often and we always went. The sort of shop you dream of – tweeds, of course, and country things, but dresses too, lovely things by Bernat Klein. Do you know who I mean? And hats and gloves and scarves and bags. A royal warrant outside. Everything a Highland lady might need. And it's exactly what she wears. Well, it would have been . . . Oh, Jaeger . . . Jaeger, Jaeger, Jaeger . . .'

The sound of a car in the drive made Daniel look up. It was the Biddles' campervan. Hilda stirred at his feet and Cosmo jumped off the Sofa of Tears, pushed at the study door, and ran past Audrey who was trying to talk and see who it was. Daniel took Hilda and showed Cosmo into the drawing room and closed the door.

'Mum,' he whispered, 'it's the Biddles . . .'

'Jane, I have to go. I'll see you at Harvest Festival. Are you on pudding? Yes? Jolly good. Bye! Bye, bye!

. . . Daniel, I'll be in the drawing room. Do you want anything?'

'Perhaps. I'll say if I do.'

There was a ring on the bell and the sound of barking intensified from behind the drawing-room door. It was Chris Biddle, alone. He looked terrible.

'Come in. Can I take your coat?'

'Thanks.' He sort of shrugged off his duffel coat releasing a whiff of unwashed body, which Daniel tried to ignore. He looked thin and underlaundered, and his blond curls looked as if he'd just come in from the rain.

'Would you like something, Chris? I can put the kettle on.'

'I'd love a cup of tea.'

Daniel showed him into his study and put him on the Sofa of Tears. 'I won't be a minute.' He put his head round the drawing-room door. 'Mum, it's Chris Biddle, would you make us a cup of tea?'

She got up, casting the pages of the *Daily Telegraph* from her lap in a little avalanche of newsprint. 'Will he want cake? A biscuit?'

'I don't know. Biscuits?'

Cosmo made a run for the door, but Daniel managed to close it before the little dog could get th rough, swerve into the study and, ignorant of human woe, throw himself at Chris. Some people like that – it reminds them of a world untouched by what has taken their world apart – but Daniel did not think Chris would be one of them. He turned his desk chair around and sat down. Chris looked smaller, suddenly, crumpled into the sofa, like he was being consumed by the upholstery.

Daniel said, 'How are you?'

Chris looked at him coldly. 'Never ask someone how they are.'

Daniel said nothing.

'I'm . . . awful. We're all awful. The whole thing is awful.'

'What can I do for you?'

Chris looked down at his feet. 'We need to discuss the funeral, work matters.'

'Don't worry about work matters, Chris. Everything is taken care of.'

'I have confirmation classes. I forgot about them. I've never done a confirmation class; we didn't do them where I was before.'

Daniel wondered for a moment what they did instead. He said, 'Don't worry about it, we'll take care of everything. But you must have done them. Your own?'

'Years ago, at school. I don't remember much about it. Except I got a new cricket bat from my uncle. But . . . I should postpone them?'

'Difficult to postpone, Chris, the bishop is booked. Let me take them – some of them. Until you're ready to think about work.'

'What will you tell them?'

'Children or adults?'

'Both. I think there are about fifteen.'

'I'll go through the Creed with them, the outline. Then the Bible.'

'I'd rather postpone it, if you don't mind,' he said flatly.

'I don't think we can. We only get the bishop once a year, and we have to fit in with his diary.'

'Maybe he could make an exception? Under the circumstances?'

Daniel knew that the bishop, and more likely his smooth but steely chaplain Gareth, would be most unwilling to make any exceptions at all. 'I could ask, if you like.'

'I would. Thanks.'

Daniel decided not to ask why he wanted to postpone because he thought he already knew the answer. Chris did not trust him to do it, did not trust him to give an adequate account of the faith. And this was not something he could discuss with him now. 'You're thinking about the funeral?'

'Yes. My dad's staying – did I say?'

'And he will want to officiate? Of course, that's fine. Do you know when it might happen?'

'It won't be here, Daniel. We'll take him home.'

'To Lower Badsaddle? Of course.'

'No, home home.'

Daniel faltered. 'But this is your . . .'

Chris looked up again. 'No. I mean *home*. My dad will do it. I will . . . do something.'

'I'm glad your father is able to officiate.'

'Are you? I don't know . . .'

'What do you mean?'

'I couldn't do it. He's his grandfather.'

'Some people cope that way.'

'One of my first memories of Dad was sitting in our pew at the church where he was vicar and . . . I must have been about seven . . . he preached on Abraham and Isaac, and how Abraham's faith was so strong he was prepared to sacrifice his own son rather than refuse God. Think what it's like to hear that when you're seven from your own father.'

'I can only imagine. It's not what we would call "good parenting" today.'

'No, it isn't. But are we really any better? Today's standards?'

Daniel said nothing for a moment. Then he asked, 'Do you have any idea when you may be able to proceed?' The coroner would need to release the body, but he had learnt not to say phrases like 'release the body' to grieving people.

'Not yet. "The investigation is ongoing," as they say.'

There was silence.

'Sal wants to see him. The undertaker . . . I think he . . . doesn't think it's a good idea.'

Daniel thought of the cuts to his throat. 'I would perhaps be guided by the undertaker.'

Chris shivered. 'The police . . . they want to help, but they have to investigate. They keep asking questions. I've told them over and over again, but they keep coming back . . .'

'It's the way it works, Chris. They have to keep evaluating evidence against evidence, seeing how different accounts match, or don't match. It's an objective process, not personal.'

'For them. It is a horrible feeling when you realise they are talking to you as suspects, not victims. What does your friend DS Vanloo say?'

'Nothing definitive. But the investigation, of necessity, husbands its findings very carefully.'

'What does that mean?'

'I'm not a police officer, Chris.'

'But they interviewed you. You were there.'

'I was able to identify Josh. And answer some questions about the circumstances.'

'That's what I want to know about.'

'About the chapel? Did you know about it?'

'You took Lydia there when you were walking the dogs. She mentioned it.'

'You've been there?'

'To the airfield, yes.'

'To the chapel?'

'No, I've never been inside any of the buildings. Josh would have loved it, though, a derelict chapel. Lyds said they were going to take some pictures there for the band.'

Daniel thought of the forensic team, the exploding flashes of the photographers sketching for a split second the terrible spectacle of Josh's dead and defiled body, like stills from a ghoulish old horror film. The door opened and Audrey was there with a tray of tea things.

'Chris, I don't know how you take it, so I've brought milk and sugar. And there are some biscuits.' She had made a little pile on a plate out of the Uniteds normally reserved for Theo. 'I'm so sorry about Josh. We're all devastated.'

Chris turned his blank look to her. 'Thank you.'

She put the tray down and said, 'Does Sally need anything? Are you all right for meals? Please say if there's anything we can do.'

'Oh, yes, I've got your casserole and a pie dish in the camper – I forgot to bring it in. Remind me, Daniel, to leave it with you?'

Audrey said, 'Oh, keep them,' with the pointless generosity that people offer to those visited by tragedy.

'There is something,' said Chris to Daniel. 'Could you come and see Lyds?'

'Yes. Of course.'

'Maybe you could bring the dogs? She's very . . . closed down. She sits in her room playing the same record over and over again. If we try to talk to her, she just goes silent. Then she cries. She likes you, she loves the dogs. Sal thought if you took her out, she might be able to . . . open up?'

'Let me know when I can do that.'

'Any time. We're not going anywhere'. He took a biscuit. 'I haven't had one of these in a while. "You'll be delighted with United", wasn't that the advert?' He unwrapped it with an oddly careful delicacy. 'These were Josh's favourites when he was a little boy. He used to unwrap the silver paper and eat the biscuit and then refold it so it looked like it was still intact, and then put it back in the wrapper as a prank.'

Nobody said anything.

6

The United biscuit that Josh had so carefully undone
had undone Chris. He had sat on the sofa and shaken
with grief, which had arrived like seizures. Audrey and
Daniel were with him, in the same space, but all knew
instinctively that they were not close enough to him to
offer the comfort of touch. After it had subsided, Daniel
offered to drive him home, but the offer was declined.
He had rather fussed over Chris as he walked him from
the door to the campervan and taken the casserole and
the pie dish that had been carefully washed up and left
neatly on the bench seat at the back. He'd felt again the
pathos of small, kind gestures made from an ocean of
suffering.

After supper he had gone back to his study to read
and had found that Chris's grief was still faintly there,
like smoked cigarettes. Perhaps that was why he could
not sleep that night. The wind was up, and the tossing
of the trees around the rectory and the wet slap of leaves
against his windows matched his feelings of unease and

restlessness. So he got up and went downstairs in his pyjamas and dressing gown, to the delight of the dogs, who started from their bed like children on Christmas morning. He took a little pan and some milk and left it to warm up gently on the hot plate while he found a tin of drinking chocolate in the cupboard his mother had arranged according to her own system, which bracketed arrowroot and Bemax, but divided honey and marmalade.

He made the hot chocolate in the way his mother made it, remembering at the end to whisk it, for 'whisking improves the flavour of this luxurious drink' – his mother always quoted this from the label with a laboured French accent, for no indulgence could pass without some sort of disavowal. Audrey loved treats, but treats, for her, who had victualled a family through the war, could be as modest as a buttered crumpet. As a boy Daniel had found his untrammelled delight in such things soon trammelled, so that now he could not eat a sausage roll without feeling, in some obscure part of his consciousness, that it needed to be negotiated with a Calvinist vegetarian. He sat at the kitchen table in a pool of light cast by the single shaded bulb above it, while Hilda circled his slippered feet and then settled on them. Cosmo, the frequency of the wags of his tail decreasing, realised an unexpected trip out was not going to happen and went back to his bed.

The murder of Josh, the devastation it had caused

his family, and the dread that event had triggered in so many, was like a hurricane offshore, an unimaginable chaotic event whose energies intensified more distant weather systems: Mrs Hawkins at the Manor, the mysterious Miss March, the Mohawk bride. Daniel imagined those three suddenly tousled and untidy and wet-faced, as if they had been caught in storms themselves. He needed to keep them separate, to direct his thoughts and time and attention proportionately to the urgency and difficulty of each matter discretely. But the wind lashed at the windows, and he knew that beyond them the rectory lawn and Champton's park and the village's back gardens and allotments would be in disarray when the sun rose at an hour that every autumn surprised him with its lateness. All things are in a state of flux, he thought, *panta chorei* – Heraclitus, remembered from his first philosophy lectures. He now thought Heraclitus had missed something, that the person stepping into the flowing river is also a flowing river; there is no coherent self, no fixedness from which to observe and judge. We, too, are in states of perpetual change, and no matter how diligent we are at mowing the lawn, clipping the borders, weeding the garden, tiling the roof, disorder increases because we are caught in the inescapable dynamics of life and existence. Sometimes it churns deep beneath the surface, sometimes it erupts like a volcano. Sometimes, Daniel believed, it is worked by an agency beyond anything we can conjure or even conceive. He was not someone in whom fear of the devil came readily. His temperament was one of gentle scepticism; his theology could admit no rival to the omnipotence of God, but some deep, intact part of him still smelled sulphur and saw deliberate action in what at first sight looked like the haphazard workings of chance. Was it chance when it dismantled people, piece by piece, by turning their virtues to their detriment rather than to their benefit? No one ever more effectively destroyed themselves than when they thought they were doing good rather than evil.

He had smelled sulphur in the chapel. It was not just the cruelty of attacking the boy, the terrible slashes, nor even the spectacle that had been made of it; it was something more than that, a quality of agency in it that he recognised. The devil's work, people said, the grip of demons – too convenient, too neat an explanation, intended to shield us from our own excited dreads and delights. But he had felt a more ancient fear than the fear of our hidden selves; a fear wired into our brains and sensory apparatus, like our fear of snakes and fire – a necessary alarm circuit to preserve life and herd. We still know to run from snakes and fire, but that other ancient fear plays out now in horror films or ghost stories, or when we are all alone at night and are suddenly seized by a dread that makes us look behind us and quicken our pace.

Daniel said out loud the last verse of 'A Safe Stronghold Our God Is Still':

'And were this world all devils o'er,
and watching to devour us,
we lay it not to heart so sore;
they cannot overpower us.'

Daniel woke later than usual. Perhaps the extra half-hour was merited after his sleeplessness, or perhaps the drinking chocolate had soporific properties? Whatever the reason, it was past seven o'clock when he opened the curtains and looked out across the front lawn. It seemed a giant game of Pelmanism had been played on it; there were branches, flowerpots, an empty box of Cash & Carry Vim and plastic bags scattered randomly all over the grass by the force of the wind the night before. There was a tap at his door.

'I've brought you your coffee, Dan. Are you up?'

Before he could answer, his mother, dressed in a nylon quilted dressing gown printed with exuberant pink and purple flowers that dated from that short-lived attempt to get with-it in the Sixties, approached with a mug of coffee. 'You're late, unusually. And I see that you were up in the night. Troubled conscience?'

'No, it was the wind. Didn't you hear it?'

'Not a thing,' said Audrey, who had the enviable gift of being able to fall asleep anywhere, any time. 'Do you want breakfast?'

'Just some toast,' he said. 'I'll come down now.'

'I've let the dogs out,' she said, 'so you needn't rush.'

In the kitchen the wireless was tuned to what his

mother insisted on calling the Home Service. He listened for a while, to a report about the Guildford Four, released after fourteen years in jail on fabricated evidence. The trial judge had apparently wanted them to be charged with treason, which still carried the death penalty, a preference which surely called into question his impartiality. Daniel, as a student, had been sent on placement to one of the prisons where the last hangings in Britain were performed, and the death penalty filled him with revulsion. The report reminded him why: because to string people up was barbaric, and irreversible, and would be inflicted on the innocent because the anger of their accusers was unbearable. Last year Ned Thwaite had been one of Kath Sharman's victims, having stumbled into a truth she could not bear to be told. He remembered Ned's daughter Angela telling him that she wanted whoever had killed him to suffer no less a penalty. He wondered what the Biddles would want for the person who murdered their son – would they want an eye for his eye, a tooth for his tooth, or would they want to be forgiving? Would they feel honour-bound to forgive, or appear to forgive, because everything they did had to be a sermon, had to reveal God's love at work, and demonstrate their conviction of God's favour and their faithfulness to it, even if what had just happened seemed to definitively disprove and discourage them?

News then of the growing crisis in East Germany, a Communist dictator who had seemed impregnable suddenly seeming vulnerable, explained away as illness, but everywhere the unthinkable was beginning to form in people's minds, in the west and in the east too.

Earth's proud empires pass away, he thought. Then the telephone rang. A rectory telephone ringing at half past seven in the morning is as reliable a herald of death as a cowled figure with a scythe. It was Dora Sharman.

'She's died.'

'Mrs Hawkins?'

'Yes, found her dead first thing. Doctor's coming. I've called the police too. Can you come?'

'Yes, I'll be a few minutes. Can you make sure that nobody touches anything?'

'Too late. Jean Tailby's all but laid her out.'

'Try to keep her away from the body.'

'Easier said than done, Rector.'

When Daniel tried the bathroom door he discovered that Audrey was already in there. She was singing 'Early One Morning' so tunelessly that for a moment he thought it something by Schoenberg, but he could tell from the brio of the performance that her complicated levée was only half done. He washed and shaved in the sink in his room and thought, as he thought nearly every day, how he would like to restore the rectory's amenities to the harmonious beauty they enjoyed before the needs of the parson's family and the means to fulfil them became so burdensome that everything became a botch job – the plumbing, the wiring, the roof. He finished in a cloud of talcum powder, bought by his mother in bulk from the Cash & Carry and scented, the tin said, with Lily of the Valley. What a shy little flower, he thought, to produce a perfume so assertive.

The dogs greeted him at the foot of the stairs, their tails wagging in undaunted anticipation of an outing. He was putting his coat on when Audrey peered over the landing. 'Where are you off to?'

'Upper Badsaddle Manor.'

'Grim Reaper?'

'Yes. Would you mind taking any messages?'

'I'm not your ruddy secretary, Daniel. I'm off to Braunstonbury with Jane Thwaite this morning.'

'I know you're not my secretary. Have a lovely day.'

The dogs wailed as he closed the front door on them. Their walk would have to wait. As he drove through the branch-strewn back roads to the Badsaddles he wondered what the Tailbys had managed to wrest from Mrs Hawkins. Dora had kept a sharp eye, he was sure, but if anyone could tear the rings from a cooling corpse's fingers it would be Jean and Roy.

He arrived at the Manor just as Neil also arrived. 'Hello, Dan. Shall we?'

As they waited at the door Daniel said, 'Why are you here? It's not a job for a DS, is it?'

'Not usually. But I would like the Tailbys to know that any death on their watch gets a detective.'

Roy opened the door. 'Morning, Vicar, Officer. Come together?'

He ushered them in. 'She's gone in the night, poor thing. Doctor only saw her yesterday, if that's what you're wondering.'

'Did the doctor give Mrs Hawkins anything?'

'She had morphine when she needed it, to help with the pain. But she's been so poorly she could have gone at any moment.'

Jean came down the stairs. 'Reverend Daniel, I'm sorry you're too late. She went in the night, like a lamb.'

'I would like to see her, if I may.'

'You'll have to get past Dora. She's being quite the Greyfriars Bobby this morning. And it's the detective sergeant from Braunstonbury!'

'Mrs Tailby. The doctor has been informed?'

'Yes, he's on his way. He only saw her yesterday and he said the end could come at any time.'

Daniel left Neil to deal with the Tailbys and went up to Mrs Hawkins's bedroom. The curtains were half drawn and in the pale light of the morning she looked tiny in the bed – her hands and head brown against the white of the pillows and the sheets, and wrinkled, which made Daniel think of a walnut. Her mouth was open, which made her look gormless; how she would have disliked that, and she had no teeth, which she would have disliked even more.

Dora Sharman sat by the bedside crocheting, which she did with such automatic expertise she did not need light or even to look. 'Morning, Rector. She's gone.'

'Were you with her, Dora?'

'No, it was in the middle of the night. Found her dead first thing.'

'Any concerns?'

'Jean Tailby, you mean?'

'Any concerns?'

'The doctor came yesterday, and the district nurse, and they put her on some sort of automatic injection thingy, which gave her the morphine because she was feeling it.'

'Yes, a syringe driver, it gives a regulated dose. Was she suffering?'

'Not much after Jean Tailby emptied most of it into her with the booster button.' There was a button on the machine that, when pressed, gave a small increase to the dose.

'How long did that take?'

'She kept jabbing at it. The nurse said to do that if she showed any signs of distress. I told her to lay off, but she said she was suffering and she had to. The old lady went to sleep, and so we went to bed.'

'Did Mrs Tailby interfere with Mrs Hawkins at all, as far as you could tell?'

'Not while I was in the room. But I wasn't always in the room.' She paused and looked at her crochet. 'It's not murder, Rector, it's thieving you need to watch out for with her.'

Daniel said, 'I'll just anoint her.' Dora put her head down and sat up straight, hands folded in her lap and her eyes closed. He took a little stole he used for visiting and hung it round his neck. It was the size of a belt and had been made for him by a pious lady of his last parish. It was a rich purple brocade, which she had adorned with heavy golden tassels at each end to stop it from flying around (beauty and utility, he thought, every time he put it on). He took an oil stock from his pocket, unscrewed it, moistened his thumb on the oily wadding and made the sign of the cross on Mrs Hawkins's forehead.

> 'Go forth upon thy journey from this world,
>   O Christian soul.
> Go in the name of God the Father Almighty who
>   created thee,
> In the name of Jesus Christ, his Son, who suffered
>   for thee,
> In the name of the Holy Ghost who strengthened
>   thee.
> In communion with the blessed saints and
>   accompanied by angels and archangels and all the
>   armies of the Heavenly Host,
> May thy portion this day be peace. And thy
>   dwelling in the heavenly Jerusalem. Amen.'

'Amen,' said Dora and picked up her crochet again. 'It's not too late, you don't think?'

'Too late for what?'

'For prayers to make a difference?'

'I don't think it is ever too late to pray, Dora.'

There was the sound of a car in the drive and Dora got up and looked out. 'It's Dr Barrett.'

Jean Tailby brought him upstairs. He was in his forties and looked tired, as GPs on house calls do. He nodded at Daniel in the way of those with professional interests at such things and went to examine the body.

Jean Tailby tiptoed in with an exaggerated effort at delicacy. 'She went quietly in her sleep. It's what she wanted, bless her. I nursed her to the end. It's a great privilege, you know.'

'You are a nurse, Mrs Tailby?'

'I've nursed all my life.'

'A qualified nurse?'

'Oh dear, you can't get qualifications in what I give my patients. I give them love.' Tears appeared in the corners of her eyes and she looked towards Mrs Hawkins on her deathbed. 'Muriel was a very special lady. We got to be . . . close.'

Dora said, 'You only knew her three weeks.'

'I know, dear, but it's a very special time when some-one gets to the end of their time here on earth.'

'Well, you would know, you've done more death-beds than the rector and the doctor.'

'Mine is a gift. And I give too. Who toileted her, who held her hand, who cleaned up her sick? Me, that's who. And I'd do it again.'

The doctor approached. 'Who is the next of kin?'

'There is no one,' said Daniel, 'but I am executor of her will.'

'Your parishioner?'

'Technically, but this parish is in the care of my . . . colleague. He's on compassionate leave.'

'The father of the boy they found murdered at the airfield?'

'Yes. So I've been looking after Mrs Hawkins. I wonder, Doctor, if I may speak to you . . .?' Daniel indicated the landing. Dr Barrett nodded and followed him out. 'Are you minded to issue a death certificate?'

'Unless you can give me a reason not to. I saw her yesterday and she was on her way out. But I see there's a police officer downstairs.'

Daniel said, 'There have been some concerns about the carer. She has a history of attaching herself to people who are alone and dying, and some say she takes advantage. According to Miss Sharman, she emptied the automatic syringe into her last night after the district nurse had gone.'

The doctor nodded. 'It won't have made much difference. There's not enough diamorphine in it to kill.'

'Double effect?'

'Not in any significant sense. I gather she's not a qualified nurse?'

'No. Would that make a difference?'

'It could, possibly, but only if she was in charge, and she wasn't – the district nurse was.'

Daniel thought for a moment. 'Are there any signs she might have been interfered with?'

'Interfered with? Not that I can see, apart from being tidied up. It would need a more thorough examination, and that's a matter for the coroner, but I have no concerns.' He looked towards the stairs.

'Thank you, Doctor,' said Daniel. 'I think the detective sergeant might want a word.'

He nodded with a hint of irritation and left.

Jean Tailby appeared at his side. 'Did I hear you say she made you her executor?'

'That's right, Mrs Tailby, co-executor.'

'Only Mrs Hawkins, who was a very generous lady, did say there were one or two things she wanted me and Roy to have. As a thank-you.'

'Perhaps you have a note of these things, and some authority from Mrs Hawkins?'

'Bless you, dear, we never thought to ask! Only there was something in particular she thought would suit me; it's only a little thing – a cameo brooch – but I would like to have it to remember her by.'

'I'm afraid, Mrs Tailby, without authority from Mrs Hawkins I cannot allow you to have it.'

Jean tilted her head to one side and said, 'Oh, that is good of you, to take such care of her things, but she did say I was to have it, and in front of a witness.'

'Who might that be?'

'My husband.'

'We would need more than that. Signed authority, I'm afraid.'

She said nothing at first, then tilted her head to the

other side and gave a little laugh. 'Such a suspicious world!' She went to sit in the chair at Mrs Hawkins's bedside and reached for her hand, which she squeezed as she mouthed the word 'goodbye'.

Dora said, 'Touching, isn't it?'

'Dora, do you know where Mrs Hawkins keeps her jewellery box?'

'I've hidden it.'

'Keep it hidden a little longer.'

Downstairs Neil was talking to the doctor at the door. Roy was leaning against the sideboard. He had the eye, Daniel thought, of a professional appraiser. 'Who's in charge now, Reverend?'

'Of Mrs Hawkins's affairs?'

'Yes. I have to put in my bill.'

'Her solicitor, and then it will be a matter for the estate.'

'Will it take long?'

'I don't know. Haven't you done this before?'

Roy looked at him suspiciously. 'We do run up expenses when we take care of someone. She knew that. We had an understanding.'

'As I said, that's for the solicitor.'

Jean was coming downstairs. 'Oh, Roy, it's the Reverend who's the executor of Muriel's will.'

'You are?'

'One of them.'

'Would you like a cup of tea? I'll ask Dora. Dora? Would you be an angel and make us all a cup of tea?'

Dora appeared at the landing. 'Make it yourself. I'm not the lady's maid.'

'I know, dear, only we have to deal with the . . . official matters. Would you?'

Dora looked at Daniel and Daniel nodded. 'All right,' she said, 'what harm can it do now?' She pushed past Jean on the stairs, who followed her down.

'Executor, Reverend? So you'll be in charge of the will and everything?'

'Co-executor.'

'Who's the other?' said Roy.

'My mother, as a matter of fact.'

Roy exchanged a look with Jean. 'I see. Very convenient. Legacy for the church got anything to do with that?'

'I cannot discuss the contents of Mrs Hawkins's will, not least because I haven't seen it. And if I had, I would not discuss it with you, unless of course you were legatees.'

Roy sneered. 'So quick to look accusingly at us, who took care of her, when all you really want is your cut. For singing a few hymns and saying a prayer? What's that worth? New roof? Maybe new curtains for the vicarage? Nice work.'

Neil was listening. 'Mr Tailby, I don't think you want to go around saying things like that.'

'Everyone can have a pop at us, and we can't say nothing?'

'No one's having a pop except you, and it's a very serious accusation you're making.'

Roy stood up straight. 'I'll be putting in my bill.'

'And mine,' said Jean.

'By all means,' said Daniel. 'I look forward to giving them my fullest and closest attention.'

Roy looked him up and down. 'Call yourself a man of the cloth?'

Daniel had never called himself a man of the cloth. No one in the trade called themselves a man of the cloth; it was a phrase used by those outside, and when he heard it all he thought was: this is a person whose views I need not take seriously.

'I don't think there's any point in continuing this conversation . . .' Outside, Daniel noticed that a glossy black 'private ambulance' had arrived and Mr Williams, the undertaker from Braunstonbury, emerged from it in a short coat and salt-and-pepper trousers, looking like a consultant on his rounds in the days before the National Health Service. One of his men fetched the trolley from the back, which unfolded like a concertina, and on which the lifeless patients for whose exclusive use it was reserved were conveyed from their deathbeds into the systems of waste management and bureaucracy that attend us as faithfully as the flights of angels winging us to our rest.

'Morning, Daniel. Morning, Detective Sergeant.' He nodded at the Tailbys. 'What have you got for us?'

'Mrs Hawkins,' said Daniel.

'Can I have a word?' said Neil. He went off to one side with Mr Williams, leaving Daniel with the Tailbys.

Jean said, 'It's not very nice, Reverend Daniel, to think of people saying such nasty things about you.'

'I expect not, Mrs Tailby.'

'All I ever wanted for Muriel was to do right by her, and all she wanted was to do right by us.'

Daniel wondered why Neil and Mr Williams had bothered to stand to one side because their conversation could be heard by everyone. Perhaps it was intended that way; the private conversation that is meant to be heard, like in a play or the opera?

'Deceased is Muriel Angela Hawkins?' Mr Williams said. 'DOB 09.04.04?'

Oh, thought Daniel, just after the signing of the Entente Cordiale. The ink would hardly have been dry.

'You're jumping the gun. The coroner might want this one,' said Neil.

'Might?'

'Yes. I don't know whether to call it in or not.'

'What did the doc say?'

'He's signed it off. So you're good to go, but there are . . . not *suspicions*, questions.'

'We're the coroner's appointed undertakers,' said Mr Williams, 'so we might as well take her. It's all the same. If he wants the body, we'll take her to the mortuary, but she can stay with us for now.' He looked over to Daniel and the Tailbys. 'Perhaps you good people would like to find somewhere to sit while we fetch her out?'

Jean said, 'Don't look at me. I don't want to be accused of trying to pinch the sugar tongs.'

'You're not coming in the kitchen,' said Roy. 'It's private.'

'It's not your kitchen,' said Neil.

'It was given to us for our use by Mrs Hawkins—' Jean gave him a look and an almost imperceptible shake of the head. 'And . . . and . . .'

'There's no need to be mardy,' said Jean, smiling again. 'I think we're all just a bit upset. Why don't you go and sit in the dining room, and I'll see where Dora's got to with that cup of tea?' She turned and extended her arms like a shepherd trying to pen sheep. 'Dining room's through there, but it's all at sixes and sevens, so you'll have to take us as you find us.'

Daniel thought how unhesitatingly she awarded herself the role of hostess, but then the speed with which she did it, the tiny nod to her husband, made him think perhaps it was not entitlement but tactics.

The dining room went from the front of the house to the back. It was panelled in oak, a Victorian simulacrum of medieval linenfold. It looked a bit peculiar, for it had not darkened with age like medieval woodwork, and it made Daniel think of Liberty. There were family portraits on the wall, but nothing earlier than the last century – perhaps they had been lost in the fire? – and nothing of decent quality. There was a long sideboard (not as well dusted as it might have been), heavy dark curtains hanging from tall windows (transomed and mullioned) and a fireplace big enough to stand up in, but dominating the room was an enormous dining table – six pedestals, he thought, at least – with perhaps two dozen chairs set round it. The far end was bare, save two candelabras, but the near end was covered in papers: piles of foolscap, another big pile of what looked like unfolded maps, and two big wicker trays labelled 'IN' and 'OUT', one full of opened letters, the other full of what he assumed were replies, in sealed stamped and addressed envelopes. He did not think Mrs Hawkins would have had such a voluminous correspondence and he wondered if it were going to be a more onerous task than he had thought to order her affairs post-mortem.

Neil, with the instinct of the detective, went to cast his eye over the letters, but the sound of an altercation came from the hall. He looked at Daniel and together they went to see what was causing it. Dora Sharman had been blocked by Roy Tailby. He was standing in front of her, towering over her, holding out his hand. She was holding something behind her back. Both had a look of non-negotiable determination.

'Give it here, Dora!' he hissed.

'It en't yourn,' she replied, in the accent and dialect of the county to which she reverted in moments of drama.

'It en't *yourn*,' he replied, and went to grab her arm.

Neil intervened. He used, Daniel noticed, the same technique as Katrina Gauchet at the primary school:

instead of going loud, he went soft. 'Mr Tailby, Miss Sharman, can we just pause for a moment? OK? What's the problem here?'

Roy said, 'Dora's been going through our personal things. Which isn't very nice, is it?'

'Your things? They're *her* things.'

'What things?' asked Neil.

Dora produced from behind her back a brooch. 'This cameo brooch, one of her favourites. It was on her bedside table, until it weren't.'

'She said Jean was to have it,' said Roy, and he tried to snatch it away, but Dora was too quick.

'If it were yourn, why did I find it in the tea caddy? Funny place to keep a brooch?'

'Not when someone like you's in the house. Always around, Dora, with your . . . long nose.'

'Need one when it's you and Jean. You're thieving magpies, Roy Tailby, and everyone knows it.'

Neil said, 'I'll take that, Miss Sharman.'

She handed over the brooch. He handed it on to Daniel. 'Canon Clement is an executor of Mrs Hawkins's will. I'll leave it with him for safekeeping. If you have any claim on it, apply to him.'

Jean was standing in the doorway to the kitchen. 'How can we? It was a gift from a friend to a friend. I think it's very sad that counts for nothing, but like I've always said, no good deed goes unpunished.'

There was a noise from the stairs. Mr Williams and his man were descending step by step with a canvas-covered stretcher. Strapped within it was the body of Mrs Hawkins – not a big woman, but a body is heavier than you might think, and bends in the middle, risking an unseemly spectacle. Daniel, in an attempt to assert seemliness, crossed himself; Dora lowered her eyes to the floor; Neil sort of stood to attention; the Tailbys watched impassively in a tableau vivant until the undertakers had placed the body on the trolley and wheeled it slowly out. As soon as the front door closed hostilities resumed and concluded with a spiteful coda.

'No need for the cup of tea now,' said Jean. 'And anyway, I don't have a pen so I can't issue you with a bill or a receipt.' And she left the hall.

Roy followed. 'Nasty, nasty piece of work,' he said to Dora.

Daniel said, 'How did you find it, Dora?'

'I came down to make a cup of tea and found it in there. She's had her eye on it for a while now, and that was quick work. Mrs R kept it on her all the time, wearing it, or in her bag, and like I said, it was on the bedside table until this morning.'

Daniel went to stand in the window where the light was good. The brooch sat in the palm of his hand. It was an oval, about two inches in length, mounted in gold with a gold pin on a hinge. The background was some sort of gemstone in brownish red, and on it, in pale stone the colour of bone, was the most exquisite cameo of a young man – no, a young god, he thought.

Hermes, wearing a helmet, with winged feet, holding a staff entwined with snakes. He looked like he was about to take off, his right arm extended over his head, his left leg kicking out behind him. Hermes, the messenger of the gods, Mercury to the Romans, god of travellers, and of thieves. He thought it must be Roman or Greek, but then noticed a carved signature beneath the god's feet. It was far too small for him to make out, but it meant it could not be Greek or Roman. A jeweller's effort, perhaps two hundred years ago, to re-create a treasure of two thousand years ago? Whenever it had been made, it was beautiful and Daniel mentally complimented Jean Tailby on her magpie eye.

Neil came to have a look. 'Not a piece of junk, I take it?'

'No, I don't think so. I'm not an expert, but I think this is by an Italian jeweller, probably late eighteenth century. It's lovely.'

'Who is it?'

'Hermes. See the winged feet?'

'I thought that was Mercury.'

'It is. That's his Roman name.'

'Valuable?'

'I think so. The quality is wonderful.'

'If anyone could spot quality, it's Jean Tailby,' said Dora. 'I should get my coat and hat. Do you need me for anything, Sergeant?'

'I'll let you know if I do.'

Daniel wrapped the cameo in his handkerchief and

put it in his pocket. Then the door opened. It was Roy Tailby.

'Who do we leave the keys with? The *executor*?' he said, with exaggerated courtesy.

Daniel said, 'You are leaving?'

'Of course we are.'

'Now?'

'As soon as we've packed. Do you want to check our bags?'

Daniel thought that was quite a good idea.

'I've checked everywhere,' said Dora. 'Nothing missing. Of value.'

Roy gave her a foul look. 'You're more like your sister than I thought, Dora Sharman. It makes sense. Bad blood and all that.' He looked coldly at Daniel. 'And you should know better. We'll leave the keys on the kitchen table.' And he went, slamming the door to the kitchen behind him.

'Oh dear,' said Daniel. 'I wonder if we have seen the last of Roy and Jean? And thank you, Dora. If it weren't for you, I expect the estate of Mrs Hawkins would be missing more than a cameo brooch.'

'I was glad to do it, Rector. Pair of vultures.'

'May I take you home?'

'Thank you. But what about here? No Tailbys, no me?'

Daniel thought about it. 'I suppose it is the responsibility of the executors now.'

'What are you going to do?' asked Neil.

Daniel thought some more. 'I'm going to take Dora home, pick up my mother, come back, and see what we can do to make everything safe.'

'I'll stay,' said Dora. 'I know where things are. You go and get Mrs Clement.'

Neil said, 'I can stay too. Until the Tailbys have gone.'

Daniel had not known his mother to enjoy herself so much in ages. First, to have free access to Upper Badsaddle Manor, not just the drawing room and hall and dining room, but the bedrooms, the kitchen, the attics. Second, Daniel had shown her the pile of papers on the dining-room table and asked her to put them in order. This access into the home and affairs of Mrs Hawkins provided rich pickings indeed. It began with a tour of the house, starting with the bedroom in which the old lady had died. Dora had restored to Mrs Hawkins's dressing table the jewel box withheld from the appraising interest of the Tailbys. It was not just any jewel box, more a cabinet, in dark-red leather and gold tooling, with doors that opened outwards and drawers that pulled out.

'Good GOD!' said Audrey. 'It makes Nancy Cunard look like Pam Ayres!'

There were rings and bracelets and earrings that flashed with sapphires and emeralds and rubies, and sparkled with diamonds, and gleamed with gold and platinum. There were three ropes of pearls and a pair of gold-mounted ovals of ivory showing Napoleon and his empress, Josephine, she thought, done with extraordinary delicacy. But when she pulled open the main drawer she gasped. There, on a dark velvet cushion, rested a necklace of diamonds and what looked like blushing sapphires, so magnificent it would not have disgraced the empress's breast.

'Can you have sapphires this colour?'

'I don't know,' said Daniel. 'Aren't they normally blue?'

'Like mine,' said Audrey, waving in front of him her engagement ring, a sapphire surrounded by diamonds. 'Toy from a Christmas cracker compared with this. I had no idea Muriel Hawkins was so well provided for.'

Daniel was often struck by the oblique way of English middle-class speech when we talk about wealth. Well provided for, well-to-do, comfortably off. If you transliterated it into any other language, it would be nonsense. *Bien à faire? Gut versorgt für? Commode . . .* off?

'She loved her jewels,' said Dora. 'Used to like to wear them when she was feeling poorly, made her feel better.'

'What torture that must have been for the Tailbys,' said Audrey. 'But I never saw her wearing anything as splendid as these. Mind you, three ropes of pearls might be a bit much for the League of Charity Summer Fork Buffet . . .'

'I don't think she wore them out, Mrs Clement. I think she liked them for herself, not for others.'

Audrey slid the glittering jewels back into the cabinet. 'Well, that will keep the Distressed Gentlefolk in tea and crumpets till Doomsday.'

After the tour of the house, Audrey assigned Dora and Daniel the task of making an inventory of anything of value in the house, working from the attics down, while she made a start on Mrs Hawkins's papers.

Two hours later, having heard nothing from Audrey, Daniel put his head round the dining-room door. 'We've finished, Mum.'

'Good, good . . .' muttered Audrey without looking up from the papers, which she had begun to arrange into fans and piles.

'I should go soon. Will you be much longer?'

'What?'

'We have to go in a minute.'

'Oh. I'm just getting started.'

'Anything of significance?'

'No. Not really. I might just take some of this home, though. There's a lot to get through. Give me ten minutes, darling, would you? And would you find me an empty box?'

Audrey's 'ten minutes' became an hour, and her 'empty box' became six, stowed in the back of the Land Rover along with another for the jewel box, to be stored in the vestry safe. They drove home via the post office, because Audrey needed to pick up 'some playing cards', an item she took a minute to think of because she did not need playing cards, Daniel knew very well, but she needed to fire up the gossipy circuits of Champton with news of the treasures of Upper Badsaddle and her appointment. He parked outside and waited in the Land Rover, unwilling to leave the fabulous trove unguarded even for a minute, for her to do her shopping and pass on the news, which took longer than he had hoped, for the arrival of another customer required another précis of events, or an extension to her conversation with Mrs Braines, and Anne Dollinger, and Dot Staveley, and Margaret Porteous, into which she could drop the salient points for the benefit of the newcomer. Eventually she was done and emerged without playing cards but with a Kit Kat instead, which she liked not particularly as confectionery but more for the foil wrapper, which she sliced open by drawing her thumbnail down the centre line like they did in the adverts.

They drove down Main Street, past the lodges at the gates to Champton House.

'Oh,' said Audrey, 'looks like your policeman is visiting Alex.'

'Is he?'

'Yes, that's his car.'

Daniel never noticed cars and would have missed it had it not been for his mother's sharp eye. What was Neil doing at the lodge? And why had Daniel not been consulted? Normally Neil's first call was to him if something of interest happened in Champton. There must have been a development.

At the rectory he was greeted by Cosmo and made a fuss of him, for the dogs had been on their own all morning. Hilda waddled out of the drawing room to see what was happening and then waddled back to the nest of cushions Audrey had made for her next to her armchair. She was looking very pregnant, and he noticed his mother looking at her in what he thought was a comradely way now the birth was approaching. She had made plans for 'the confinement' and was on the telephone to country friends every day reporting the changes in Hilda's size and manner and bearing and asking for advice about puppy husbandry.

That afternoon, however, she had other priorities. She opened her bureau, for the first time since her husband's death, and arranged the boxes of Mrs Hawkins's correspondence around it in a semi-circle. She was going through them one by one, and Daniel heard her occasionally chuckling to herself – what was making her laugh? And how good it was to see her laughing, and engaged with a project, and being busy, as she loved to be and found harder to be as age made her world smaller. Age and reduced means. Twice a year Audrey would go to town on the train and have lunch with the circle of friends she had made at school more than half a century ago. They met at the Goring Hotel near Buckingham Palace, and over the years and decades that twice-yearly luncheon had become one of the steadiest elements in lives that were less steady as history – and economics – upset the patterns they had been born into. That had also created distance – a growing distance – between those who had been fortunate, in marriage and life, and those who had been not so fortunate. Audrey was in the latter camp, not where she wished to be, made worse by having dropped in the ranks from a strong start when they were all getting married. She had married into trade, which was not ideal, but the trade she had married into was a prosperous one and she rather enjoyed the cut of her clothes and the extravagance of her bill, which some in her circle were unable to match. But her husband's wealth had declined sharply when the shoe factories had all closed in the Seventies, and then he'd died without having made for her the provision she expected.

Audrey noticed, biannually, the decline in her circumstances: no new hat, no new bag, a glance at the menu – not for the food, but the prices. Worst, she was being overtaken by some she had once surpassed. No one said anything, no one needed to, but the gaps widened, and there came a terrible day when a woman she had never particularly liked arrived as *Lady* X thanks to her husband acquiring an honour when he retired from the gas board (*and* there was shot in her pheasant that day). Now, living in retirement with her parson son, the two luncheons taking more of her budget each year, she wondered if she could even afford to go at all. Daniel had not noticed, for it was not the kind of thing he noticed, not unless someone's salvation was involved, and if she asked, she was sure he would unhesitatingly insist she must go, and find the means to allow it. But she did not want to ask, any more than she would have accepted the tactful but humiliating offer of subsidy from her friends.

Daniel was in his study. He wanted to order his thoughts and read through his notes after the brisk inventory of Upper Badsaddle Manor. The cameo brooch? He had forgotten it was in his pocket, so he found it and unwrapped it and looked at it again in the palm of his hand. It was reassuringly cool – he remembered reading somewhere that a real cameo should feel cool to the touch – and seemed to glow even away from the window. He noticed again the tiny signature, so he took the magnifying glass that had once belonged to his grandmother from the Habitat salt pig he had adapted for stationery items of suitable shape, size, style, and frequency of use (letter knife, ruler, larger scissors). He held the cameo up to the light and in the convex lens the letters MORELLI came into focus. He made a note to consult the antiques dealer in the cathedral close at Stow and put the cameo to one side, so he would remember to take it to church for Evensong and put it in the safe with the rest of Mrs Muriel Hawkins's jewels. He took a new notebook – ruled A4, spiral-bound – from the left-hand second-down drawer, and two fountain pens from the little tray reserved for them, one a Conway Stewart No.60 filled with black ink, the other a Blackbird with a medium italic nib filled with red ink. He wrote at the top of the first page in capitals

'INVENTORY, UPPER BADSADDLE MANOR, 20.10.89', and underlined it in red ink.

Daniel and his mother settled into their tasks, each in their own domain, each applying order to the sudden disruption of death. Every item had to be given a value; not a pecuniary value yet, but a new value now Muriel Hawkins's departure had deprived them of their significance. Sometimes that was clear – a tatty doll from childhood, a souvenir from a trip no one remembered. Sometimes a finer judgement was required, for a document whose relevance was not clear, or a portrait of an anonymous sailor or parson who may not be anonymous in a circle beyond hers.

He was just considering whether a well-used and incomplete Spode dinner service merited conservation when he saw a car turning into the drive. It was Miss March, in her smart little motor – 'the Van der Valk', as Audrey called it.

He met her at the door. She was dressed in a neat and tidy grey skirt and jacket, in one of the milder sorts of tweed. Norland Nanny, he thought again; it looked like a uniform, and it matched the grey of her eyes – if anything, making them look greyer. They flickered when Cosmo barrelled out of the drawing room barking and Daniel had to restrain him by the collar.

'He won't bite, Miss March,' he said in a dog lover's tone that was intended to be reassuring but sounded more like a criticism.

'*What* a noise he makes!'

'Please come in. I'll just put him back in the drawing room.' She waited while Daniel, stooping awkwardly, ushered Cosmo towards the door.

'Who is it?' asked Audrey from within.

'It's Miss March. From the dress shop,' he said.

'Business or pleasure?'

'Business,' she said to Daniel, unnecessarily.

'We'll be in the study, Mum,' he said, and closed the door. 'May I take your hat? Your coat? Your gloves?'

Miss March divested herself of these things and handed them to Daniel. They were, he noticed, impeccable but softened by use.

He invited Miss March in and sat her down on the Sofa of Tears. It was a little low for her, being tall and in a narrow skirt, and she had to trim and adjust as she settled.

'What can I do for you, Miss March?'

She opened her mouth to speak and then froze. Her grey eyes, he noticed, were fixed on his desk. He looked behind him where she was looking and saw the cameo brooch.

'So . . .' she said eventually, '. . . you know.'

'Yes,' he said as gently as he could. 'I was called this morning to Upper Badsaddle Manor.'

She collected herself. 'Why?'

'To do . . . what we do.'

She frowned. 'Some sort of exorcism?'

Now he looked puzzled. 'No, not exactly. I said a prayer and anointed her.'

'She allowed you to do that?'

'She was dead, Miss March.'

She gasped and put her hand to her mouth. 'Dead? No! No, no, no, no. She can't be dead!'

'I'm afraid so,' he said. She blinked and patted at her chest. He said, 'Would you like a glass of water? A tissue?' She shook her head.

After a few seconds she composed herself again. 'I'm sorry. It was a shock.'

'Forgive me,' he said. 'I thought you knew. The brooch?'

'I recognised the brooch, yes.'

'But – again, forgive me – what did you think it meant?'

She blinked again and looked at her hands in her lap. He thought not of a Modigliani this time, but a Gwen John.

'The brooch . . . may I ask why it is here?'

'I cannot tell you precisely why, but I can tell you that my mother and I are co-executors of Mrs Hawkins's estate.'

'Oh. I was executor of my father's estate. It is more work than you think.'

'So I have found.'

'Rector, I understand Mrs Hawkins has no family?'

'I don't think so.'

'And, in that case, might her effects be sent for sale?'

'I expect so.'

'Would you think it forward, or improper, of me to ask, if the brooch were to be sold, that it be offered to me?'

Daniel thought about it. 'I don't know, Miss March. If this brooch might be of significance to others, then it would not be in order for me to offer it to you on preferential terms. I'm sure you understand.'

The grey in her eyes turned to steel. 'I am prepared to offer a more than fair price. If you would let me take it now, you could name it.'

Daniel said softly, 'That would not be acceptable.'

'Cash.'

Daniel said nothing.

'I see,' she said. 'Perhaps you would let me know if an opportunity should arise?' She stood up.

'I will. But . . .'

'Yes?'

'I don't understand why this brooch is so desirable. I can see it is a beautiful thing, and I expect a valuable thing. But it seems to have the same effect on people as the Rhinegold on Alberich.' He could see she did not understand the reference.

'A great jewel', she said, 'has a peculiar magic. Muriel Hawkins understood that. Women do. I expect your mother does.'

He handed her things to her in the hall. 'I think you gave notice at church that Harvest Festival is this Sunday, Rector?'

'Yes, at Champton. Ten-thirty. There's a harvest

lunch afterwards in the village hall if you would like to come.'

'Yes, please. Do I need to let anyone know?'

'You just did, Miss March.'

As he opened the door a gust of wind blew in a little bouquet of fallen leaves.

Miss March said, 'All is safely gathered in, ere the winter storms begin.'

'You did WHAT?'

'I refused.'

'Why?'

'Mum!'

Audrey threw the *Radio Times* to the floor. 'Daniel! A cash buyer, and she's got plenty, and you're going to have to sell it anyway, and the brooch would be . . . going to a good home. If Dora Sharman hadn't had her wits about her, Jean Tailby would be wearing it to the bingo! Really! How *could* you be so dense?'

Nothing exasperated his mother more than his refusal to bend his scruples. She used to pretend to admire it, but over time she had come to see how they caused her and others inconvenience or worse. Last year he had risked prison rather than give the police information about the murders. Where would that have left her? One of the reasons she had moved into the rectory was to pool scarce resources, and she could not possibly live in a house as splendid as this if he were not the incumbent. She picked up the *Radio Times* again and

pretended to be interested in an article about a titan of
light entertainment, whom she once described as being
'about as funny as shingles'.

Daniel was not unsympathetic to his mother's frus-
tration, but he simply could not, even if he wanted to,
compromise when trust or integrity were involved. If
he couldn't be trusted then what use was he? The best
work he had done as a priest, he supposed, was when
he had reached into the pit to grab hold of someone
who had fallen in, and once or twice even hauled them
out. He kept in his wallet a little playing-card-sized
reproduction of the anastasis, the icon of Orthodox
tradition, which shows what the Western Church calls
'the harrowing of hell', a picturesque if unbiblical
episode that fills the gap between the Crucifixion on
Good Friday and the Resurrection on Easter Sunday.
According to this tradition Jesus visited hell – actually,
he *invaded* hell – trampled down the gates and reached
into the abyss to yank Adam and Moses from perdition
to glory, and with them all who, of necessity, had not
been saved, for salvation had not yet arrived; but here
it was, and the chains and locks that had once bound
them fell away with an echoing rattle and clank. If he
was to be Jesus' yanking hand – for Christians are called
to be his hands, his feet, his words, his deeds – then he
had to be worthy of that charge and worthy of trust.

Audrey put the *Radio Times* down again. 'Daniel, I
really think in future you should let me take care of
this sort of thing. You are an innocent, a Daniel – how

apt! – in a den of lions. Only I see little evidence that Jehovah is minded to save you from their snapping jaws.'

'I'm not sure that would be wise.'

'No, I'll tell you what is unwise: to imagine that you can go through life without ever having to compromise your precious faith or get a bit dirty and bruised like the rest of us, and without a thought for how we are expected – *I* am expected – to pay the price for it too!'

Audrey had never said this before, or not so directly, and in the surprised silence that followed, the thought that Daniel's unquestioning faithfulness to his priestly vocation was far easier for him than for her acquired sharper focus in his mind.

'Mum, it's not our money.'

She said nothing, but Hilda, alerted by this change of mood, uncoiled herself at her feet and looked up from her nest of blankets. Then she curled up again.

Then Audrey said, 'I have work to do,' and got out of the chair on the third attempt, making Hilda growl gently as she settled. She shuffled over to the bureau, lavishly spread with papers, sat down and switched on the lamp. After a minute Daniel could hear that her breathing had slowed and she was calm again, and after two she chuckled.

Daniel went back to his study and started to write a sermon for the Festival of Christ the King, the last

Sunday of the Church's year at the end of November. Daniel rather disliked it, for it was new-fangled, formalised in the 1920s when a pope felt it necessary to dress Christ in robe and crown and sit him on a throne. Rather unnecessary, thought Daniel, for the King of All Creation, and each year he found it a struggle to find something novel to say. Not this year. Mrs Hawkins's fabulous hoard flashed and sparkled in his imagination, and he started to write about the glitter and glister of jewels and gold and the crown of thorns and a cross for a throne. He was just working on a paragraph about the more dazzling adornments of the Counter-Reformation when he was dazzled himself by headlights turning into the now-darkening drive.

It was Neil. 'We have something,' he said, walking past Daniel and into the study without the formality of an invitation. He sat on the sofa in his coat.

'Can I get you anything?' asked Daniel.

'I'm not stopping,' he said. 'I just wanted to fill you in.'

'Go on.'

'Forensics got back to us about Josh's guitar case. Traces of amphetamine sulphate, cannabis, cocaine and Ecstasy.'

'Traces?'

'That's quite a cocktail. And in quantities which are unlikely to be for personal use.'

'Josh was dealing?'

'Somebody was. Using him, at least, to carry gear around. We found the bass in his bedroom.'

'I can just about imagine Josh taking drugs – well, smoking a joint – but a drug dealer? Do you really think so?'

'Don't know. Could be just fetching and carrying, helping someone out, maybe for a gram of coke and a couple of Es. If he *was* dealing, then who to?'

Daniel thought, but did not say, 'to whom'. 'He was only sixteen. The other boys in the band? School?'

'What sort of teenager deals amphetamine sulphate to his classmates?'

Brandon Redding, thought Daniel.

'But', Neil went on, 'this looks more organised than that.'

'I'm just trying to think of where the market is for class A drugs in Upper and Lower Badsaddle.'

'You'd be surprised, Daniel.'

Daniel would not. One of his former parishioners, a respectable pharmacist and Rotarian, was currently halfway through a long stretch after obliging some businessmen from Margate with ingredients for their enterprise, for which they had paid cash.

Neil said, 'It's in schools, colleges, the pubs, the music scene, and I dare say even in the pastoral enclaves of Champton and the Badsaddles.'

Now Daniel was thinking of Alex de Floures, and how he might provide for his entertainments when he was in Champton rather than Soho. A thought

occurred to Daniel. He suspected it had occurred to
Neil too. And that it would explain something that had
been niggling him all day.

'Anyway, just wanted to fill you in,' said Neil, 'see
if there was anything you would like to share – your
thoughts, ideas.'

'Nothing very formed yet. Let me give it some
thought.'

'OK. I'll see you at Harvest Festival. Church and
dinner. I mean lunch.'

'You can make it?'

'"We Plough the Fields and Scatter" and a pie?
Wouldn't miss that for the world.'

7

Daniel rather liked Harvest Festival too. It was not a festival of the Church in the way that the Ascension or All Saints were, but a nineteenth-century innovation, a made-up celebration of an agrarian England that was already fading when Parson Hawker, Vicar of Morwenstow, who invented it, stuck the first cauliflower on a windowsill. Ancient or modern, at Champton they liked to observe all things properly, and they retained the tradition of the harvest loaf. The wife of the first farmer to cut his wheat for the harvest made flour from it and baked a loaf of bread in the shape of a bound sheaf of corn with a little mouse perched on one of the stalks. At Champton the harvest loaf was actually baked by Kath Sharman, but Kath had died in the terrible Ascensiontide of last year, so the task now fell for the first time to Mrs Shorely. It had been some time since she had baked bread and this year's loaf, propped up in front of the altar, was not quite the splendid egg-glazed offering of former years. It looked grey and droopy, the

255

mouse like a blob, but Daniel would still rather that than the one they displayed at St Martin's Kinnerton Square, donated by a magnificent department store, which harvested money in extraordinary amounts from its prosperous customers, who were no more rural than the Number 14 bus. Also looking a little bedraggled were the corn dollies made by the children at the primary school, another picturesque custom that had not quite delivered on its promise. 'They look like they've been made for voodoo rites, Daniel,' was his mother's remark.

Another custom they retained was the mell supper, conveniently shifted to midday and renamed harvest lunch. It was held at the village hall, and cooked and served by a team under Margaret Porteous, a custom, like Bonfire Night, embedded in the life of the village. Daniel often wondered how long it would be before it disappeared, like Oak Apple Day and the churching of women.

An offer of food, free to the poor, and supported by donations from the better-off, could still draw a crowd, and the village hall was busy each year, the village and friends packed in between the pitch-pine walls under the corrugated-iron roof. At that moment, in the hall's kitchen, aluminium basins of beef stew plopped on the burners, peeled potatoes bobbed in their pans and a 'medley', as Dot Staveley called it, of cabbage and carrots and runner beans and leeks were skinned and trimmed and made ready to cook. The pudding was Audrey's department, 'Rectory Bramble and Apple Pie', though the apples were not entirely her Bramleys, for they were especially maggoty that year and she had to supplement them with Cox's Pippins from Bernard's trees. The meagre showing of blackberries from the churchyard had also been supplemented by punnets from Sainsbury's, but, as she rightly observed, 'menus need not be comprehensive nor exhaustive'. Jugs awaited their dole of custard, so thick and glutinous it could have insulated the building, which had been erected by the Free French stationed at Champton House during the war, made from whatever materials they could find in straitened times, and to a spec which Audrey thought more suitable to the balmy South than the windy East Midlands in autumn.

This banquet was to come, but another, more important banquet was first: the feast of God in bread and wine, to which the village was summoned by bells tolling from the tower. They came up the lane in their Sunday best: the farmers from the outlying parts of the parish with their families on one of the three compulsory attendances of the year (Christmas and Easter being the others); the estate workers (the handful now employed) and the retired, who still touched their caps to Bernard; and those whose harvests were a pension, or wages, or stocks and shares, and their children and grandchildren. His mother was there, talking to Angela Thwaite, down for the weekend from town. Neil was there, uncomfortable in his suit, talking to PC Scott in his regimental blazer. And there was Miss March, all in grey, only a sort of Sunday grey, who took her place on the north side at the edge, in a 'last shall be first and first shall be last' manner.

Daniel was in the chancel, in his cassock but not yet his vestments, doing what his first vicar called the pre-flight checks: ensuring the lectionary was turned to the right page, the bread box stocked with sufficient wafers, and the linens – the purificators and lavabo towel and corporal – were all in place.

And then he sensed, rather than saw, a stir in the congregation, a change of conversational note, a light rise in volume, a rustling, as people turned in their pews.

Bernard and Honoria and Alex had arrived at the south door, and with them Hugh and a young woman. She was dark haired, and darker skinned than her mottled pink hosts, and Daniel could see even from the chancel that she was unusually beautiful. Next to each other, she and Honoria looked like the yin and yang of feminine beauty: red hair, peach skin and blue eyes, with jet black, bronze and deep brown.

His mother was suddenly at his side. 'Daniel, *look!*'

'I saw; that must be Miss Giasson.'

'Giasson?'

'Michelle Giasson. She's Canadian.'

'She's no more Canadian than Minnehaha.'

'Mother! And actually, Hiawatha was of the Mohawk

people, who live in Canada, or some of them – and so, I believe, is Miss Giasson.'

'You knew and you didn't tell me?'

'Tell you what?'

'That Hugh has a prospective . . . squaw.'

'Really not funny, Mum. She's not a caricature.'

'Yes, yes, yes, I know. Mistress of Champton too . . . What does Bernard have to say about that?'

If Bernard had something to say he did not show it but greeted people in his customary way, showed Michelle to the family pew at the front, took his place and dropped to his knees in prayer, shading his eyes with his right hand as if he had a migraine in that way the English upper classes have when communicating with God. Hugh sat up stiffly and then whispered something to Michelle, which made her smile.

Audrey scooted down to the nave, giving a rather exaggerated smile of welcome to the newcomer, and Daniel retreated to the vestry to get dressed. Two of the children from Junior Church were torchbearers, already dressed in black cassocks that had to be belted, for they were too long and had to be hitched over their shoes. They were holding the processional candles to lead the way with the crucifer, Bob Achurch, who was waiting down at the west end for the choir to line up.

Daniel said the vestry prayers and they set off for the other end of the church, Daniel smiling in a vicarish way at those who smiled at him from the pews as the mini-procession passed down the south-side aisle. The choir arrived in their blue cassocks and surplices, not as tidily as Daniel would have liked, but he had got used to that, and there were a couple of late-arriving sopranos still getting dressed in the choir vestry; still, the quarter bell chimed the half-hour and Daniel signalled to Jane Thwaite to strike up with 'Come, Ye Thankful People, Come' on the organ. The sound of a familiar hymn was enough to distract the congregation from their conversations, or most of them, and make them stand – the regulars confidently, the visitors with the mildly paralysing anxiety of infrequent church attenders. The choir began to sing and the procession moved off.

> *'Come, ye thankful people, come,*
> *raise the song of harvest home . . .'*

A soprano, puffing from a rushed arrival, interposed herself into the front of the procession as it passed.

> *'. . . all is safely gathered in,*
> *ere the winter storms begin . . .'*

Daniel caught Miss March's eye and she looked down at her hymn book.

> *'God our Maker doth provide*
> *for our wants to be supplied . . .'*

He noticed that Jane Thwaite had left her pinny draped over the organ stool so she could make a quick getaway after church and be ready for the harvest homers at the village hall.

> '. . . come to God's own temple, come,
> raise the song of harvest home.'

'For aa-aa-all his love!'

The last chorus of 'We Plough the Fields and Scatter' was delivered with double gusto – first, as a familiar tune they only got to sing once a year, and second, because it meant the service was over – as Bob and the torchbearers led the choir out. Daniel brought up the rear, adding his own tenor to the uncertain and overtested performance by the gentlemen apportioned that part because they were game rather than suitable.

He prayed the choir out at the crossing, then took up his place at the south porch to catch people as they left. Normally some would hurry past with a smile and a wave – acknowledgement rather than interaction – others would stop to tell him the achievements of a granddaughter, the condition of a housebound neighbour or – most common of all – their ailments. Country parsons, he had discovered, were richly schooled in the treatment of swollen ankles, the burden of maintaining foot health, and the vexing and imprecise art of catheter care. Today's exit was different, partly because of the awkwardness of knowing that half of them he was about to see again in the village hall, and partly because the de Floures were in, and would be first out, because even now people held back deferentially to allow Bernard and his party to leave. Daniel could see the ladies of Champton, his mother principal among them, poised like athletes at the starting line to intercept Hugh and Michelle in the churchyard. Audrey had a useful advantage here, for she could exercise her rights as the rector's mother and leave by the vestry door, come round the west end of the church and position herself on the path between the south porch and the lychgate.

Bernard lumbered up to Daniel. 'Good morning, Rector. Thank you so much for your interesting sermon. Very good to see the church so full. We look forward to joining you for lunch,' he said in the singsong way of a formula often spoken, and with no gaps to allow any reply.

Hugh and Michelle followed. 'Hi, Daniel,' Hugh said. 'This is my fiancée, Michelle.'

'Hello, Miss . . . is it Giasson?'

'It is,' she said, 'but please call me Michelle. I have heard such nice things about you.' A frown for a second tensed her brow. 'But what do I call you?'

'Daniel.'

'Daniel.' She smiled.

'Are you coming to harvest lunch?'

'I think so.' She looked at Hugh, who nodded.

Alex interjected: 'We'll just walk Daddy home and pour him a Bloody Mary first. Dan, can Honoria and I come too?'

'Yes, you will all be very welcome, but I need to tell Jane . . .'

Jane Thwaite was already at the door, pinny in hand. 'Five from the house, plus Jean Shorely. We can manage that!' She beamed at Michelle and Hugh as she slid past but at a velocity that did not allow for introductions.

Bernard looked irritated, like a man whose effort to get away early had been thwarted, and he gestured testily to encourage the others to get a move-on. He was too late to dodge Audrey, who had nipped out of the vestry door before he had even reached the south porch, and appeared, a little breathlessly, round the north transept at that very moment, coming up on his blind side. He turned, and there she was, blocking his way, like Wade Dooley on a rugby pitch churned with Welsh blood.

'Audrey,' he said, but with an emphasis on the first syllable of her name, which made it sound a bit like a growl.

'Wasn't it lovely to see the church so full?' she said, and extended her arms in a general benison, but with the actual purpose of funnelling the de Floures party towards her. 'Honoria, good morning. Alex, good morning – what's your T-shirt all about today, dear? "Meat Is Murder"? And Hugh, how lovely to see you again! And . . .?'

'This is Michelle, Audrey, my fiancée. Michelle Giasson. And this, Michelle, is Audrey . . . I've forgotten your last name . . .'

'It's Audrey Clement, I'm the rector's mother. We're all *so pleased* to meet you.'

'Thank you. I'm really pleased to meet you too.'

'And such good timing to be here for Harvest Festival! You will find our customs rather quaint!'

'Oh, not really. We have something like this at home too.'

'Harvest Festival?'

'Yes, it's an old tradition, to hold a thanksgiving for the harvest and for all the land has given us.'

'And do you . . . gather . . . your people?'

'Yes, like you; it's quite a big occasion. And we have special food too.'

'Around the campfire?'

'Excuse me?'

'Your people. Around the fire?'

'No, in the dining room.'

Audrey pretended not to have made a faux pas. 'Oh, yes, I see, the dining room.'

'There's a furnace. In the basement. It . . . ducts warm air around the house. It can get pretty cold in Canada in the fall.'

'Oh, yes. And bears.'

'Bears?'

'Don't they get into your bins?'

'Not really. In the cities.'

'Ah. We have a similar problem with foxes, you see.'

There was silence. Then Audrey said, 'Are you here for long?'

'Just a few days.'

'Well, I hope you have the most splendid time. Champton is at its loveliest in the autumn.'

Bernard interrupted. 'Audrey, you'll forgive us if we go?'

She moved to one side. 'Of course, I'm so sorry. See you . . . very soon.'

Bernard led his party down the path, just as the churchyard started to fill with clumps of people all keen to see what the future Lady de Floures looked like but not wanting to be obvious about it.

Audrey was still smarting because of her clumsiness. 'Daniel! Campfire! Why on earth would a woman wearing a Barbour jacket and corduroy trousers meet "her people" round a campfire?'

'What happened?'

'I've just put my foot in it with our next chatelaine. She was talking about some thanksgiving ritual at home and I asked if they met round a campfire, that's all. That's what you see them do. I know it's just the films, and no one really lives like that, but she did say it was an old custom, so . . .'

'What did she say in response?'

'She said they met in the dining room.'

'Did you think they made a circle of their teepees and roasted a bison?'

Audrey's habit in a corner was always to attempt magnificence. 'Sarcasm, Daniel, does not become you, or your calling.'

Daniel saw Neil emerge from the porch. He nodded at Daniel and mouthed something. 'Mum, I just need to catch someone . . .'

He left Audrey in the middle of her magnificence. Neil drew him to one side and said, 'There's something I need to discuss with you.'

'Can it wait until after lunch?'

'Best now, if you can.'

Daniel told him to wait at the rectory, went into the church, used the north aisle to dodge the stragglers and made the vestry in one uninterrupted manoeuvre. He pulled the chasuble over his head like a poncho, left it in a heap on the vestment chest and was out of the vestry door before Bob Achurch had herded the servers back to get changed.

Neil was at the back door of the rectory, with Cosmo on the other side barking in a frenzy of alarm. 'It's open,' said Daniel.

'I thought I'd wait. Didn't want to induce labour.'

They went into the study followed by Cosmo and Hilda, who waddled out of the drawing room to see who it was.

'Do you want a coffee?'

'No, thanks, I won't stay long. But there's another development in the Josh Biddle case.'

'Go on.'

'The 999 call.'

'The anonymous person who discovered the body?'

'You know we record them now?'

'The 999 calls?'

'Yes, big tape machine, records everything that comes through the switchboard — we've just got one. I want to play the call to you. It's not the best quality, but that's got a cassette player?' He gestured towards the music centre and, before Daniel could think, was taking a cassette out of a brown envelope and inserting it into the machine. He switched the selector to TAPE, but then paused and appeared to be thinking about something. Then he pressed play.

There was a voice, indistinct and scratchy, but audible. 'There's been a murder. I just found a body . . . No, I don't want to give my name . . . Just send someone soon as you can. It's in the chapel on the old airfield up at Badsaddle . . . I don't know the name of the road — they'll know it . . . won't need an ambulance, he's dead . . . I don't want to give my name . . .' and there was a click and silence.

Neil looked at Daniel.

Daniel said, 'Yes, I think so too. It's Nathan.' Nathan Liversedge, the gypsy lad who lived on the estate with his grandfather, Edgy, working as unofficial gamekeepers and fixers. They had disappeared after the murders last year: both had historic matters to discuss with the police, and Nathan, it was discovered to the surprise of everyone, had been having an affair — a love affair — with Alex de Floures.

'So *that's* why you were at Alex's?'

Neil looked up. 'How did you know that?'

'We drove past on the way back from Mrs Hawkins's and saw you parked outside the lodge.'

A faint tinge spread across Neil's face.

'Yes. I called in. I wasn't keeping it from you, Dan . . .'

'You don't need my permission.'

'I know, only . . .'

'But that's not important. Actually, it makes sense of something that was puzzling me. I called in last Sunday to see Alex and Honoria and there were two places laid on the dining table. I assumed the other was for her, but she asked for a lift back to the house. What did Alex say?'

'Not in. I waited for a bit, then left. I decided to talk to you first. He trusts you.'

'Who?'

'Nathan. And Alex. But I need to talk to Nathan, and I don't want to scare him off.'

'Alex will be at the lunch later, I think.'

'Will you talk to him?'

'Yes. I may need to pick my moment.'

'OK. Shall we head down to the village hall now?'

Daniel thought for a second. 'You go first. It may not look right to Alex if we turn up together.'

'OK, I'll see you there.'

Neil made to go and then Daniel remembered the cassette. 'Do you need that tape back?' He took it out of the machine, and then saw what Neil had seen. On the turntable he had left the record he had played before he went to bed. 'Something's Gotten Hold of My Heart', by Marc Almond featuring Gene Pitney.

It was his turn to blush.

The village hall was packed. Three long trestle tables were laid along its length with another at the head. There sat Bernard and Hugh and Michelle and Honoria. Alex had not come, which had messed up Margaret Porteous's seating plan and made her tut.

Bernard had welcomed everyone and thanked them for their hard work, which seemed a little odd considering only a handful actually worked on the estate, but he saw no reason to change what he had said every year – and his father and grandfather before him – merely because the circumstances of the present moment did not precisely match the text. No one put their scythe to the corn any more, fair waving or not; it was mostly oilseed rape now, or winter barley, which was harvested by contractors, and milkmaids and swineherds were few. It was not only Bernard who saw no necessity to adapt to the present if the past was still serviceable. Canon Dolben, Daniel's ancient predecessor, was known to refer to 'our brave boys home from Mafeking' well into the 1970s. No one minded, perhaps because it would not have occurred to them to contradict squire or parson, or perhaps because there was comfort and security in the litany of the familiar. There is a peculiar forgetfulness of our age, thought

Daniel, so enchanted with novelty and the extraordinary success of science and technology, that the longer story of the evolution of the values and institutions and virtues that have long shaped our lives gets lost. He once asked Alex, with his gleeful denunciations of the status quo and the customs and traditions that formed him, why he thought his generation was uniquely and sufficiently competent to sit in judgement on the sum of human history, to which Alex answered, 'Fuck history, let's dance.'

Perhaps that was why Alex had chosen not to come, as a protest of some kind, or perhaps he could not be bothered to be nice to the tenantry when there were barely any tenantry left to be nice to. It was interesting that Hugh, who did not want his heritage and would much rather be out on a prairie with Michelle than exercising noblesse oblige on the family estate, nevertheless turned up to do his duty, even if his smile was fixed and his eye strayed to the clock over the door too frequently.

Every other eye was on Michelle, of course, inventorying, assessing and judging. She knew this but was the model of gracious charm, happily introducing herself to people in the melee, laughing at their jokes and not flinching when they, like Audrey, blundered around the matter of her heritage.

When they did all sit down, Michelle was on Bernard's right with Daniel on hers, an alteration to the original placement, which Audrey had quietly requested. After

Bernard's speech, Daniel said grace, and the ladies of the catering team pushed their trolleys down the aisles between the tables – trolleys laden with plated-up stew and mash with their accompanying 'medley of seasonal vegetables'. There was cider to drink, made not from the estate's apples but industrially in Herefordshire, with pop for those who were wary even of the cider's feeble intoxicants.

As Cynthia Achurch went along the top table doling out the plated mains, Daniel turned to Michelle. 'It is so nice to meet you,' he said. 'I hope it is not too much to be the object of so much fascination.'

'No, it's fine,' she said. 'It's kind of what Hugh told me to expect. It's not something that happens so much, I guess: a new candidate for the post of mistress of Champton.'

'No, though your father-in-law-to-be has had three.'

'So far.'

'Indeed so. I hope you have not been made to feel too much like an exotic for other reasons?'

'I suppose half the people here think I have a head-dress and a tomahawk at home.'

'You met my mother?'

'The lady who asked me if we circled our teepees round the campfire when we bring in the crops?'

'Yes.'

'I guess that's what's in everyone's mind.'

'I think also it may be nerves. They are so anxious

not to say the wrong thing, it becomes inevitable that they do.'

Michelle smiled. 'But this is fun!'

Along the trestle tables Champtonians were digging in, not only to the food, but to their neighbours, a semi-commonwealth on such an occasion, for apart from the top table, with squire and parson arrayed in all their glory, everybody was huggermugger, regardless of status or locality. Neil was wedged – it was an almost uncomfortably busy board – between Bob Achurch and Dot Staveley; Miss March, on the centre table, had Gilbert Drage to her right, who had the manners of a Viking, and Christian Staniland, who had the conversation of a Trappist. She looked even more like a putty-pale Gwen John portrait.

Daniel turned to Margaret Porteous on his right, top-tabled by virtue of her status as churchwarden. She was not only churchwarden, but organiser of the harvest lunch, so had set herself the tricky choreography of running the kitchen and the servers while simultaneously performing her duties as the congregation's 'senior member', as she liked to describe herself, but without any authority to do so at all. She had replaced Anthony Bowness after his murder last year, and had glowed a little unattractively when she was asked if she would care to stand for election to that office – one she had long coveted not only for the prestige, but because it allowed her more involvement in the life of the house and its residents. Anthony had been the patron's warden, and his cousin too, and so Margaret thought it only proper to call on Bernard weekly to discuss liturgical matters or items lost from the terrier, the inventory of the church's chattels or contraventions of the bylaws concerning monuments in the church-yard, until one day Bernard had snarled that unless the church had been set on fire by a passing band of insurrectionists, she should kindly deal with all matters herself.

Bernard, even two places away, was radiating dis-pleasure tempered by obligation. He observed the courtly rule of turning to face one way for the first course and the other way for the second, so those sit-ting to his left and right, Hugh and Michelle, got equal shares of his attention. His attention, however, was a mixed blessing when he was in the best of moods, and even from the side Daniel could tell that he was stiff with Michelle and terse with Hugh.

Margaret Porteous leaned into him confidentially. 'Rector, do you think it appropriate that I should perhaps say a few words of welcome on behalf of the parish to Miss Giasson?'

'Are you sure that's necessary, Margaret? I wonder if it would not be better to maintain the informality of the occasion. I think until the announcement is made officially?'

'Oh, but she's here, isn't she? Wouldn't it look rude if the parish did not acknowledge her presence? It's the first time she's been!'

The arrival of the Rectory Bramble and Apple Pie interrupted them, so chewy and sticky in its thick blanket of custard that there was a discernible drop in the decibel level as mouths once loud with chat were stopped by Audrey's pudding. Then 'tea or coffee' was served in green Woods Beryl Ware cups and saucers – as essential a component of English parish life as hassocks and gossip.

One tinkled when Margaret tapped at it with her spoon, silencing the hall place by place as she stood. 'Thank you, everyone,' she said, inclining her head in a way that she thought gracious but actually made it look like she had ricked her neck. 'As senior churchwarden' – she's not senior churchwarden, thought Daniel – 'it falls to me to express on behalf of the parish our most warm and heartfelt welcome to Miss Giasson.' Grunts of approval followed from the trestle tables. Michelle smiled. Bernard frowned. 'Miss Giasson . . .'

Michelle nodded. 'Michelle, please!'

'Miss Giasson, you have travelled far from a distant land, a land of forests and lakes and mountains and prairies, to join us here in our beloved Champton for our Harvest Festival. Our food may seem strange to you, our customs new, but I feel sure that you can be in no doubt of our genuine delight to meet you. And we hope that when you return to your proud homeland you will do so knowing that no matter how distant our lives and traditions, we are *all* united in *assuring* you that under the skin we are the same, God's children, and—'

At that moment Bernard, who could bear it no longer, rose and said, 'Thank you, Mrs Porteous, and now the rector will finish with a prayer.'

Daniel, for the second time that day, positioned himself near the exit to catch people as they left. Bernard already had, taking Hugh and Michelle with him, and Daniel knew he would have to call at Champton House later with a dole of harvest balm rather than bread. Michelle seemed to have made an excellent first impression, not flinching at the well-intentioned but clumsy welcome of those whom she would one day live among, and if there were any questions on their part that she would not be able to fulfil the role of chatelaine of Champton, in the judgement of the village she could not have seemed more poised and more gracious.

He went to thank the ladies in the kitchen, did the compulsory stint helping to wash up, WI pinny over his cassock, and then made his way to the gatehouse along the brook and through the main gates. A thread of wood smoke rose from the chimney and two pairs of boots had been left in front of the woodpile neatly stacked at the door.

Daniel knocked. Nothing happened. He knocked again. Again, nothing, so he did what he would not normally do and let himself in. He nearly tripped in the corridor that led to the drawing room, which made enough noise to alert anyone there of his presence.

Alex and Nathan were lying on the sofa, Nathan with his head against Alex's chest, their legs resting on the ottoman. Nathan got up in a hurry and blushed.

'Don't you knock?' asked Alex.

'I did.'

'And when there's no answer you take that as a "come in"?'

'I would not normally, Alex, but I need to talk to you. Both.'

'Rector,' said Nathan, 'I was going to come to see you . . .'

'I know, Nathan, and you're not in trouble, but there is something you need to know.'

Nathan sat down again. Alex did not even stir but indicated the armchair as an invitation to Daniel to sit too.

'Thank you. Nathan, we know it was you who called in the discovery of the body.'

Nathan made to answer, but Alex held up a hand.

'Who is "we"? And how do you know?'

'The police.'

'You mean Neil?'

'Neil is the police.'

'I know, but he is becoming rather a feature in our quaint little world. Hard to tell whether he is off duty or on sometimes,' said Alex in a knowing tone.

'Which is why I am here rather than the police. And we know—'

'*We* . . . Are you turning into Father Brown?'

'We know because the 999 call was recorded and it is your voice, Nathan, unmistakably.'

'So I *am* in trouble.'

'No, you're not in trouble, and you did the right thing, but you will need to answer some questions.'

Daniel knew that any encounter with the police was to be avoided, because for Nathan and his grandfather there was always the option of flight into the network of gypsy families that they came from. That had happened last year after his relationship with Alex was discovered. Daniel had always known he would be back, or he had when he realised their liaison was not a taboo knee trembler behind the woodshed, but a true love affair. He also knew that Alex would not thank him for driving Nathan away. 'No one is interested in what happened last year, Nathan. We just need to know about what happened to Joshua Biddle. You would only need to talk to DS Vanloo . . .'

'And then what?' said Alex. 'How can you promise us that it won't go further? It's a murder inquiry and we know better than most how that works.'

'Because the inquiry is focused on how Josh died, not on Nathan or Edgy and the past. And it is better that we manage it ourselves rather than set the machinery of the criminal justice system in motion.'

Alex thought about it. 'OK. What happens next?'

'Nathan, why don't you call round at the rectory after Evensong? Say seven? I'll arrange for Neil to meet us there.'

Alex saw Daniel to the door. 'Did you know?'

'I suspected.'

'Why?'

'Two places laid for a dinner for one? And the logs. Only Nathan stacked them that way.'

'*Very* Father Brown.'

'And, if I may say so, love sometimes conquers fear. It is one of the few things that can.'

'Love?' Bernard almost snarled. 'Love? It's not fucking Romeo and fucking Juliet.'

They were in his study, the loveliest room in Champton House, where Bernard liked to retreat when he felt the world was against him. Daniel had let himself in and found him there, sitting in his armchair by the fire, which Mrs Shorely had lit. On his lap sat Jove, carpeting his tweed with his white fur, but Bernard preferred the cat to any dog, for its dark nature and indifference to suffering. He looked to Daniel for a moment like Blofeld stroking his white cat in the Bond films, only without the diamond collar. Bernard had barely looked up, had greeted Daniel with testy impatience, and had not even offered him a drink, though he was on his second brandy.

'Well, that's not a particularly helpful comparison, if I may say so . . .'

'No, it's the house of Montague and the house of fucking Hiawatha.' He paused and calmed a little. 'I mean no offence to Michelle, Daniel, but it is not about our personal feelings, it is about . . . the requirements of the role.'

'I understand that you have to think of such things. But she would not be the first outsider to marry into this family. There are precedents.'

'You mean my third wife? Italian nobility. My grand-mother? She was a railroad heiress from Baltimore, Daniel. With a million dollars, not a fucking peace pipe.'

'But my point is, she learnt how to do it. Indeed, she was a great success.'

'Yes, but she grew up with wealth, position – it wasn't such a big jump. And while she was learning how to be presented at court, Michelle's grandmother was shooting fucking bows and arrows at trains.'

Daniel let the anger subside. Then he said, 'What do you want for Hugh?'

Bernard took a slurp of brandy. 'I want someone suitable, from a suitable family, suitable background, who will help him keep this show on the road. It is complicated, it requires experience and judgement. Do you understand?'

'Who would bring that?'

'Some dim earl's daughter from a shire county or Scottish shooting estate, or a . . . I'd settle for a fucking nancy-boy gypsy had not primogeniture fucked it up.' He took another long slurp of brandy.

Daniel could see the brooding mood begin to settle on him. It came more frequently upon him now. It used to be towards the end of a marriage, or on those occasions when the house and park were open to the public under the terms of the arrangement he had made with the tax man. He was at his bleakest when he felt his inheritance of title, estate and history was most precarious, most threatened by the failure of the present to provide for the future. A gay son in love with a gypsy gamekeeper, a daughter working for her living and now – hardest blow of all – an heir who did not want his inheritance and who had brought back to Champton a bride-to-be who was not cut from the right cloth.

'What do you think of her personally?' Daniel asked.

'Personally? I think she's absolutely fine. More than fine – charming and beautiful. But that's irrelevant.'

'Not irrelevant to Hugh. And Hugh's happiness.'

Bernard sighed. 'For fuck's sake, Daniel. Have you ever been in love?'

Daniel did not know what to say. He blushed.

'Thought not, though even parsons must have their passions. Is it dogs with you? Doing pretty services? But love is . . . a palm court orchestra, a rose in bloom, it's your favourite pudding. It's *not* running this estate. It's *not* being a de Floures. Why am I having to tell you about this? You should know. I've always thought it absurd that a bachelor parson should pontificate about

marital matters, let alone dynastic matters. What quali-
fies you to do that?'

Daniel blinked. 'Detachment.'

'The detachment of the non-combatant?'

'If you like. But also, I am outside your world,
Bernard, and perhaps I can see what you cannot see.
The world is changing. Think how different life is
on the estate now compared with when you were a
boy. Or when your grandfather brought his American bride back from Baltimore. Perhaps Hugh and
Michelle will have the necessary elements to adapt to
change.'

Bernard snorted. 'Do not be beguiled by the promise of change. First lesson they teach you when you are
born into something like this.'

'But change will happen. Look at the world, Bernard.
Look at what is happening in Hungary, East Germany,
Romania. The Communist world, impregnable? Not
so impregnable now. The old order passeth.'

'Perhaps the old order returneth and the commissars
will face their own firing squads. Hasten the day!'

'I don't know, but it will not be the old order again.
The Wettins restored to the throne of Saxony? Trianon
reversed?'

Bernard made a noise between a growl and a sigh
and went to pour himself another brandy. Jove, dis-
placed from his lap, gave an irritable little miaow and
stalked away.

★

He had barely got out of the Land Rover when his mother's bedroom window flew open.

'Daniel!' she shouted. 'Get in here!' and she slammed the window down again.

Daniel wondered what the cause could be of not only the urgency, but the location. His mother's bedroom was out of bounds, her sanctuary, her boudoir, that part of the rectory into which neither he nor any other authority could stray without a very clear and very infrequently issued invitation. He could not remember the last time he had been inside it; he could recall only the doctor getting past the door when his mother had shingles after she bit off more than she could chew for the League of Charity Centenary Party. So he rushed inside and, while hardly taking the stairs at a bound – 'A good priest never runs!' his tutor at theological college had told him – he was puffing when he arrived at the door. Cosmo was lying in front of it, his snout almost on the paintwork. Daniel tapped on it gently.

'Come in, quick!' was the reply. He held Cosmo back with his foot and went in. His mother was kneeling beside a mound of cushions and pillows and towels, which she had heaped inside what she called 'the whelping box' but which he had improvised from the cardboard boxes he had taken from Upper Badsaddle Manor. In it, Hilda, the size of a small seal, lay on her side.

'Puppies!' his mother exclaimed. 'They're *coming*!'

'Oh, good Lord,' said Daniel, 'should I telephone the vet?'

'Nonsense! Easiest thing in the world, Daniel. Leave nature to her work!'

'So what do you want me to do?'

'Make me a cup of tea.'

'May I just see Hilda?' He knelt next to his mother and stroked Hilda's flank. 'Beautiful girl,' he said, 'beautiful girl!' She stirred slightly, and he supposed she was preoccupied with the business of parturition, although she looked like she was resting. Then there was a jostle from inside her. 'Mum!' he said. 'They're moving!'

'Of course they're moving, they're ready to pop out. Now get me that cup of tea!'

Daniel, flustered like a grandparent outside a delivery suite, forgot to fill the kettle before he put it on the hob, confirming the old adage, but in a new way, that a watched kettle never boils. He picked things up and put them down in a random ritual of orderliness before he pulled himself together. He carried a tray upstairs set with two mugs of strong tea (he thought a mug rather than a cup and saucer more suitable to the hard work of midwifery) and a plate of nourishing digestives, which he took from the biscuit tin that had provided for him since childhood, and indeed for others before he arrived – and for that reason, and because of the promise of new life imminently to come, tears began to blur his vision and he had to compose himself again.

The bedroom was hot and charged somehow: hot because Audrey had ignited the ugly portable Calor gas heater which she had wheeled in from the dampest of the guest bedrooms, normally reserved for Daniel's brother, Theo; charged because the great drama of birth was unfolding. Audrey, who had given birth to Daniel – a feat which she thought, very privately, her greatest work – was almost unable to contain her excitement. Her eyes were shining, her colour was up, and there was a sort of repressed whinny, if there can be such a thing, with every contraction.

'Look, Daniel,' she said, and pointed to Hilda's rear end, where something that looked to Daniel like a fleshy hot cross bun appeared to be about to pop out.

'What is it?' he asked anxiously.

'It's a vulva, Daniel. What were you expecting, the archangel Gabriel?'

'Is it normally like that? Shouldn't we fetch someone?'

'No, it's meant to be like that. And before long we will have, I think, three puppies.'

'What shall we do with them?'

'Keep them, of course.'

'How can we possibly keep them?'

'Oh, Daniel, if you have two, what's another three?'

'The expense, Mum?'

'I will take care of that.'

'How?'

'Oh, do stop fussing, Da— oh, *look*!'

Hilda tried to heave herself onto her paws and then

lifted her tail. A tiny head appeared, with a squashed snout and closed eyes, covered in a sort of juice, which Hilda curled round to lick off. And then what was left of the tiny creature emerged, covered in wet, dark fur; it plopped onto the towel, and Hilda licked it and it gave a sort of squeak, like a toy. She licked and licked, and nuzzled it towards her belly, and it latched on to one of her teats, which were the size, Daniel noticed, of raisins.

'Oh, my goodness!' he said.

Audrey sat up and said, like the grocer's daughter from Grantham, 'We are a grandmother.'

Forty minutes later another was about to arrive, but the bell for Evensong rang and Daniel had to go. 'Send for me, Mum, if you need me,' he said.

'Send my lady's maid? A groom? A gamekeeper? Just hurry back!'

The office hymn at Evensong was 'Creator of the Stars of Night', good for Harvest as well as for Advent, when it was usually sung, and especially apt that day:

> 'When earth was near its evening hour,
> Thou didst, in love's redeeming power,
> Like bridegroom from his chamber, come
> Forth from a virgin-mother's womb.'

Hardly a virgin mother; the father of Hilda's puppies was thought to be Siegfried, a black-and-tan dachshund, who belonged to one of Theo's friends. He was less than a year old when Theo came to look after the dogs so Daniel could take his mother to the funeral of a cousin in Scotland. He invited his friend to stay at the rectory and to bring his little puppy too, and in a quiet and unobserved moment the little dog must have mated with Hilda. Daniel was so distracted by the outcome of their congress he could barely concentrate and nearly beseeched God to endue his ministers with righteousness twice.

By the time he got home, Hilda was about to give birth to a third. He marvelled at her composure and the easy arrival of each pup, so unlike human child-birth – noisy, agonising and dangerous. He had been summoned to perinatal intensive care sometimes to baptise a very premature baby only a little larger than the two puppies now greedily sucking at Hilda's teats. They fluttered between living and dying, so vulnera-ble, so tiny, and once, when he was asked to scatter the ashes of a premature baby, he had quietly added some he had made himself by burning the little charcoal bri-quettes for a thurible, so that there would be enough for the parents to grieve. He wondered if childbirth was a design flaw, not a curse inflicted on the daughters of Eve after she ate of the fruit of the tree of knowledge, but something to do with bipedalism? The cost of our striving upwards? Chris Biddle came into his mind, or rather the conversation he would not want to have with him about the truth of Bible stories, for Chris would insist on them being true in a way that Daniel did not, could not – and anyway, he thought we owed the Bible more than the literal truth that those who thought themselves its defenders allowed.

The doorbell rang. Audrey jumped up from the floor and threw the window up again. 'Who is it?'

A voice floated up from the drive. 'It's Alex. And Nathan!'

'I'm up to my elbows in placenta!'

'I'm sorry?'

'You will have to come back another time!'

Daniel stuck his head out of the window. 'Hold on, I'll be down in a moment . . . Mum, this is important, I have to deal with it.'

She said, 'Did he say Nathan? Nathan Liversedge?'

'Yes, he did.'

'Well! The wanderer returns! You had better see what's the matter. I've been managing perfectly well on my own so far. And I don't think there will be any problems. We'd know by now if there were.'

Daniel was nearly at the foot of the stairs when she shouted, 'Daniel!'

He turned and rushed back to her bedroom.

She was wiping her hands on a towel. 'Ask Nathan if he can fix those loose slates, rehang the gates and paint the windows?'

'Mum, it's not really the time.'

'Cash!'

'We don't have the money – and he's helping the police with their inquiries, not doing bob-a-job.'

He left his mother to her ministrations and went

downstairs to let in Nathan and Alex. Cosmo, he noticed, remained *en garde* outside the bedroom door instead of coming to bark at the people.

Daniel showed them into the study. Nathan looked around uncomfortably, then said, 'Your windows need doing.'

'That's just what my mother was saying.'

'Mrs Clement all right?'

'Yes, being a midwife.'

'A what?' said Alex.

'Hilda's puppies are coming.'

'Oh, how are they doing?'

'They're fine. But how are you doing, Nathan? Sit down . . . please.'

Alex and Nathan sat side by side on the Sofa of Tears. Daniel could tell just from the way they reacted to each other physically that their relationship had been not only recently revived; he supposed their enforced claustration, out of sight of Champton, had accelerated the accommodation of another, which comes when people form couples.

Nathan looked briefly at Alex and said, 'OK, Rector. I had to come back because I wanted to see Alex, but I couldn't tell no one.'

'How is your grandfather?'

'He's all right. His hands are really bad. But he's staying with some of our people Essex way.'

'Does he know you are here?'

'I told him and he went mad, said it would cause

more trouble and that I couldn't come, but I came anyway.'

'What have you been doing?'

'I've been with Alex. And out round the estate and the farms. Places I used to go, like the airfield. That's where I found him, like.'

Alex said, 'He's been unlucky, hasn't he, Daniel, with murder victims? One last year and another this year. People will talk. Oh, they already *were* talking.'

'Would you like a drink?'

'While we wait for the Detective Sergeant? It's a yes from me. Have you got anything apart from sherry?'

'There's wine, there's whisky, there's Noilly Prat.'

'I wouldn't dream of raiding your mother's vermouth. Do you have anything white open?'

Daniel nodded. 'Not open, but I can open it. What about you, Nathan? I think there's a bottle of beer somewhere.'

'I'll have a white wine as well, please.'

'Oh. Chardonnay all right?'

'Not too oaky. I don't like it too oaky . . .'

'Oh, I'm quite the Henry Higgins, Daniel, in an E. M. Forster sort of way.'

Daniel went to fetch the bottle and some glasses from the kitchen. When he got back Alex was standing at his desk and holding up Mrs Hawkins's cameo brooch to the light.

'This is a bit special.'

'Is it? It used to belong to Mrs Hawkins.'

'What a nice present.'

'Not a present. I'm an executor of the will.'

'I could see your mother wearing this.'

'So could she.'

Alex turned the brooch in his hand. 'It's Hermes, isn't it? The winged god. Early nineteenth century, Italian, I think. We've got drawers of them. But this is very special. Was Mrs Hawkins a collector?'

'That's more my mother's department than mine.'

'Perhaps she was a jewel thief? Perhaps this was one of ours? Over the roof by night she came in a black jumpsuit and balaclava . . .'

Daniel handed him a glass. 'I don't think Muriel Hawkins was ever that athletic.'

'Nobody would have noticed if she had.'

Nathan sipped his wine. 'That's quite nice,' he said.

They sat in silence for a moment, then Alex said, 'What will the police want to know?'

'About the discovery of the body. When, where, why – the usual things. But you need not worry about last year, Nathan, they're not interested in that.'

'Gramps said we could never come back because they would start asking questions and there would be no end to it then.'

'You are not your grandfather, Nathan. I can assure you the police will only be interested in this case, not anything else.'

'Did you fix that with your friendly plod, Dan?' said Alex.

'If you mean DS Vanloo . . .'

'Oh, I do.'

'I don't fix things. But I have his assurance. Think about it, Alex; what's the priority here? It's who killed Josh Biddle, not a hangover from a case that was closed a year ago.'

'You *are* a trusting soul, Dan.'

A shout came from the hall. 'Daniel, *help*! HELP!'

Audrey was standing on the landing. 'The third one's arrived! It's not breathing!'

Nathan rushed past Daniel and went up the stairs, two at a time. 'Where are they, Mrs Clement?'

Audrey pointed to her bedroom door. 'In here. Can you help?'

He went in; she followed; Daniel and Alex after them.

Nathan had the tiny puppy wrapped in a towel in his big hands and was delicately clearing its snout of mucus. He rubbed the puppy briskly with the towel and checked for breathing, but there was nothing. Then he cupped it in his hand, placed his other hand over it and raised the puppy over his shoulder. He looked like he was going to dash it to the floor.

'Stop!' shouted Daniel, but Nathan flung his arms down with all the force he could muster, holding on tightly to the puppy; once, twice. After the third time a tiny mewl followed as the force cleared the gummy stuff from its lungs. The puppy peeped again and writhed and Nathan, with a lovely delicacy, placed it back in the whelping box. Hilda nuzzled it towards a spare teat, and it suckled alongside its siblings. Cosmo went and put his snout over the side of the box and watched, like Joseph, Daniel thought, at the stable in Bethlehem.

'Nathan, you hero!' said Audrey.

'It's just what you do when they won't start breathing.'

'But should we call the vet?' asked Daniel.

'No need,' said Audrey. 'Once it's breathing, it's breathing. But, Nathan, thank you. We've missed you.'

A ring on the doorbell. 'That will be Neil, I think,' said Daniel and he went downstairs.

'I suppose we had better go and do our duty,' said Alex.

Nathan was kneeling next to Audrey, both of them fascinated by the squirming trio.

'How many puppies is it, Mrs Clement?'

'Three.'

'Is that all of them?'

'I think so.'

Alex peered into the box too. For a while even he was quiet. 'Three little wrigglers,' he said eventually. 'Shall we name them after the Rhinemaidens in honour of their German heritage?'

'It's two girls and a boy, dear.'

'Hitler, Himmler and Eva Braun, then.'

'Don't be silly, Alex. We should call one of the boys Nathan. Isn't that what you do, name the baby after the doctor who delivered him?'

'They'd all be called Abdul now, Audrey, if we did that . . .'

Then the door opened and there was Daniel with Neil and two uniformed officers.

Daniel began to say something, but Neil interrupted. 'Nathan Liversedge, I am arresting you on suspicion of the murder of Joshua Biddle. You do not have to say anything, but it may harm your defence if you do not mention when questioned something which you may later rely on in court. Anything you do say may be given in evidence.'

For a moment there was total silence, save the mewling of the puppies. Then Alex said, 'You *promised*! Daniel?'

Before Daniel could answer, Neil said, 'Alexander de Floures, I am arresting you on suspicion of the murder of Joshua Biddle. Consider yourself cautioned too.'

'Me? Arrested?'

'In my *bedroom*?' said Audrey.

Audrey decided to keep Hilda and the puppies close to her, both for their benefit and for hers, for she was unsettled by what had turned out to be an unexpectedly dramatic day. First, the births; second, the appearance of Nathan, the gypsy lad missing for over a year; third, his arrest and the arrest of the Hon. Alexander

Arthur John Wellbeck de Floures, his boyfriend, in her bedroom. 'What a turbulent world those puppies must think they've been born into,' she said to Daniel, and retired to her room with a mug of Ovaltine and the *Sunday Telegraph*.

Daniel had gone to church to say the night prayer, but had been so distracted, so angry, he could not concentrate. Distracted trying to work out why Neil had arrested two people whom he thought – knew – to be incapable of the crime. And angry that Neil had used him to get Nathan and Alex to walk into a trap. That he had made him look like he had broken a promise, been unworthy of trust, lied. Daniel knew enough of human nature to no longer be surprised when people did not behave as they ought to behave. Very few of us, in a corner, acquit ourselves with credit, for we are weak, and scared, and flawed. And very few of us, if offered the world, would not at least consider leasing our soul to the devil.

But this was Neil: he had given him his trust, and received trust in return, and they had come to know each other, and to spend time together, and had shared the things about themselves they wished to be known, but, most importantly, the things they wished not to be known. For he knew, and Neil knew, that the friendship, which had surprised both of them, demanded it; it wanted to go places, and would take whatever it needed for wherever it was going. Daniel – he found this difficult to admit, but it was true – had never given anyone more than he wanted to give, so this was new, and exciting, and challenging. And to be betrayed was crushing.

He went back to the rectory and sat at his desk. Cosmo, with the innate sense dogs have for human distress, came to find him and curled up at his feet. And then he uncurled and ran to the door, and Daniel saw headlights in the drive.

Neil stood on the doorstep. 'Can I come in?'

Daniel let him in. Neil went straight into the study and waited for Daniel to follow and close the door. Daniel said, on reflex, 'Would you like anything to drink?' but as he did, he felt the corners of his mouth begin to turn down and his voice trembled.

'I'm sorry, Dan. It wasn't what I meant to happen, but I had to.'

'Had to?'

'Yes. Do you want to sit down?'

'Normally the host invites the guest to sit.'

Neil said nothing. Daniel indicated the sofa.

'I wasn't misleading you, Dan. I only wanted a statement from Nathan. But there's new evidence.'

'What evidence?'

'Wellingtons. Two pairs of Dunlops. Did you notice anything outside the lodge?'

Daniel remembered the pairs of black wellingtons left next to the woodpile. Two clues, not one.

'One size ten, one size nine. And from what I can

see, the tread is identical to the tread from the crime scene.'

'Everyone has wellingtons – all the estate people, all the farmers, have the same kind, the black ones, like theirs.'

'Size nine and a size ten? It could connect them to the crime. And remember, Nathan is technically a fugitive. He has suspected involvement in a crime of violence . . .'

'*Suspected*, and he was a boy, and it was nothing like this . . .'

'. . . and his grandfather has a suspected involvement in a number of murders, with victims who had their throats cut. What do you think my superiors expect me to do with that?'

'But Nathan didn't kill Josh Biddle. Of course he didn't.'

'I don't think he did – I don't think he's capable. But Alex?'

'Why on earth would he want to kill Josh Biddle? He might like a spectacle, he might seem cold-hearted, vicious even, but why would he want to kill someone?'

'There's more evidence. We think Alex has been using cocaine bought in Braunstonbury rather than brought from London . . .'

'Why?'

'We've been hearing about one especially entrepreneurial dealer, young guy, active in the local music scene.'

'Works in the record shop?'

'You know him?'

'Brandon Redding. Do you remember him?'

'From where?'

'He was the surly boy sitting behind us at the football.'

'I didn't make the connection.'

'He didn't threaten you. Nor me, exactly, but I recognised him at Our Price.'

'What were you doing at Our Price?'

'It doesn't matter.'

'Oh. OK. But Redding and Josh Biddle knew each other through the local music scene. We think Josh might be the connection to Alex.'

Daniel thought for a moment. 'But it doesn't make sense, Neil. I know Nathan could not kill someone that way. I don't think Alex could either.'

'There's a difference between know and think.'

Daniel thought about that too. 'There's quite a gap between having a hunch and arresting people on suspicion of murder.'

'Only way we could keep Nathan where we need him. And if we nicked him, we had to nick Alex too. Murder inquiry? Class A drug connection? Not how I wanted it to go, but it's out of my hands. And I'm sorry.'

'What am I supposed to say to Bernard? What sort of relationship will I have with Alex and Nathan when you release them, as you surely will?'

'Are you sure?'

'As sure as someone like me can be.'

'I need to be surer than that.'

Daniel thought how that could have come from Chris Biddle, who needed to be surer than him too. Perhaps it was unacknowledged fundamentalist Christianity that drove Neil too. Then he felt a wave of sadness fall on him, as if he had lost something he had thought he was about to gain.

Neil was looking at him. 'I'm really sorry, Dan. I hope this won't . . . affect things between us?'

Daniel said nothing.

'Well, I must be going. Are you free at all . . . in the . . . week?'

Daniel said, 'Not this week, no.'

And Neil looked sad too. 'OK.'

Daniel went with him to the door.

'How are Hilda and the puppies doing, by the way?'

'All well, thank you.'

'Have you decided what you're going to do with them?'

'Not really. Mum wants to keep them, but I don't see how that would work.'

'I'd take one if I could. But I can't.'

'We must all learn to live with the possible.'

They stood for a moment in silence on the steps. And then another set of headlights appeared in the drive. A Land Rover came to a halt in a slither of gravel. Honoria got out and slammed the door. She stood at the bottom of the steps and just said, 'How could you? How could you?'

Daniel said, 'Honoria . . .'

But she turned and got back into the Land Rover and drove away.

8

The hall table was the place where rectory correspondence lay before being claimed by the recipient or taken
to the post box. Normally the traffic was moderate: for
Audrey, letters from friends so regular, and of such long
standing, that Daniel recognised them from the cancel-
lation stamp; for Daniel, letters from friends too, from
quiet little country parishes to grand royal peculiars,
from Canon Dolben down the road, to mission priests
in the townships round Johannesburg; and there were
letters from people to whom he gave counsel, household bills, communications from the diocese, and from
church organisations to which he had a connection:
the Additional Curates Society, the Prayer Book Society, the Society of the Faith – and St Martin's League,
of which he was secretary and treasurer (and which had
not met since 1902 but nevertheless existed thanks to a
very eccentric but generous High Church cousin of the
benevolent duke who originally funded it to promote
the spiritual and material wellbeing of postmen).

That morning the table was covered in envelopes, half going out, in his mother's hand, addressed neatly in rows, and then a pile coming in, in as many hands as there were envelopes, all to A. H. D. Clement, Secretary, TCS, with no address, but a post office box number in Stow instead. Daniel decided not to arrange them for his mother to pick up after her breakfast but scooped them up – there were more than a dozen, from plain brown little diamond flaps to smart tissue-lined tucks – and brought them to her in the kitchen.

'Mum,' he said, 'quite a delivery from the postman this morning.'

Audrey rather slurped on her second mug of 'déca'. 'Oh, couldn't you leave them on the table, Dan?'

'There are so many – to go as well as delivered. Nearly all for you, and from a post office box number. Is there anything you want to tell me?'

'Why on earth would I want to tell you anything?'

He coughed. 'It's just a bit mysterious, that's all, and people . . . might wonder what it's all about.'

'The postman might, you mean?'

'Anything you can tell me? What is TCS?'

'I could tell you to mind your own business, and perhaps I should, but it is nothing to be mysterious about. It's the correspondence concerning Muriel Hawkins's estate, and it is turning out to be extensive. As you have, typically, noticed.'

'But what is TCS?'

'What does it matter?'

'I don't know, can't you tell me?'

'It stands for Total Co-executrix Services, if you must know.'

'What on earth is that?'

'It is what I provide for people with an interest in Muriel's estate.'

Daniel's eyes narrowed. 'So many?'

'Muriel had lots of friends and lots of interests.' She adopted her magnificent voice. 'Does it surprise you that a widowed woman of riper years might have a full life? It would do you little credit if it did.'

Daniel knew when the matter was closed as far as Audrey was concerned, but silently he vowed vigilance.

'And another thing,' she said, 'I'm going away for the weekend of the eighteenth and nineteenth. Just so you know.'

'Oh, anywhere nice?'

'I am spending the weekend in town. With the girls. If you need me, I will be at the Goring.'

There was a silence. Then Daniel said, 'Have you won the pools?'

'Don't be ridiculous. Or impertinent. But what about you?'

'I have no plans for a splendid weekend in town.'

'I meant for the day.'

'I have Muriel Hawkins's funeral this morning, and Lydia Biddle is coming to see the puppies later.' A thought occurred to him. 'That is, if you haven't sold them?'

'I have not. But they are going to need their vaccinations soon and perhaps you could arrange an appointment with that nice girl, what's her name?'

'It was Dorcas, but she goes by Lizzie now.'

'I bet she does. But I didn't know it was Muriel's funeral today.'

'She wanted something very small and private. And it's not in church, it's at the crem at ten-thirty.'

'Why didn't you tell me?'

'I thought you knew. You've seen the instructions — no fuss, ashes to be scattered in the Garden of Remembrance.'

'I should come.'

'There's no need. Or expectation.'

'I am co-executrix of her estate. I'll come with you.'

'I shall be leaving at a quarter to ten.'

'I shall be ready. And what time is the Biddle girl coming?'

'After school.'

'Don't let her get too close, as they've not had their jabs yet.'

'You make her sound like Typhoid Mary.'

'Better safe than sorry, Dan, with such tiny things. I've picked their names, by the way.'

'Have you?'

'I'm not naming them after those ghastly Wagnerians that sound like *Schweinhund*. Imagine calling that out in the park? No, Nathan for the reddy brown one, the black and tan girl is Bramble after my pudding, and the little one is Muriel.'

'Mum, you cannot call a dog Muriel.'

'I can call them what I bloody well like – and it's Muriel.'

Daniel was surprised by Mrs Hawkins's request that her death be observed with the smallest ceremony, not in the midst of God's holy temple but in the municipal grey of Braunstonbury Crematorium. But she was a tidy woman, as his mother observed, and her instructions were clear and simple. The briefest of services – said, not sung – at the crematorium, no music, no flowers, no notice in the paper, no mourners. In this last item she had been disappointed, for standing to greet her coffin as it came in, borne by Mr Williams's men, was his mother, Miss March, and Roy and Jean Tailby, sitting as far from each other as could decently be managed. All were in black, his mother and Miss March with hat and gloves, dressed, he thought, for St Paul's Cathedral rather than the Walter Butlin chapel, the smaller of the two the council provided for the extinction of its electorate. The coffin went silently onto the catafalque, the organ mute, without the comfortless accomplishment of what undertakers called 'suitable music' lest the congregation hear instead the straining of the bearers, and the scrape of the coffin before it hit the rollers, and distantly, behind the curtain separating front of house from back, the clang of a furnace door.

'Man, that is born of a woman, hath but a short time to live, and is full of misery. He cometh up, and is cut down, like a flower; he fleeth as it were a shadow, and never continueth in one stay . . .'

Mrs Hawkins had asked for the burial service from the Book of Common Prayer, words of antiquity and loveliness, but they soon became unsuitable for a body about to be consigned to flames rather than worms.

'Forasmuch as it hath pleased Almighty God of his great mercy to take unto himself the soul of our dear sister here departed: we therefore commit her body to the ground; earth to earth, ashes to ashes, dust to dust . . .' Daniel pressed the button on the last 'dust', which did two things: first, set in motion the curtain, which began slowly and sombrely to encircle the catafalque; second, alerted the boys on the other side that the next job was almost ready for collection.

'. . . in sure and certain hope of the Resurrection to eternal life, through our Lord Jesus Christ; who shall change our vile body, that it may be like unto his glori-ous body, according to the mighty working, whereby he is able to subdue all things to himself.'

What a job the Lord Jesus Christ would have, he often thought, changing our vile bodies unto his body, glorious, radiant, incorruptible, not lost to time and strife and our own undoing.

Muriel Hawkins's coffin, spattered with holy water from his pocket-sized aspergillum, rolled away to-wards the radiance of the cremator. One of the crem boys told him, half gleefully, that when he looked through the spy hole as the jets of fire were ignited, the sprinkling evaporated in an instant, not water for a soul's refreshment but useless vapour as the flames took hold.

Mr Williams solemnly bowed to the closed curtains with pointless ceremony, and Daniel followed him through an opened side door to the yard outside where floral tributes awaited the inspection of the mourners. On a busy day, as soon as the last mourners had departed via the side door, the main doors opened to admit the next batch of the bereaved, and he remembered when he was a curate pressing not the button to close the curtains, but the one that flashed a light indicating to the awaiting undertaker that the chapel was now vacant and they had filed in, pressed forward by mourners unaware that the catafalque was still occupied.

He waited for the mourners to file out, his mother first, conscious that her status as a co-executrix had earned her principal place in the hierarchy – so conscious, in fact, that she had interposed herself in front of Jean Tailby, who had attempted to assume the role for herself.

'Lovely service, Rector,' said Jean as she manoeuvred her way past Audrey, who had decided to monopolise her son or at least form a human barrier between him and the Tailbys. Once they were both safely blocked and had gone to pretend to look at the flowers – there were no flowers save a bunch of calla lilies with a handwritten card — Miss March appeared in front of him, like mist on an autumn morning.

'It was kind of you to come, Miss March.'

'Of course I came.'

'But how did you know? There was no notice.'

'I checked the lists posted outside.'

'Every day?'

'Yes, every day. And I wasn't the only one.' She indicated the Tailbys, who were now talking to Audrey. Audrey looked at them with the smiling condescension she would use for people on the same ward as her in hospital, people whose company she would not normally endure, though under the circumstances had no choice but to.

'It is not difficult to see why the Tailbys would take the trouble to come to Mrs Hawkins's funeral,' Daniel said.

'No. But why did I?'

'I would not dream of asking.'

Miss March turned away from Daniel and looked towards the Tailbys and Audrey admiring the single bunch of lilies.

'Were they from you?' Daniel asked.

'Yes. I was indebted to Muriel Hawkins, Rector. She was a remarkable woman.'

'She was. I can see that she was very important to you . . . but I don't fully understand why.'

Miss March turned back to him and her grey eyes narrowed. 'Curiosity is a tricky thing. You never know what it will turn up. But I must get back to the shop. Goodbye, Rector, and thank you for doing this.'

'Goodbye, Miss March.'

She went to say goodbye to Audrey, who inclined her head to one side and smiled as they shook hands. Jean Tailby went to do the same, but just got a curt nod.

Mr Williams emerged from the chapel. 'No refreshments to follow, Rector?'

'No, Mr Williams, not so much as a cup of tea. In accordance with her wishes.'

'The Tailbys won't like it. They practically live on funeral meats. But I didn't expect to see Miss March.'

'You know her?'

'Knew her father from the Chamber of Commerce. The shop was like something from Dickens. He was like something from Dickens. I think he liked us because we're like something from Dickens. Can't help but feel sorry for her.'

'Sorry for her? Why?'

'She never got over his death. It was a terrible thing.'

'What happened?'

'Tried to be a good citizen. Some rowdy kids in the street at night outside the shop woke him up, so he shouted at them and they gave him lip. He went downstairs to give them a piece of his mind and one of them hit him and he had a heart attack. Died in the street. We came to pick him up. In his pyjamas and dressing gown – looked like Ebenezer Scrooge.'

'Did they catch the boy who hit him?'

'Don't think so. But she didn't want to carry on without him. Her mother died years ago, so she's on her own. Anyway, she sold the shop and the house is up for sale, I hear. End of an era.'

Daniel thanked him and was about to go when he remembered Josh. 'Any news on the coroner and Joshua Biddle?'

'Body released, I think, but we haven't got him. He's at the mortuary. Another family destroyed though, eh?'

Daniel went to collect his mother. Jean Tailby got in there first. 'Reverend Daniel, a sad day, I'm sorry to say.'

'It is indeed a sad day, Mrs Tailby.'

Roy came over. 'Not much of a funeral, really.'

Daniel bridled. 'In accordance with Mrs Hawkins's wishes.'

'Can't have cost much. The basic package. Are you writing the cheques?'

'I wonder what you mean, Mr Tailby?'

'Don't mean a thing. If it ain't got that swing,' he said.

Jean said, 'Lovely brooch, Mrs Clement. Are those real pearls?'

Audrey smiled her most deadly smile. 'It's a mourning pin, pearls on onyx, set in gold – so charming, don't you think?' She leaned forward so Jean could see it. 'If you were wondering, it was my great-grandmother's. So nice to have things passed down from generation to generation, don't you think, Mrs Tailby? Keep things in the family?'

Jean was not easily cowed. 'I wondered if it was one of Mrs Hawkins's, only she had so many no one would ever know.'

'Each one carefully accounted for, let me assure you. I believe you were particularly interested in the little cameo brooch? Of Hermes? It's going to auction at Reynolds & Reynolds, the Stow branch. I can't re-member when, but I'm sure they can tell you. Good luck with your bid!'

Roy said, 'Come on, Jean, don't give her the satisfaction.'

Audrey continued smiling at their retreat. 'The second-most enjoyable moment today.'

'What's the first?'

'The card with the lilies.'

'From Miss March?'

'Yes. *Kimberley* March. No wonder she insists on Miss . . .'

Since Audrey had taken on the job as co-executrix of Muriel Hawkins's will, life at Champton Rectory had acquired a new pattern. She sat at the bureau in the drawing room after breakfast, with a pile of doc-uments to left and right, and Hilda's whelping box at her feet. Hilda, who gave no sign in her maidenhood of a maternal character, had transformed into the most diligent of mothers, feeding, nuzzling, shepherding the three, whose eyes were beginning to open and were twice the size already. If anyone called or telephoned, Daniel was to say his mother was 'busy with her correspondence' and take a message. And she was indeed busy with her correspondence – letters came and went thickly every day, so many that he wondered if she might be fatigued by the responsibility he had rather dumped on her. But it had the opposite effect; the more she did, the more she wanted to do, and Daniel had been surprised once or twice to hear her through the door singing as she worked – 'The Cobbler's Song' from *Chu Chin Chow*, which had been his shoemaker grandfather's party piece.

> 'The stouter I cobble the less I earn,
> For the soles never crack nor the uppers turn,
> The better my work, the less my pay,
> But work can only be done . . . one . . . wa-a-a-y.'

Daniel, with his critic's ear for song, marvelled that in what was really an untaxing tessitura she managed to go from a shrieking and sharp treble to a rumbling basso in just a few lines. But if Audrey was singing it meant she was contented, and that was pleasing not only for her sake, but for his.

She emerged for elevenses, a cup of tea and perhaps a slice of the everyday cake she made for sustenance rather than delight, to a wartime recipe that required barely any marge, eggs or milk, and came out looking like compressed sawdust. After that, to the village for shopping and gossip, and then back for lunch, eaten in the kitchen, and her nap. Then she would return to the bureau and work until it was time for the six o'clock news on the wireless and *The Archers* just after seven, when she would make supper. Afternoon Bridge with the Porteouses was suspended, trips to town curtailed, 'for', she said, 'the Sisyphean task of sorting out Muriel's affairs comes first'. Daniel thought she must mean Herculean rather than Sisyphean, for there was an end to them, which must, surely, come soon?

The year, too, was ending. October was about to turn into November; autumn was advanced and the trees mostly relieved of the burden they had borne since May. There was a coldness in the morning and evening, a taster for the frosts yet to come, and the smell of woodsmoke and wet leaves made Daniel nostalgic, for the new school year, the summer done. He was in the minority in this, but there were compensations for those who missed the sunshine and the holidays: Bonfire Night for one, with its Guy and pyre and fireworks and toffee apples. For Daniel the Church offered the feasts of All Saints and All Souls, the latter marked with an Evening Prayer for Remembrance instead of Evensong. He had started this and invited to church everyone who had been bereaved in the previous twelve months, originally for a sober and reflective service of prayer, but it had taken off and accretions had occurred: the lighting of candles, which were brought up to the altar by a family member or friend, and – Stella Harper's unnegotiated intervention – the presentation of a bronze chrysanthemum on their return journey to the pew, 'for *remembrance*' she used to say, as if it were an accomplishment rather than a fate.

At four o'clock, when daylight was beginning to dim a little, the Biddles' campervan came up the drive. Daniel opened the door to Sal and Lydia. 'Come in, come in.'

'Thanks, Daniel, I'm just dropping her off.' She noticed the table covered with envelopes. 'Are you having a big do?'

'No, it's my mother's correspondence – abundant correspondence.'

Sal looked puzzled for a moment. 'Oh . . . Are you sure you're OK to bring Lyds back?'

'Yes, of course. But won't you come and see the puppies before you go?'

They stood in the hall while Daniel put his head round the drawing-room door.

'What?' said Audrey.

'Mum, it's Sal and Lydia Biddle. They want to see the puppies.'

'Show them in.'

Lydia almost ran to the whelping box. 'Oh, they're *beautiful*,' she said as the puppies wriggled and wrestled to get in closer to Hilda, who stirred and lifted her head at the interruption. Daniel again thought of the Nativity, that moment of silence when the visitors and the animals are all arranged round the manger looking at a baby and beginning to understand something for the first time.

But not Sal, who stood in the background and seemed uncomfortable. He was about to ask if she wanted to look into the box but realised, with a jarring feeling, that a mother who had lost a child might not want to bill and coo over another who had just had three.

'Can I see you out, Sal?' he said as gently as he could.

She nodded and without saying anything walked away. In the hall she said, 'Thank you for doing this, Daniel. It makes a difference, the small things.'

'Is there anything I can do for you, small or big?'

'I just want him to walk through the door. Like Lazarus. Jesus did it for him, why not for me?'

'I don't know.'

'That's a relief. I am surrounded by people who are absolutely certain of the loving, if mysterious, purposes of God, and far more concerned to assure me of that than ask me how I feel. I think they worry I might not feel so assured and let the side down.'

'That can be . . . very difficult.'

'Yes. Maybe I prefer your way. It's not all done and dusted. Our prayers can make a difference. Josh will be . . .' She faltered. 'It's not our tradition at all and if I try to talk about it to Chris, he just gets . . . well, he can't do it.'

'We have a service on Sunday, for All Souls.'

'What's that?'

'It's the day after All Hallows – sorry, old name for

All Saints — when we commemorate the souls of the
. . . departed.'

'Hallowe'en?'

'No, absolutely not, that's Eve of All Hallows, and
this is the day after. And it's not dressing up as ghosts
and ghouls. It's to remember those we have lost, and to
pray for them, if that's what you want to do. We will
be praying for Josh.'

'I've never heard of it.'

'A casualty of the Reformation, but it came back in
again. Well, for some. It's six o'clock on Sunday.'

Sal looked troubled for a moment, then she sighed.
'I can't, Daniel. I just can't,' and before he could say
anything she had gone.

In the drawing room Audrey was explaining the
elements of dog midwifery to Lydia.

'Their eyes are open, but they're not really *seeing*,
Lydia, or not yet. The world, which is basically Hilda's
teats at the moment, or rather her milk, is only just
beginning to open up. And soon they will have their
jabs, and then we can introduce them to the parish.'

'Are you going to keep them?'

Audrey glanced at Daniel. 'Not quite decided yet,
dear.'

'If you want homes for them, please, please let me
take one.'

'Well, not decided, Lydia . . . and that would of
course be up to your mother and father . . .'

One of the puppies started making the mewing noise

they made when they were hungry and that made the others join in too. Hilda shifted to give them more room to suckle and then settled again.

'So cute!' said Lydia. 'How long before they start to eat solid food?'

'They're starting now, morsels, eating some of Hilda's food, and drinking from her water bowl. And that means we have to train them to go to the lavatory on the newspaper.'

'The *Daily Telegraph*, I hope,' said Lydia.

'Why don't I make some tea and find some cake?'

Daniel sat and watched Lydia become completely absorbed in the playfulness and purposefulness of the puppies. She reminded him of his brother, Theo, who as a child had the same capacity to become completely fascinated by something he found on his toddling excursions round the back garden. He would suddenly squat and watch with unblinking fascination a leaf of clover, a raindrop like a jewel, snails mating with all the passionate urgency of an archdeacon granting a faculty.

Was Theo aware of what had happened? How awkward it would be for him, as Daniel's brother but also Alex's and Honoria's friend – a friendship that had a life of its own in London, separate from their Champton friendship. And, Daniel thought with faint alarm, how much Theo would enjoy the drama.

At least Alex was now at liberty, obliged to endure only a single night in the cells. He had been released without charge the next morning when Bernard's solicitor from Braunstonbury had come to collect him. At first, he had refused to go without Nathan, but Nathan was not so fortunate, and for him the wheels of justice had further to grind. Bernard had shouted at Alex when he'd arrived back at Champton and been taken not to his lodge at the gates but to the offices at the back of the main house, where his father was waiting to see him. 'Are you going to actually horse-whip me, Daddy?' he had said, according to Mrs Shorely, who had told Mrs Braines, who had told Audrey. Daniel had called round to the lodge later, but there had been no reply to the knock on the door, and no reply to the note he left either. When he'd got home there had been a note for him too, from Neil – 'SORRY, CALL ME' – but he had not called him; and that night in Champton Rectory and Champton Lodge and Braunstonbury Police Station and its Custody Suite the protagonists in that drama had sat solitary vigils.

After an hour of raptures, and refreshments, and reflections, Daniel said it was time to take Lydia home. Cosmo came along for the ride, sitting on her lap and letting her stroke his ears as Daniel drove even more slowly than usual along the darkening lanes.

'You can come whenever you want, Lydia,' he said. 'When they're older you can take them out for walks if you like.'

'I'd love to.' She was suddenly silent. Then she said, 'If I can. I don't know what we're going to do, Daniel.'

'What you are going to do?'

'If we'll stay. I don't think Mum could stand it.'

'And your father?'

She was silent again. 'I don't know what Dad wants. He's very . . . He doesn't talk about how he feels. Mum says he can't.'

'Not everyone can.'

'But he shouldn't bottle things up. It'll do his head in.'

'Some people cope better by not talking about things.'

'And I think he feels guilty.'

'Why?'

'Because he and Josh used to argue so much. And now he can't do anything about it.'

'Parents and children always argue, Lydia.'

'But this wasn't like normal arguments. This was . . . *biblical*.'

'Like David and Absalom?'

'No, it was *about* the Bible. When Dad quoted a Scripture at Josh when he was angry with him − usually that bit in Ephesians that goes on about honouring your father and mother and servants and masters . . .'

'Ephesians six.'

'. . . yes, that, and Josh would quote one back, one of the crazy verses from Deuteronomy about castration and mixed fibres. It drove Dad mad.'

'What happened then?'

'Mum would calm him down.'

'When your father's angry . . . does he talk to your mother?'

'I don't know. He's very' – she looked for an expression – 'buttoned up. But that's his background.'

'He seems so open.'

'No, he's not. But he was sent away to boarding school when he was seven. And I think they all buried their emotions, and then when he was older he was beaten at Eton. It was vicious then.'

'Eton?' said Daniel, surprised.

'I know. His mother's family is posh and they paid for it. He hates the public school system now.'

'I was at boarding school too,' said Daniel. 'Not one as grand as Eton, but even I got beaten.'

'You?'

'Yes.'

'What for?'

'Nothing. I took the blame for something I did not do to protect someone else.'

Daniel remembered then the violence of that beating. And how he had tried not to cry but the tears still came to his eyes, and the glass of sherry the master who had beaten him insisted he have with him after the punishment, and how he had sat on smarting buttocks drinking this horrible drink and wondering if he was bleeding and if it would stain the cushions.

'It wasn't the same for Dad. He was part of a Christian organisation at school and they went away to summer camp, and there was someone there who ran the camp

. . . I don't know the whole story, but I think he really hurt Dad. Not just Dad – there were other boys.'

'How awful.'

'No one did anything about it. I don't know if he even told his parents.'

Daniel thought of his own school, and the odd sadist who liked to hurt little boys, and those who liked little boys too much, and unexplained absences from the Senior Common Room at the beginning of term, and the omertà of masters.

They drove in silence for a while. Then suddenly there was a whizz and a bang and a burst of light. Daniel glanced at Lydia and saw there were tears on her cheeks. 'Early Bonfire Night for somebody,' he said.

Cosmo shifted on her lap and let out a sound between a gurgle and a sigh.

When Daniel dropped Lydia off at the vicarage he did not expect to call in. He normally would, to see how the bereaved were doing, but he hesitated with Chris because the conversation so easily turned to theological disagreement, which was notoriously potent between religious professionals. It even had a name – *odium theologicum* – and Daniel felt it rise behind the faint but unworthy triumph of discovering that Chris, so earnest, so virtuous, was a beneficiary of the very privilege he deplored. How he would enjoy telling Bernard that the man 'in overalls of Lincoln green' was also an Old Etonian.

He was thinking about this when Sal tapped on his window. 'Hello, Daniel,' she said as he wound the window down. 'What are you smiling about?'

'Nothing,' he said, 'nothing in particular.'

'I like to see people smiling,' she said, 'but perhaps it doesn't become a grieving mother. Would you like to come in?'

'No, thank you,' he said, 'unless you want me?'

Sal didn't move. 'You've been good to Lydia, thank you. I just wonder . . . if she has said anything I might . . . need to know?'

'No, I don't think so. She may be a bit anxious about the future. Where you're going to go. What you're going to do.'

'I don't suppose we will stay here. You see that?'

'Yes.'

'It's not just about what's happened, Dan. It's about who we are. And how that fits here. I don't think it does fit here.'

'You would know better than me, and forgive me for talking shop, but you have barely arrived and your life has been brutally wrenched out of shape. People always say not to take big decisions when you are in the pit of bereavement.'

'The pit. That's good. We are deep in the pit.'

'But not lost to it.' He thought of the little card showing the anastasis in his wallet, and Jesus yanking out of the pit the souls thought lost. 'Sal, we talk a lot about Chris's ministry, but not about yours. I wanted you to know how much I value it, and how much I am looking forward to your priestly ministry, too, when the old order finally gives way to the new.'

'Priestly?'

'Yes, when you're priested. It's coming.'

'No, it isn't.'

'I think it will come. Five years maybe?'

'Not for me. I don't want to be a priest. I can't be a priest.'

'Why ever not?'

'Because it is not biblical.'

'Oh, I see. I assumed you were . . . on the way.'

'No. Headship is for men, not women. One Timothy – I'm sure you know the text: "I do not permit a woman to teach or to have authority over a man." And I can make myself useful doing what I do.'

'You look like you're in authority when you do it.'

She gave a little grimace. Then she said, 'Have you ever noticed how things fall apart when we go against God?'

'I have. But I don't think women in authority go against God.'

Sal said nothing for a moment. Then she said, 'How is your mother?'

Daniel did not know what to say for a moment. 'She's fine. She's busy – puppies, Mrs Hawkins's estate.'

'Tell her . . . God is our judge.'

'I don't think I understand.'

But Sal was walking away.

★

When Daniel arrived home he found, parked in its usual spot in the rectory drive, his brother's gunmetal-grey Golf GTI. The sound of the front door opening brought Theo from the drawing room with Cosmo scampering after him. As Daniel squatted to greet the dog Theo said, 'Oh, hello, Dan. Isn't he a good boy, and a clever boy, becoming a father . . .?'

'Not Cosmo's work, Theo,' said Daniel.

'Really? Then whose?'

'Your friend's. His dog's, I mean – Siegfried, that black-and-tan you brought to stay when I took Mum to Scotland.'

'Don't think so, Dan. In fact, it would be impossible. Siegfried had the snip.'

'Are you sure?'

'I think so. Why are you so sure it's not Cosmo?'

'Same reason. He could not, although the procedure has done nothing to cool his ardour.'

'So I see,' said Theo as Cosmo rolled onto his back, presenting unmistakable signs of arousal. 'I hope you won't be asking for child support?'

Audrey appeared from the kitchen. 'How long are you staying?'

'As long as it takes, Mum, or maybe just tonight.'

'As long as what takes?' asked Daniel.

'I am here on a mission of reconciliation!'

Daniel's eyes narrowed.

'I have come to make peace between you and Alex

and Honoria and Neil and Nathan and anyone else who needs it.' He put on a Mrs Thatcher voice: 'Where there is discord, let me bring harmony, where there is error let me bring truth . . .'

Daniel said with obvious sharpness, 'I would rather you didn't.'

Theo looked surprised. 'Why? What's the problem?'

'Please don't interfere, Theo. It's delicate and it's complicated and sometimes people need to let things settle before they try to put right what's gone wrong.' His voice faltered – not much, but enough for Theo to notice.

He was silent for a moment and then he said, 'Dan, are you OK?'

'I'm absolutely fine. I just don't want anyone meddling in this.'

'Oh dear,' said Theo.

'What do you mean, "oh dear"?'

'I've sort of already meddled in it.'

'How?'

'Honoria called me. Told me the whole story. I'm going round to the lodge later for supper with her and Alex.'

'Why? How?'

'I am allowed to have my *own* relationship with Honoria and Alex and—'

'But that doesn't give you the right to get involved!'

'It's not about rights, Dan. I'm your brother. I'm their friend. I stand with a foot in Champton and the other in Soho. They're London friends as well as friends from here. Who better to talk to them? The sooner we get this going the better.'

'He thinks I betrayed his lover to the police when I promised I wouldn't. You think you can fix that over a fish pie and a Chenin Blanc?'

'Let your brother do something for you. For once,' said Audrey.

'I'm not completely stupid, Dan. I'm just going to find out . . . very gently, very carefully . . . what they're thinking. You don't think it would be good to try to re-establish normal relations? And remember, Bonfire Night is coming up and you're going to have to make nice for that.'

'I don't think you understand how tricky this is. There may be more to come. I don't know. And I don't want to begin to make things better only for them to fall apart again. It's a murder inquiry, Theo, anything can happen. Don't you remember from last time?'

'But we all know Alex didn't do it. Nor Nathan!'

'I'm not saying they did. I am saying there's an investigation and that has to be conducted without fear or favour, and that can conflict with . . . personal matters.'

Audrey said, 'Is this because of your policeman?'

'He's not *my* policeman, and . . . yes, it is awkward because Neil and I have become friends.'

'Friends?' said Audrey. 'You're practically Morecambe and Wise.'

'I got Nathan to come to the rectory to talk to Neil, who turned up with two uniformed officers and arrested both of them.'

'Yes, I heard,' said Theo. 'How mean of Neil.'

'Between arranging it with me and arresting them, Neil discovered some evidence, which changed things. He didn't tell me because, I suppose, he knew I would not go along with it, and he couldn't risk losing his chance to question them.'

'What was the evidence?'

'I can't say, but it wasn't enough to detain Alex. I don't see how it can be enough to detain Nathan. But it looks like I deceived them.'

'It was your policeman who deceived them. And deceived you.'

'Yes, in a way.'

'What does he have to say about it?'

'We haven't spoken. He left me a note. Apologising. But I haven't replied.'

'It's not like you, Daniel, to be slow to forgive.'

'Forgiveness isn't the problem. It's how to discharge our responsibilities properly that is the problem.'

'Oh, that's one of our storylines in *Clerical and Medical*. Turf wars between the vicar and the doctor.'

'That's a television drama, Theo, it's not real. And if it were, they are both pastoral roles. Neil's role is not pastoral.'

'I see. What are you going to do?'

Daniel said nothing.

326

Then another pair of headlights appeared in the drive and a car came to a halt on the other side of the steps from Daniel's Land Rover and Theo's Golf.

'Blimey, is this the copper, right on cue?' said Theo, but Audrey said, 'No, it's Miss March in her Van der Valk.'

Daniel opened the door as she approached. 'Miss March, we saw you arrive.'

She looked slightly ambushed, but she often did. 'Rector. I see I am interrupting something. Mrs Clement.' She nodded.

'Good evening, Miss March. This is Daniel's brother, Theo.'

'Good evening, but I think we have met?'

'I don't think so,' said Theo, shaking her hand. 'Are you new in the parish?'

'Fairly new,' she said. 'But I recognise you, I think, from the television. Aren't you PC Heseltine from *Appletree End*?'

'Indeed, I am,' said Theo, in the courtly way he used when accepting a compliment, but it was followed by silence from Miss March.

'What an extraordinarily talented family you are,' she said eventually. 'I wonder if someone might distract the dog?'

Cosmo was sniffing her shoes with the scent hound's intense concentration, so Theo picked him up and tucked him under his arm in the hold miniature dachshunds seem designed for especially.

Daniel said, 'What can I do for you, Miss March?'

'I am sorry', she said, 'to call without an appointment, but I really need to see your mother.'

'Me?' said Audrey.

'If you could spare me a few minutes?'

'Of course. Why don't you come into the drawing room?'

'Thank you,' she said. Daniel took her hat and coat – 'Thank you, Rector. Mr Clement,' she nodded again at Theo, and Audrey ushered her behind the door, which she closed. Cosmo wriggled in Theo's arm.

'Blimey,' said Theo, 'who is Miss March?'

'She keeps the dress shop in the village.'

'Stella's High Class Ladies' Fashion?'

'It's now called Elite Fashions. She's from Stow. Her father kept the shoe shop near the cathedral. I took you there once.'

'Oh, yes, wonderful shop, like going back in time but in a good way. I bought a gorgeous pair of Derby boots. Didn't you say they used to take ours?'

'They did. Her father knew our father. She told me he had a pair of brown Oxfords of ours made in the Fifties, which he was still wearing when he died.'

'She looks like she's just stepped out of the 1950s too.'

'Yes, she must have settled on a way of presenting herself to the world and never felt the need to revise it.'

'That's very C of E.'

'We are the natural habitat of the nostalgist. Or at least

that's what nostalgists think. Only we're not, and when they discover that they get disappointed and spend the rest of their lives complaining about everything.'

Theo thought about this for a moment. 'That's interesting . . . I felt like that sometimes when I was at the RSC. That audiences came because they thought we were the custodians of an ancient tradition, a priesthood almost, but that's not what we thought we were doing.'

'What did you think you were doing?'

'Exploring the possibilities of now.'

'Now?'

'You know, Coriolanus in Brutus jeans and Ariel on a hang-glider, but . . . if it doesn't connect with something real, what's the point?'

Daniel wondered what it would be like for once to see a production of *The Tempest* or *The Rhinegold* that didn't attempt to connect with something real.

Daniel's mental excursion was interrupted by the sound of disagreement coming, rather surprisingly, from behind the drawing-room door.

Audrey and Miss March were having an argument – not the passive-aggressive exchange of ambiguous pleasantries that Audrey normally enjoyed, but direct, and explicit, and loud. Daniel and Theo were so surprised they did not know what to do, but then the door swung open and Miss March appeared with two patches of rose blooming on her grey face, as if someone had slapped Whistler's mother.

'My hat and coat, please, Rector,' she said, her voice shaky with anger.

'Oh dear, what's happened?'

She fixed him with a look. 'It is no matter,' she said and almost snatched her things from his hands.

'Mr Clement,' she said to Theo. 'Rector.' And she went.

Audrey poked her head round the drawing-room door. 'Has she gone?'

The sound of the Vanden Plas skidding on the gravel told her that she had.

'What an unusually quick temper that woman has. It's like porridge exploding.'

'But why?'

'Business matters.'

'What sort of business matters?'

'Mind your own business matters.' And she went back into the drawing room, closing the door behind her.

'This is very peculiar,' said Daniel. 'And someone just asked me to remind Mum that God is our judge.'

'What an odd thing to say. Even for vicars.'

'This was not a vicar, exactly.'

'This reminds me of last year,' said Theo.

'How do you mean?'

'Everyone short-tempered and anxious. I suppose it's because there's a murderer on the loose. There must be a sort of mechanism for self-preservation programmed into the herd or something.'

He was right, thought Daniel; the murders at first caused shock and excitement, but in time there were other effects that began to appear, like a damp patch after the rainstorm has passed.

'I must go, Dan. Supper. Do you have a bottle of wine I can take?'

'Take one from the pantry fridge. Not an oaky Chardonnay.'

'Oh, is Alex picky?'

'Alex's taste is more for a Chablis. But I don't think we have any of that.'

'Then I shall be the wine of amity and reconciliation and all things fine.'

'If you could try not to make things worse.'

'I think you could feel more optimistic, Dan. They wouldn't have me round if it were a permafrost.'

9

You might think that someone like Daniel, a war baby, would have an aversion to bangs and flashes, but he did not. He sometimes thought his earliest memory, though he could not possibly have remembered it, was a red sky to the east of Braunstonbury as Norwich burnt in the Baedeker Blitz. It was his mother's memory, so vivid as she looked anxiously out of the nursery windows at Grey Gables, that it had gone into him in the womb. Audrey, like many who had seen bombs and fire and their terrible effects, hated bangs and flashes, and Bonfire Night for her was almost as traumatic as it was for the dogs. Every year she would stay in with Hilda and Cosmo, their basket moved for one night into her drawing room. She would tune the television to *Juliet Bravo* and turn it up to try to mask the exploding rockets and traffic lights and jumping jacks and bangers from the village bonfire, which Daniel was obliged to attend *ex officio*.

Daniel liked fireworks. Their power to cast light on

unexpected landscapes, to burst in a shower of red and gold sparks, to leave a pungent odour in the frosty air was entertainment indeed for someone of High Church sensibility, and a bonfire, were it merely for warmth and light and toffee apples and sparklers, would instantly make him feel *en fête*. But it was a bonfire – originally bone fire – commemorating not a cheery celebration of light in darkness, but the burning of heretics; he could not enjoy that, especially when it culminated in the burning of a Roman Catholic in effigy, Guy Fawkes, paraded around towns and villages on a barrow before being fixed to the top of the pyre.

It was one of the main festivals in Champton's year, and had been for as long as anyone could remember. The de Floures were always for the king rather than any rival authority, and in church one of the most enthusiastic congregations of the year was for the old Service of Prayer with Thanksgiving, 'to be used yearly upon the Fifth day of November; for the happy deliverance of King James I and the three Estates of England, from the most Traiterous and bloody-intended Massacre by Gunpowder'.

That was no longer in the Prayer Book, but the popular celebration endured and every year, on the nearest Friday (Friday, he supposed, because of the association with the Crucifixion), there was a bonfire in the park, lit by Bernard, built by the Bonfire Committee, which also arranged a fireworks display and suitable refreshments. The committee had been chaired, extremely effectively, by Ned Thwaite, but he had been murdered by Kath Sharman and there were no obvious successors and scant enthusiasm for a job that demanded much and returned little. In a flash of inspiration, or desperation, Daniel had asked Alex if he would take it on, shrewdly predicting that he would find such a spectacle irresistible, and he had said yes. The bonfire would be a triumph, the fireworks extraordinary, but the orderly administration of the parking and the toffee apples and the St John Ambulance was less sure, so they had been taken on, under protest, by Nicholas Meldrum, the estate manager, who had passed the operational responsibilities on to Bob Achurch.

Daniel was in the hall, in his second-best cassock, which he reserved for Bonfire Night, pet blessings and the long procession at Walsingham, over which he was wearing the floor-length black Melton cloak that had been given to him by a now-deceased canon of Stow, making Daniel the fifth canon of Stow to wear it. He was putting on his wellingtons, not the smart green kind but the serviceable black kind, which all the farmers round here wore, with turned-down tops to make them easier, he assumed, to take on and off, though it was actually to stop them flapping against the calves in an unpleasant way, which had an unfortunate depilatory effect. Then he felt a little peak of anxiety, for it was wellingtons that had caused his unintended betrayal of Nathan, and tonight Alex and Honoria would be on their first public outing since the arrests.

Daniel was, for once, grateful for his brother's interference. He had returned from supper at the lodge with moderately good news. Alex, perhaps anticipating too the forced detente for Bonfire Night, had indicated a willingness to resume civilities. Honoria had been harder to persuade, but with her years of experience in reconciling difficult families for wedding receptions, she was competent in behaving *toujours* with *la politesse*. Daniel had then felt able to telephone Alex and invite him to elevenses, often the most propitious opportunity, he had discovered, to effect reconciliation; not too early for slow starters, but preceding luncheon drinks, which could provoke ignoble impulses. Alex had come. There was stiffness; there was halting conversation; Audrey had appeared during a silence she had detected from just outside the study door with a tray of coffee and some out-of-date United biscuits disrobed of their wrappers. The intervention was beautifully judged, arriving in one of those silent tipping points in a difficult conversation that could go either way; the indulgence of refreshments nudged it down the way of peace and friendship. Alex was not ready to forgive yet, but he saw that Daniel had been more sinned against than sinning, thanks to the perfidy of Neil Vanloo, and in time, if he perhaps tried to be less innocent of the ways of men, then the cordiality of the past might be restored. This summary was Daniel's to his mother; Alex's actual words were briefer, more direct and grainier, and for Daniel one of the brief moments when he saw Bernard in his second son.

'Dan, have you gone yet?' – his mother's voice came from the drawing room.

'Not yet, I'm just putting on my wellies. Do you want something?'

'Would you mind?'

He pulled on the second wellington and put his head round the drawing-room door. 'What is it? Only I need to get going.'

'The puppies.'

'What about them?'

'Do you think they will be all right in the blitzkrieg?'

'I don't know. I would put their bed in the knee hole under the bureau; they should feel safe there. You remember how Hilda was last year?'

'She cowered, poor thing, but I expect her maternal instinct is stronger than a few whizz bangs. Mine were as the bombs fell on poor Norwich.'

'A hundred miles away, Mum.'

'And the doodlebugs.'

'Not over Braunstonbury.'

'Over *London*. And you try a bloody Blitz and see how you like it.'

'I must go.'

'Hope it goes well with Alex and Honoria!'

'Thank you.'

'And bring me some of Jane Thwaite's parkin!'

It was dark and cold outside, and the wind rustling through the trees sounded like distant trains. The smell of woodsmoke was in the air, from the fire now burning in the drawing-room grate, anticipating the bonfire that was soon to be lit.

Daniel walked through the park to the house, where the spectacle took place on the grassy field that went beyond the ha-ha separating garden from park and the lake beyond. Guests at the house had the option to join the melee round the bonfire or watch from the terrace outside the west wing. This had the advantage of not only the reflective properties of the lake when the fire was roaring and the fireworks were bursting, but also of refreshments made in a proper kitchen rather than roasted imperfectly on barbecues, so the spectacle was amplified and the risk of food poisoning reduced.

Some preferred to be part of the crowd, gathering from Champton and the surrounding villages and from Braunstonbury. Daniel could see the headlights of cars being parked in the next field, and then the erratic swing of hand-held torches as people made their way towards the unlit bonfire, and then the tiny bright spurts of sparklers, darting like fireflies, anticipating the pyrotechnics to come.

Mr Meldrum had organised a beer and cider bar made out of trestle tables, corralled by a pair of burger vans from Stow. The smell of hot grease and onions blew towards Daniel as the wind changed direction; not too much wind, he hoped, for the bonfire was large and Alex's enthusiasm for heaping it high did not encourage confidence in its structural integrity.

337

There was a group of boys and girls, teenagers or not much older, who were sharing cans of lager and drinking from a bottle. If they were village kids, should he say something? He thought probably not. At first it was too dark to make out who they were, but then two of them lit sparklers and in the bright-white light he saw that some were Goth kids from Braunstonbury, and the boy with the bottle was Brandon Redding. He looked quite Goth himself, thought Daniel, like a cowled monk, until he saw it was a hooded sweatshirt. One of the kids was waving the sparkler around and making the others laugh. Daniel could not see why, and then he worked out in mirror writing that he was spelling the word 'tits'. Then Brandon saw Daniel.

'Eyup, Vicar,' he said.

'It's Brandon, I think?'

'You remember me from the shop?'

'I do.'

'And from the football?'

'I remember that too.'

'Do you want a drink?' He offered Daniel the bottle.

'What is it?'

'Vodka.'

'I'm all right. Should you be sharing that with these kids, Brandon?'

'Why not?'

'They're not old enough to drink, and you should know better.'

'You can't tell me what to do . . .'

'I'm not. I'm asking you a question.'

Another sparkler flared up and all the kids seemed bewitched by its light. A girl made patterns with hers, garlands and spirals that burnt so brightly and so briefly that when they faded they left a ghost image on the retina.

'It's not only vodka I've been sharing, Vicar,' said Brandon, who leaned into him in a way that was both confidential and menacing.

'What else?' he said in as level a voice as he could muster. There was something very unnerving about this man.

Brandon leaned in nearer, so close that Daniel could feel his hot breath on his ear and smell the vodka on his breath, and said, 'We've done magic mushrooms. Do you know what they are?'

'I don't.'

'Liberty caps, little mushrooms, pointy little bonnet on them, grow in the fields round here in the autumn, famous as a natural source of psilocybin.'

'I don't know what that is.'

'It's a hallucinogen. It makes the world go psychedelic, Vicar, and it makes us go psychedelic as well.'

'A hallucinogenic drug?'

'It's a mushroom — all natural, nothing illegal. It was taken by the Aztecs in their religious ceremonies. Maybe you should try it in church on Sunday?'

'Why would I do that, Brandon?'

'Because it would be fucking mental.'

He started laughing and then began to move around Daniel in a way that was half dancer, half boxer. 'Do you like dancing, Vicar?'

'No.'

'Dance with me. Let your hair down.' The kids were watching him now.

'I don't want to dance with you, Brandon,' said Daniel, backing away.

'Just a little dance. I think you'd like it, I think you really would.'

One of the kids laughed.

'I would not. I do have a question for you, Brandon.'

'Fire away.'

'Is Lydia Biddle with you?'

'She was.'

'Where is she now?'

Brandon waved the bottle at the crowd. 'Somewhere here.'

'You left her to it?'

'She left us to it. The mushrooms. Not her cup of tea.'

'But you offered?'

'She's not a kid. She can make her own choices.'

'She's sixteen. Legally a child. Maybe you could leave her alone?'

Brandon pushed his face into Daniel's. 'Maybe you could fuck off?' he said.

Daniel walked away.

'Say a little prayer for me, Vicar,' Brandon said as he went. His friends laughed.

Daniel made his way through the thickening crowd. He could not see Lydia anywhere, but it was hard to pick out a Goth in a crowd on Bonfire Night, and when he saw Bernard standing on a dais at the edge of the crowd he remembered he had a job to do. Honoria and Alex and Theo were on the dais too, sharing a flask of something stronger than beer or cider. Hugh and Michelle were standing slightly apart from them.

Daniel went to greet them first. 'Hello,' he said, 'you're doing rather well for our quaint customs.'

'Oh, this is great,' said Michelle. 'I love fireworks. And Bernard asked me to light the bonfire . . .'

'That's a very great honour.'

'. . . but I volunteered you.'

'Me?'

'Yes. Hugh felt a little uncomfortable about me being on parade.'

'Oh, I see. But why me?'

'Isn't it a religious thing?'

'Not now. It was, but not now. It's rather jarring to modern sensibilities. The anti-Catholic sentiments. Burning effigies. At Lewes, a little town in Sussex, there's a famous bonfire celebration with parades and they burn the pope himself in effigy.'

'That seems a little . . . medieval.'

'Not really. Early modern. And the plotters we

commemorate weren't burnt, they were hanged, drawn and quartered.'

'Progress.'

'An update, perhaps.'

'Interesting.' She looked thoughtful. 'We're off next week, Daniel. Back to the New World. Can we come and see you before we go? We have some wedding questions.'

'Yes, of course. Monday? Tea? Elevenses?'

'Tea, I think. When is that?'

'At four?'

Michelle turned to Hugh and said something. He nodded. 'See you at four on Monday.'

Daniel braced himself and went to say hello to Alex and Honoria.

'Hello, Daniel,' said Alex. 'Ready for this?'

He wasn't sure what he meant for a moment. 'Alex, Honoria . . .' She gave him a nod. 'Ready for what?'

'Lighting the bonfire.'

'Isn't that your father's job?'

'He'll do the speech, but he's delegated the actual lighting to you.'

'Are you sure?'

Bernard was talking to Bob Achurch, who was in charge of the Tannoy system – two little steel horns on a pole connected to an amplifier connected to a small generator. It looked like something from a First World War airfield. Daniel touched Bernard's arm and said, 'Bernard, am I supposed to light this thing?'

'I'll give the speech, then when I give the count-down you light the bonfire. It's what Michelle wants. And it saves me having to arse around with that.' Bob was holding a stick with a petrol-soaked rag wrapped round the end.

'All right. Bob, what do I do?'

'Stand next to me and I'll light this when he starts the countdown, then you take it to the fire and you'll see we've made a gap. Stick the torch in there and back off. It'll catch straight away; we've made sure of that.'

'Is it safe?'

'Unless you're an idiot, I'd say so.'

Bernard looked at his watch. 'It's seven o'clock, so let's get on with it, Achurch.'

'Yes m'lord.'

Daniel followed Bob to the edge of the dais, where he turned some knobs on the amplifier and then gave Bernard a nod.

'A very good evening to you all,' he said, and waited for the crowd noise to subside. 'A very good evening . . . A VERY GOOD EVENING TO YOU ALL . . . We meet again on Guy Fawkes Day to mark, and to celebrate, the deliverance of the king from the hands of those who would overthrow the throne, our parlia-ment, and our way of life. The plotters came to their deserved fate, as may all enemies of England and of our Sovereign Lady, Queen Elizabeth, today!'

He's drunk, Daniel thought as he joined in the applause.

343

'Let us never forget that those enemies rise today, but they will fall also – not far from here, in East Germany, and in Hungary and in Peking, socialist tyrants hold sway over their people, and if it were up to me it would be the effigies of Herr Honecker and Chairman what's-his-name, and that awful Polish general Kowalski, or whatever it is, who would be sitting on top of our pyre . . . May they this night quake and tremble as people . . . join hands . . . and light bonfires . . . as we do today . . . to celebrate the freedoms we all too easily – *all too easily* – take for granted. Champton has stood up to tyranny throughout its long history, and stands, too, for loyalty to the Crown, and so I say three cheers for Her Majesty Queen Elizabeth the Second! Hip-hip . . .'

The hoorays were half-hearted, not for any lack of sincerity, but from wondering what his lordship was going to say next.

'And so, it gives me great pleasure to invite the rector to light the bonfire . . .'

Honoria whispered something to him.

'Oh, but before he does that, let me thank everyone who has worked so hard to make this evening such a success, in the house, in the village, and . . . so on. But now – Rector, let there be light!'

Bob Achurch held his Zippo lighter to the fuel-soaked rags, which ignited with a whoomph that nearly took off Daniel's eyebrows.

'Ten!' said Bernard.

344

'NINE!' answered the crowd, and Daniel carried the flaming torch to the bonfire. I hope all the hedgehogs have escaped, he thought.

'EIGHT! . . . SEVEN! . . . SIX! . . .'

He saw Brandon Redding in the crowd blinking as if he could not believe his eyes.

'FIVE! . . . FOUR! . . .'

There was the gap at the base of the pile of old pallets and offcuts and junk.

'THREE! . . . TWO! . . . ONE! . . .'

To the sound of cheers, he thrust the torch into the gap and immediately a ball of bright-orange flames burst inside the stack. He turned and felt the heat on the back of his neck as the fire caught hold. There was a gust of wind and he saw everyone on the dais looking up as the flames suddenly began to climb, and then there was another, far bigger whoomph, and the whole stack was ablaze.

Then the crowd, instead of a cheer, made a noise like a gasp. Daniel looked up and saw, perched on top of the bonfire, lit from below, an effigy not of Guy Fawkes, but of another unmistakable figure, dressed in a coat and a crocheted hat, and sitting in the same attentive pose as in church and in the mural at the old bath house, before she set fire to it, and burnt to death in it, after murdering three of their neighbours last year.

It was an effigy of Kath Sharman.

Daniel was speechless.

Bernard looked angrily at his son. 'Alex, what the hell are you playing at?'

Alex, even angrier, said, '*That's* what a fucking murderer looks like.'

Bernard stormed off as the effigy of Kath Sharman burnt. Some began to cheer, others looked away. Michelle and Hugh looked embarrassed. Honoria was giving Alex a dressing-down. Bob Achurch started the fireworks and soon there were oohs and aahs as the big rockets exploded overhead and the traffic lights popped in red and amber and green and the Catherine wheels whistled and span – another horrible martyrdom commemorated, Daniel thought.

Daniel went to the refreshment tables. Dora Sharman was on the toffee apples, but people would have to wait for theirs because she was staring at the bonfire.

'Dora . . .'

'Was this Mr Alex's idea?'

'I think it was.'

'I thought so. Why would he do that?'

'To make a point, Dora.'

'He never thinks about what others feel.'

The effigy of her sister collapsed into the fire and a plume of red sparks went into the air.

'I suppose that's what lots of people want, Kath burning again, or burning forever, in hell.'

Daniel saw that there were tears in her eyes, picked out by the red of the now-dwindling fire. 'Some, Dora.

Not lots. People are on the whole more generous than we expect,' he said, not adding Dr Johnson's qualification, 'but less kind'.

'Do you think she's burning in hell?'

'I don't think so, no. How could anyone blame Kath beyond any hope of redemption when they knew what she had suffered? And the state of her mind?'

'You're a gentle soul, Rector. In the past she would have had hellfire.'

'There's a saint I'm rather fond of, Dora – not one of ours, but of the Eastern Church – Cyril of Jerusalem. He lived in the fourth century in a time of great trouble and peril, but he said – I paraphrase – "Our wounds surpass not the great physician's skill." If we tell God what ails us, we will be healed. And saved. No matter what we've done. I think Kath knew what ailed her. That's why she died like she did. And I am sure she is beyond the reach of flames now.'

Dora wiped her eyes. 'Smokey, ennit, with the bonfire.'

He stood and watched the end of the display, which rose in a crescendo as rockets fired in salvoes exploded into starbursts in the black night sky, reflected in the black waters of the lake.

'Ooh! Aah!' they went, and then he saw among the red and yellow and green and white a flash of bright blue, and then another, and another, and distantly the sound of a siren.

In the kaleidoscope of colours faces froze, captured

for a split second in the bursts of light. There was Dora, the jewel-bright tears still in the corners of her eyes; there was Brandon Redding, who seemed to have his own personal kaleidoscope happening as well as everyone else's; there were Alex and Honoria de Floures, who seemed to be having their own fireworks; and there was Neil Vanloo, rushing towards him in the strobing freeze-frame of the bursting rockets.

'Daniel, you need to come with me.'

'Why?'

'Your rectory is on fire.'

IO

Two fire engines and an ambulance were parked in the drive – untidily, was Daniel's first thought, blocking in the Land Rover and Theo's Golf. Figures in the bright-yellow trousers and helmets of the fire brigade were walking in and out of the house, which looked as though a small but dirty explosion had blown open its doors and windows. Daniel gulped to see it, but then noticed that the firemen were working without urgency, and the hoses connected to the appliances lay on the gravel like sleeping serpents.

'Looks worse than it is, Daniel,' said Neil.

'The ambulance?'

'Precautionary. They're looking after your mother and Miss March.'

'Miss March?'

'You're surprised?'

'She and my mother had an argument a few days ago. I don't know why.' Daniel had a sudden thought. 'What about the puppies? The dogs?'

'I don't know.'

Daniel leapt out of the car and ran as fast as his billowing cloak allowed to the ambulance. His mother
and Miss March, with red blankets laid over their
shoulders, were sitting on the step holding mugs of tea.

'Hello, darling,' his mother said. 'There's been rather
an incident.'

'Are you all right?'

'Fine, though they put sugar in this tea and it's
disgusting.'

'Miss March?'

'I think it is recommended if people are in shock.'

'No, are you all right?'

'Yes. Quite all right.'

'If it weren't for Miss March, Daniel, we would all
be dead.'

'Oh! The dogs?'

Audrey gestured behind her and Daniel looked into
the ambulance where Hilda and the puppies had been
stowed in their basket and were now being rather fussed
over by the paramedics. One had Cosmo on his knee.

'Oh, thank God,' said Daniel.

'Are you all right, darling? Do you want the rest of
this filthy tea?'

'No, I'll be all right in a moment, I'm just . . . relieved you're all safe. But what happened?'

'I suppose it was one of those awful rockets. The fireman said it happens all the time around Bonfire Night.'

'Tell me the whole story.'

'Well, I was sitting at the bureau, working. Hilda and Cosmo were curled up under my feet with the puppies, in the knee hole, like you suggested. Poor thing, I could feel Hilda trembling through my slippers. It really is too much, these awful bangs going off . . . Anyway, she got up and barked. Then she waddled to the door and barked again. I thought you had come home at first, but she wouldn't normally do that, not while the puppies are still so tiny. She kept barking, and then started scratching at the door, so I let her out and she ran to the front door and sat there barking, and she did that same funny thing she did when she was pregnant, rolling over like a barrel, and then started barking again. I suppose she was frightened and wanted to be let out, but I wasn't going to do that, so I picked her up and brought her back into the drawing room. But she wouldn't settle. Actually, she got more and more agitated and I had to scold her. Then suddenly there was a furious knocking on the French windows and Cosmo went bananas. So I drew back the curtains and it was Miss March!'

'I hope I didn't give you a fright . . .'

'A little — it was unexpected, and you were rather abrupt, my dear, when you last called in, but that's by the by.'

Daniel said, 'But why were you banging on the windows?'

'Because I saw the flames in the hall. It was too risky to try to get through the front door, so I went round into the garden. I knew your mother would be in the drawing room, and she could have fallen asleep, or not noticed. I banged on the French windows and tried to open them, but they were locked, and then your mother appeared, and I shouted at her to climb out of the window.'

'I said, "Why on earth would I want to do that?" and Miss March said there was a fire. So I telephoned the fire brigade, which I thought sensible, but perhaps it wasn't because she was most insistent that I come. So I managed to get a window half open and she managed to hoist it up as high as it would go, and I passed the dogs through to her, and then I pushed the armchair over, and passed Miss March some cushions to break my fall, if I should fall, and I climbed onto it and then sort of rolled out of the window, and Miss March caught me, and then we put the dogs in the shed and sat there with them shivering until the fire engine arrived.'

'Miss March, thank you so much, I don't know what to say.'

'It was nothing, really.'

'I don't know how I can possibly repay you.'

Miss March was silent for a moment, and then said, 'I do.'

'How?'

'You could sell me that brooch.'

'You can have the brooch,' said Audrey.

'But didn't you send it to auction?' said Daniel.

'No, I only said that to annoy Jean Tailby. It's in my

bureau, unless it's been reduced to ash or one of those firemen has pinched it.'

'They don't pinch things, Mum.'

'Oh, you would be surprised by who would try to pinch things,' Audrey said, and there was a telling silence, only Daniel did not know what it told.

'The brooch, Mrs Clement – I would be quite happy to pay, as I have said, several times . . .'

'No need, you may have it as a present.'

'Mum, strictly speaking it's not ours to give . . .'

'Daniel, if it were not for Miss March, your mother and dogs would now be burnt to cinders. Look the other way.'

'. . . Only I wonder if I might take it now?'

'Now?' said Audrey. 'The rectory, unless I'm very much mistaken, is still sizzling.'

'Perhaps one of the firemen would just have a quick look?'

Neil approached. He looked on duty. 'Miss March, I wonder if I could have a word?'

'You may.'

'Daniel, do you have a key to the vestry?'

'Yes. What do you need from the vestry?'

'Somewhere to talk.'

Daniel gave him the key.

'Thanks. Would you come with me, please?'

Miss March started to say something but stopped herself. She stood up, slipped the blanket off her shoulders and patted down her grey skirt. 'Of course, Detective

Sergeant. You won't forget, Mrs Clement, about the brooch?'

'I certainly won't, dear. Is everything . . . all right?'

'Is anything ever all right?'

Neil, with the lightest pressure on her arm, led her away.

'I wondered when he'd arrive with his little note-book,' said Audrey.

'You mean there are questions to answer?'

'*Aren't* there!'

'What did she tell you she was doing here tonight?'

'She said she was just passing. But where is her Van der Valk, Daniel? It's not parked in the drive. Why? And I am very grateful for the rescue, really, I am, but my first thought when I saw her banging on the window was that she'd come to take Muriel's brooch.'

'Mum, what's going on?'

Audrey looked over his shoulder and said, 'Where shall we live while this is put right?'

'I'm sure Bernard will find something for us. But you're avoiding my question.'

'So many questions. You're like Mr Magnusson from *Mastermind*.'

'What is it about the brooch? It's not just a piece of jewellery, is it?'

Audrey sighed. 'All right, it is all going to come out anyway. But don't interrupt, let me finish, and don't be pompous about it.'

Daniel nodded.

Audrey pulled the blanket more tightly round her shoulders. 'You wondered how Muriel managed to collect such splendid jewels? I can tell you. She was a successful businesswoman. A *very* successful business-woman. When you asked me to be co-executrix of her affairs I discovered just how clever and entrepreneurial she was. You remember all those papers on the dining-room table?'

'I do.'

'The tip of the iceberg!'

'The tip of the iceberg of what?'

'Don't have an attack of the vapours, Daniel, but . . . well, she was a medium.'

'A what?'

'A medium. She was Caduceus. The foundress and chief prophetess of the Caduceus Society. You know what the caduceus is?'

'The serpent-entwined staff carried by the god Hermes.'

'Yes – don't interrupt. Hermes, the god of divination and prophecy.'

'TCS. Something Co-executrix Services?'

'The Caduceus Society, that's what TCS actually stands for. What a flash of inspiration to come up with Total Co-executrix Services when you put me on the spot, don't you think?'

'Inspired. So, Muriel was conducting . . . seances? There must have been lots of them if she turned it into such a lucrative business.'

'She was not. That's the clever part, Dan. She was a medium by correspondence.'

'I don't follow.'

'She communicated with her clientele by letter. No table turning or gazing into crystal balls, no ectoplasm, no queues at the door, no cup of tea afterwards. They wrote to her and she replied with a clairvoyant summary of whatever the spirit wanted to communicate. Clever, isn't it? A medium you did not have to visit! A boon for the shy or embarrassed! And the *revenue*! A lot more than crossing her palm with silver.'

'If I consulted a medium, I would want to know how they communicated – is that the word? – with the spirit world.'

'I can tell you how she did it. She placed the letter face-down upon her table, covered it with her right hand, then placed her left on the brooch, which was pinned over her breast. It was a . . . I don't know – a juju, or lucky charm . . . and anyway, then she invoked Hermes.'

'Oh. How exactly did she do that?'

'The same way you do, dear. I don't suppose the Virgin Mary is really much different.'

Daniel let that pass.

'And then she jotted down her conversation with Hermes and sent it to them.'

'Were they billed per prophecy?'

'Per consultation, at first, but then she had them sign up to a course – Gold Members, or, best of all, a subscription: a monthly consultation in perpetuity – Diamond Members. That was what made the money. She really was very clever.'

'No wonder you've been so busy. How many subscriptions have you had to cancel so far?'

Audrey said nothing.

'Mum?'

'It's not that simple.'

Daniel thought, then froze, then spoke. 'Mum, have you cancelled any at all?'

'I said not to get pompous.'

'Mum, have you actually informed any of these poor people that the chief prophetess has . . . passed over to the spirit world?'

'Or sarcastic.'

Daniel thought for a moment, then said, 'What do you need to tell me?'

Audrey gave him a look, a squaring-up, an assessment of an enemy, a challenge. 'Daniel. I see no need to deprive these unfortunate people of a source of great solace and satisfaction. Many of them are deeply troubled by the loss of a husband, or a parent . . . or a *child*. They turn to Caduceus for comfort and hope. And you would have me deny them?'

'It's not really me denying them, is it? Muriel Hawkins has died. Caduceus is no more. They need to make other arrangements if they wish to continue to communicate with their dear departed.'

'There are more things in heaven and earth, Daniel, than are dreamt of in your philosophy.'

An awful realisation fell on Daniel. 'Mum, are you trying to tell me that you . . . have taken on that role?'

Audrey said, 'Muriel's mantle has happened to fall on my shoulders. Rather like this hospital blanket,' and she pulled it up once again.

'Mother,' said Daniel, quietly but clearly, 'you cannot conduct seances from Champton Rectory. You cannot take advantage of vulnerable people for pecuniary gain from Champton Rectory, or indeed anywhere else. It is dishonest, it is fraudulent. It is . . . *wicked*.'

'Oh, don't be so—'

'No, *you* listen for a change. These people are bereaved, they are suffering, and you mean to take advantage of that? For gain?'

'You do.'

'I do?'

'Yes. Mr Tailby has a point, hasn't he? Why do you make such a fuss of the old widows, Dan?'

'I am the vicar. I am charged with their spiritual care.'

'Very nice. And I expect they are so grateful.'

'You think I am like Jean and Roy Tailby?'

'I—'

'How could you say that?'

'Don't be so prim and pro—'

'You live with me. You see what I do. You think I do it for financial gain? How could you?'

'I wish you bloody did!' Audrey suddenly burst into tears. 'We are so hard up, Daniel. *So* hard up! You think God will provide? The Church Commissioners provide, from investments, and income, like everybody else, like Norwich Union my pension, only neither provide very much, and it is *impossible* to make ends meet, and neither you nor God do anything about it. So don't blame me if I—'

'If you defraud people who are wretched with grief and pretend to be their dead parents? Their *children*?'

Neil Vanloo appeared with Bernard and Honoria and Theo following him.

'Are you all right, Audrey?' he said.

Daniel said, 'She's had a shock. We all have.'

Theo said, 'Blimey, this doesn't happen very often. Do you want some more tea? Isn't it sweet tea when someone's in shock?'

'Earl Grey,' she said, suddenly recovered, 'with lemon.'

'Daniel, I need you, please,' said Neil.

'We will return to this later,' he said to Audrey.

Bernard interjected: 'Dear lady, may we offer you accommodation at the house?'

'We've got plenty of room – and I'm sure everything you would need if you can't get into the rectory,' added Honoria.

Audrey couldn't help but express a little squeak of pleasure at the thought of being accommodated in the splendour of Champton House.

'So kind!'

'Are you all right, Theo?' said Daniel.

Theo looked confused. 'Yes, I'm fine, but someone's burnt your house down.'

'It's not that bad. Mum's fine, she's here. Will you take care of her?'

'Yes,' he said, blinking, as if he could not quite take in what was happening around him. 'Could I have a word?'

Daniel took Theo off to a part of the drive shaded by laurels. 'What is it?'

'Dan, I'm afraid I seem to have taken some magic mushrooms.'

'You've done what?'

'They're like a mild form of acid, LSD – although not that mild. I've been having quite a firework display actually.'

'I know what they are. Where did you get them?'

'I bought them from some dodgy lad who Alex . . . knows.'

'Is he on them too?'

'No, he had to be compos mentis for the bonfire spectacle.'

'What are you going to do? I can't look after you, and you're not telling Mum.'

Honoria appeared out of the darkness with Neil. 'Dan,' she said, 'I'll look after him, and your mother. You're needed.'

'Now, Daniel,' said Neil.

'Leave them to us, Dan' – Honoria's recent froideur seemed entirely to have melted – 'and those *divine* puppies. We'll see you later.'

Neil led Dan away. 'Miss March wants to talk to you.'

'What about?'

'As a priest. I'll let her explain.'

'Is she in any trouble?'

'I don't think so. Are you all right, by the way?'

'Um, as well as any man whose house has just caught fire with his mother and his dogs inside can be.'

'*Set* on fire.'

'What? Are you sure?'

'Petrol-soaked rags, the fire chief says. And you had a visitor.'

'Miss March?'

'Another visitor. She saw him – she thinks a him; a figure in dark clothes, wearing a hooded sweatshirt – put them through your door.'

'Oh. But what was she doing there?'

'It's an interesting story, but I'll let her tell you. I think it will check out.' Neil opened the vestry door. 'I'll leave you to it. Can we talk later? I would like to.'

'Yes. I would too.'

Miss March was sitting in a chair by the vestment press looking like one of the wise virgins awaiting the bridegroom.

'Miss March, you wanted to see me?'

'Bless me, Father, for I have sinned.'

'Haven't we all? But what did you want to tell me?'

'My sins. I actually do want to make my confession.'

'Oh. Forgive me, only people aren't normally so formal. Or not C of E people.'

'I was secretary of the Guild of St Mary at St Saviour's Stow for twenty-five years, Rector, I know the difference between Canterbury and Rome, and I want to make my confession. My last was in Lent.'

Daniel pulled open the 'Lent & Advent' drawer in the vestment press and took out the purple stole folded on top of a chasuble in the same fabric. He wasn't quite sure how to do this in the vestry rather than in church or in his study, and he placed it round his neck so it hung down his cloak in rather an awkward way. But the sign of his priesthood was the important thing and, vested in it, he said what he always said when people wanted the Church's absolution for their sins.

'Almighty God, unto whom all hearts be open, all desires known, and from whom no secrets are hid: cleanse the thoughts of our hearts by the inspiration of thy Holy Spirit, that we may perfectly love thee, and worthily magnify thy holy name; through Christ our Lord.'

'Amen,' said Miss March. 'Now, Rector – as I think you may know, my father was killed, murdered, some time ago. He and I were very close, especially after my mother . . . disappeared from our lives . . . and I have found it extremely difficult to manage without him. I have turned to the Church and found sympathy, patience, solicitude, but what I really want is for my father to be alive again, in the here and now, rather than in some . . . theological way. I know that our Saviour does not dole out individual resurrections to order, but that does not diminish the pain of loss. I have tried to speak to my father in prayer, and to get a priest to speak to him too, to be an intermediary, but . . . nothing. And then one of my customers told me about Caduceus.' She looked at Daniel to see if there was any reaction.

'I see,' he said, pressing his fingertips together and closing his eyes.

'Rector, I am not in the habit of consulting clair-voyants or mediums or seers. Quite the opposite; I am aware of the prohibitions in Scripture and the serious-ness of the offence – thou shalt not suffer a witch to live, as it says in Exodus, I think?'

Daniel looked surprised. 'Yes, it's part of the Book of the Covenant and there's something similar in the Holiness Code, but so are lots of things and, um, some context is necessary to under—'

'Of course. I was not suggesting we should stone Mystic Meg to death, but Caduceus, I was assured, was a Christian and nothing in his practice was contrary to the Gospel. And I am afraid I was so desperate I wrote to him. And he wrote back – such a reassuring letter, and with words of such comfort . . . and with a message from my father, a message that no one could possibly have made up, for it used an endearment only he used, and was entirely private to him and to me.'

'I see.'

'And there was something else . . .'

'Go on.'

'I recognised Caduceus's handwriting.'

'Whose was it?'

'It was Mrs Hawkins's. She was a customer of ours and I once corresponded with her when she wanted a pair of court shoes resoled – tan crocodile, Bally, lovely – and I remembered her handwriting.'

'Were you concerned to discover that Caduceus was not a seer, but a widow from Upper Badsaddle?'

'No. I only felt grateful that I had at last heard from my father.'

'I understand. So you became a regular correspondent?'

'Yes, and . . . I don't actually believe in divination or anything like that, but the accuracy of what Caduceus relayed, and the loveliness of what my father said through her, was irresistible. And then I noticed . . . a falling-off.'

'What do you mean?'

'The slowness of the replies, the content, the hand. Imagine how it felt, how it feels, to think that the connection, once found, is now lost?'

'So what did you do?'

'Caduceus wrote a preface to a divination saying that the needs of his growing band of followers had obliged him to commune with the spirit world rather more than was good for him and he was feeling enervated – an excuse, but I thought it obvious that Muriel was ill, seriously ill, so I went to see her. But she refused to see me. Or rather, that dreadful woman and her even more dreadful husband would not let me see her.'

'The Tailbys.'

'The Tailbys, who are notorious, as you know, for preying on widows. So I made sure they knew I was keeping an eye on her, and on them.'

'It was you who notified the police about them?'

'Yes. I make no apology for it.'

'Why then?'

'I was genuinely concerned for her welfare. And I suppose I wanted them to know that they were being watched. Is that a waste of police time? I don't think it is.'

Daniel nodded. 'May I ask . . . the brooch?'

Miss March went red. 'I knew that Muriel's talisman – is that the word? – was the brooch, the brooch of Hermes carrying the caduceus, and I knew that Jean Tailby would have it in a shot, even though I am sure she did not know its true value. So I did what I had to do to . . . bat them away.'

'And when Muriel died . . .'

'. . . I did what I could to obtain it.'

A late rocket exploded in the night sky and through the vestry window cast a sparkling net over Miss March's face.

'It is yours now.'

'Thank you.'

'Thank my mother. You did know, I take it, that she has taken on Caduceus's mantle?'

'I did know, yes, I worked that out. It made me very angry, so I came to see her about it, to tell her I knew she was pretending to be Muriel. We had some sharp words, do you remember?'

'Of course. Did you come tonight to steal it?'

'To protect it.'

'I must remind you, Miss March, that if you want absolution, you must tell me the truth.'

'I offered a fair price. Any price.'

'Which we could not accept.'

'Your mother could, and would, but you were intransigent.'

Daniel said nothing but looked at her steadily. The red patches in her cheeks intensified a little – always a good sign in a confession, he thought – and she looked away.

'Am I correct in thinking that everything we have said is under the seal of confession?'

'You are.'

'So nothing I have said you may report to the Detective Sergeant?'

'Not a single word.'

'And no one need know about my arrangement with Caduceus?'

'No one. As I think you very well know, Miss March.'

'Then, yes. I would have stolen it. But it did not turn out that way.'

'How providential.'

'Providence indeed.'

They were both silent for a moment. Then she said, 'That's all, I think.'

Daniel said, 'Thank you.'

'Are you able to offer me absolution?'

'That depends.'

'On what?'

'Your resolution not to sin again.'

She was silent for a while. 'I cannot promise anything.'

'I'm not asking you to promise anything, I am asking if you are resolved not to sin again.'

She thought again. 'If I understand you correctly, then yes.'

'Good. And I must give you your penance first.' He thought for a minute. 'Would you read the hymn "Lord Jesus, Think on Me"? And I think a generous donation to a prison charity, if you are able? The Howard League perhaps?'

'Yes. Thank you.'

Daniel raised his hand in blessing and said, 'Our Lord Jesus Christ, who hath left power to his Church to absolve all sinners who truly repent and believe in him, of his great mercy forgive thee thine offences: and by his authority committed to me, I absolve thee from all thy sins, in the name of the Father, and of the Son, and of the Holy Ghost. Amen.'

'Amen.'

'And pray for me, a sinner.'

'I shall. And is there anything else I can do for you?'

'You have already done me a very great service, Miss March.'

'Have I?'

'Yes. You have solved a mystery.'

Daniel found Neil on the lawn in front of the rectory talking to the white-helmeted fireman he assumed was in charge. There was only one appliance left now, its job done, but there were still one or two crew coming in and out of the hall. Through the door he could see soot and water everywhere, and the disarray that uniquely comes when your domestic space becomes a crime scene.

'Dan, this is Keith,' said Neil. 'He's in charge.'

'Vicar,' said the fireman, a man in his fifties with a seen-it-all air about him. 'A sorry sight. No serious damage, but it's a mess. Will take a while to put right.'

'Thank you for coming so quickly. And for rescuing my mother and the dogs.'

'That was the lady – Miss what's-her-name. You were lucky. Actually, not so lucky; someone just tried to burn your house down.'

'You're sure?'

'Yes. It wasn't a very accomplished effort. Petrol-soaked rags through the letter box. Not the height of sophistication.'

'Well, thank you anyway.'

'All part of the service. Especially on Bonfire Night. On to the next one.' As he walked off another rocket fizzed up into the sky over Champton House, burst and faded.

'Neil, we need to talk.'

'I know. Is now the right time? You're probably in shock.'

'Not that sort of a talk. I know who did it.'

'Started the fire?'

'Yes. And who killed Josh Biddle. And why.'

There was still, distantly, the sound of the odd rocket
exploding, and little bursts of sparks low in the sky; not
the municipally bought kind – the splendid pyrotechnics of the organised displays – but the back-garden
fireworks bought in boxes from Woolworths in Braunstonbury, and illegally by kids from corner shops.

Daniel wondered if behind the ceremonies of Bonfire Night another, even more spectacular event was
still dimly remembered or lodged in the unconscious
– Michaelmas, where the events that had led to this
moment had begun. The Feast of St Michael and All
Angels celebrates the fiery archangel's cosmic battle
with Satan, the winged hordes of light in combat with
the winged hordes of darkness; what fireworks there
must have been, as Satan, vanquished, fell to earth
like a spent rocket. Tradition had it that he landed in a
blackberry bush and peed on it, which is why Audrey
observed the custom of picking hers before that day.
The Church weaves heaven into earth through these

traditions and binds the Gospel into the lives of people. There's a lot in that, he thought, and not all of it benign. Human sin and greed and violence can dress itself in gospel robes and proclaim righteousness for the most depraved of deeds: the blessing of slave ships, the witch trials, the ruin of people whose love and desire did not fit the rigour of the law – and disguising psychopathic violence as the execution of God's will.

And now he and Neil were standing on the doorstep.

'Are you ready for this, Dan? We don't have to do it this way. I can get uniform?'

'There won't be any trouble. And this limits the damage to others, if you see what I mean.'

'I understand.'

He pressed the knob and a bell rang deep in the house. A door opened, and there was Sal Biddle half in light from the kitchen. She looked anxiously at the outline of two figures on her doorstep and it occurred to Daniel that every time it happened she must recall the time she had answered the door to him to discover her son was dead.

She had been baking; it was all she could manage since Josh's murder, and she wiped her hands on her apron. 'Daniel. Detective Sergeant Vanloo.' She looked suddenly alert. 'What do you want? Have you caught someone?'

'Sal, is Chris in?'

'Yes, he's just got back from Champton. Didn't you see him at the bonfire?'

'I didn't.'

'He's in his study, writing a sermon probably.'

'Could I see him?'

She looked worried. 'Yes, but – you know – maybe call first?'

'Sorry, didn't have time.'

'Daniel, what's going on?'

'I need to talk to him. Is Lydia in?'

'She went to the bonfire.'

Neil intervened. 'Mrs Biddle, could we wait in the kitchen while Daniel talks to your husband?'

Daniel saw her take a breath and then she let out a sigh. 'Yes. I can put the kettle on.'

Daniel tapped on the study door.

'What is it?' shouted Chris, with impatience.

Daniel walked in. Chris was sitting at his desk. Daniel noticed he was working on a word processor, an Amstrad PCW 9512; he could tell because the type was white on black, rather than green.

'Chris, I need to talk to you.'

'What about?'

'DS Vanloo is here to arrest you. You know why. I wonder if we could do this in a way that causes the least distress to your family.'

Chris seemed to freeze. Then he said, 'You should have worked it out ages ago.'

'I did, eventually. I suppose I did not want to think that someone would do what you have done.'

'What? Be obedient to the Bible? You should try it.'

'I don't think anyone can be obedient to the Bible in the way you mean, even if we should. How can we, when it obliges us to be opposite things simultaneously?'

'You think so? I don't.'

'Now is not the time to argue hermeneutics . . . we should . . .'

'What if I confess my sins to you?'

'You don't believe in confession, Chris.'

'You shouldn't either. Or any fond thing vainly invented, and grounded upon no warranty of Scripture, as the rules say. But not binding on you?'

'A lot has happened since the Reformation.'

'I want to unburden myself.'

'It would be better, if you did, to talk to someone else.'

'Why? Aren't I a sheep of your fold?'

'Yes, but I want to be free to give the evidence I need to give, and I don't want you to tell me anything relevant under the seal.'

'So why am I talking to you?'

'I wanted to see you. I wanted you to see me. I don't understand how you could have looked at Josh, your own son, and killed him.'

'I find it extraordinary that I should have to explain that to you. Even you must be familiar with Genesis twenty-two.'

'Take now thine only son Isaac, whom thou lovest, and get thee into the land of Moriah; and offer him there for a burnt offering . . .'

'Gold star for Bible study.'

'You're not the only person who knows the Bible, Chris. And he didn't kill his son.'

'He was prepared to. And Isaac was an innocent.'

'And Josh wasn't?'

'He was . . . lost.'

'Lost?'

'You don't have children. Of course you don't. You have little dogs instead. If you did, how do you think you would feel if they rejected heaven and chose hell?'

'I wouldn't want to kill them.'

'But then you are lost too.'

'I rather thought I was saved.'

'You would say so, but you're a false prophet, Daniel, and you deceive not only others but yourself.'

'It's a very tidy world you live in, Chris. No ambiguity, no uncertainty . . . and no mercy. Not for Josh, not for my mother.'

'You were going to be next. Originally, I was hoping to get you and your mother together, root and branch, you see? Every tree that does not bear good fruit is cut down and thrown into the fire. But it is surprisingly complicated doing away with people. Or it is if you want to keep at it.'

'Justice tempered with pragmatism.'

'If you like.'

'What about Sal and Lydia?'

'They still have . . . godliness.'

'I didn't mean why have you spared them. I mean what happens to them when you are brought to justice?'

'There is only one judge, Daniel.'

'Murdering your teenage son and attempting to murder by arson your brothers and sisters in Christ might require some explaining when you stand before the throne of grace, don't you think?'

'In Christ? You are not in Christ. Your mother conducts seances in your rectory. Did you know that?'

'My mother does *not* conduct seances in the rectory or anywhere . . .'

'My wife is one of her clients. She couldn't bear the thought – grief can make you mad, you know? – she couldn't bear the thought that Josh was gone, and she . . . she went to the Spiritualists in Braunstonbury and they told her about the prophet. So she wrote to her by that demonic name – Beelzebub or whatever it is – but it is your mother. She replied, and quite deliberately fed her fear. Fed her fear for her own enrichment and yours. And came between her and her one hope of salvation. Sal called round at the rectory and saw her own letter on the table in your hall, and all the other letters from all the other grieving parents and husbands and wives.'

'I did not know.'

'You should know. You would know if you did what you are supposed to do . . . "sanctify the lives of you and yours, and fashion them after the rule and doctrine of Christ, that ye may be wholesome and godly

examples and patterns for the people to follow." How
do you think you have done?'

'You killed your son.'

'He was already dead.'

They sat in silence for a while. Then Daniel said, 'It's
time to go. DS Vanloo's waiting in the kitchen.'

'Another of your conquests.'

'I beg your pardon?'

'Another soul won for Satan. Nice work. Or do you
have other plans for him?'

'Enough.'

'I thought you might.'

Daniel stood up, went to the door and opened it. 'I
hope, Chris, you will one day understand what you
have done. And repent of your sins and know that you
are forgiven.'

'I know exactly what I've done. I'd worry about
your own salvation if I were you.'

Neil appeared in the doorway. 'If you would come
with us, sir?'

Sal appeared behind him. 'Why do they want to
question you? What have you done?'

'I'm sorry, Sal,' he said. 'To God be the glory,' and he
pointed towards the ceiling.

Daniel noticed a crack running from cornice to
cornice.

In the library at Champton House the fire was piled
high and burning hot, which struck Audrey as being

in poor taste after the ordeal she had just endured. She flinched from it a little obviously, but nobody noticed. Far more important, and she would make sure this was noticed by as many as possible, was that she and Daniel were staying with the de Floures in the splendour of Champton House until a cottage on the estate was made ready for their temporary accommodation. Audrey had her eye on the old gardener's cottage, a lovely little Palladian building next to the walled garden that was built when the de Floures were especially rich and restless for home improvements. Alex had wanted it for himself, but his father had said no, and it had not been occupied since Bernard's Aunt Boots had died there during an enforced blackout in the three-day week of 1974.

But for now they were in the house, Audrey in Queen Charlotte's Bedroom, for it was provided with its own bathroom in what was once the dressing room, and Daniel in the Chinese Bedroom, named for its wallpaper, and chosen by Bernard because it was said to be haunted and he thought that especially suitable for clergy.

They were sitting on sofas round the fire, Alex on the fender, flicking the ash from his cigarette into the fire, but not Nathan, for that was still somehow unthinkable, who was back at the lodge with a toffee apple and a bottle of Amarone della Valpolicella Classico. Honoria was lying on the rug with Hilda and the puppies, and Cosmo had jumped onto Daniel's cassocked lap and curled up. Jove was on the library steps, to where he had fled when the dogs came running in, and he stared with yellow-eyed disdain at them from his eyrie. Michelle and Hugh were sitting on the sofa opposite Daniel with Audrey, who tried to catch his eye when she noticed they were holding hands. Theo was sitting slightly apart from the rest of them, looking into the fire like a man hypnotised. Bernard was going round the room supplying them with drinks, which he mixed at the table Mrs Shorely had prepared for the unexpected houseful.

Then she appeared at the door from the hall. 'The Detective Sergeant is here, m'lord.'

'Show him in at once and then – finally, Daniel – you can tell us what's going on?'

'At *last*,' said Alex.

Neil looked distracted, like a man who had too many things to think about; when he did he looked untidy, which Daniel found rather charming. He felt his affection for his friend returning – normal service resuming, he hoped, after the almost unbearable tension of the past couple of weeks.

'Good evening, everyone,' said Neil.

'What news from the nick, Neil?' said Alex.

'I can tell you that a man has been arrested and charged with the murder of Joshua Biddle and attempting to murder you, Mrs Clement. He's in custody.'

'Would you like a drink?' asked Bernard. 'And perhaps then you can tell us who?'

'Do you have a beer?'

'No.'

'Just a bitter lemon or anything soft then, please.'

'We've got ginger ale,' said Honoria.

'Fine.'

She got up to get it, and everyone settled into an unusual attentiveness for the library at Champton, which normally accommodated several conversations simultaneously, and Neil for a moment rather enjoyed the rare experience of the de Floures and their guests having to wait for him instead of the other way round.

Honoria handed him a tumbler. 'Ice, how you like it?' she said.

'Thanks.' He waited for her to sit down, then said, 'This is obviously not for publication just yet, but it's Chris Biddle.'

'The boy's father?' said Alex.

'Oh my God,' said Michelle, 'his *father*?'

There was a silence as they took in the news, the name, and imagined what it would have been like.

Bernard broke it. 'I *told* you,' he said. 'I told you there was something very wrong about that man.'

'You were right, Lord de Floures, but the credit for discovering how wrong goes not to me, but to Daniel. Again.'

Daniel said, 'I just connected some items of information.'

Bernard sat down in the leather armchair he always

379

sat in, which in the years since he had succeeded had moulded to fit him exactly. 'Tell us the damn story, Daniel.'

Daniel sat forward. 'It took me far too long, till this evening, in fact, to work out first who, then why. And for that the credit really goes to Miss March . . .'

'Miss who?' said Bernard.

'Daddy, she's that peculiar lady at the dress shop who looks like she's in *Dr Finlay's Casebook*.'

'Yes, Miss March. She gave me the why, but not the who.'

He paused, slightly enjoying the drama of the moment too, until Audrey said, 'Oh, for goodness' sake, Daniel, who gave you the who?'

'It was Hilda.'

'Who is Hilda?' said Bernard.

'That dog,' said Audrey, pointing to the mound of dachshunds on the rug in front of the fire. 'The mother of the puppies.'

'Yes. You were telling me that earlier tonight when the visitor came to the door it roused Hilda from her bed, and from the puppies – most unusual – and then you said she "did that same funny thing she did when she was pregnant", she rolled over "like a barrel". She had only ever done that once before: when she first encountered Chris Biddle. I remember thinking how peculiar it was, a barrel roll, like a trick, but she doesn't do tricks. And then we discovered she was pregnant and I put it down to that.'

Michelle said, 'Yes, I would have too. But dogs try to communicate with us when they sense danger, or a threat, or a person who means to harm us. They need to let us know — it's in the adaptation of species to species. I've seen something like it with hunters and their dogs.'

'I don't know, but it stuck in the back of my mind. Chris was, of course, always technically a suspect — no alibi for when the murder took place — but he was not the only one; there were likelier candidates, and I suppose a part of me did not want to admit the thought that he could have done . . . what he has done. It was only tonight that things fell into place. I couldn't see why he might kill his own son, until Miss March answered that question.'

'How?'

'Something she said to me earlier. We were talking about the Covenant Code in Exodus, and she quoted from chapter twenty-two, verse eighteen, I think: *thou shalt not suffer a witch to live.* And my mother, as you may or may not know . . . took over the late Mrs Hawkins's business as a correspondence medium.'

'Audrey!' said Honoria. 'A medium! Oh, that's too good!'

'It was just an entertainment, really,' said Audrey, 'just letters written to lonely people, hardly witchcraft.'

'Not an entertainment to Sal Biddle, who was grieving the loss of her son, and suddenly here was an opportunity to commune with his spirit.'

Audrey opened her mouth to speak but decided not to.

'And then she discovered the medium was in fact my mother. She saw her own letter on the hall table in the rectory. Of course, that was why she asked me to remind you, Mum, that God is our judge. I thought it was grief speaking, but it was anger. She told her husband, and he did what he always tried to do: be faithful to the will of God as set out in Scripture.'

'Oh, that's *horrible*,' said Hugh.

'He tried to kill Audrey for being a Basildon Bond Madame Arcati?'

'Yes, Alex, he did, but he had already killed his own son, and for a similar reason.'

'But why kill Josh?' said Honoria.

'When Miss March quoted from the Old Testament, I remembered seeing Josh's body, crumpled on what had been the altar, in what had been the chapel at the airfield, his throat . . . well, you don't need the forensics . . . and I remembered what I had thought when I first saw it: that it reminded me of a sacrificial victim, like the boys the Aztecs sacrificed at the top of their pyramids to propitiate Tlaloc, the god of rain. That boy, Brandon Redding – whose interest in Lydia Biddle was so sinister – reminded me of that earlier this evening, out of his wits on hallucinogenic toadstools like the Aztecs. But then I thought of Abraham, the pious man, who was prepared to sacrifice his own son, Isaac, on the mountain at Moriah because God commanded it. And at the last moment, when Abraham raised the knife to strike him, God produced a ram caught in a thicket to take his place.'

'Only in this case there was no substitute,' said Alex, 'which was unfortunate.'

'But the poor man,' said Michelle, 'thinking God would intervene. Do you think he lost his mind?'

'It sounds insane', said Alex, 'to kill someone because God forgot to organise a sheep as a substitute.'

'I'm afraid not,' said Daniel. 'I think his intention was always to kill Josh.'

'Why?' said Neil.

'Because he was already dead. His words.'

'What does *that* mean?' said Alex.

'Chris believed that Josh had repudiated heaven for hell, turned away from Christ and chosen the works of the devil.'

'You make him sound like a paragon of depravity. He wasn't anything like that,' said Alex. 'He was a *teenager.*'

'He was rebellion. It is the worst thing. For it corrupts not only the person who rebels but implants rebellion in the hearts of others. "Whosoever shall offend one of these little ones that believe in me, it is better for him that a millstone were hanged about his neck, and he were cast into the sea."'

'Lydia?'

'Yes, and Sal. Perhaps even Chris himself.'

'But he was the incorruptible, wasn't he? The good and faithful servant?'

'If you are, imagine what it must be like when the spirit of rebellion flickers within you?'

'They used to beat it out of us at school,' said Bernard, 'or they tried to.'

'Yes, they tried to beat it out of Chris there too – same school, Bernard . . .'

'Oh dear, Daddy,' said Alex, 'one of us.'

Bernard winced.

'I remember', Alex went on, 'the earnest Christians used to go on these awful summer camps, like boot camps, but the Drill Sergeant was Jesus. And there were rumours.'

'Not just rumours,' said Hugh, 'there were injuries. To the lower halves.'

'Yes, some of those beatings were . . . well, bespoke. For the prettiest boys.'

Bernard winced again and mumbled, 'But people get over such things.'

'They don't always, Bernard,' said Daniel. 'There's a world of difference between a caning for disobedience and a savage and prolonged and repeated beating – with, as Alex says, bespoke elements – in some debased pseudo-religious ritual.'

'And on a teenager,' said Michelle, 'inflicted by adults.'

'And in the name of Jesus Christ,' said Hugh. 'Michelle, what must you think of us?'

'It wasn't just you,' she said. 'We have something like it at home in our residential schools.'

'Boarding schools?' said Daniel.

'Yes, but not Eton. For First Nation people – some of my folks went. They were set up to beat the "Injun" out of us. Well intended, their defenders say. There's a huge scandal right now.'

'But Josh was beyond salvation,' said Daniel, 'already dead, so there was nothing to do but excise the corruption.'

'He was MAD,' said Theo, still staring into the fire. 'He'll plead insanity, balance of mind and all that . . .' He meant to flick his ash into the burning logs but absentmindedly threw the whole cigarette in.

'I don't think so.'

'Why not?'

'Premeditation.'

'He intended to kill him?'

'Yes. Otherwise, why did he wear wellington boots that were two sizes too big for him? And leave prints that happened to be the same size and pattern as Nathan's?'

Neil interrupted. 'We checked the shoe sizes of everyone at the vicarage, and none matched, nor did the prints on their wellington boots. We think he must have taken a pair of boots too big for him as a disguise.'

'And to make it look like someone else was responsible for the murder,' said Daniel.

'He knew about Nathan?' said Alex.

'I don't think so. I don't know.'

385

'But you're saying he took my boots? I don't think he can have; I would have noticed.'

'He didn't need to. There are dozens of pairs of boots all over the estate and this house. And all the same, all Dunlops.'

'We buy them from a supplier,' said Bernard, 'for the estate. And for our guests. They're in the cloakroom, stowed by shoe size. You think he nicked a pair?'

'Maybe. But he knew he needed to conceal what he was about to do. And then tonight, while we were all at the bonfire, he dropped off Lydia, and then made his way across the park to the rectory, hooded sweatshirt pulled up, like all the kids do now, and pushed burning rags through the door. If it hadn't been for the vigilance of Miss March, it could have been a different outcome.'

Audrey said, 'But how did he know I would be at home?'

'Who would leave a dog with her new puppies alone on Bonfire Night?'

There was silence. Then Neil said, 'Yes. He's confessed.'

'That poor woman,' said Audrey. 'Lost her son, and now discovers her husband was his murderer!'

'And the *daughter* . . .' said Honoria.

'They're at the station,' said Neil. 'Sal's sister's coming to take care of them.'

Bernard sighed. 'I suppose we'll be on the news *again*.'

★

The fire was burning lower when Bernard announced, after three brandies, that he was going to bed and wished them all good night. Theo almost jumped up and announced he was staying with Alex and Nathan at the lodge and seemed to want to hurry Alex along. Before Audrey could annexe them, Hugh and Michelle said they were going up, too, so Audrey declared she would also. Honoria offered to show her to her room, which was through the salon and up the staircase, which was so wide that when Audrey aimed for the centre, in her Gloria Swanson way, she had to climb without the support of banisters, a risky enterprise for a woman of riper years and half a bottle of sherry down. Honoria had scooped up the puppies in their bed and so had her arms full, but Audrey managed to reach the summit, if, like an alpinist, low on oxygen. Hilda waddled up beside them. Then Cosmo, who was allowed to sleep on Daniel's bed in these unusual circumstances, got into a squabble with Jove, so he decided to take him out for a pee before bedtime. 'Wee-wees and bo-bos,' he said, the force of routine making him forget how ridiculous this sounded, and he made his way to the Rudnam Room where French windows opened onto the terrace. There, he could keep an eye on Cosmo lest he roam into the way of deer or sheep.

It was dark, but he did not need to find a light switch, for there was enough moonlight coming in through the high windows, gleaming on the varnished surfaces and gilded frames of the paintings of Farmer Hugh's shorthorns. Perhaps, he thought, this is why stories of ghosts in houses like this proliferated: candlelight flickering across the faces of ancestors catching you unawares. The heavy glazed door opened outwards, and Cosmo scampered off across the terrace to sniff the base of the balustrade that separated it from the park beyond. Daniel walked slowly behind him to check he did what needed to be done, and barely heard the gentle creak of the door opening a little wider.

'Dan?' It was Neil. 'Dan, can we talk. Please?'

Daniel thought how tired he looked, less crumpled and more dishevelled with the lateness of the hour. There was something schoolboyish about him, an unusual vulnerability, and he felt another lurch of affection, despite himself.

'Yes.'

He sat on the balustrade and invited Neil to sit next to him, facing the house, with its unshuttered Georgian windows, and beyond it the outline of the older parts of the house, the oldest of all at the heart, with the silhouette of gables and crenellations and a cupola heaped against the sky like a stagey backdrop. Some of the windows were lit, and he wondered who was behind them – Mrs Shorely in her quarters, a corridor connecting a Tudor landing with a Baroque stair, Honoria brushing her hair.

'This has happened before, Dan, hasn't it?'

'You mean business clashing with the personal?'

'Yes. I hate it.'

'I don't like it either, but ... we have our commitments.'

'We do. The last time it actually made us closer in the long run, didn't it?'

'But here we are again. And it's more difficult now, I think.'

'Why?'

'Because, Neil, we are not strangers to each other. And the closer we become, the harder the adjustments we have to make. And, I have to say, the more painful, at least for me . . .'

They were silent for a while.

'But you know, Dan, it's going to be painful sometimes, because that's what happens. We knock into each other, we take chunks out of each other. Adjusting our life to another's life . . . it's wrestling.'

An image of Alan Bates and Oliver Reed wrestling naked by firelight in the film of *Women in Love* flashed into his mind, but he did not want to think about that and immediately put it out again.

Daniel said, 'It's also about the shape of our lives, how they are different and distinct. You put people in prison, I visit people in prison. There will always, always be that tension, Neil, you can see that? Your bond of trust with the sinned-against cuts across my bond of trust with the sinner. And when that happens it makes us less able to do what we have to do. And it makes us foes, not friends.'

'You could never be my foe, Dan. Never . . .'

'But it does . . .' His voice shook a little. 'And it . . . it is hard to bear.'

'You think it's easy for me?'

'I don't know.'

'Do you think you're the only one who feels pain?'

'No. But . . . I am finding it very difficult . . .'

'Dan, what are you trying to say?'

There was a sudden shaft of light as curtains were pulled back and then came the sound of a window being hauled open. Another little spurt of light caught the copper of Honoria's hair as she leaned out and lit a cigarette. Cosmo, startled, began barking – his angry, insistent intruder bark. Daniel jumped up. 'Cosmo, *Cosmo*, no barking! No barking!' – a fruitless request for a dog defending its pack, so he went out, picked him up and tucked him under his arm, saying, 'Who's a good boy? Who's a good boy?' into his ear, until he grew calmer and quieter.

'What I'm saying is . . .'

But Neil had gone.

12

God said, 'Let there be light': and there was light.
And God saw the light, that it was good: and God
divided the light from the darkness.

The Bible began with this, Daniel thought, and ever since the faithful have been fascinated by the opposition of the two. In the old religions it was the eternal battle between good and evil, and so powerful was that idea that it had never really been eradicated, even after Jesus Christ came along and destroyed the power of darkness forever. It was not even that it was destroyed; it was another order of thing, the light that shines in the darkness, and the darkness comprehended it not. But it still captivated people – at Bonfire Night, with its terrible history of blood and fire, and at All Souls tonight. The church was in semi darkness, and busy, for it was the custom in the parish for everyone who had lost someone in the last twelve months to be invited to come to church to remember them and all those who had gone into the eternity that awaits us. Their names would be read out, and a representative of the family or a friend would come and light a candle and place it on the altar while the choir sang 'The Souls of the Righteous'. Like Christingle – another tricky service with candles riskily held in the unsteady hands of children – it brought a congregation rarely seen.

Daniel began by singing into the dark church the plainsong antiphon *Requiem aeternam*, a custom he had picked up in the monastery where he had lived for two years before he was ordained. It was spare and lean and spoke what needed to be spoken into the darkness. He sometimes felt plainsong was like a fishing line, cast into the sea of human strife, and when you reeled it back, fear and trouble and fight came with it, flapping like mackerel.

The choir led the congregation in the first hymn, 'Let All Mortal Flesh Keep Silence', which he had insisted on despite the annual complaints from those in the congregation who found it too gloomy and thought that a legitimate theological argument. He had once mischievously suggested they could have 'All Things Bright and Beautiful' instead and Stella Harper hadn't realised he was joking and had given her approval.

> 'Rank on rank the host of heaven
> Spreads its vanguard on the way,
> As the Light of light descendeth
> From the realms of endless day,

That the powers of hell may vanish
As the darkness clears away.'

In the half-cleared darkness he could make out
Anne Dollinger mourning for Stella, and Miss March
for Muriel Hawkins. The Tailbys were there too, and
Dora Sharman, for her sister, and Jane Thwaite and her
daughters for Ned, who had died at Kath's hand, and
in the de Floures pew his brother and his delighted
mother, sitting with Alex and Honoria, and Michelle
and Hugh, who were there for cousin Anthony, but
not Bernard, who found these things mawkish, if not
ghoulish, and thought services should be more like the
church parade he remembered from the army rather
than a 'fucking Scouts jamboree'.

Daniel led the congregation and the choir carefully through prayer and music until they reached the
moment when he read out the roll call of death, the
names of the departed, and people came up, one by
one, or sometimes in a group of two or three, to receive a candle in a glass holder and be guided to the
altar to light it and leave it there.

'*The souls of the righteous are in the hand of God . . .*'
sang the choir.

The de Floures and the de Floures-to-be, first in line
to mourn, as in everything else, came up, took a candle
and went to the altar.

'*. . . and there shall no torment touch them . . .*'

Dora Sharman came up alone.

'. . . *but they are in peace . . .*'

The Thwaites followed, Jane weeping, Angela and Gillian on either side.

'. . . *For though they be punished in the sight of men, yet is their hope full of immortality . . .*'

Daniel read out the name 'Joshua Biddle', for it had to be read out, but to compound the wretchedness of his death, there was no family there, no friends, and no one, he thought, to take the candle up in his memory, so he had asked his mother to do it. Before she could, someone emerged from the dark at the back of the church. It was Neil. He took the candle and lit it, and his face brightened in its soft glow. Daniel thought of the lovely *Nativity at Night* by Geertgen tot Sint Jans in the National Gallery, painted at the end of the fifteenth century, with Mary's face illuminated by the radiance of her infant son, the baby in the manger. There was something about this depiction of private devotion at an event of infinite importance that moved him deeply – and the knowledge of what lay in store for this child. He thought of Sal Biddle, mother of a son lost to a rage too dark to comprehend. Too dark for human comprehension, but not for God.

Neil carried the candle to the altar and placed it alongside all the others, flickering in the darkened church, and in silence, save the sound of an occasional sob from the pews.

The silence held for two minutes, more powerful than anything he could say, or preach, or sing, and then

Katrina turned on the nave lights and Mrs Buckhurst, deputed for the day, started the final hymn on the organ, and they stood to sing.

> *'The king of love my shepherd is,*
> *Whose goodness faileth never,*
> *I nothing lack if I am His*
> *And He is mine forever.'*

The words were both familiar and unfamiliar, a lovely version of Psalm 23 by the Revd Sir Henry Williams Baker Bt, a country parson in Herefordshire. They were sung to an even lovelier tune, *Dominus regit me*, the essence of the Church of England, or the Church of England Daniel liked, distilled into melody and harmony, and composed by a man with the most Church of England of names, the Revd John Bacchus Dykes, a parson from the diocese of Durham who went mad in the Ritualist controversies of the 1860s and died in the asylum.

> *'Perverse and foolish oft I strayed,*
> *But yet in love He sought me,*
> *And on His shoulder gently laid,*
> *And home, rejoicing, brought me.'*

Perverse and foolish, the flock he was called to shepherd, but so was he, who had taken too long to see what needed to be seen. Thinking about the mystery of the murder, the perpetrator and the motive had not entirely eclipsed his own hidden truths, the aspects of himself he had not yet admitted to the light, although he knew it would have to be done, and in the end all would be well, even if it filled him with dread.

> '*In death's dark vale I fear no ill*
> *With Thee, dear Lord, beside me;*
> *Thy rod and staff my comfort still,*
> *Thy cross before to guide me.*'

And then he felt something he rarely felt: a swell of resistance, a surge of revolt, against the vocation God had seen fit to send him, which demanded so much, and took so much – his leisure, his fulfilment, his liberty – and put him here with these people, mourners at gravesides, with wreaths of lilies and yew trees, and their lives out of shape because of misfortune, the cruelty of fate, the inevitable end that comes to us all, whether we look at it with fear or equanimity. He wanted – so badly then that he felt almost breathless – to stand in the light, not in the shade; to run into it, to truly live, fully, not the half-life he feared he lived because that was all the church, his family, his parishioners, his diligence, his fear would allow.

> '*And so through all the length of days*
> *Thy goodness faileth never;*
> *Good Shepherd, may I sing Thy praise*
> *Within Thy house forever.*'

And then he saw Neil looking at him, and he was not singing either.

★

It was the one service of the year where there was
no press at the door, because no one wanted to talk.
Not many were even able to speak, and they smiled
at Daniel the imperfect smile of the bereaved, for the
effort to summon affection summoned instead the grief
that was nearer the surface.

Last out was Neil. He had waited for those others to
go so he could have Daniel to himself. 'Hello,' he said.

'Hello,' said Daniel. 'Thanks for coming up for Josh
Biddle. That was good of you.'

'When you said his name no one was there.'

'You were there. I'm not the only one who does
pastoral care.'

Neil looked at his feet, then looked up again. 'Let's
not talk shop.'

'Let's not. Do you want to come back to the big
house?'

'I would rather we spoke somewhere more private.'

'The vestry?'

'Not the vestry. It's like me talking to you in an in-
terview room.'

'There's the rectory. It's a mess.'

'I don't care about that.'

Daniel locked up and they walked together through
the churchyard. He felt an almost unmanageable sense
of anticipation. He knew that Neil thought the same
thing. Whatever was going to happen was about to
happen.

He let Neil in through the kitchen door. There was no electricity since the fire, so no light, but he knew where there were matches and a candle on the dresser, and he lit it. His hand, he was glad to see, was steady. Light flickered around the room. It was in a mess. The firemen had shifted things out of the hall, and the floor was dirty from their boots and what had been outside that was now inside, and the gallons and gallons of water that had drenched most of the ground floor.

Daniel put the candle down on the kitchen table, which he thought he might just move so it wasn't at an awkward angle to the wall, and he started to say something but Neil interrupted.

'I just need to say this, Dan. I need to tell you something.'

'OK.' His throat was dry and the word came out like a cough.

'I think you know what I am going to say. You are not stupid. And although you always look like nothing can flap you, I know that these things are not easy, even for you. Especially for you.'

Daniel nodded. He couldn't speak, but Neil had more to say.

'I know that people round here have had a lot to get used to in not much time at all, and that makes things more difficult for someone like you, because you are the still centre of a turning world, you know? And people come to rely on that when things are turbulent – they couldn't have been more turbulent in the past year or two, and people want stability, they want someone who isn't going to give them surprises. Right?'

'Yes, I think so too.'

'But life just happens regardless . . . and love just happens. We long for it, or most of us do. We try to charm it down from the sky, we delude ourselves about it, we deny it, we try to make it into something else . . . I'm police, Dan, no one knows the madness of it better than us, except perhaps you. But it *happens*. And you have to acknowledge that, accept that. Because it's worse if you don't.'

'Even if it costs the earth?'

'I'm not pretending this is easy. But you know . . . I know you know . . . that sometimes you have to do what you have to do.'

Daniel said, 'How do you think Bernard will take to another surprise? After Alex and Nathan? How do you think the parish will?'

'I think it will be fine. In the end. It has to be.'

They were facing each other. The candle guttered in a draught from the open door, then recovered. As the light steadied Daniel thought he could almost feel the warmth from Neil's body. And he was steady.

'We haven't actually said what we're talking about.'

'No,' said Neil.

'The love that dare not speak its name?'

'Until now.'

'Say it.'
'I love . . . I love . . .'
'Say it.'
'I love Honoria.'

Acknowledgements

Thanks to:
  Kate Albert
  Kitty Muirden
  Dr Catherine Cargill
  Jonathan Abbott
  The Earl and Countess Spencer
  Cllr Andy Coles
  Tim Bates and all at PFD
  Federico Andornino and all at Orion
  and special thanks to Jack Dorsey

MURDER BEFORE EVENSONG

AVAILABLE NOW

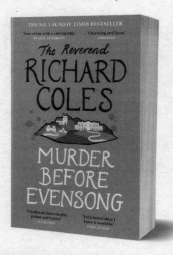

'I've been waiting for a novel with vicars, rude old ladies, murder and sausage dogs . . . et voilà!'
DAWN FRENCH

Canon Daniel Clement is Rector of Champton, where he lives alongside his widowed mother - opinionated, fearless, occasionally annoying Audrey - and his two dachshunds, Cosmo and Hilda.

When Daniel announces a plan to install a lavatory in the church, the parish is suddenly (and unexpectedly) divided: as lines are drawn, long-buried secrets come dangerously close to destroying the apparent calm of the village.

And then Anthony Bowness - cousin to Bernard de Floures, patron of Champton - is found dead at the back of the church. As the police move in and the bodies start piling up, Daniel is the only one who can try and keep his community together . . . and catch a killer.

Turn the page for the first chapter . . .

I

Canon Daniel Clement AKC, Rector of Champton St Mary, stood in his pulpit, looking down on his parishioners. His text was taken from the Book of Numbers, the story of the Israelites turning against Moses for leading them not into the Promised Land but into a wilderness. A resonant story, not only for him but, he felt sure, for all fifty-eight of his predecessors, for flocks, then and now, were apt to turn. Moses averts mutiny by striking a rock, and a cataract of water miraculously pours forth, so his thirsty and restive people may drink; a resourceful tactic that suited Daniel's purposes too.

'Like Moses and the footsore of Israel,' he preached, 'we too must learn to live in hope, to look to the future, and to find in our present circumstances the resources to meet its challenge. As Moses struck the rock of Meribah and lo, a crystal stream poured forth, we too must allow new waters to flow, or rather to flush: my dear people, we need to install a lavatory.'

A frisson went through the congregation, mirroring

the reverberation of that last, loaded word. It was as if someone had actually flushed something unmentionable in their midst.

St Mary's, a jewel of English Perpendicular, singled out for architectural merit and pastoral beauty, had managed without a lavatory for four centuries. Numberless Champtonians down the centuries had endured services of far greater length and frequency than today's without mishap; and the clergy, even those who lasted into their leaky nineties, managed too. Daniel suspected he was not the first incumbent of the parish to have discovered the corner between buttress and north wall (not visible from the path) in which a parson, unobserved, might take care of necessities while awaiting an overdue bride.

The frisson had settled by the communion, and Daniel waited at the centre of the altar steps, consecrated host in hand, for his flock to arrive at the rail. This always took longer than necessary. St Mary's, like so many churches, filled up from the back, leaving the front pews for the feeble, so that they could see and hear better (once the whistling of hearing-aid feedback had died down).

'Draw near with faith,' Daniel declaimed, not entirely suppressing a tone of mild exasperation, 'receive the body of Our Lord Jesus Christ which he gave for you, and his blood which he shed for you.'

Those hungry for eternal life would hurry, you might think, to accept so generous an offer. The choir was up in good order to be nourished before a swift return to their stalls to sing the anthem, but on the other side of the chancel arch no one moved until Lord de Floures – patron, landowner, employer, frequent absentee, but here today at Daniel's request – moved. Squeezing out of the family pew at the front, emblazoned with the de Floures circlet of flowers, he led an unsteady way through the chancel arch, wearing his Sunday tweeds (venerable would be a charitable word to describe them, thought Daniel, and wondered if they had strained to contain his father before him). It was the effects of last night's refreshment, rather than Bernard's fifty-seven years, that made him slowish, and he slightly stumbled as he passed the family tombs in the chapel on his left, where his ancestors lay in effigy, awaiting his own arrival.

Falling in behind him was Margaret Porteous, who overtook the other occupant of the de Floures pew, Anthony Bowness, Bernard's cousin and the recently appointed archivist at Champton, looking like Philip Larkin after a particularly bleak day at the library. She scooted past him at the chancel step, in tweeds too, but not so ancient as Bernard's and Anthony's, and with a Liberty headscarf over her shoulders. Margaret was not of the family, nor of the village; she was somewhere between the two, responsible for coordinating the volunteers who showed visitors round Champton House and its treasures on the two months a year his lordship opened it to the public – an arrangement agreed with the Inland Revenue to mitigate death duties (no wonder he seems gloomy, thought Daniel, with his grave on one side, death duties the other). Mrs Porteous, nimble in moccasins, caught up with Bernard at the rail so they arrived side by side, and knelt together. A slow crocodile of the faithful followed and spread and knelt, filling the rail from left to right, like text on a page – a text that told the story of Champton, its hierarchy, its light and shade, those who were in, those who were out, the fortunate, the unfortunate, the saintly and the works in progress.

There was Norman Staveley, county councillor, in cords and a blazer, to whom the world's estimation was important, striding to the rail a little too eagerly. Katrina Gauchet came next, head teacher at the primary school, with her two boys, but not her atheist husband, Hervé, who was at home making brunch (a Bloody Mary, poured when the ding of the sacring bell from the tower gave a fifteen-minute warning of her return). The Misses Sharman, Dora and Kath, twin spinsters, tiny too in stiff Sunday best, squeezed in next to the wriggling Gauchet boys.

Daniel worked his way down the line, doling out their Incarnate Lord.

'The body of Christ . . .'

'Amen.'

'The body of Christ . . .'

'Amen.'

'The body of Christ . . .'

'Thank you . . .' said Norman politely, as if he had been handed a canapé.

The organist, Jane Thwaite, married to Ned, who always attended but never received communion, struck up with the opening bars of the communion anthem, 'Thou Visitest the Earth', one of Daniel's favourites, the eighteenth-century C of E at its perkiest.

'Thou crooow-nest the yeear, the yeear with thy goo-oo-dness . . .'

And the year felt good indeed, as the spring sunshine flooded through the clerestory and the motes danced in it, and the queue for communion stretched the length of the nave. Up the people came – knelt, received and departed – most back to their pews, but one or two walked past their places and left, to avoid having to meet their neighbours – or the rector – at the door.

As the final hymn faded and the vestry prayers were said, Daniel went outside to take up his position by the porch. He looked out across the churchyard with its headstones – most now illegible, rearranged in orderly lines to make it easier for the sexton to mow – and beyond, over the ha-ha into the park, made fashionably disorderly by Humphry Repton in the 1790s when the lake was dug and follies built for a de Floures in thrall to the Romantick spirit of the age.

His successor, the present Lord de Floures, was first out, as always. 'Lavatory, Dan? They looked like you'd sworn at them.'

'Yes, odd, wasn't it? Why do you think they flinched like that?'

'Wee-wees and poo-poos. Don't want to think about that in church. We might have a fight on our hands, I fear. Come and see me this afternoon? Tea? Do bring your mother.'

'Thank you.'

Margaret Porteous, faithful follower of the master, was second out. 'Rector,' she said, glancing at him, 'such a lovely service!' as she sped past to catch up with Bernard.

The flower department followed, the formidable Mrs Stella Harper and her sidekick Mrs Anne Dollinger. Like many of their kind they had become flowery almost to the exclusion of everything else and appeared in related – if not quite matching – floral-print Sunday dresses, bought at cost from Mrs Harper's shop. As a badge of rank she had a silk flower corsage pinned wiltingly to the lapel of her jacket. Nature, alas, had not bestowed on either lady the freshness of spring; Mrs Harper was thin and stringy and thistly, described by Daniel's mother once as looking like 'an embittered cardoon'; Mrs Dollinger was bulky and square and slightly slobbery ('a knackerman's dog in drag'). They were stalwarts of the village scene, dutiful attenders at church but not consumed with interest in the items of the Nicene Creed, nor the liturgical proprieties of whatever season the church happened to declare; for them, it was really all about the flowers. There had been tensions in Lent as there were every year when Mrs Dollinger sought to undermine the No Flowers rule for this most austere season. In her view 'the more sombre kind of hyacinth' was not an infringement, and Daniel had been obliged to insist that it was. He sometimes thought they had started to think of the church primarily as a sort of giant flowerpot – the font a convenient oasis, the altar a giant stand for displaying arrangements, the village children walking pedestals for Mayday, carrying hoops wound with blossom and a bouquet for the crowning of the May queen. The Gauchet children, as if in training for the coronation procession, were doing circuits of the churchyard, propelled by energies stored up during the enforced stillness of the service. Stella Harper wrinkled her nose.

'Good morning, Rector,' she said, formal suddenly. 'These . . . improvements. Any idea of when?'

'Not yet, Stella. It's just a proposal at the moment for the parish church council to consider. What do you think?'

'Quite unnecessary. And the plumbing would be very difficult.'

'I think others would disagree. Many churches have loos now and the plumbing seems to present no difficulty. You have a tap and a sink, after all, for flowers.'

'Yes, but that's *quite* different. The noises, Daniel, the *noises*. No one wants to hear flushing during divine worship.'

'No one,' added Mrs Dollinger, with emphasis.

'No complaints in my last parish when we installed a lavatory there. Quite the opposite. People were glad to have it,' said Daniel.

'*There* is not *here*,' said Mrs Harper.

'Should we follow, like lemmings?' asked Mrs Dollinger.

'And where is it meant to go? In your vestry, perhaps, or the belfry?'

'There's plenty of room, Stella, at the back. We have far more seating than we need. Think of what we could do with that space—'

'I knew it!' said Stella. 'Why do you vicars hate pews so much? I've never met one who didn't want to turn them into matchwood.'

'They are our *heritage*,' added Mrs Dollinger.

'They're Victorian, mostly, so quite recent heritage. People managed without them for hundreds of years.'

'So where did they sit?'

'They didn't. Well, most of them, anyway. They just stood around, as best they could. It's where the expression the weak shall go to the wall comes from. The old and the feeble sat on benches against the walls,' explained Daniel.

'So you will tear out our lovely pews and force us to stand for Evensong?'

'No, just a couple of rows of pews at the back. But, as I said, everything is to be discussed,' said Daniel, flapping his hands in what he thought was an emollient way. 'Won't you stay for coffee?'

Anthony Bowness, on coffee duty that day with the Misses Sharman, was dispensing steaming water from an urn into styrofoam cups given a degree of dignity by dainty plastic holders.

It was not enough to pacify Mrs Harper. 'More discussions? Until you get your way? Your mind is made up, I suppose. Why will *no one* listen to us?'

'I am listening to you, Stella. I'm listening to everyone. It's a proposal. If the people don't want it, we won't do it.'

'You would say that! But you can't just get rid of pews willy-nilly. They're historical artefacts. What do you think English Heritage would have to say?'

'Victorian,' said Ned Thwaite, former headmaster of the junior school, who had spotted Stella from the porch and decided to intervene, 'nothing special, Stella.'

'Thank you, Ned,' she said, without looking at him, 'but I am speaking to the rector.'

Ned, a Boycott-blunt Yorkshireman when it suited him, said, 'I'm on the PCC, Stella, and this is a PCC matter. If you have a problem, stop bothering the rector and raise it with the PCC.'

Ned stuck his chin out and jangled his keys, which hung on a clip on his belt, an accessory so freighted with pouches and clips and penknives and the 'bumbag' a daughter had bought him for a joke in San Francisco that Daniel wondered how it did not pull his many-pocketed trousers down rather than keep them up.

It was enough. 'Oh, I shall, I shall,' said Stella. 'Don't forget, Rector, it's the flower guild AGM tomorrow evening. There's an item on the agenda that might give you pause.' She did not quite harrumph, but her departing look told Daniel that he did not have as much goodwill in the bank as he thought he had. He felt a little spike of anxiety.

'Told you,' said Ned.

'Told me?'

'Told you this would cause a fuss. It's *change*.'

A new case
for
Canon Daniel Clement

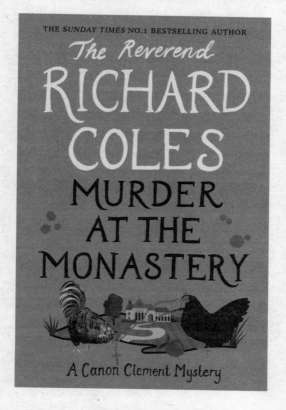
PRE-ORDER NOW